KV-389-329

WILLOW HARVEST

Was it purely by chance that the Nash family, newcomers to that part of the West Country, should share the same surname as the evil man who long ago had been put to the gallows at Beech Cross? But it was enough for the village folk to regard these strong-willed craftsmen with suspicion and dread. And though many lusted after young Rosie Nash, they could not rid themselves of their ancient fears.

Willow Harvest is the unforgettable story of jealousy and hatred, love and romance.

WILLOW HARVEST

WILLOW HARVEST

by
Rowena Summers

Magna Large Print Books
Long Preston, North Yorkshire,
England.

British Library Cataloguing in Publication Data.

Summers, Rowena
  Willow harvest.

  A catalogue record for this book is
  available from the British Library

  ISBN 0-7505-0760-8

First published in Great Britain by Severn House Publishers
Ltd., 1984

Copyright © 1984 by Jean Saunders

Published in Large Print March 1995 by arrangement with
Jean Saunders.

All rights reserved. No part of this publication may be
reproduced, stored in a retrieval system, or transmitted in any
form or by any means, electronic, mechanical, photocopying,
recording or otherwise, without the prior permission of the
Copyright owner.

Magna Large Print is an imprint of
Library Magna Books Ltd.
Printed and bound in Great Britain by
T.J. Press (Padstow) Ltd., Cornwall, PL28 8RW.

Publisher's Note

This novel is a work of fiction. Names, characters, places and incidents are either the product of the author's imagination or are used fictitiously, and any resemblance to actual persons, living or dead, events, or locales is entirely coincidental.

Prologue

A single newcomer in the isolated village of Moule would have been a curiosity. A whole family of them drew suspicion and speculation, especially to a community that hadn't seen the strangers at church in the three weeks since their arrival among them.

The people of Moule were mostly God-fearing folk. Partly as a result of their stentorian vicar's powerful personality; and partly as their heritage in living in that part of the Somerset Levels that had once known bloody carnage in the Duking Days of Monmouth's Rebellion. The slaughter in those far-off days had been brought to its climax in the wild and lonely area where Moule had seemed to spring up like a fully-fledged moth from a chrysalis.

Its inhabitants were an odd mixture of the fey, who swore that on dull and misty nights they could still hear the anguished cries of the dying, the breaking of heads, the stealthy rustle of an unseen enemy...and the brash and lawless, who seemed to epitomise the brooding enmity of those days of two centuries before, and whom Vicar Washbourne tried vainly to bring back to the Christian fold.

There were those who had already glimpsed the three people come recently to live at Briar Cottage alongside the rhine. The strangers might have felt disturbed to know how often they had been discussed in the smoke-filled taproom of the Moule Inn.

There, the old men pondered darkly on folk who moved about the country like gypsies, for to those who rarely strayed from their rustic environment, all others were likened to the broom squires.

'There's two men, I'm told,' one would say, trying to appear knowledgeable over his foaming jug of sweet-smelling cider. 'And a pretty maid.'

' 'Ave 'ee seen her, Tom?' another would add, the thought of the girl coarsening and broadening his dialect. 'A fine looking wench she be, a real fiery one by the looks on 'er, all plimmed out and ripe for plucking, I'd say. There's a fine bit o' bed-sport for a lusty young feller-me-lad to wed.'

'A pity you ain't fit for the job then, Isaac,' the raucous laughter filled the fetid atmosphere of the Inn. 'I reckon 'tis a few years since they creaking bones 'ave climbed aboard a pretty maid!'

'I can still mind it well enough,' the

10

old man snorted. 'And I'd still give young Rosie Nash a minute or two's gamin', if not a whole night...'

What he said from then on didn't matter. He knew he'd set the cat among the pigeons by mentioning the pretty maid's name. And none on 'em knew it afore he did, he thought gleefully. That was clear from the way the rest of them sat suddenly straighter on the benches, their beetroot faces paying more attention to old Isaac Hale than they normally did.

'Nash, you say, you old gorm? Her name's Rosie *Nash?*'

Isaac preened himself. 'Ain't you going to ask how I know it? 'Twas Vicar himself that told me, see. He went over to Briar Cottage to see 'em today and came away sore miffed. I seen 'im and paid my respects, an' he told me.'

'Suckin' up to 'im, more like.'

But nobody was really listening. It dawned on Isaac's slow-witted brain that his brief moment of glory was over. The rest of them were glancing at each other and then away again, as if each had thoughts of his own he didn't care to transmit.

' 'Tis not a good omen,' Tom Kitch said at last.

'That it ain't. Vicar won't know what to make on it.'

'One thing's for certain sure. We'll get a longer sermon than usual next Sunday,' came the gloomy comment. 'He'll want to make sure the Lord's on his side.'

Isaac's rheumy old eyes shifted from one to another of his drinking companions. When he belched loudly, wiping the froth from his mouth with the back of one mittened hand, they glared at him, as if this new turn of events that so far had him mystified was all his fault. And if he'd unknowingly stirred up a nest of emmets, he reckoned he had a right to know about it.

'Are you buggers goin' to tell me what you'm on about?' he demanded.

Tom Kitch took on the role of spokesman for the group, since the rest seemed reluctant to open their mouths.

'You'd find it in the church if you took as much interest in its innards as young wenches, you old has-been. How long since you cast your eyes on the board of martyrs of this parish? The name of Nash can't have escaped your notice, nor the crumbling gallows at Beech Cross you pass every day. I know you can't read much, but even your dummy brain must listen when Vicar reads out the names and points to 'em for the benefit of thick-noddles like yourself once a year!'

Tom spoke with all the lofty superiority

of church caretaker, and was well able to read more than the simple items within the hallowed walls, if these half-wits weren't. He overlooked the fact that he often did so in order to relieve the boredom of his task.

Isaac felt a slow crawling down his spine as the other's voice grew stern, and memory of ancient tales stirred inside him.

' 'Tis all past history now, Tom.'

'Aye, so 'tis. But the fact remains that a Henry Nash of this parish—mebbe livin' on the very spot where Briar Cottage now stands—was put to death by the hanging judge not more'n half a mile from where we sit. You know what they did to 'em in them days, don't 'ee, Isaac? They hung 'em in front of their family and friends, then they quartered 'em, and after they'd soaked 'em in cauldrons of boiling pitch they hung 'em out to dry in the streets as a dire warning. They say you could hear their bones clattering in the wind for months afterwards...'

Isaac heard no more. The bile rose in his mouth in a great acid gob, and he clamped his hand across it, his scrawny cheeks bulging with the effort not to spew up his guts at the graphic description. Tom always did have a vivid turn of the tongue. He heard the rest of his companions chuckle uneasily as he fought down the urge to vomit and finally mastered it.

The night was chill and vaporous in the flat shallow saucer of the Levels, and he had no fancy for lurching out into it alone after hearing such a tale. It was all too easy to miss a footing and go headlong into the dank waters of the rhine, or wander in a muzz until the blessed daylight had mercy on a man.

It happened to Isaac more than once after a night's drinking, when he'd stepped out with false bravado, only to be mist-weirded and near crazed by morning. The fear of lunacy was sharpened even more by seeming to float on a sea of shapeless, writhing spume, without even the landmark of the distant, mystical Tor of Glastonbury for guidance.

It was easy then, in that soundless hell with only his own harsh breathing for company, to imagine himself back in the Duking Days, when the Levels had run with blood. And the sudden fearful hot gushing of his own urine only added to the illusion.

There was a snap of fingers beneath his nose, and Isaac breathed a little more easily. This was no ill-wished moor, but the cloying, familiar atmosphere of the Moule Inn taproom, and he was among friends. If he waited long enough his

14

grandson Cyrus would come looking for him from his own cider-supping corner of the Inn, and the crowd of them would stumble out together into the cold night air. The ghosts of the past were well and truly laid...only it seemed that Tom wasn't inclined to let them rest.

'What did Vicar tell 'ee about these strangers then, Isaac? Seein' as how he chose to confide in such a nonse as you. Or is it all in your head as usual?'

'I ain't a'fairyin'!' Isaac said indignantly. 'Vicar was all put about, and only said summat about 'em bein' basket-makers, which is a respectable enough jobbin', and much sought after in the towns, Vicar said, as if I didn't know that already. An' that he hoped little Rosie Nash 'ould come to church on Sunday and persuade her father and brother to do likewise, that's all.'

His companions looked at him thoughtfully.

'Little Rosie Nash,' Perce Guppey ruminated, pinching his thin nostrils together the way he always did when there was something to puzzle over. 'There don't sound nothin' sinister about a pretty maid wi' a pretty name, I daresay. And if her menfolk are basket-makers, I reckon they'm here to do a buying-for-work with the withy growers. That'll be it, Tom.'

'It still don't explain how they came

15

here out of nowhere, do it?' Tom's grey eyes were remote, as they were when he gave the impression of seeing things other folk didn't, whatever the truth of it. 'Folk won't like it. 'Tis too much of a chancing. The name and the place and the timing of it all. The midsummer month of the slaughter, and a family called Nash have come back among us. 'Tis a bad omen, and I'm thinkin' the sooner Vicar gets 'em to church or the devil chases 'em out, the better 'twill be for all on us.'

Chapter 1
1850

For the first time since Rosie and her menfolk had come to live at Moule, she felt able to leave Briar Cottage with an easy mind. Now that the worst of her father's severe bout of influenza was over he was at his most irritable, and her brother Edwin urged her to take a walk on such a warm and golden afternoon.

Scorning doctors with all the bitter memories of the futile attempts to save his wife from the throes of childbed fever some three years ago, Dunstan Nash had been a difficult patient for his children to nurse. An irate one too, when the vicar of their new parish had voiced his hopes in less than pious tones that the family would soon make their appearance in church and become part of the greater family of God.

Rosie's soft mouth twisted wryly as she stepped out of the cosy cottage with its snug stone walls and roof of thatch. She had fallen in love with the cottage at first sight, but Vicar Washbourne had chosen a bad time to come calling. Her father was at his most frustrated from enforced inactivity, and from the weakness still keeping him indoors when he too would like to explore this flat countryside that was now home, before applying himself eagerly to the craft that was his life and his joy.

Poor Vicar, Rosie thought fleetingly. To be told in no uncertain terms that God hadn't done overmuch for the Nash family in recent years, and that they could manage very well without Him now, was almost blasphemous. Rosie recalled the vicar's pale gaunt features turning puce as he promised curtly to say special prayers for God's lost children on Sunday.

Her brief sympathy towards the vicar vanished. What did he know about lost children, except in vague general terms? He knew nothing about the loss of a beloved wife and mother, and the rearing of the weak premature child for two years afterwards, until their sweet Dorcas had toddled towards the edge of the cliffs, unknown to the rest of them, to be found cold and lifeless on the rocks below a whole day and night later...no, he couldn't know the pain of it...

Rosie swallowed back the lump in her throat that came with remembering. The past was behind them, and they must begin a new life. Edwin had been insistent on the sense of it, after their father seemed to be half-demented by this new tragedy. And now that the strain of the past three weeks was over, Rosie felt the first stirrings of interest in her new surroundings.

She was too young, at seventeen, to mourn for ever. Her innate optimism and indomitable spirit had done much to keep her father going, and now, with the July sunshine warm on her face, and lifting the long silky strands of her dark hair to a blue-black sheen from her shoulders, she had to admit she found the new village a welcoming sight. The charm of the square-towered church and the winding street, even the criss-cross of rhines over the moor, some of them carpeted with a deceptive growth of mossy weed hiding the dank water beneath, all added to the lushness of the area around Moule.

Rosie hesitated. She should be seeking out the school-room, where she intended offering herself to the head teacher as a teacher of letters and drawing and needlework, if required. It wasn't what she would have chosen to do, but she thrust to the back of her mind the wild episode in the spring, when the gypsies had encamped on the moor near their Minehead home, and she had become bewitched by a young gypsy boy with night-black hair and flashing eyes, and a way of taming horses that was uncanny. It was her brother Edwin then who had talked to her long into the night about the way the Nash family was taking the road to destruction.

'Do you think Mother would have liked to see this wanton look in your eyes, Rosie?' He'd been blunt with her. 'Did she insist on us having a proper education so that you could run wild with the gypsies?'

'If Pa doesn't mind, why should you?' she had said angrily, the truth of his words stinging her to round on him, despite the fact that he was three years older and a foot taller than herself. She tilted her face to look up at him, her firm young breasts heaving, a pulse beating in her throat, and a fine red flush on her cheeks, and Edwin sighed, knowing just what the gypsy boy found in her to quicken his blood.

'It's Pa I'm thinking about,' Edwin slowed down his speech deliberately. 'Haven't you seen the way he looks so vague at times lately? I'm afraid for him, Rosie. This whole place holds too many memories for him now, and the bad ones outweigh the good. We should get him away from here before he does himself a mischief or just gives up on the will to go on living.'

Her heart had leaped in her chest as his

words sank in. In a trice she reverted to the child on the brink of womanhood, with all the trust in her brother showing in her appealing sea-green eyes that could melt a man's heart.

'What can we do, Edwin?' she whispered. 'We both love him, and I couldn't bear it if anything happened to Pa...' She caught her breath, remembering the bad times with a sharpness that took her unawares. Her soft expressive eyes blurred, and she dashed the tears away with her long slim fingers.

'The best way is to remove ourselves from this place to a new environment,' Edwin said ruthlessly. 'We must get him away from the sight of the sea that Mother loved so well, and from the moorland cliffs where we lost Dorcas. It's all too much of a reminder, Rosie. His eyes stray there too often, and sometimes he cocks his head as if listening for Mother's footsteps. Haven't you noticed?'

To her shame, Rosie knew she hadn't. She had been too busy discovering the delights of being seventeen and the object of a young man's admiration, and one who was ardent in his embraces. In her heart she knew it was an association that had no future, but the taste of it was sweet, because it was her first young love, and the gypsy was a new and exciting experience...

'I don't know,' she stammered now. 'Where would we go, Edwin. Pa has his work...'

'I've thought it all out. Will you back me up when I suggest it to him, Rosie? I've even made some enquiries, and there's a place we can look at. Do you agree?'

She trusted him, her tall, strong brother, and nodded. And the next evening over supper, Edwin put the proposal to their father.

'Father, it's time we left Minehead.' Edwin was never reticent when it came to voicing his thoughts, and Rosie knew the truth of his words to her when she saw the vague look in her father's eyes. It was as if only half his mind was with them.

'Left Minehead? Who's leaving, boy? Not you and Rosie?'

'All of us, Pa,' Edwin went on urgently. 'I'm thinking we could do a lot better with the business than we do here. The fashion for basket furniture has grown apace recently as you know, and we're not getting the best of the trade.'

A flicker of interest was kindled by Edwin's enthusiasm. At twenty, Edwin was a mirror-image of how Dunstan himself had looked at that age, tall and broad, and darkly handsome. In those far-off days he had wooed and won his lovely

Marjorie with the ease of butter melting in the sun. He strove to give his son all his attention.

'How could we do better? We do well enough with our baskets and stools and have a steady business.'

'But we have to pay such a price for the withies to be transported all this way, Pa. It's the middling man who makes the bigger profit.'

'Edwin's right, Pa.' Rosie added weight to their discussion, her nimble mind appreciating all that her brother said.

Dunstan looked at her, his darling, his slender girl-child, who was so subtly emerging into womanhood that he had hardly noticed the changes in her lately. He registered them now, the wide eyes and generous full-lipped mouth with the mutinous little chin when she wanted her own way, and the dark gleaming hair like satin that would be a delight for some lucky young man to entwine himself in, as his Marjorie's had been for him. Dunstan was aware of a fleeting envy for the unknown suitor, and dragged his thoughts back to Edwin.

It had been all too easy for him to drift away lately, into melancholy, to a place where Marjorie and then Dorcas had gone, to which he could not follow. But for these two, whom he loved so dearly, he might have been tempted to hasten the day, to hurry the eventual meeting in paradise.

That he could even contemplate such a meeting was some reassurance in his saner moments that he had come a little way back from the torment he'd suffered, even to renouncing his God and all who professed to be His servants. Just a little way...

'Are you listening, Pa?' Edwin said sharply. 'I've had thoughts on this for weeks now. We could sell up here and find a place nearer the withy fields on the Levels. We could do a buying-for-work with one of the farmers. Once he's harvested the withies we can take them straight away and do our own stripping and boiling of the rods. That way we can be sure of getting the colour variations we want for the work, without relying on what's brought to us by the middling man. We can set up an exclusive brand of basketware. We might even become famous. Perhaps even the Queen would buy from Nash and Son!'

Edwin's voice grew reckless as he saw he'd caught his father's full attention. Dunstan was shrewd enough to know the idea was a sound one. And Edwin still had one last card to play.

'Mother would approve, Pa. She'd like to know her legacy to us was a cottage business in the country. And if it prospered, mebbe we could buy a shop in a nearby town. Bridgwater's a fine place for selling, they say, and our Rosie can set herself up as a teacher. Mother would have liked that.'

This time she glared at her brother. It was what Marjorie had wanted, but it seemed too rigid an occupation for Rosie's own free spirit. But she bit her lip as Edwin nudged her, seeing that her father was letting the suggestions sink into his mind.

'I'll need time to consider it,' was all he would say at that time. But a few weeks later he'd instructed Edwin to make fuller enquiries as to a cottage with workshop alongside, in easy reach of a farmer willing to supply them with the willow rods they needed for the basket work in which they were both employed. The withies were transformed beneath their expert hands into items of beauty and usefulness, strong and supple as the wood they worked so lovingly.

The outcome of Edwin's enquiries was that the Nash family left Minehead early one Saturday evening, with all their belongings in two carts, resting for the night at a wayside inn, and reaching Briar Cottage on the outskirts of Moule in the middle of Sunday morning, when all the good inhabitants of the village were singing their hearts out in Vicar Washbourne's church.

Rosie stumbled a little in her stroll across the marshes, breathing in the heady scents of grasses and wild blossoms, a little reminiscent of home without the tang of the sea...*this* was home now, she reminded herself. A lingering pang for the richly carpeted moorland above the town of Minehead salted her eyes for a moment, but her chin lifted resolutely. Tears were for children, and she and Edwin had formed an undaunting pact to put the sparkle back into their father's life once more. That he had been stricken down with the grim bout of influenza from the day they arrived here had taxed them to the utmost, but it was over now, and things could only get better. Rosie's natural optimism asserted itself.

Besides—her soft mouth curved into an upward tilt—there hadn't been time yet to begin the new business, and no question of her finding the village school and taking up a post as teacher...but inevitably, Edwin had become anxious about the farmer with whom he'd done a deal for the withies, and a week ago he'd voiced his worries.

'I'm afraid Farmer Merrick will think we're fly ones if we don't let him know what's happened, Pa,' he said to Dunstan.

'I think I should go there and explain that it's taken more time than we expected to get settled, or else he'll be selling the withies elsewhere.'

'Can't I go?' Rosie said at once. 'I feel stifled in here, and I promise I won't be any longer than I can help. If the farmer's feeling out of sorts at your non-appearance, he might take more kindly to a pretty face!' she added teasingly. 'And I can take the cart and get some eggs and cheese at the same time. Oh, do say I can go, Pa.'

'You don't know the place, Rosie, and you're a stranger here.'

'I know the name. It's Merrick Farm, and Edwin pointed it out when we came here,' she pouted. 'It's in a straight line from the village, and I can't miss it, even though it's two miles away. What's that, anyway? I've walked twice as far for eggs before now. And what can happen in the country? It's so sleepy it's almost dead. Without even the sound of the sea to liven things up...'

'All right, you can go,' Edwin said at once, his mouth tightening at her tactless reference to the sea. 'She'll be all right, Pa, and she can take the dog with her for protection. Not that I think she'll need it. One look from those glowing eyes of hers when she wants to quell anybody, and

27

there's no one who'd dare to argue with our Rosie!'

He was exaggerating to put her father's mind at rest, Rosie thought. At least, she hoped so. She wasn't as dogmatic as Edwin suggested, was she...? Remembering the gypsy boy on the moors, she knew that she had inherited all her mother's melting femininity with Dunstan's strength, and the result was an intriguing blend of softness and haughtiness...but the gypsy, Cory, had seen right through her to the budding flower that she was.

His aggressive weight had crushed her into the soft bed of the moorland that last evening before the gypsy caravans were to move on. It was wrong, and Rosie knew it was, but the new sensations he awoke in her were too exquisite to be denied. His rough, calloused hands had sought the softness of her breasts in her unlaced bodice, moulding them and touching their peaks with his lips in a way that sent wave after wave of a pulsing fire through her limbs. He kindled a matching flame deep inside her that as yet she was too innocent to know how to handle. Despite her yearning, she had struggled against any more familiar embraces, and Cory had reluctantly let her go, his black eyes hot with desire as he gazed at her captive little body beneath him.

'If there was only time, I would break you with all the delight of breaking in a new mare.' His words, coarse and whispered, his mouth against her skin, had sent a new thrill coursing through her veins. It was the first time she had been wanted—and loved—outside the family, and however mismatched, she knew she would never forget him, and this night. Velvet dark the sky, diamond-studded with stars, and Cory's arms holding her close...but he had reluctantly let her go as the sounds of his own family's impending departure made it necessary for him to go.

'Will I ever see you again?' Rosie had asked, her voice catching a little. His hand had taken a thick strand of her hair and twisted it around his wrist, where it gleamed like ebony in the moonlight.

'As sure as we breathe, my sweet Rosie,' and then he had let her hair go, and he was gone, swallowed up in the night.

The pain of parting had lessened over the months, and Rosie had set out on her journey to Merrick Farm with the dog they simply called Boy. It wasn't a joy-ride and she had an object to her mission, but it was good to get away from the sick-room where her father still lay, immune to the acid odours of staleness that made her wrinkle her nose each time she entered it.

It was an easy ride to Merrick Farm,

and Rosie paused as she reached the great beds of withies, growing tall and straight, their olive green leaves whispering in the breeze. Nurtured by the waters of the muddy river Parrett and the rhines in the Levels, they were an ancient crop, but Edwin had informed her that it was only since early this century, with the Enclosure Act of parliament, that there had been laying-down of cultivated beds. Before then it had been a haphazard growth. Now, the beds were fine and square and certainly flourishing, and Rosie turned the horse and cart onto the Merrick land.

The next hour had been one of pleasure. Farmer Merrick and his wife were full of concern for her father's welfare, and insisted on sending more than the eggs and cheese she had come to buy, piling the cart with fresh vegetables grown on the farm, and a bunch of sweet-smelling roses for herself.

' 'Tis your name, I believe, my dear?' Mrs Merrick's round apple-cheeks broke into a smile. 'Your brother told us all about you, and a fine and pretty maid you be. You'll be having the young men knocking at your door afore long wi' such a winnin' smile, won't she, Faither?'

'That she will,' Farmer Merrick said comfortably. 'Unless she'm already spoken for, which 'ouldn't surprise me for certain sure!'

'Nor me neither,' Mrs Merrick agreed. 'A comely young maid can always put the sparkle in a young man's eyes. I bet our Rosie's courtin'...'

They had a way of talking about her as if she wasn't there, but with a quaint rustic charm that brought a smile to Rosie's face as she sat in the warm farmhouse kitchen and watched Mrs Merrick pound the bread dough with competent hands, twisting it deftly into a huge thick plait to be left to prove before baking.

'No, I'm not,' she began.

'Then there's hope for our Will yet, Missus,' Farmer Merrick said cheerfully. He bade Rosie good-day for the present, banged out the clay pipe against the large black range and clumped across the stone-flagged floor to be about his business. When he'd gone Mrs Merrick offered Rosie a second drink of raspberry cordial, for the afternoon was hot. Rosie spoke with studied casualness.

'Is Will your son, Mrs Merrick? Would that be the boy I glimpsed at the withy fields? I thought it was Farmer Merrick with him.'

The amply-proportioned farmer's wife chuckled, every bit of her seeming to shake like ripples on a pond. She was a very stout, good-hearted woman, and Rosie had taken to her at once.

'Aye, that'll be our Will, me dear. Tall as his father, but half as wide, which is what catches the eye of a maid these days, I'm told. Takes more'n a regular shape to find a good partner, though. I was never anywhere near your size, with your pretty little waist and nice soft curves, but I still caught me a good man!'

Rosie couldn't take offence at the odd compliment. 'Your Will's not courting then?' She hid a smile as she realised she had already dropped into the country way of talking.

Mrs Merrick gave a despairing snort. 'That one's bidin' his time, Rosie. Farmer an' me 'ould like to see strong healthy grandbabbies about the place, but our Will don't seem in no hurry to oblige.'

'Are you still trying to arrange my life, Ma?' A lazy masculine voice spoke from the doorway, making Rosie jump. She looked up quickly. He seemed to fill the open space of the doorway, and from the darker interior the image of him was of dark against light. For a second Rosie felt her heart thud, and then Will Merrick came farther into the room and she saw his face clearly.

He was rugged rather than handsome, but when he smiled the creases on his cheeks and around his eyes made her want to smile back. His eyes were bluer than her own, his jawline strong. Rosie guessed instantly that nobody was going to arrange Will Merrick's life except Will Merrick.

'Sit you down if you've got a minute to spare and make the time of day with Miss Rosie Nash,' his mother said tartly. ' 'Tis her folks who've come to live over at Briar Cottage and are doin' a buying-for-work wi' us for the withies.'

'I know it.' Will's eyes never left her face, yet Rosie sensed that he was registering every line and curve of her. She should be annoyed, yet she didn't find the experience entirely unpleasant. Even though he was only a farmer's boy, and she was all set to be the village teacher...her brief feeling of superiority faded, because if the truth were told, she would far rather be doing a job that didn't have to comply with rules and regulations... She remembered Cory, and a faint flush heightened her cheeks. After the heady moments she had shared with the gypsy boy, she felt a brief shame for her class-awareness. Here in the heart of the country such things seemed less important. If the whispers of their new abode were to be believed, Vicar Washbourne seemed to be king, and all the rest his minions. And since her own menfolk were to be so closely connected with the Merricks from now on

33

in the course of their business dealings, it would be churlish to try to put on airs.

Rosie held out a dainty hand towards Will, the pink-tipped fingers touching the square male hand that he reached out to her automatically without thinking to wipe off the grime of the day beforehand.

His mother tut-tutted at once, muttering something about fine manners to show when they had a visitor in the house, and foraging about for a towel for Rosie to clean her hands on. It hardly mattered to her. What did matter was the sudden warmth she felt at the contact between herself and Will. The sensation that he didn't merely grasp her hand, but her whole body. It was something to do with the intensity of his gaze that seemed to try and penetrate beyond the pretty picture she made in her muslin calling dress and bonnet. Trying to see into the soul of her...

Rosie shook herself. Such nonsense to be imagining thoughts like that from a farm-boy...as if to rid herself of the shame of the recurrent phrase in her mind, she gave him a brilliant smile and told him a bit of dirt wouldn't kill her, but that she must be getting back to the village soon, or her father would be anxious.

'Mr Nash has been ill,' Mrs Merrick commented. 'A nasty bout of the influenza that needed careful nursin' these past weeks.'

'Oh aye.' Will answered his mother evenly enough, but truth to tell he was startled to see the sudden spreading of a smile like sunlight on Rosie Nash's face. As lovely and dewy-fresh as the flower of her name. Will's eyes shifted direction slightly to take in the satin bloom of her cheeks, and the wide eyes that reminded him of the picture of the sea in his bedroom. Will wasn't given to poetry, but he was stirred by the sight of the stranger, and it irritated him to know that she was aware of it.

He wasn't gettin' caught in no wedded trap for many a year yet, and that was something he'd definitely made his mind up about. He chose his female companions with care. Some for chaffing and some for sporting...but a sixth sense told him this one would want the heart and soul of a man. She looked as fragile as glass, yet he sensed she was made of stronger stuff than she looked. There was fire in her, as yet unlit.

What in God's name was the matter with him, Will asked himself angrily? It wasn't like him to be afraid of any man or woman on this earth, but when Rosie Nash looked at him in that certain way with that angelic smile on her face, it was almost like knowing himself for a marked man. And Will didn't like the feel of it one little bit. It made him more caustic with her than he intended.

'Well, Miss Rosie Nash, I daresay our paths will cross again sometime,' he said abruptly. 'I'll look forward to seein' your father as soon as he's well again, and to jawin' with your brother. Mebbe he'd care to meet with me at the Moule Inn one night. I daresay he's found his way there by now.'

'No, he hasn't, as a matter of fact. There's been too much to do at the cottage, and with my father being so ill we've hardly dared to leave him alone,' she replied, aware that he was acting oddly restrained towards her and intrigued to know why. It wasn't that she was at all interested in him. She could fly her kite far higher if she wanted to! She got up to leave, knowing full well that Mrs Merrick was still glaring at her son for his surliness. It didn't matter, Rosie kept averring to herself all the way home. It didn't matter one scrap.

It was odd how the thought of Will Merrick kept intruding into her mind in the days that followed. He was as unlike Cory as it was possible to be, except for the darkness of their hair, yet she was aware of similar sensations affecting her whenever she thought of either of them. Except that in Cory's case it was still with a twinge of nostalgia, and in Will's, it was with irritation. She couldn't really explain why he irritated her so, but he did.

She hadn't seen him since that day at the farm, but Edwin had. It had been his turn to leave the cottage while she remained in sole charge of her father's health, and he'd gone to Merrick Farm to discuss business and the coming withy auctions, offering a put-down price to be sure of obtaining enough rods to see them through the next season. The auction usually gave the right for the buyer to cut the withies after the fall of the leaf in the winter, but since this was new to the Nashes, there might be a compromise needed.

She hadn't seen Will...but she had thought about him... They could hardly avoid seeing each other in the future, and it would be far easier on their two families if the young ones were at least sociable. At least...maybe there was little need for her and Will to meet at all! Once she was established at the village school...

Rosie sighed, flexing her back muscles on the first real day of freedom she had since coming here. Even the ride to Will's farm had been on an errand. Today she could laze as long as she wished, knowing her father was pottering about in the cottage now, and burning to get out into the workshop and among his beloved baskets. Tomorrow, Edwin had told him. Just wait one more day, until you feel really fit again...

She really should turn back and find the schoolhouse, but she was reluctant to break the spell of enchantment this soft green spread of land was having on her. Overhead the sky was blue, with barely a drift of fleecy cloud to mar its serenity. The scent of wild blossom tingled her nose, and alongside the rhine where she walked were clusters of pale mauve and white water-violets, each with a golden star in its centre. Who would dream that beneath the carpet of flowers and herbage was a sodden mass of weed and dank water? A huge crane-fly skimmed across the surface, the tiny green bits of weed sticking to its legs like miniature boots, and Rosie laughed out loud as she leaned forward to see where it went.

She suddenly felt herself gripped from behind by two strong arms, and gave a frightened gasp as a shadow fell across the rhine in front of her. She'd heard no one approach, since she'd been so engrossed in the sheer simplicity of nature, and the next minute she heard a rough guttural voice in her ear.

'You want to be careful, pretty maid,

leaning for'ard like that. These rhines be deep and it 'ould be a pity to get that pretty dark hair all tangled up in they water-weeds.'

Rosie twisted out of the fellow's arms without losing her footing, and stepped quickly back from the edge of the rhine. Her pulse was racing, more from the unexpectedness of finding herself no longer alone than from any real fear. But the feeling changed as she found herself looking into a fleshy face that was florid and slackly made, the dark eyes small for the size of the cheeks, the mouth over-prominent. It made her want to squirm, that mouth. There was a whiff of smoke about him, and over his shapeless clothes he wore a sleeveless leather jacket. On the ground nearby was a newly-fashioned iron cooking-pot, and Rosie surmised that the fellow was a blacksmith and delivering some of his work. She forced herself to be civil, though the smell of his hands was still on her arms, and she could see out of the corners of her eye that his hands had left a mark on her dress.

'Thank you kindly. Now, if you'll excuse me...'

He made no attempt to move, merely stood there with a leering grin on his face. When she moved a pace he stepped sideways as well, to bar her way. Rosie lifted her chin, her eyes flashing.

'Would you let me pass, please? I have to get home.'

'An' where would home be, I'm wonderin'? Briar Cot, if I'm not wrong, and you'll be Miss Rosie Nash that my ol' simpleton of a Granpappy thinks so threatenin'!'

Rosie looked at him in astonishment, her fear of him allayed for a moment by his words. 'I don't know what you're talking about, nor how you know my name, but I've got more things to do than stand talking to the likes of you all day.'

The crowing look on the rough fellow's face angered her more than anything. As if he knew all about her, whereas she knew nothing about him, and decided he must be as daft as his Granpappy, if he could do nothing better than stand there grinning at her.

'You tak' a look in the church, my pretty, an' you'll be as knowin' as me,' he chortled smugly. 'But now I've saved 'ee from the rhine, I expects my reward, my pretty!'

'You didn't save me. I was never in danger of falling in,' she said crossly. 'If you don't let me pass this instant, I shall call for my brother.'

'You'll 'ave to call a long way,' he sniggered, and glancing over his shoulder,

40

Rosie saw how far she had come. The land was a vast flat saucer, but she hadn't gauged the distance she had walked, and the village church was a distant square turret now, and a hazy ground mist was beginning to spangle the lush green meadows. She felt a spurt of panic, wanting to be safely indoors.

The oaf suddenly grabbed her and pressed his fleshy mouth to hers before she could stop him. She struggled in vain, and though it was only seconds that he held her fast, it felt like an eternity. When he chose to set her free, she scrubbed furiously to rid herself of the taste of him on her lips, and his dark eyes suddenly glowed like the coals in which he worked.

'Don't you dare come near me again, you hear?' Rosie hissed at him, too furious even to shout. 'If you do, you'll be sorry.'

For the briefest instant she thought he looked alarmed, but then he swaggered away from her, scooping up the iron pot as if it was made of paper. He threw one last comment over his shoulder as he strode off along the rhine away from her.

'Maybe Granpappy ain't so dippy after all then. Mebbe we'd all better be hangin' garlic over our doorsteps to safeguard us all!'

41

His words were carried away on the breeze, and Rosie couldn't be bothered to try to understand them. Not until later.

Chapter 2

Cyrus Hale was the centre of his small group of drinking cronies at the Moule Inn that night. Somewhere in the taproom his Granpappy was yarning the night away with the old sticks of the village, but down here Cyrus was king among the lusty young yokels.

'I tell 'ee I 'ad a kiss from 'er,' he was insisting to the disbelieving drinkers. 'All soft and rosy she was, like 'er name. An' fitted into my arms as snug as a tick on a sheep's back.'

'Who do 'ee think 'ould kiss a mutt-head like you, Cyrus Hale?' Seth Weaver grunted. 'A maid 'ould need to be cross-eyed afore she fancied the likes of you! Did 'ee brand 'er or summat, wi' your iron?'

Guffaws of laughter stopped any reply Cyrus might have made. His little eyes glinted darkly at being made to sound a fool when he'd done exactly as he said, and kissed the pretty maid, which was more than any of these louts had done.

'It's true, you weavils!' he shouted. 'An' she liked it too. I could tell, despite what she said.'

'What was that then?' Seth slurped his ale and looked inquiringly at the flush-faced blacksmith.

'Well, I reckon as how she weren't none too pleased at bein' taken by surprise, if truth were told,' he blathered on, 'an' said she didn't want no more, or I'd be sorry. Now don't that just prove that I kissed 'er, or else why would she have said that!'

He beamed round at the little group, glad he'd thought to add that last bit so that he didn't entirely lose face. The response was a mixture of grunts and suspicion.

'You mind she don't ill-wish 'ee, Cy,' one growled. 'You've heard the tales old Tom Kitch be puttin' round about they Nashes.'

'Who's taking notice of an old fool like him!' Strengthened by the ale inside him, and his own burly stature as village blacksmith, Cyrus flexed his muscles.

'Well, your Granpappy for one,' Seth grinned. 'I heard tell as how he don't like passin' Briar Cottage no more for fear he might hear strange goings-on.'

'The only strange goings-on you'm likely to hear is if Miss Rosie Nash gets herself a

43

fine fellow-me-lad, and I ain't sure if I ain't aimin' to be the one,' Cyrus chuckled.

His words were drowned in raucous laughter and thumping of ale pots on the stained wooden table.

'We'd need to see it to believe it,' Seth announced. 'Ain't that right, boys?'

They nodded assent, and before Cyrus could protest they were putting bets on it. Cyrus Hale and Rosie Nash...it didn't sound too bad a combination to him, even though his mates were sniggering that it was more likely to see a snowball in hell than see old Cy kissing Rosie Nash. He'd show 'em, he thought darkly. And mebbe it would be more than kissing too. The flicker of interest the thought was producing in his loins was too pleasurable to be ignored, and such sport among the village wenches was not to be compared with laying with the snooty young maid with the mouth like ripe cherries and the fire in her eyes. And a fire in her belly too, if Cy knew anything about females, he thought knowingly.

The evening was passing in its usual haze as the back room became smoky and the talk more bawdy. Moule Inn was a meeting-place for young and old for some distance around, though generally the two factions observed an unwritten rule to keep well apart. Among the older clientele of the

Inn the talk was of the daily business of a farming community, where the biggest non-feeding crop was the basket willows; and the biggest dependant industry of west Somerset was the basket-making, which was enjoying a great boom now, since the ladies and gentlemen of fashion in the towns had discovered its versatility.

Not only was the humble carrying basket sought nowadays, but there was a demand for theatrical baskets, and even larger ones, since the willow had both lightness and strength. And from small items like birdcages and log baskets, long used by country folk, the townsfolk suddenly demanded basket chairs and baby cribs, chaises longues and picnic baskets. In fact the upsurge in inventive items produced and requested was like manna to the basket-maker, even if the purists among them deplored the idea of such finicky requests as dolls' furniture and plant pot holders alongside the wicker trays and shoe baskets. Country needs were more robust and functional, potato baskets and rug beaters, but the boom in basketry lent both dignity and farce to some of the resulting products.

Dunstan Nash was already feeling the need to immerse himself in the familiar surroundings of his workshop after his enforced inactivity. It wasn't a state that he enjoyed. He needed to be active, to be industriously cocooned in his own workshop once more, with the familiar whiff of dampness from the pre-soaked withy rods, kept under damp cloths until ready for working, and to test the whip of the withy in his experienced hands.

He needed the familiarity of seating himself on his plank, his lap board before him, and applying his skills to the raw natural material he loved, until it emerged in front of his eyes as a thing of beauty and usefulness. It was his joy that his son Edwin had inherited the same enthusiasm for the craft as himself, and between them they had earned a fine local reputation as basket-makers in a county that was famed for them.

Especially here, where the withy beds flourished, and every other man was partial to trying a dab hand at fashioning a basket or two, even if he wasn't employed full-time in the craft. But Dunstan was confident of his own and Edwin's expertise. It took more than a knowledge of randing and waling the rods into a given shape...it took years of careful application to symmetry and perfection and an innate love of intricate pattern and design that made a cratsman's work as individual as himself.

Dunstan had finally thrown off the pall

of lassitude inflicted on him by his illness, insisting to Edwin that he wanted to inspect the workshop for himself on that afternoon when Rosie had gone exploring. The July day was warm, and it could do no harm to stay in the confines of his own piece of land. Edwin agreed, relieved enough to see the keen light back in his father's eyes again, and certain he had done the only possible thing in suggesting the family move to Moule, away from the sad memories of their old home.

He had toured their humble new estate with his father at first, pointing out the merits of the extra small shed where they could do their own boiling of the withies, and showing Dunstan how he had stacked their present stock of rods, brought with them from Minehead, in neat sheaves against the workshop walls. At last, exasperated, Dunstan turned to his son irritably.

'Will you stop treating me as if I was born yesterday, boy! I can see it all for myself, and I've already inspected the place when it was empty. I appreciate that you've had a busy enough time, getting it all ready for working order, but just let me be for a while, will you? I want to get the feel of the place on my own, without having you wet-nursing me.'

'All right, Pa,' Edwin grinned as he

caught sight of his father's hands rubbing slightly together, the left thumb absently caressing the toughened heel of his right hand as if it itched to be working the rods and hammering them into place with the sheer strength of his fist. 'I'll leave you inside. I reckon as how we'll be starting work very soon now you're well again, so I'll be looking out the sign board and nailing it in place to let folk know we're in business.'

Edwin went out into the sunlight, whistling, thankful to his soul that Dunstan seemed to be coming out of his personal long dark tunnel at last. And maybe Vicar Washbourne wouldn't be too pleased to know it, but the little exchange the reverend had had with his father yesterday had done much to restore his fighting spirit and put him on the mend. His Ma, who had had more of a religious inclination than her husband, had frequently noted that God worked in mysterious ways, and Edwin reckoned it was pretty much the case if that pompous old vicar had been able to rouse his father into being more like his old self!

He left Dunstan in the middle of the workshop, and the older man was already thinking the place was too clinical to be worthy of the name, with the stone floor empty of its usual rough matting made by

48

the cut ends of withy that he and Edwin discarded. His spirit soared. Tomorrow he would get back to work, and for now he would find his own basket of tools and see to the sharpening and readying of them...

If Edwin had been five minutes later leaving the workshop Rosie would have got back inside the cottage without being seen, after speeding back along the arrowed length of the rhine. As it was she came face to face with her brother just as she reached the back door and, knowing she had guiltily hoped to avoid being seen until she had composed herself, sent an even wilder flush to her cheeks. Edwin had seen her something like this months before, after the gypsy encounter...but there was a difference here, he realised almost as he would have snapped at her. Rosie looked more agitated than on those nights when she had slipped into the small house after dark, and her pretty blue dress was dirtied as if rough hands had held her. On her face, too, there was a smudge of grime around her mouth. Before saying a word, he bundled her inside the cottage, glad that his father was safely elsewhere for the moment.

'What's happened?' Edwin said abruptly. 'The truth now, Rosie.'

Her soft mouth trembled. 'Edwin, why

would anybody hang garlic outside the door?'

Her reply took him by surprise. It wasn't what he'd expected to hear, not to have his question countered by another one that seemingly bore no reference to his. Or did it? His eyes narrowed. He had left the cottage on one or two evenings now to call in at the Inn, but he must have called there on slack nights, for there had been little conversation, and none who seemed inclined to jaw with a stranger. At the time Edwin hadn't thought it odd, knowing a countryman's natural suspicion until he's got the measure of a man from outside his own boundary, but now he wasn't so sure.

'Who's been talking about hanging garlic outside doors?' he asked carefully.

'A hateful oaf,' Rosie's blue eyes smarted at the memory of how Cyrus had gripped her and pulled her in close to him. Edwin was strong, but that lout had a bull-like strength that made her shiver, and as yet she hadn't rid herself of the smell of him on her skin. 'I think he was a blacksmith, and he tried—he tried—'

'Did he hurt you, Rosie?' Edwin had the light of battle in his eyes now. 'You know well enough what I mean.'

'No, no,' she said quickly. 'He—he kissed me as some kind of payment when he supposedly stopped me falling into the rhine, though there was never any danger of that. He was only jesting, I suppose, but when I told him he'd be sorry if he did it again, he said something stupid about hanging garlic outside the door. You do know what it means, don't you, Edwin? I can see that you do!'

'It's no more than old-fashioned superstition, that's all,' his voice was rough-edged. 'An old country safeguard against witches, if you must know. The oaf was only trying to frighten you, Rosie.'

Her mouth dropped open. 'You don't mean he thought I was a witch!' She started to laugh, yet there was a primitive panic in the sound. She thought back to exactly what had been said. 'Edwin, he also said I should take a look in the church.'

'That'll be it then. Vicar Washbourne will have spread the word about the three sinners who have been here for weeks and never set foot inside the place!' Edwin's voice was hearty, trying to reassure her, but she wasn't entirely fooled. She knew him too well.'We'd better turn up on Sunday, now that Pa's better, and prove to them all that we're as normal as they are! You'll be pleased to hear that Pa couldn't keep away from the workshop a minute longer, and he's talking about starting work again tomorrow. It'll be good to get our hands working again.'

He was turning the subject neatly, Rosie realised, but she could see the sense in what he said too. The sooner they all got to know their new parish, the sooner they would all become part of it. It was never comfortable to feel the outsider. But she still didn't like the inference that she had anything to do with the black arts. Nothing could be farther from the truth, she thought incredulously, and why folk should even think it, she couldn't imagine. She was about to probe into it more deeply with Edwin when she heard her father clumping back to the cottage, and decided to go and change out of her soiled dress instead before any more questions were asked, and to wash her face and hands before preparing their evening meal.

Later, she heard Edwin say casually that he supposed they had best do as Vicar Washbourne requested, and go to church on Sunday. Dunstan put down his knife and fork with a clatter.

'We choose our own time to go a'churching, boy, not when the preacher says we will!' he said loudly, his granite jaw a match for the vicar's at that moment. It cheered Edwin rather than dismayed him. At least it showed that his father was back to his normal spirits, and the change of scene was to his benefit, even though Dunstan had seen little of it himself as yet.

'And Rosie and me have chosen this Sunday,' Edwin went on firmly. 'We don't want folk to think we're hermits, do we Pa? And if we want folk roundabout to buy our baskets, it would be foolish to act as if we thought we were too good for them, wouldn't it?'

Dunstan looked at him thoughtfully. 'That tutor your mother insisted you and Rosie had has got a lot to answer for,' he said finally. 'There's no empty space in that head of yours, is there, boy? Very well then. It makes sense, I daresay. We'll go to church on Sunday.'

It was a satisfying exchange of words, not least because it was the first time Dunstan had referred to his late wife in an easy manner, and Edwin breathed more easily, half wondering if he'd been all set to encounter his father's wrath at being so insistent. He was a strong young man, but his father was still his father, and had all the strength and tenderness in his hands that his work had produced. And Edwin had also felt the back of them when his father's anger was aroused.

'I think I'll make a start on getting to know our neighbours,' Edwin went on easily. 'I thought I'd spend an hour at the Inn tonight, Pa, and start to break the ice.'

Dunstan agreed, though Rosie was a little surprised. Her brother wasn't a drinking man, and too much of the potent stuff made his head reel, but she made no comment, suddenly realising that Edwin must be as much in need of other company as she was herself. Suddenly she missed the gossip of other female company. There had always been someone with whom to pass the time of day at Minehead, and several girls of her own age lived nearby. Here they were very isolated, despite the fact that the village was no more than a stone's throw away.

In fact, apart from Farmer Merrick's wife, the only young woman she had seen since coming to Moule had been the girl who came round the village with the milk churns on a farm cart, and had called to see if they needed any. She had been about Edwin's age, maybe a little older, pretty and fair-haired, though with a premature tension about her mobile mouth. Behind her in the cart a small fair-haired child had sat between the milk churns.

'Hello, and what's your name?' Rosie had smiled at the small girl at once. She didn't answer, her mouth pursed mutinously.

'I'm sorry, miss, she won't speak,' the

girl said apologetically. 'Her name's Daisy and I'm Jess-Jessica Lawrence.'

It was clear she didn't want to linger, and Rosie had bought a large jug of milk and reluctantly seen her leave. Since then she had called several times a week, but still with the same air of declining conversation. It had taken Edwin to bring a smile to Jess's face with some witty remark, and then Rosie had been startled to see how beautiful the other really was. Edwin had seen it too, she noticed, and had taken to buying the milk from the cart himself this past week, even though it was women's work.

The conversation at the Moule Inn died down a little as the tall stranger pushed his way purposefully through the crowd of farmers and villagers in the taproom, nodding to one and then another, and occasionally getting a grunt in response. It wasn't going to be easy, Edwin saw at once. And now he thought he knew why. On his way here he had gone into the church, where an ancient man who told him his name was Tom Kitch had looked at him warily over the broom with which he was supposedly sweeping the stone floor.

'I heard that my family is causing a bit of a stir in Moule, Mr Kitch,' Edwin said without preamble. 'Have you any idea why that should be?'

Tom's eyes shifted involuntarily to the large board inside the entrance of the church. He hawked his throat before he spoke. 'Could be folk don't take kindly to foreign folk appearing out o' nowhere, especially on the Lord's Day,' Tom grunted. 'Then again, could be they'm afeared of any mindings of the Duking Days, and a Nash stirred up a bit o' worry, see?'

His scrawny finger pointed out the name at the top of the Martyrs' Board. Edwin read it quickly. All below were hanged, drawn and quartered on July 26th at Beech Cross Gallows, he read, and heading the list was a Henry Nash of this parish.

His blood felt heated as he read. Not with any superstitious anxiety such as this old dolt might be feeding to his cronies, but that they should be so stupid. This Henry Nash had nothing at all to do with him or his family. And some lout of a blacksmith had scared Rosie because of it. He felt his hackles rise in defence.

And now he was at the Inn, ordering a jug of cider and swilling half of it down far faster than he should do, in order to make these suspicious yokels think he was one of them. He needed their good opinion, he repeatedly told himself. The living of his family depended on it. He forced himself to look agreeable for the time being, and when the cider was nearly gone he asked where the blacksmith could be found.

' 'E'll be in yon back room, young sir,' one red-faced farmer slurred, clearly curious. Edwin nodded, and strode through, the cider jug held firmly in his hand. Cyrus Hale and his cronies stopped chin-wagging as Edwin's tall figure was framed in the doorway, and after glancing round the group his gaze settled unerringly on Cyrus.

'Are you the blacksmith?' he snapped.

An uneasy chuckle behind Cyrus put an added bravado in his voice when he answered. He had brawn enough to be a match for the stranger, he was thinking, and if he'd come spoiling for a fight, then he'd come to the right place...

'What if I be?' He leaned back on the bench and looked insolently at Edwin. Poncy basket-maker, the look said. 'An' who wants to know?'

Edwin stepped nearer. 'I think you know bloody well who I am, Cyrus Hale, just as I've learned your name. And I understand you've met my sister too.'

This time the chuckles were more raucous, and there was an undercurrent of excitement among Cyrus's friends. If they were lucky, Cy would goad the stranger on

57

to a fist fight, they were thinking hopefully, and they'd lay odds on Cy beating the shirt off this one.

Cyrus banged his jug down on the table, folding his arms across his chest and letting his tongue revolve around his fleshy lips, as if he was savouring the memory of something more than the cider he'd just drunk. His voice was thick and guttural.

'That I 'ave, and a choice meeting it was too. Told 'ee about it, did she? A right luscious little handful she be—'

He said no more, because Edwin was across the small space between them, his strong hands closing around the fellow's throat in one fast movement. The action took the blacksmith so much by surprise, as did the strength of Edwin's grip, that for a moment he didn't even struggle, his little eyes suddenly bulging in his purple face.

'If you ever come near my sister again, it'll be the worse for you,' Edwin shouted right in the other's face. 'You keep your filthy hands to yourself in future.'

Cyrus suddenly came to life and let fly a vicious punch with the butt of his knuckles into Edwin's groin. It had the full force and length of the blacksmith's arm behind it, and Edwin reeled backwards. He involuntarily clutched at himself, as the searing pain shot through him, his eyes seeing stars. A fierce wave of nausea gripped him.

'Fight! Fight! All takers at the ready! Get 'em outside and put some wagers on 'em!'

As if from a long way away he heard the sharp excitement in a dozen voices, and fought to shake off the sickly feeling in his gut. He tried to ignore the excruciating throb in his lower regions, and hoped grimly that this cow-turd hadn't emasculated him. The room seemed to be filled with a sea of faces, all egging the combatants on to come outside and put up their fists.

And though God knew he hadn't come here to fist-fight, Edwin would rather die than let himself be seen for a coward. He let himself be pushed and pulled outside as if swept along by a tidal wave. Out into the clean night air, bawled at by the innkeeper who wanted no drunken skirmishing inside his establishment.

Edwin felt himself propelled towards a wide open space near one of the rhines. The next minute he heard the jingle of coins as wagers were made, and then he and Cyrus were encircled by those who'd come to watch the sport. He flexed his muscles and eyed the blacksmith warily. He wouldn't fight fair, but Edwin had brains as well as strength, and hoped that the combination would serve him well enough to keep his vulnerable tender regions well away from any more vicious jabs.

The side of his head suddenly rocked, his cheek stinging as it was split open by Cyrus's clenched fist. He hadn't been ready for it, but now he was. Now, all the blood was singing painfully in Edwin's veins, and though he could feel the effects of the jug of cider he'd drunk too quickly, he lashed out at the blacksmith, bobbing and weaving to avoid the wild arms coming at him like an octopus. And he realised his own fists were connecting with more success than his opponent's. He could tell it by the muttering among the crowd, who half wanted Cyrus to win, and half wanted him to get what many of them would like to do to him.

'Have you had enough yet, you bastard?' Edwin gasped, knowing this was the only language the lout would understand.

The reply was a cuff beneath the chin that all but broke Edwin's jaw. Somehow he stayed on his feet, knowing that once he staggered the fight would be called over, and any wagers on him would be lost.

'Not until I've given you summat to remember me by, my fine bucko,' Cyrus grated back. Edwin leapt backwards as another blow would have caught his groin again, and somehow Cyrus lost his balance at that moment and sprawled headlong on the dusty ground.

At once there was a roar of approval that the fight had been settled, but it wasn't conclusive enough for the two contestants. As if to make these yokels know it wasn't a mere fluke that he had won, Edwin hauled the blacksmith to his feet and frogmarched him towards the rhine. Edwin was head and shoulders taller than the other, and Cyrus's eyes were promising murder as the onlookers bellowed with laughter at the sight of him.

Once at the rhine, Edward dunked the blackmsith's head under the stinking water for several minutes, bringing it out covered in the slimy green water-weed. Encouraged by the slow clapping of the crowd he did it several more times, until Cyrus was spluttering and shouting for mercy.

How long he would have continued with the torture Edwin didn't know, but a sudden arrival from the direction of the Inn put an end to it. Running feet and a hoarsely shouting voice made everybody pause and turn round sharply.

'You'd best come quick, Cyrus Hale. Old Isaac's had a funny turn, and is sitting at the taproom gaspin' like a fish out o' water and callin' for 'ee.'

Edwin let him go, and Cyrus scrambled

to his feet, shaking the weeds from his head like an angry dog. The crowd scattered.

'Aye, I'll come,' he growled, his eyes still murderous. 'But this won't be our last encounter, Nash, not by a long chalk. I ain't never lost a fight yet. So I reckon 'tis true what they'm saying, and the devil was on your side tonight!'

Murmurs filled the air with a slow buzz as the blacksmith strode back to the Inn to see what ailed his grandfather, and to Edwin's reeling vision, the crowd seemed to melt away into the darkness, leaving him alone. A fat lot he'd accomplished, he thought bitterly. He'd come here intending to put a firm but not unfriendly warning to the blacksmith not to molest his sister, and all he'd succeeded in doing was undoubtedly making an enemy.

Chapter 3

'Don't think you'm getting out of coming to church by tellin' me there's work to do, Will,' Mrs Merrick scolded her son roundly on Sunday morning. 'Me and your Pa know all about cleanin' the withies of weeds and what a boring, back-aching job it be, and why you should think to prefer it to listenin' to Vicar Washbourne's sermon, I can't imagine! The weeds'll still be there when we get back, and 'twill give 'ee summat to ponder on to mull over Vicar's words this afternoon.' Her voice was tart. Young people nowadays...

Will groaned. His mother could be rock solid when she put her mind to it, but privately he thought that nurturing their precious crop was a mite more important than listening to the intonations of Vicar Washbourne. If only the preacher didn't go on endlessly about the evils of drink and fornication and the wickedness of man against man...putting more ideas into receptive minds than were ever there before, to Will's way of thinking.

And always ending up with the pious urge to his flock to forgive their fellow-men, as the good Lord decreed. Will sometimes thought that some of Vicar Washbourne's so-called bible quotations were self-composed to suit the occasion, though he knew his Ma would think it blasphemous if he dared to say so. And there was no help for it, he sighed. He would have to go. Even his Pa never missed a Sunday morning unless he was ailing, and lately Jess Lawrence and her little daughter had taken to coming along with them in the big farm calling-cart, since the vicar had apparently decided that seven years of being ostracised by most of the village was a long enough penance for a fallen woman. Bearing a child out of wedlock was the devil's doing, the vicar had impressed upon his congregation at that time, though Will himself hardly remembered the day, being only twelve years old at the time. And since the child had hardly uttered a word since the day she was born, it had seemed to uphold the vicar's judgement.

Lately, however, he had taken pity on poor Jess, since she seemed to be doing no one any harm, and the child sat like a mute in the village school, neither co-operating nor disrupting. And since Jess's tiny cottage was on the way between Merrick Farm and Moule church, Mrs Merrick's generous heart had decreed that the farm calling-cart would stop and pick up the young woman whom they employed to deliver their milk, and her pretty little silent daughter, and allow them to accompany them to church on Sunday mornings.

On that particular Sunday, however, as Will filed into the pew behind his parents, nobody was bothering to note that Jess Lawrence and her child seemed to be developing into suitably docile members of the community. All eyes had already turned to register the appearance of the three strangers from Briar Cottage, and all voices were buzzing like subdued bees as they took their places in a vacant pew near the front of the village church.

Will noticed them at once. At least, he noticed the cream bonnet with the flower sprigs across the top and the trailing pink ribbons beneath. He noticed the long tendrils of gleaming hair curling softly on her slender shoulders, and how straight-backed she sat on the hard wooden seat, with the poise of a princess. He noticed the delicacy of her profile as she sat across the aisle of the church from the Merrick pew; the fresh, soft curve of her cheek and the tip-tilted nose. He noticed how long her lashes were as she lowered her head to study her prayer-book, the dark crescent of them brushing her cheek. He noticed the womanly shape of her, and the way one slim finger brushed away a strand of hair from her face.

Will felt a new and raging need somewhere deep inside him, that had best be severely controlled in this place of worship. If Vicar Washbourne ever suspected that one of his flock was fighting off the urges of the flesh in a way that was physically painful, under the guise of singing the chosen hymns, then he would wash his hands of him, Will thought almost desperately.

For himself, he didn't care, but his Ma

and Pa would be disgraced if it ever happened, and he thought too much of them for that. Anyway, the singing hadn't started yet. If he just sat here and kept his muscles rigid, maybe the sweet savage urges would subside... But the thought of Rosie Nash's sensitive slim fingers touching his own skin was almost sending him into spasms of ecstasy...

Rosie was perfectly aware of the rustle of interest at the Nash family's appearance in church that morning. Edwin had instructed her to keep her head high but not defiant; to let the village of Moule see that the strangers were as God-fearing as any among them...though it was hard for Edwin himself to feel over-pious that morning, with a painful split cheek that stung like vinegar when the breeze touched it, and an ache in his groin that was dull and throbbing. The one small recompense was that he had caught sight of Cyrus Hale sitting with his grandfather, apparently recovered from his funny turn, and the blacksmith was sporting an eye the colour of an over-ripe plum.

Every now and then Rosie managed a surreptitious glance at the rest of the community, and knew the moment that the Merricks arrived in the church, together with the milk girl and the child.

She glanced Will's way several times more before the vicar appeared, and felt a strangely plunging sensation in the pit of her stomach at the almost fierce look on Will Merrick's face. It seemed to be directed at her. As if he hated her for some reason. If she wasn't in a place of worship and knew she was very much in the public eye that morning, Rosie would have flounced her long dark hair and stuck her nose in the air. As it was, she continued to sit demurely, burning inside with a rage she couldn't explain at the apparent slight.

Edwin too had glanced around the small church, filled to capacity as the strains of music began to subdue the buzz of sound from the congregation. And his eyes had met those of the milk girl, registering with a little shock that in her Sunday best instead of the homely spun garment she wore when delivering the milk, Jess Lawrence was a very comely young woman. Beside her the small child sat in a docile manner, a pretty, fair-haired replica of her mother.

A sudden crashing of chords from the pianist brought every head to the front, and Vicar Washbourne mounted the steps to the pulpit, his eyes seeming to take in every aspect of his flock in one sweeping appraisal. And Will Merrick hid a smirk as the vicar's first words upheld his own belief that the vicar spouted more words out of the bible in God's name than were ever in it.

'We will start with the hymn singing, good folk of Moule,' his resonant voice boomed out, 'and while you sing, will you ponder on today's text, if you please. God has brought many sinners into this world to test us. Do we turn our backs on them, or do we welcome them into our hearts as He would have done? Today we welcome newcomers to Moule into the house of God, so let us do so with gladsome voices as we sing hymn number twenty-four, or for those who cannot read they will recognise the tune as "Fight the Good Fight".'

Rosie dared not look at Edwin. She was fighting already. Fighting the urge not to laugh at the clumsy attempts of Vicar Washbourne to welcome the Nash family, while making it perfectly clear it was not before time that they showed up in church.

But long before the next hour and a half was over, she was fidgeting on her hard wooden seat along with many another that morning. The vicar had a captive audience, and as usual he made the most of it. The sermon was long and seemed interminably pompous, as if he was the sole instrument of God, and these simple country folk the worst sinners that ever lived. Rosie found her mind wandering, asking herself desperately if this was the kind of Sunday morning they were destined for in future, or if it was particularly cumbersome for their benefit today.

Out of the corner of her eye she could see that the fierce look on Will Merrick's face had subsided, so presumably he was more entranced by the vicar's words than she was, a fact that surprised her. She wouldn't have taken Will for an especially religious young man. He had the same earthiness about him that Cory had...involuntarily Rosie gave a deep sigh, remembering for a heady moment the way the gypsy boy had swung her off her feet in the soft damp bracken and rained kisses on her unresisting lips. Would she ever see him again...he had promised that she would, but she wasn't born yesterday. She knew that such promises came easily to Cory, and were as unreliable as a will o' the wisp...

Edwin's elbow dug into her side as the sigh became audible, and Rosie's cheeks flamed as she saw Vicar Washbourne's eyes fixed firmly on her. For a moment she felt pinned to her seat by that icy stare, and wondered how a man who professed such piety could look so disagreeable.

'Do we begrudge the minutes spent in the house of God?' the voice thundered on, aimed directly at Rosie, she was certain. 'Would we deny Him all the attention he deserves when He has given us life? A little moment in eternity to spend on earth before we join Him in the glorious great beyond? I tell you, my friends, it is our duty to be humble, as He was humble, to love as He loved, to serve as He served. Join with me now in the final hymn to the glory of God the Father. Raise your voices to the rafters, and be sure that He is listening, now and evermore.'

'Amen,' came the lusty reply, said more with relief than anything else as the congregation rose in one fluid movement from the numbing seats. Ten minutes later they spilled out into the sunlight, their duty done, to be shaken by the hand by the vicar as each one filed out of the church.

'So good to see you today.' He leaned towards them as Rosie and her menfolk appeared, and she couldn't help comparing him to a gaunt black eagle hovering above them. Her father and Edwin were tall, but Vicar Washbourne was the tallest man in the community, which gave him added authority. 'I trust this will herald a regular attendance in future? We are proud of our total commitment to the church at Moule, and like to think of ourselves as God's family here, of which each individual family plays a small part to make up the whole.'

Rosie's eyes were becoming glazed. It seemed they were due for another small sermon outside the church as penance for their tardy appearance. But at last he let them go, to speak with other folk, and she breathed a long sigh of relief, not daring to comment to her brother just yet how appalling she had found the entire morning. He wasn't paying attention to her anyway. Her father was talking to several people who were wanting to make his acquaintance and enquire after his health, since it appeared everyone in the village now knew he had had influenza.

And Edwin was talking with the Merrick family. Though from the way his eyes seemed to rest on the milk girl more often than on Mrs Merrick's rotund figure, Rosie realised he was more interested in her at that moment. Her gaze took in the small child clinging to the milk girl's hand. Shy-eyed and oddly appealing in an elfin way, Rosie could have taken to her at once, but for one thing. It was one reason she had no wish to follow the teaching role her mother had dearly wished for her, and which her father also wanted her to follow.

Couldn't they see, any of them, that each time she looked at a small child like this one, in effect she was seeing the way her little sister Dorcas might have grown? Was she the only one of any sensitivity on that score? The only one who still mourned and silently wept for their bright-eyed moppet who had been taken from them so cruelly...?

'Rosie, there's someone asking to meet you, my lamb.' The comfortable tones of Mrs Merrick broke into the painful memory, and she turned almost with relief at that moment as the farmer's wife stood back a little deferentially from the tall good-looking man, neither young nor old, but clearly more polished than most of Moule's congregation. His clothes were more fashionable, yet not so flashy as to upset Vicar Washbourne. His eyes were smiling and grey, his dark hair dusted with a becoming speckling of white that on him looked distinguished. He was obviously not a farmer, and she felt a quickening of interest as the man took her outstretched hand in his for a brief moment.

'This here's Mr Bennett Naylor, Rosie, our school teacher. Lived in London, he did, and came down here to live among us four year ago now. I told 'im you might be interested in helpin' him out at the village school, so you two just get acquainted now.'

'I'm delighted to meet you, Miss Nash.'

It wasn't an over-cultivated voice, and Rosie suspected that if it had been, it wouldn't have gone down too well with these country people, who were always suspicious of a posh townie. It was just a pleasant voice to listen to, and her mouth curved into a smile as she echoed his words, taking in the fine cut of his clothes and the unmistakable mark of a gentleman in his manner.

'And you're interested in a teaching post, I understand?' Bennett Naylor went on. 'I could certainly use an assistant, Miss Nash, and if you are willing, I would be very happy to show you around the school this morning if you have the time. Perhaps you would ask your father or brother to accompany you if you wish?'

'You seem to know all about us, Mr Naylor,' she hedged a little, feeling uneasily that she was being propelled into the very situation she didn't really want. Yet unable to deny that the man was charming, and far from being a village clod. It would be a pleasure to work with him, she was sure. But the memory of Dorcas still remained too vivid in her mind to agree immediately. She heard the man laugh, and his rather correctly genteel features became more animated.

'I assure you that when you've lived here a little while, my dear Miss Nash, you'll realise it's a country trait to discover everything about one's neighbours with all possible speed!'

'Like the fact that we're viewed with slight suspicion because of our name, and the one-time martyr of this parish, Mr Naylor?' She couldn't resist asking, hoping that she had imagined it all, and that he would look at her with amusement that she had ever taken notice of it all. Instead, he eyed her gravely.

'You must give them time, my dear young lady. I have been here four years, and it's only recently that I have been accepted fully among them. There's a saying that Rome wasn't built in a day, and the same could be applied to the thinking of these people. They view us all with suspicion until we've proved ourselves worthy of their trust. And it would almost certainly hasten the process in your family's case if you were to become my assistant. A teacher has a certain standing in a community.'

As long as some of the more uncouth and short-sighted among them didn't think a witch was taking over the education of their children...the thought churned around Rosie's head before she could stop it, and at the same moment she caught sight of Cyrus Hale farther along the church path with an old man and several of his cronies. Cyrus was grinning her way, and she knew at once that he was talking about her. He made her cringe inside, remembering the way he'd forced himself upon her, and she deliberately turned her back on him.

'If you would care to show me the school, I'd love to see it, Mr Naylor.' She spoke with a breathless quickening of her voice. 'I'm sure my father will have no objection to my going there alone with you, since if we are to work together I can hardly have a daily chaperone, can I? Will you come and be introduced to him and my brother?'

It was clearly the pattern of a Sunday morning for groups to linger on the church path and grassy boundaries, and Rosie was quite aware that Will was scowling her way now as she spoke prettily with the school teacher. Well, it just served him right, she thought. She had really liked him, and from the way he had been glaring at her in church, it would do him no harm at all to think she was interested in someone else! Particularly a gentleman like Bennett Naylor.

As her father gave his permission for Rosie to go along to the school for half an hour, she suddenly realised how much she was enjoying the conversation with the teacher. For too long she had been starved of any kind of stimulating talk, since the tutor she and Edwin had had at Minehead had moved on, and Rosie's world had shrunk with the death of her lively-minded mother and then with that of Dorcas, sending the whole family into a kind of introverted misery, wanting little contact with anyone outside the house. The men had their work, and business hadn't been affected, but for Rosie herself the misery had gone on, and she hadn't realised until now that she too had needed to get away from the scene of painful memories and begin life anew.

She walked along the village street with the school teacher, allowing her fingers to rest lightly on the arm he proffered her, and hoping such an act wouldn't be misconstrued. They were barely acquainted, but tomorrow they would be working together. Even before he had shown her around the little schoolroom with its row of benches and tables and the familiar smell of chalk, Rosie knew she was going to accept the post. When she told Bennett Naylor so, he shook her hand delightedly.

'I couldn't be more pleased, Miss Nash—or may I call you Rosie? It's such a pretty name and suits you so well. As long as you don't think it too presumptuous of me...'

'Oh no, I prefer it.' Her mouth curved into a wide smile. She couldn't help it. His admiring looks made her feel more mature, more of a woman than the young girl she was. His use of her Christian name did nothing to lessen that effect as it sometimes did. It gave their working relationship a little more intimacy that must be good for the children. That was what she told herself.

'And I'd be pleased if you would call me Bennett except in school time, of course,' he went on. 'Do you object? You seem to look at me a little quizzically.'

Rosie felt her face flush. 'I'd like it,' she said honestly. 'No—I was just wondering how you could adjust so well to living in the country, that's all. It's obvious you're much respected here, but it must be vastly different after London!'

'It is!' Bennett laughed. 'And I'm not pretending I had the kind of inner voices attributed to St Joan that sent me here, but there was some kind of compulsion all the same. I found the city too stifling in some ways, though my sister did her best to dissuade me from leaving. I've never regretted it though. There's a feeling of space and freedom, and a oneness with the earth that I find difficult to explain, but I know I'm nearer to it here than I ever was in London. And now you'll think

I'm mad, and it's something I've never told another living soul!'

'Then I'm deeply honoured that you've trusted me with your innermost thoughts,' Rosie murmured, her admiration for this deep-thinking man rising even more. She was dazzled by his articulate way of talking, and the fact that she was to share in his life and perhaps indulge in more stimulating discussions than she had expected to find at Moule was becoming more attractive every second. Before she began to look for reasons, she realised that she had been here long enough, and that her father would begin wondering about her.

'I really must leave,' she said regretfully, 'but I shall look forward to seeing you tomorrow morning, Bennett.'

She spoke his name shyly, and was rewarded by the pleasure in the man's grey eyes. It gave her heart an odd little jolt. He offered to walk her home, but she said quickly that she would prefer to go alone, that perhaps one sight of them together in the village was enough for one day, and that anyway she was still enjoying her private exploration of her new environment.

'I know that feeling exactly,' he smiled, 'and that you are unerringly right about the other matter! Until tomorrow then, Rosie. I know the children will be charmed by having such a lovely young lady in their midst.'

As Rosie stepped away from the school-house, she knew very well it wasn't only the children to whom Bennett Naylor referred. The thought put a little extra lift into her step, and a growing feeling of self-confidence. Right now she could pooh-pooh all the nonsense that the oafish Cyrus Hale had put into her mind. She could tilt her chin at the little snub she felt Will Merrick had directed her way that morning.

She could even begin to view the handsome gypsy boy's departure from her life a mite more dispassionately for a moment, now that a new interest was beckoning her. Whether it was the teaching post or the man, she didn't yet question. What mattered right now was that she felt just a little less disorientated, and she would be grateful to anyone who had provided the means of helping her to achieve it.

'It's not that I don't love you any more, Cory,' the sweet thought whispered through her mind as she walked homewards. 'Nor that I'll ever forget you. How could I, when you and I were as close as any two people could ever be? But I have to be realistic, Cory. I can't live on dreams.'

Her lips moved as if she said the words aloud, the way they sometimes did when she held an imaginary conversation with him, willing him nearer, as if some bond of telepathy between them would send her message to him over the ether, drawing them close...

'Who are you puttin' a spell on now, my pretty?' a voice she knew jarred into Rosie's thoughts. She was hardly noticing where she walked as long as it was in the general direction of Briar Cottage, but now she saw that she was outside the smithy, and that Cyrus Hale lounged against one of the charred oak beams, back in his more familiar blacksmith's garb from his Sunday clothes. He wasn't working, of course. Rosie guessed that even he would balk at the vicar's displeasure at working on a Sunday, but it was clear that Cyrus felt more at ease in working clobber. The ring of the anvil was silent, the glow of the coals absent. And he was out for any kind of sport he could get to relieve the boredom of the day.

Rosie's temper snapped as she saw the jeering look in his eyes and, bolstered by her new position in the village and the backing of a man of influence, her blue eyes flashed like liquid sapphires as she stepped towards him from the village street, her firm young breasts heaving with anger and indignation.

'It's time you and I got a few things

straight, Cyrus Hale,' she burst out. 'Once and for all, you can stop thinking my family has anything at all to do with Henry Nash! I'd never even heard of him until I saw his name in the church. My family has no connection with Sedgemoor and I'll thank you not to spread evil gossip about us. And I know what's meant by hanging garlic over a door, so you can stop all that sinful talk as well. You've already had one taste of my brother's anger, and it will only take one word from me for you to get another. You may think you're the village strong man, but a basket-maker's hands are equally as strong.'

'Women's work!' He was glowering at her now, for being reminded of Edwin's triumph over him. ' 'Tis nearly as mincey as sewin' a seam. I seen 'em threadin' the withy rods in an' out, sat on their planks afore now. There's plenty o' basket-makers around these parts, my pretty, and your men 'ould need to be gurt good to make any sales.'

'They *are* good!' Pride in her menfolk made Rosie's voice shake for a moment. 'And you just better not try to stop folk buying from them, that's all.'

'He suddenly moved towards her, his arms circling her waist before she could stop them. They were inside the overhang of the smithy, and there were no onlookers at that time of day, and Rosie squirmed to free herself in vain.

'An' what will you give me in return, little Rosie?' His voice coarsened. 'I don't do summat for nothin', an' 'twill give me gurt satisfaction to pleasure 'ee. I don't need to tell 'ee what I mean, do I? 'Tis all there in thy pretty blue eyes and thy luscious tits. I seen 'em all stuck out like hat-pegs in church 'smorning. Fair made my mouth water, they did.'

Rosie shoved him away from her with all her strength. 'You pig!' she ground out. 'I've already told you to keep away from me, and you'd better in future. I'm to work with Mr Naylor at the schoolhouse, and you'd better be more respectful towards me.'

'Oh! School teacherin', is it?' If she had thought to overawe him, she failed miserably. The lustful leer was still in his face, his eyes darkened by a desire he didn't bother to hide. 'Well, when you get tired of our fancy school teaching man's talk, you mind an' see what a real man can teach 'ee, my pretty. There's more sport to be learned out of the schoolroom than inside it, you take it from me!'

'I don't want to take anything from you,' Rosie began savagely, which brought forth a roar of laughter and a crude gesture from the blacksmith's forearm.

'You'll soon change your mind when you get it, girlie!'

She turned and hurried away from him, her cheeks scarlet with fury. All her pleasure in the interlude with Bennett was evaporating, and her eyes smarted with humiliation. Yet she didn't want to go blundering home to Edwin again and provoke another fight between him and Cyrus Hale. It wasn't fair to store up enmity on her account, and instead she had walked through the fresh green fields until she felt composed enough to go home. She had already been away far longer than she should have been, she thought guiltily, and the Sunday meal wouldn't cook itself. She just hoped the fact of her doing what her father wanted and taking on the teaching post would allay any questioning as to where she had been all this time.

She needn't have worried. The two men had also had their spirits restored that morning, despite the vicar's ponderous sermon. Dunstan Nash had been more amused than irritated by the continual snide references to strangers among them, who had at last been brought joyfully into the fold, to use the vicar's own colourful phrase. And Edwin...Edwin had been stirred by a completely different kind of emotion that had taken him totally by surprise.

While Rosie had been looking around the schoolhouse and reversing her ideas about working there, the Merrick calling-cart had jolted off through the village in the direction of the farm, and Mrs Merrick had cast a thoughtful eye over her son. Not one for wasting her words, she said exactly what was on her mind.

'Well, what a fine state of affairs we'm finding ourselves in now, my boy, with you sittin' in church and glaring at that pretty young maid as if she was no better'n she should be, beggin' your pardon, Jess, my dear.'

The milk girl's cheeks were stained pink by the aside, but Mrs Merrick was too intent on railing at Will to notice the slight tightening of the girl's mouth. Would they never forget...?

'I never glared at no one,' Will began, his voice surly.

His mother gave a loud sniff. ' 'Tis your mother you'm talking to, my boy, not a new-born babby,' she said acidly. 'And the Nashes are to be business acquaintances, for all the silly nonsense that's been going the rounds about 'em. I don't hold wi' none of it, and nor should you, if that's what's worriting you.'

'You talk in riddles sometimes, Ma.' Will was angry now. 'And I choose my own friends, no matter what the rest of the village thinks about 'em, the same as Rosie Nash.'

He didn't quite manage to hide the slight annoyance as he spoke her name, because truth to tell he'd been all for suggesting she came over to the farm for tea next Sunday afternoon with her father and brother, knowing his Ma would readily agree, only to see Rosie's face suddenly light up as if a candle had been lit behind her eyes as she shook the hand of the school teacher. And his own Ma had been the one to introduce the two of them. So if she'd had any thoughts about himself and Rosie Nash, she may as well forget 'em, Will thought furiously. He could read and write as well as the next, but he was no competition for a man like Bennett Naylor, and he was clever enough to know it. But the fact did nothing to lighten his temper as he thought of the two of them together, and the brushing of Rosie's glossy dark hair across the school teacher's hand as they leaned forward to study the school books together. It put him in a raging mood for the rest of the day, and he for one was damned if he was going to heed Vicar Washbourne's intonations about not working on the Sabbath. What he needed was the seclusion of the deep and secret withy beds, dense and shadowy, where he could hack away at the encroaching weeds with his mattock, undisturbed except by the rustling of the snipe that favoured it as a hiding-place. There Will could work out his frustrations on weeding out the withies until he felt in a better humour.

That was what he would do once the midday meal was over, he decided. He'd work until he'd got Miss Rosie Nash and her tempting blue eyes and soft red mouth out of his conscious thinking. He concentrated so hard on planning the rest of his day that he hardly noticed when the cart jerked to a halt to let Jess Lawrence and the child dismount. He leapt down automatically to give Jess his hand, and to lift the silent Daisy down after her, and then jumped back on the cart again with only a careless wave of the hand. He had other things on his mind that needed all his attention.

Chapter 4

Jess let go of the child's hand and let her scamper over the grass to the humble cottage they shared. She had little to thank Vicar Washbourne for, but at least when he had condemned her as a fallen woman, he had told the parish he had no wish to deprive her of her home as well. Jess had known of other women who had been hounded out of close-knit villages like this one for committing the awful crime of bearing a child out of wedlock. Especially when refusing to name the father...

How could she name him, she thought bitterly? She didn't even know the name of the travelling-man who had knocked on her door late one night begging a drink of water, and seized the chance to rape a helpless young girl, and neither did she want to know it.

The midwife who had delivered the child had been sorry for her agony, and informed the village that the girl had paid in full for her sin, but it had been a long, lonely time before the village finally relented. And Daisy's silence had been one more punishment Jess had to bear. The child was capable of speech, a doctor had told her, but she suffered a strange reluctance to do so.

It was a mark of shame, Jess believed, brandishing her child as different from the rest. Now that she was seven years old and was allowed to attend the village school, Jess had hoped desperately that words would come from her delicate little daughter's lips, but they never did. And in an attempt to stop the vicar's constant reminders to his congregation that a strumpet walked among them, she had burst into a passionate tirade against the wickedness of men that completely took him by surprise.

Vicar Washbourne had looked at the abject figure before him in the empty church, where Jess had confronted him two years previously, and thought about the Lord's forgiveness.

'Do you repent absolutely your mortal sin?' he had demanded of her at that time, his eyes seeming to pierce into her very mind to see the truth of it.

Jess's misery had flooded out, uncaring whether or not she shocked a man of the cloth. 'If you mean do I repent of allowing my body to be used in lust, then I do, a thousand-fold! Not that I did allow it, never willingly, and never since! I fought with every bit of my strength against the fiend who abused me, hating the feel and the stench of him, and the violation I felt. And the pain too, Vicar! If that was the act that results in procreation, then surely God must be laughing somewhere up there in his heaven, because it was more like the piercing of my flesh with a red-hot needle than an experience to be enjoyed!'

'Will you please hold your tongue and remember where you are, woman!' The vicar had been outraged, his face almost convulsed. 'What you speak is blasphemy.'

'If it is, then I think God would have struck me dead before now, because I've thought it enough times since my daughter was born,' Jess said bitterly. 'You say your God is a caring God, who welcomes sinners into his arms and forgives them. Haven't I sinned enough, Vicar? Don't I qualify for His forgiveness even yet? Or must I pay for the rest of my life? Isn't it enough that every time a man comes near me I flinch because of what happened to me, and that I'm doomed to remain an outcast because of it? Oh, I've got work, because of the kindness of the Merricks, but as for love, I can no longer feel it except for my little Daisy. Wouldn't you say that was punishment enough, Vicar?'

No one had ever spoken to him that way before, nor since. As if to emphasise her words, when he had put one hand on her shoulder, whether to turn her out of his church or show a brief sympathy he didn't rightly know, he felt her visibly tremble at his touch. In one movement she turned and ran out of the place, leaving him with her words still ringing in his ears and an examination of his own interpretation of the Lord's work.

The following Sunday, seeing the girl at her habitual place at the back of the church, the child beside her, Vicar

Washbourne had made a momentous decision, and the sermon that followed left his congregation in no doubt that a sinner who was condemned by man would find even greater solace with God. From that day on Jess Lawrence was no longer so ostracised, and Moule had accepted her, if a trifle cautiously.

And it was true, Jess thought now, as she let herself and Daisy into the cottage. No man had ever touched her since that terrible night, nor had she wanted them to. In effect, she was still as virginal as before the thing had happened. She still thought of herself that way. If it hadn't been for the constant reminder of Daisy...ah, but how could she condemn Daisy for reminding her, when the child had brought warmth and lightness back into her life? Without her, Jess knew she would have shrivelled and died long ago. As it was...she was still a woman, deep down, and still capable of a woman's longings, however submerged they had been all these long years.

She had been as bright and pert as the young girl at Briar Cottage, who had been in church that day with her father and brother. Jess had hardly seen any of them before today. She had delivered the milk when it was needed, and sometimes it was the young girl who had answered, and several times the young man. But always they had seemed preoccupied and anxious, and knowing now that it had been on account of the father's health, Jess had thought wistfully how wonderful it must be to be cared for so much.

And then today... She moved quickly into the scullery to see if the meat pie and potatoes that she and Daisy were having for their Sunday meal was cooked, and caught sight of herself in the old looking-glass above the sink—really looked at herself as if through a man's eyes, which was something Jess hadn't done for a very long time.

How had she appeared to him that morning, she wondered tremulously? She was still a young woman, though she sometimes felt the ravages of her past had stamped her indelibly. But the softness was still in her skin and the bloom of youth still there. Her eyes were large, like Daisy's, and her shape still womanly enough to stir a man's heart, maybe...

Jess turned away, her limbs suddenly trembling with a wild emotion she had never felt in her life before. She had heard his name that morning, spoken on Farmer Merrick's lips. It was a strong name, a name she liked. Edwin. Edwin Nash. She gave a sudden little laugh that caught in her throat and had a hint of heartbreak in it. How foolish she was. How foolish even to dream of him, and even more so to think he would ever look at *her*.

Dunstan didn't conceal his pleasure when Rosie made her announcement on her return from the village. If her eyes were a little bright he didn't comment on it. He wasn't quite as unknowing of Rosie's devotion to her little sister's memory as his daughter believed, and privately thought that the best therapy for Rosie was to surround herself with other children. The girl was a born teacher, Dunstan thought proudly, and one day she would marry and have lots of babies of her own. At least, it was his firm hope that it would be so.

'And the school teacher? A fine man, by the looks of him,' Dunstan remarked, his eyes on his daughter. She laughed at his blatant questioning, her eyes mischievous.

'Oh, very fine, Pa. I liked him enormously, and I'm sure we're going to have lots of interesting conversations in the future. He's from London, you know, and I gather he has a sister who still lives there.'

'Is that so? A dirty, smoky place, they tell me.'

'I can't imagine Bennett living anywhere but the most fashionable area.'

'Bennett already, is it?' Edwin put in. 'It didn't take you long to get acquainted,

Rosie, but I must say, I prefer your choice of companion to the other one.'

She turned away, her face flushed as Edwin fingered the split cheek that was smarting like hell right now. Edwin wouldn't be too pleased to know she had had another little brush with Cyrus Hale, and she decided to keep that bit of knowledge to herself. In a burst of tit for tat she looked at him teasingly.

'I noticed you had your own reasons for lingering around the Merricks this morning, Edwin. Shall I ask her name the next time she calls with the milk?'

'I think I can manage to do that for myself,' Edwin told her, not bothering to say he already knew it. He was intrigued by the sight of those sad eyes, and he sensed the girl's background hadn't been easy, though as yet he was oblivious of her true circumstances. The child was a little charmer, even though she remained quiet and docile, but she would grow up to be as good-looking as her mother, Edwin thought. Yes, he was definitely intrigued, and wanting to know more about the girl. He would make it his business to find out as soon as possible. If there was a husband around then that would alter his intentions, if he had any. But a sixth sense told him there wasn't—that, and a quick glance at her left hand, which was quite ringless. A widow, perhaps, which was a tragedy in one so young and attractive...

'Wake up, Edwin,' Rosie's knowing eyes were laughing at him. 'Why don't we take a walk over to Merrick farm after our meal and take a look around? Mrs Merrick said we could go any time we liked, didn't she? And you'll want to see the withy beds properly.'

'And you'll want to see our Will,' Edwin grinned.

Rosie tossed her head. The glossy fall of dark hair spun out around her head as she did so, as angry as a horse's mane, Edwin thought with a hidden smile. She was transparent to him, if to no one else, and he knew she was piqued by the apparent snubbing of the Merrick boy, and would be burning to find out the cause of it.

'I'm not interested in him really,' she said casually. 'Bennett is far more interesting. He's a gentleman.'

'Oh Rosie, Rosie,' Edwin chuckled. 'Since when did a man need to be a gentleman to turn your pretty head? I remember not so long ago...'

'Well, I don't want to remember,' she said crossly, knowing he referred to the gypsy, and thankful that her father had gone out to the workshop among his beloved withies. 'That's all in the past,

Edwin, and I'm not going to think about it.'

A small feeling of betrayal crept into her mind even as she said the words. Cory had been so very much a part of her...but the practical side of her knew it was no good, that a liaison between them could never be. Even if her father allowed it, the gypsy people would not. There was no place for her in Cory's world.

Once their meal was over, Dunstan decided to rest for the afternoon. Though nearly back to full strength, there was still a hint of weakness in his chest that the damp atmosphere of the Levels didn't help. Thankfully the influenza had caught him in mid-summer. If it had happened in winter, when the land hereabouts was subject to flooding, it might have been much more serious.

So Rosie and Edwin set out for the exhilarating walk to Merrick farm, and once through the village they breathed in the fragrant country air, heady now with the abundance of wild flowers and trees in full leaf. The small figure of Daisy Lawrence in her print pinafore almost merged in with the background, as she darted among the grasses trying to catch a butterfly.

'Hello. What are you doing?' Edwin smiled at the child, who looked at him with wide eyes and made no response. Daisy looked from one to the other, and then turned and flew like the wind towards the cottage nearby.

'She's an odd one, Rosie. You're not going to get much conversation out of her if she's one of your pupils. She didn't say a lot outside the church, did she?'

'She didn't say anything,' Rosie said, remembering. 'Not that you were paying too much attention to the child!'

At that moment Jess appeared in the garden of the cottage, hesitating as she saw the two of them. She gave a half-smile but it was enough for Edwin. Without comment to Rosie, he strode forward and his sister was obliged to follow. At the gate of the small cottage garden he stretched out a hand to Jess.

From two steps behind Rosie had the oddest feeling she was watching all this in slow motion. Jess seemed to move towards her brother very gradually, as if drawn to him against her will, lifting her arm and placing her delicate fingers within Edwin's grasp as if the contact between them was wanted yet dreaded.

Who was becoming fanciful now, Rosie asked herself? But there was an atmosphere between these two that was almost tangible. She felt it as surely as she breathed, and it was as if she was an intruder at this significant moment in two people's lives. It was all nonsense, and she knew it, but the feeling was too strong to be denied.

'It's Jess, isn't it?' Edwin was saying softly. 'I think we may have frightened your little daughter just now. I'm sorry.'

'It's all right. She's wary of strangers, that's all.' Jess's voice was softly modulated. The words they spoke were almost stilted, as if they didn't matter. What was being said was in the holding of the glances between them and the slight colouring of Jess's fine-boned cheeks, and in the clasp of her fingers that each seemed reluctant to break.

For a moment Rosie felt oddly shut out, as if she was witnessing something too tender to evaluate, as deeply personal as the moment of conception, the fragile dawning of love between two people. Perhaps if all her own senses hadn't been so sharply aware these last few days through all the new experiences and new people in her life, she would not have sensed it so surely, but the feeling left her oddly insecure, and her voice was more jerky than she intended when she broke the spell between Jess and her brother.

'Does she attend the village school, Jess? I'm to begin a teaching post there tomorrow.'

Jess seemed to drag her gaze away from

Edwin to look at Rosie, dropping her fingers from his hand at once as if only just aware that they were still clinging to each other. But Rosie saw how she gripped her own fingers that had touched Edwin's, as if to keep the warmth of his hand captured within her grasp a little longer.

'She'll be there, miss, but you won't find her an easy pupil, I'm afraid. She doesn't talk, you see.'

Rosie's interest was caught. In the same instant she knew it was ridiculous for Jess to address her so meekly.

'My name's Rosie, Jess, and this is my brother Edwin. You already know we live at Briar Cottage,' she went on briskly. 'So why doesn't Daisy talk? Is she deaf—or mute?'

Rosie's warm heart went out to the child, who had appeared at the cottage window now, as if afraid to come too near the strangers, but intrigued by them all the same. Jess shook her head.

'The doctor says she's perfectly capable of speech, but she just won't,' she said simply. 'No one has been able to make her say more than the odd word in her life. I've just got used to it now. But please—won't you both come in and take some lemonade with us? It's a warm day for walking.'

Rosie would have said yes anyway,

wanting to know more about Daisy, but Edwin was already moving towards the cottage with Jess. The child jumped back from the window and was nowhere to be seen when they went inside. The cottage was homely, with patchwork cushions on the hard chairs and settle that Jess must have worked herself. She moved about with a grace that impressed Rosie, as if she entertained in a palace instead of the humble interior of the cottage. When she had poured them all some lemonade, she called her daughter.

The child came reluctantly, pulling a cushion from a chair and sitting on it on the rag rug. Jess laughed indulgently.

'She likes to be near the fire, even when it's not burning, and we fill the fireplace with pots of flowers from the meadows.'

'She should have a small chair especially made for her,' Edwin said at once. 'How would you like a basket chair, Daisy? Shall I make you one to fit you?'

Rosie looked at her brother in astonishment, and Jess flushed, protesting that it was out of the question, but Edwin brushed aside her objections.

'I said nothing about payment, Jess. It will be a useful exercise to make a chair for a child, and it will be give me an excuse to call on you again.' They both knew he needed no excuse, and as if the moment was charged with meaning, both looked away from each other to the child.

'Daisy would like a special chair, wouldn't you, Daisy?' Edwin asked her.

For a moment there was no response. The child looked up at him from her floor position, her small head on one side like a bird poised for flight. And then she nodded vigorously, her small hands moving like lightning towards her mother and then Edwin and then herself. Rosie looked mystified until Jess laughed and explained.

'She's very happy that you want to make her a chair, Edwin,' she spoke his name shyly for the first time. 'And she wants me to make a cushion to fit it exactly.'

Rosie could see that the thought delighted them both, because it would be something they both had a share in. She cleared her throat, suddenly wanting to be away from here, more restless than she had been since Cory went away in the spring.

'What happened to her father?' She said the words softly to Jess, and was so startled to see a look of anguish in the other girl's eyes that she was horribly embarrassed. It was clearly something dreadful, and she wished she hadn't asked.

'I've always been mother and father to Daisy,' Jess said at once, but her mouth trembled a little, and Edwin stopped any more questions by saying they had better be on their way, but that he'd call on Jess soon to decide on the measurements for Daisy's chair. He almost bundled Rosie outside, and when they had walked on in silence for some minutes she asked him if he had any ideas about the missing father.

'It was clear Jess didn't want to talk about it, and I didn't want to pry. I've no doubt we'll find out in time.'

Meanwhile Edwin didn't want to spoil the tremulous stirring of love that he knew would grow like a flower blossoming in the sun. He had known other girls, but never one he knew instinctively was the one for him, for all time. The idea of making a chair for Daisy had been an inspiration. It would be made with love, with all the tenderness of a man's love for a woman. As his hands worked the withy rods and his deft fingers caressed them into shape, the finished article would be all the more perfect because he fashioned it for Jess's child. Edwin't step was doubly jaunty as they neared Merrick farm, where the growing beds of withies spread as far as the eyes could see, and from the barns near the farmhouse the swish-swish of milk dropping into pails was a comforting reminder of the farm's secondary product. One thing Vicar Washbourne couldn't argue with was that farming work had to continue, Sunday or weekday, rain or shine. And Rosie's heart began to beat a little faster, wondering if Will was in one of the milking barns right now, and if she dared to wander around with Farmer Merrick's approval...

Mrs Merrick's beaming round face appeared at the farmhouse door to welcome them.

'Come you in, my dear, and 'tis a pleasure to see you both again,' she said, as if they hadn't so recently met at church that very morning. 'You'll take some tea and seed cake, won't you?'

'If it's no trouble, Mrs Merrick?' Rosie said at once. 'We've had some lemonade at Jess's cottage, but it's certainly a warm day, so if you're sure we're not disturbing you.'

'I'm only too glad to be disturbed, my lamb. With Will in a troublesome mood and Farmer out in the barns, 'tis a long afternoon after the excitement of the morning.'

Rosie didn't dare look at Edwin. To describe the vicar's sermon as exciting was really stretching the imagination. And Will was nowhere to be seen. She wondered just why he was in a troublesome mood. At least it proved he was a young man of spirit as well as handsome looks, she thought suddenly. She preferred that to one who was too bland and genteel, for it matched her own temperament more exactly. The image of the school teacher flitted into her head for a moment, but Bennett Naylor had other attractions, of course. He could converse so knowledgeably, and he knew all about London, which was exciting in itself...

'So you've been to call on poor Jess, 'ave 'ee, my dear?' Mrs Merrick was saying thoughtfully. Rosie's interest was caught at once, and she knew Edwin's was too, though he carefully left the talking to the womenfolk.

'Why do you call her "poor Jess", Mrs Merrick? She seems a very likeable girl, though I suppose you mean because of Daisy. It seems tragic that she won't speak.'

'Aye, Daisy.' Mrs Merrick gave a heavy sigh. 'Well, 'tis bound to come out sooner or later, so I might as well be the one to tell 'ee both. Better to come from a body who's fond o' the girl than one who's got her knife into poor Jess, and there's still some o' they about, for all their pious looks!'

Rosie felt sure it couldn't be as bad as Mrs Merrick implied, but as the woman told the tale, her own face tinged with colour, and she could sense how rigid

103

Edwin had become beside her.

' 'Tis always the woman who has to bear the shame,' Mrs Merrick said sorrowfully, when she had done. 'And poor Jess was just a child herself when it happened, living alone in that cottage since her folks died, and prey to any foul-minded brute that came her way. Fair turned her brain for a time, it did, and even now 'tis said she'll let no man touch her if she can avoid it, not even to brush her fingers. She confided to me one time that it makes her curdle inside, and none can blame 'er for feeling that way.'

Rosie could see the information had affected Edwin badly. His face was quite pale, and she plunged on quickly before the farmer's wife noticed anything.

'There's nothing wrong with the child though, is there, Mrs Merrick? Jess told us the doctor said it's nothing physical.'

The woman sighed. ' 'Tis a tragedy, and that's for certain sure. 'Tis summat else to mark her out like a punishment.'

'But what happened wasn't Jess's fault,' Edwin said, his voice tense. 'Nor Daisy's, come to that. It was the brute who forced himself on her who's to blame.'

'Oh, aye, we all know that, but 'tis a hard job convincing folk, my dear, when the evidence of a man's lust is in a woman's belly. 'Tain't the man who

104

carries the child, is it?' Her voice was reproachful, as if all men were guilty.

If it hadn't been for the fact that she knew Edwin was finding all this intensely personal, Rosie would have pursued the conversation. It was rare that anyone spoke so frankly, but she supposed that in the farming world life and death and all the processes in between were matters to be discussed as freely as any other. She changed the conversation before Mrs Merrick gleaned that Edwin was more interested in the milk girl than mere idle curiosity allowed.

'Can we look around the farm, Mrs Merrick?' she asked.

'Of course you can. Farmer's in the barns with the milking boy, and Will's somewhere out in the fields, doin' some weedin' o' the withies. Like I said, he's in a tetchy mood, so if you want to keep clear of 'im, I don't blame 'ee!'

It wasn't what Rosie wanted at all. And since it was withies and not cows that Edwin wanted to see, she was quite sure they would soon track down Will Merrick. The thought made her heart beat a little faster. She was still annoyed with him for the scowling looks he had given her in church that morning, when she knew very well she was looking her best and the new bonnet had flattered her face. But as

Edwin strode out ahead of her, it was all Rosie could do to keep up with him.

'Just a minute, Edwin,' she grumbled as her foot almost turned on the rutted ground. 'Is there a fire or something?'

He stopped walking so suddenly she cannoned into him, and as she would have snapped at him she caught sight of the look in his eyes, and she should have guessed all along...

'If I had the bastard's neck between my hands right now, I'd squeeze the life out of him, Rosie. To rape a young girl and then leave her to face the consequences is criminal. She might have been hounded out of the village. As it was—well, you can see the scars in her face, can't you? Poor sweet Jess.'

It was clear that Mrs Merrick's story had done nothing to lessen the impact the girl had had on him. Rosie trembled for her brother, remembering other things he seemed to have overlooked—that Jess was so fearful of a man's touch that the capacity to love might be lost to her forever; that Jess must see Daisy's constant presence as a reminder of what a man's lust could do, and that love and lust would be so mixed up in her mind she could never separate them. Edwin could be rushing headlong into a heartbreak situation, and knowing her brother's passionate nature there was nothing Rosie, nor anyone else could do to save him from it. Only Jess herself...

'Go slowly, Edwin, I beg you,' she said hesitantly, knowing it was indelicate to put it more clearly, and feeling embarrassed at suddenly feeling older and wiser than he. It was so obvious that Edwin had been smitten by love and was blinded by it to the exclusion of all else.

They had made a fine start in Moule, Rosie thought ruefully. They had stirred up a hornet's nest by all accounts by the very fact of their name, and by living in a cottage on the very site where an ancient battle had been fought. A village oaf had alternately hinted that she was a witch and promised to lust with her the minute he got the chance. Her brother had already had one fight with Cyrus Hale and set himself up in the village as the blacksmith's enemy. Now he had fallen in love with a girl the village had clearly banished from their midst until the vicar had relented and they had reluctantly allowed her in once more.

While Rosie herself...she had met two men who intrigued her, one with a fleeting resemblance to Cory but with a moody nature and a depth of passion in his soul she recognised as if it was part of herself...the other, a gentleman who treated her like a lady, with whom she would work and enjoy good conversation, and whom she was delighted to know, not least because he was so informative about another kind of world Rosie didn't even know.

They walked silently, each with private thoughts until they neared the withy beds, and then Rosie's eyes were searching among the rows of swaying withies, the supple stems moving in the breeze, the leaves rustling and whispering as if with a thousand muted voices to an imaginative mind. They were calling her unerringly to where a dark-haired figure worked methodically among the rows, hacking away at the encroaching weeds, and Rosie's heart leapt with a joy she couldn't ignore as Will turned and came towards them.

Chapter 5

Now that he had time to think it over, Dunstan realised it may have been a bit rash to suggest Rosie worked at the village school. It was what Marjorie had always wanted for her daughter, and the idea of it had been doggedly in Dunstan's mind ever since. There hadn't been the opportunity in their old home, but seeing the little schoolhouse at Moule, it had seemed heaven-sent. It was only now, when he was clearly recovered from his illness and seeing things more clearly, and the deed was done, that Dunstan realised there would be no woman in the cottage to clean and bake and see to the washing and the pressing of the family's clothes. Rosie could do some of it, but Dunstan was a fair man, and decided the only answer was to hire a woman from the village on a daily basis.

Not a young woman, either. A widow, perhaps, needing a little extra money. The Nashes weren't paupers. They were craftsmen and proud of it, and they could afford to pay for help in the cottage. Dunstan was well satisfied with the thought. And he would make himself agreeable to Vicar Washbourne and enquire about someone suitable, leaving the Vicar in no doubt that Dunstan Nash wasn't looking for a wife, merely a paid house-keeper.

Since Marjorie, women had had no place in Dunstan's life, nor ever would, save for his little Rosie, who was blossoming into a woman in front of his eyes. He half-smiled at the simile. Never had a child been so aptly named, and he was quite content to leave any future matrimonial prospects to his children, trusting them to choose well.

There had been a brief moment of anxiety earlier in the year when Rosie had begun to run a little wild, and Dunstan's suspicions had been aroused. But now he had every hope that she would develop into a good and dutiful daughter, and working beside the handsome and intelligent schoolteacher, who knew what might happen there! As for Edwin...Dunstan had every confidence in his son. It was Edwin who had suggested the business here, and with an ambitious head on his shoulders, there was always the chance he would catch the eye of a gentleman's daughter in due course. Dunstan's smile grew broader as he flexed the fingers of his hands and reluctantly left his workshop until Monday to go in search of the vicar with his request, blissfully ignorant of the fact that his children had very different ideas for themselves.

'Mr Nash—Mr Edwin, sir...'

Edwin and Rosie paused as they heard the shout behind them. Turning, they saw Farmer Merrick waving his arm to them from the barn.

'Can 'ee spare a minute, young sir?'

Rosie spoke quickly. 'He'll want to ask you about the withy auctions, Edwin. You'd better find out exactly what's going to happen. You go back and I'll take a walk around the fields. You can catch me up later.'

'And no doubt your walk will take you directly to our Will,' Edwin grinned. 'All right, but don't get lost among the withies, will you?'

She watched him stride out and walked on eagerly, her heart beginning to thud. It couldn't be better. Rosie shared her brother's forthrightness, and if she had done something to annoy Will Merrick then she wanted to know what it was. Even if he was a mere farm-boy, she didn't like to know he'd been glaring at her in church. The real reason was far more complex than that, of course, but Rosie pushed it to the back of her mind. She stepped into the field of tall swaying withies, nearly shoulder-high to her, and walked purposefully along the row where she could see Will's dark head. When he stood up straight, he was a good head and shoulders above her own height, and Rosie had to lift her chin to look at him. She watched him silently for a moment as he severed the weeds with the sharp blade of the mattock, ignoring her presence. Just as she was about to make some scathing remark about his lack of manners, he turned to face her, his blue eyes glinting in the sunlight.

'Only a fool 'ould go walking through

111

the withy beds in dainty shoes, or folk with more money than sense!'

Rosie's mouth opened furiously, and then she felt the damp seeping through her thin shoes, and looked down quickly, realising Will was absolutely right. The fact did nothing to endear her to him at that moment, nor did the look of triumphant arrogance on his rugged face. She registered at the same moment that he wore stout boots, the bottoms of his breeches tightly tied round with twine to keep out the damp. Rosie felt suddenly foolish, all her superiority gone. She tried vainly to regain it.

'I'm not in the habit of walking through withy beds.'

'O' course not. Your menfolk have the easy job, don't they? Playing wi' the rods and makin' them into fancy pieces for the townsfolk!'

Rosie was outraged. 'Playing with them! Is that your opinion of a skilled craftsman, Will Merrick? It takes years to perfect the art of basket-making, but any old fool can plant a few sticks and let nature do the rest!'

Her blue eyes were blazing at him, her face scarlet. How dare he belittle her father's work! And Edwin's too... If Edwin had heard that remark...but a sixth sense told Rosie it wouldn't have been said if Edwin had been there. For some reason Will Merrick wanted to get her riled. She could see it in his eyes. He wanted to get the better of her, but this time she felt they were on equal terms, as Will's mouth tightened to a hard line.

'What do you know about growin' the crop?' he snapped. 'Don't tell me those pretty fingers ever wove a withy rod to make a basket!'

Any other time Rosie would have snatched at his unwilling compliment about her pretty fingers, and noted that although he looked so angry his eyes were taking their fill of her as she stood, taut and defensive, her gleaming hair teased by the wind and a pulse beating wildly in her throat. As it was, she felt an overwhelming urge to let this clod know she wasn't as ignorant as he. She seized one of the withy rods growing beside her.

'I know which is the back of the rod when my father uses it,' she said haughtily. 'I know which is the tip and the butt, and how he assesses which rods will make the best baskets. I may not be able to work the rods, but I know how it's done, which is more than you do, I'll wager.'

'Why should I care?' Will scoffed. 'All I do is grow the crop. What's done with 'em after that is no concern o' mine.'

The fact remained that the two concerns

113

were interdependent on each other, and both of them knew it. Rosie remembered why she had come here. For the moment crowing over the merits of withy growing or basket-making could wait.

'Why did you look so cross in church this morning?' she demanded. 'Each time I caught sight of you, you looked so fierce, as if I'd done something terrible!'

Will felt the colour race up his neck as he remembered the exact reason for his discomfort that morning. Just for a moment he was tempted to tell her, knowing it would wipe the superior look off her beautiful face quicker than blinking. What would she do, Will thought briefly, if he told her bluntly he'd had such a raging hard-on and all on account of her that he'd been in danger of sitting through Vicar Washbourne's sermon in tacky breeches! The thought of her stunned reaction made him grin, even though he knew he'd never say the words, but he had to say something! While he tried to think, Rosie felt her own cheeks redden at the look on his face. He was laughing at her now, and that was something she couldn't bear. If the ground hadn't been so soggy beneath her feet, and squelching every time she moved them slightly, she would have stamped her foot in temper.

'I suppose you find it boring to sit in

church on a Sunday morning,' she said scornfully before he could speak. 'It's what I might have expected from country folk!'

'Oh? Are you so much better than we then?'

She had the grace to look shamefaced. Deep down, Rosie knew her father would be aghast at the way she was talking down to Will Merrick. She couldn't really explain it herself. It was as if she was drawn to him against her wishes, wanting to be perverse and to antagonise him for no other reason than to keep him talking. Only now she couldn't think of an answer to his aggressive question. Will answered for her.

'I saw you talking to the school teacher. He's more your mark, I daresay. I noticed how your face came to life when you looked up at him.'

Rosie saw the dark scowl on his good-looking face, and a sudden awareness swept into her mind. A feminine intuition that told her Will Merrick wasn't really as immune to her as he might pretend. Why, he was jealous, Rosie thought! And she was young enough and pretty enough to let the thought of it delight her. She smiled up at him winsomely, putting her small hand on his arm for a moment.

'Don't be jealous of Bennett Naylor, Will! I'm to work with him at the village school as his assistant, that's all! We're not walking out together or anything.'

'I never thought you were, and I wouldn't *care* if you were!' he said roughly, but he knew with a sharp twist of his gut that he would mind. If Rosie Nash was walking out with anybody, he wanted it to be him...but the thought of her being a young woman with brains enough to be a school teacher made him suddenly dumb. She took his words to heart.

'That's all right then.' She tossed her head. 'I'm glad I don't have to ask your permission if I decide to change my mind! Bennett's a very intelligent man and I like him very much already. He came here to work from London, you know.'

'Really?' Will sneered. 'I suppose he thought we savages needed educating.'

'If the cap fits...' Rosie said sweetly. 'Anyway, I'll leave you to your boring weeding now. My brother will be waiting for me.'

She intended making a grand exit away from him. Her slender body twisted, but her feet were stuck fast in the marshy ground, and a sudden cry was torn from her throat as she lost her balance. The next second she was falling, falling, against the yielding mass of withies. They whipped past her body, some scratching her soft skin, and snagging at her clothes and

116

hair, and she had the horrible sensation of plunging into a forest of unresisting wands. She closed her eyes against the sting of them on her face, and then strong hands were pulling her out of the forest, and she gasped as a searing pain shot through her ankle, the hot tears filling her eyes with the shock of it.

'Rosie, Rosie, are you hurt?' Will's voice was a rich vibrant sound deep in his chest as he held her close against him. His arms were tightly round her, and she could feel the thud of his heartbeats. ' 'Twas all my fault for goading you on so, even if you did push me into it. We're a good match when it comes to fightin' with words, Rosie, but I never meant this to happen. Have you calmed down now?'

Didn't he know she was all the more disturbed by the fact that she was held close in his arms? That her heart beat so fast it was nearer to suffocating her than the warmth of his embrace? Will's arms were the only welcome ones to hold her since Cory's...and the sweet sensations the contact evoked were so much the same, and yet so subtly different, Rosie could hardly breathe at the magic of it.

'I don't think I'm badly hurt,' her voice was a soft whisper, not wanting the moment to end, yet knowing she could hardly stand here in his embrace all afternoon. And wanting to do so with a hunger that took her by surprise. 'Oh Will, thank goodness you were there to catch me.'

Her blue eyes looked up at him, blurred with tears into mysterious pools. Her voice was catchy in her throat, her mouth still trembling from her fright, soft and parted and moistly inviting. Will's prosaic reply that if he hadn't been there in the first place she'd never have got herself into this situation died on his lips, and it was more than he could do to resist lowering his head to hers and touching his mouth to her lips.

Her arms tightened around him as she seemed to sway into his embrace. Earth and sky seemed to merge into one at the first exquisite meeting of mouths in a kiss of such tenderness Rosie knew instantly that no other could match it, before or after. This was love, the tremulous thought shivered through her senses. This finding of a soul-mate and recognising him...as the kiss deepened, she became aware of the hardening of Will's body against her, and the total masculinity of him. It should shock her, but it didn't. Instead, it exhilarated and thrilled her, because now she knew that however reluctant Will Merrick might appear towards her at times, together they were capable of igniting a flame that would burn for ever...if there was ever the remotest feeling of mysticism about Rosie Nash, it came to her at that instant that here was her destiny.

Dimly, she heard a shout from the direction of the farm, and recognised her brother's voice. It was an intrusion into a moment out of time, and as Will jerked his head away from her, she felt as torn apart as if someone had divided her flesh in two. At the sudden fleeting look of uncertainty on Will's face as Edwin began walking towards them from the far corner of the field, Rosie spoke swiftly.

'Pick me up and start moving towards him, Will. I don't think I've done more than wrench my ankle, but it pains enough for Edwin to believe that I shouldn't walk back on it.'

He looked down at her, a half-smile on his lips. Rosie could still taste them on hers, and knew the passion they held. He scooped her up in his arms as if she was weightless, and as he began walking with her arms clasped around his neck, she delighted in having made the suggestion, for now she was able to be bumped along in his arms, still close to him, still almost a part of him...

'I should have known your clever little brain would be quick enough to think of something, Rosie,' Will's voice was vibrating against her breast as he carried her, a hint of amusement in it. 'You're a little witch at heart, aren't you?'

She laughed back, snuggling even closer to him, and knowing he was enjoying this unexpected situation as much as she was. But she wished desperately he hadn't chosen those particular words to use...

'What's happened?' Edwin said at once, when he reached them. He looked suspicious for a moment, and Rosie was glad he'd been too far away from them to be absolutely sure whether Will Merrick had really been kissing his sister... She pointed to her ruined shoes, thankful that they would bear out her story.

'Will told me I shouldn't have gone walking across the withy beds in such stupid shoes,' she said quickly. 'I got so interested in watching him cut down the weeds and asking him about the farm, I didn't realise I was sinking into the mud. When I started to move I was stuck fast, and went headlong into the withies! I feel as if I'm scratched to pieces, and I wrenched my ankle as well, so Will kindly offered to carry me.'

She wasn't sure if Edwin took every bit of her story as fact, but there were enough red marks on her hands and face to uphold the fact that she had fallen. And the flush in her cheeks could be attributed to the same cause, he supposed. Her shoes were proof of her words, and Edwin allowed Will to continue carrying her until they were out of the withy field and on firmer ground. Then Rosie knew she had better not prolong the delicious contact with Will any longer, reluctant though she was for it to end. There was an earthiness about him that wasn't unpleasing. If she was completely honest the scent of his maleness so close to her was far more stimulating than the perfumed smell exuded by some so-called gentlemen. Will's smell was natural, a mixture of labour and health, though no doubt some of Rosie's contemporaries might say it was uncouth. Compared with Bennett Naylor, it probably was...compared with Cory, it certainly was not... As their images came into her mind, Rosie felt her arms tighten a moment around Will's neck before she asked to be set down to try out her ankle.

She trod gingerly, but the pain had long since subsided, and it had been no more than a sudden wrench. As long as she moved carefully, it didn't feel as if any real damage had been done.

'There's no sense in straining it more and walking back to Moule, though,' Will said gruffly. 'I'll take 'ee both back in the farm-cart, if you've no objection to travelling in it.'

'Of course not. Why should you think we would?' Rosie spoke quickly, realising Will was suddenly comparing his own shapeless working clothes with the finer ones Edwin had donned for Sunday, and her own dainty muslin dress. She suddenly saw that Will was embarrassed, and her impatient mind was irritated by the thought.

How stupid men were! As if anything mattered but the feelings between a man and a woman! She had tried to convey as much to Edwin when he upbraided her over Cory...and it had clearly slipped his mind when he had become smitten with Jess Lawrence! Where was Edwin's class-consciousness now? And it was all so silly anyway...the fact that Will seemed suddenly tongue-tied when there had been no lack of words between them a short time ago, and was now looking almost broodingly humble, the way lower folk sometimes did. It wasn't the way she wanted Will Merrick to behave towards her, and she was pretty sure it wasn't his normal demeanour either!

'Well?' Rosie demanded. 'Are we going to stand here all afternoon, or are you going to fetch the cart, Will? If not, we'll start walking, but there's no point in our going up to the farm and waiting with you when we have to pass this way again, is there? Please explain to your mother and ask her to forgive us for not calling to say goodbye. I'm sure she'll understand when you tell her what's happened.'

She didn't mean to sound imperious, but Will was making her nervous. In an instant they seemed poles apart from the two people who had found warmth and love in each others' arms. Or maybe it hadn't been the same for Will...no more than physical reaction.

'Aye, school teacher,' his voice was short, little more than a growl. 'Are there any more instructions afore I go for the cart, miss?'

'Of course not,' she answered crossly.

He swung away from her without another word. He was tall and broad-shouldered, with an aggressive set to his head. And a prickly manner that exasperated Rosie. She gave a sudden wince as her body tensed in annoyance, reminding her that she had better take no chances with her ankle if she wanted to begin her job the next day. There was an old tree trunk nearby, and she perched herself on it carefully to wait for Will. She watched his retreating back with a frown between her fine-arched brows.

'Well, that was a fine performance,' Edwin said coldly. 'You treated Will as little more than a servant, Rosie. You might remember that he'll own all this land one day, and if we're still wanting to buy withies from him, you'd better treat him like the equal he is, and not as a country yokel! I'm ashamed of you, Rosie! And so would Pa be too.'

She flinched from his angry tone, blinking back the rush of angry tears. It wasn't like that at all, she wanted to shout. She didn't think of Will as a servant... It was his own stupid manner that had made her react the way she did. If she felt herself to be superior at all, it was to men in general, to the strange vulnerability of them when their masculinity was threatened. They were far more complicated creatures than women, who knew what they wanted when they saw it and didn't let social conventions stand in the way. Rosie never stopped to consider whether she was unique in her opinions or not.

She had been nurtured in the home of two people who loved each other very much, and Rosie had always wanted her parents' idyllic happiness for herself. They had given her a yardstick, and nothing less than an all-consuming love would be enough for her...and though her mother had been far more educated than her father, such a trifle had never been allowed to stand in their way, nor ever mentioned. Marjorie had brought a dowry to her marriage far more precious than the small inheritance that had proved so useful in starting the successful basket-making business in Minehead. She had brought love and lightness and joy of living, and a burning desire in her daughter to experience such things for herself.

'I didn't mean to shame him,' she muttered now to Edwin. 'I like him well enough, and it's just my ankle paining me that made me sound so abrupt.'

It was a bending of the truth, and liking Will well enough was an understatement Rosie didn't want to think about right then. It was enough that she had displeased both young men without meaning to, and her mother's gentle chiding about her sharp tongue seemed to echo in her head at that moment. She bit her lip, and Edwin took the action as confirmation that she had indeed hurt her ankle. His expression softened.

'Poor Rosie. And your pretty shoes all spoiled too. Never mind, I'm sure Will's not the kind to take it to heart.'

She fancied she knew him better than Edwin. She guessed that he would brood over her insensitive words and take out his vengeance on more threshing about among the weeds in the withy beds when he returned from taking them to Briar

Cottage. Rosie was startled at how well she felt she understood him on so little acquaintance. But Marjorie, her mother, had always said it would be so. That there was an extra communication between two people in love that was beyond explanation; understanding moods, sharing moments of joy and sorrow in an intimacy stronger than the ties of blood; truly a union of body and spirit.

For a moment Rosie could almost hear the softly spoken words talking to her, and once more her eyes were momentarily dazzled with tears at memories of days that would never come again, and with a longing for a woman's care in the harsh world of men.

'Here he comes,' Edwin said, as the sound of the cart approached them. Will sat stiffly while Edwin helped his sister into it. She wanted to apologise to him for her curt words earlier, but the words wouldn't come and so she said nothing at all. Edwin made stilted conversation, but the afternoon was somehow spoilt, and it was a relief to all of them when Briar Cottage came into sight. The journey had been only briefly lightened by the sight of Jess and Daisy in the garden of their tiny cottage, and the mutual acknowledgement among them.

'You'd best put a cold compress on the

ankle,' Will said gruffly before he left them. 'It 'ould be a shame if you couldn't start your school teachering tomorrow. I'll bid you both good-day now.'

He had clicked at the horse and was on his way before they could thank him properly or ask him in to the cottage for some refreshment. Edwin gave a slight smile.

'He's an odd one, isn't he? Ma would like him though. He's what she used to call straight, with no side on him.'

'You mean there's half of him missing,' Rosie grinned, deliberately misunderstanding him. Edwin laughed back, their easy relationship restored as he took her arm and opened the cottage door for her. But Rosie knew instinctively that there was nothing missing in Will Merrick's make-up. Nothing at all.

Twenty minutes later Edwin had related the afternoon's events to his father, including the fact that the next withy auctions would be in a month's time at the Moule Inn, but that the Nashes had been promised one field unreservedly on a token bid. And Rosie's ankle had been tightly bound with a cold water compress, in which she found an absurd pleasure that Will had made the suggestion. The ruined shoes had had to be thrown out, and Edwin had told her he would take her to Bridgwater sometime to buy some similar ones, since she had always liked them so much. And Dunstan had news of his own to impart.

'I haven't been idle while you two have been to Merrick farm,' he announced. 'I've been to see Vicar Washbourne.'

'What!' Edwin's grin broadened. 'That must have made his day after seeing you in church today, Pa! What did you go to see him about?'

Dunsan ignored the little jibe. 'It's obvious Rosie can't be in two places at once and doing two jobs, so I went to ask the vicar to recommend a suitable woman to come here and work on a daily basis, and Mrs Guppey from the village will be here tomorrow morning to start work. I've been to see her and taken a bite and a drink with her and her husband, and she's a hard-working body, by the looks of her. I hope you two approve of my day's work!'

Edwin was mightily pleased that his father had taken the initiative after his months of non-caring about anything, even the state of the family home. If it hadn't been for Rosie looking after them...but of course, it was obvious she couldn't be expected to carry on doing the same, though she didn't look too sure about the arrangement.

'I don't know that I like the thought of another woman in the cottage when I've just got it all arranged to my liking,' she began dubiously, 'but it makes sense, I suppose, and if this Mrs Guppey doesn't suit, no doubt we can send her packing, Pa.'

'You'll find I've done the right thing in a week or two, my love. I know you well enough to know you'll be completely absorbed in your new life as school teacher, and it will be good in the wintertime for you to come home to a ready-cooked meal and a warm cottage. And I'm not so sure about finding another woman to replace her. Vicar didn't sound too hopeful when I told him what I'd come about, and Mrs Guppey was the second name he gave me. The first one was quite put out when I arrived at the door, and her man nearly as bad. A strange fellow, though I'd have thought since he was the church caretaker, he'd have been pleased the vicar had suggested the wife to take on a daily job on the vicar's own recommendation. And he didn't even ask me to step over the door.'

Dunstan was clearly a bit affronted, and his children exchanged hidden smiles.

'What excuse did he give, this caretaker then?' Edwin asked indulgently. 'You know country folk don't take kindly to strangers at first, Pa. It was probably no more than that.'

Dunstan shook his head slowly, a frown on his face. 'It was more than that, Edwin. It was as if Tom Kitch was barring me from his cottage as if he thought I was going to put a spell on it or something! And I got the feeling he wouldn't let his good wife work for us for the same kind of reason. It was probably nothing of the kind, and no doubt I was seeing things in his reactions that weren't there. Your mother always said I expected folk to be as outspoken as myself, but there are those who hide dark secrets in this world.'

'But not the church caretaker, Pa!' Edwin laughed out loud. 'You mean the old fellow who looked as if he owned the church this morning and did double-duty in handing out the hymn sheets?'

Dunstan's mouth relaxed into an answering smile. 'It does sound foolish when you put it like that, boy. Anyway, what does it matter if Mrs Kitch didn't want to clean for us? I'm sure Mrs Guppey will be satisfactory, and no doubt I've let my imagination run away with me.'

Rosie bent over her ankle to adjust the cold compress more comfortably. Perhaps it was that that was sending little trickles of fear running through her at that moment. An adding together of small incidents that in themselves amounted to nothing, but when put together sent a gnawing unease to the pit of her stomach.

There was Cyrus Hale and his idiotic words about hanging garlic at his door to ward off witches... There was Will's own teasing reference to her as a witch that had surely not been said in any meaningful way...? There was this Tom Kitch refusing to let his wife work for the Nashes, and the undoubted fact of a Henry Nash having once been put to the gallows somewhere near the very spot where Briar Cottage now stood.

There was also the sudden vivid recollection of the moment in church that morning when the old caretaker—Tom Kitch—had handed out the hymn sheets, and had been very careful not to let his fingers make the slightest contact with any of the Nash family...and the rustle of comment their appearance had evoked at Moule church that day.

Rosie didn't care for mysteries, and especially one in which she and her family moved so unsuspectingly... Her thoughts shifted a little. Tomorrow she was starting as school assistant at the village school, and surely Bennett Naylor would be the man to ask if there was anything untoward going on that the Nash family should know about. Bennett was too educated to allow a fear of village gossip, and he was the one to allay her fears if anyone could do it. Already, she was unconsciously relying on him.

Chapter 6

On Monday morning Rosie felt almost as nervous at facing over twenty village children of different ages as they did at seeing this new young woman appear in the classroom at the start of the day. Only one face was familiar among the various ones in front of Rosie, and that was the unsmiling one of Daisy Lawrence, who gave no indication of ever having seen the new teacher before. And Rosie hoped desperately that it didn't show too obviously that she was completely new to the role.

Bennett Naylor had welcomed her a few minutes before they rang the bell to admit the children, and told her briefly what her morning duties would be.

'We all sing a morning hymn together, Rosie, then say a prayer and have a reading from the bible. After that, I try to divide the school into age-groups or interests. Until now, it has been difficult and the school curriculum a little irregular, but it will be far easier now I have an assistant to help me.'

He smiled encouragingly at her, as if perfectly aware how her knees were knocking beneath the prim grey skirt and white blouse she wore, as befitted a school teacher, the dark hair neatly swathed and pinned. Bennett noted immediately how it changed her appearance, maturing her in an instant, and emphasising the determination of her neatly pointed chin. He couldn't help but approve of her efforts, and told her so, with the result that a disarming blush swept into Rosie's cheeks. The children would love her, he promised her, and he wasn't sure if he didn't already include himself in his assertion.

'What must I do after the hymn singing and prayer and bible reading, Bennett?' she murmured, feeling that it sounded more like an extension of Sunday church than the beginning of a school day.

'I suggest you take all the girls for needlework, which is something that's been lacking, as you might imagine. I've merely let them get on with it, but they need a woman's touch to guide them, Rosie. After that, we could divide up the group once more, so that you teach the little ones their letters, and I take the older ones. Between us, I can see that Moule village school is going to flourish!'

Perhaps he only said it for her benefit, to reassure her, but his words sent a glow to Rosie's heart. She was needed, for the first time in her life, she realised. Except at home, of course, and she knew how sorely she had been needed after Marjorie's death, and then that of little Dorcas...but that was a different need, a family need, while for the first time in her life Rosie felt she was doing something useful for the community. The thought reminded her of something else. But there was no time for it now. Bennett was already handing her the bell, and asking if she would like to walk outside into the school yard and summon the children inside.

And after all, that first day wasn't nearly as traumatic as Rosie had feared. The little girls were happy to stitch and snip, and prattled noisily as they did so, with the exception of Daisy, who merely did as she was told and remained silent no matter how many questions Rosie asked of her.

'She don't talk, miss,' one of the others piped up. 'Me Ma says she'm a dummy.'

'Don't be silly, Vera, and don't be unkind,' Rosie said at once. 'When Daisy wants to talk, I think she'll surprise us all, won't you, Daisy?'

The only response was a vigorous

134

shaking of Daisy's fair head, to the instant chortling of the other girls. Rosie caught a mischievous grin on Daisy's face. Why, the minx knew exactly what she was doing, Rosie thought at once. She was playing to an audience, whatever the reason for her initial silence, and somewhere in her childish mind had come the discovery that she could get whatever she wanted by continuing to play dumb. Whether it was for attention or sympathy, or just being able to slip into the background, Rosie had the feeling that Daisy's ability to speak was as developed as anyone else's. She just didn't choose to use it.

Rosie tried a score of times during that day to catch the child unawares and surprise her into a response, but all for nothing. And now there was a spark of awareness on Daisy's face that she was too immature to hide, but Rosie recognised it all the same.

'She's challenging me,' she informed Bennett when the day was over and the children had all gone home, and Bennett had invited her to a welcome cup of tea in the small back room he called his study. 'It's like a match of wills between us!'

'And she'll win.' Bennett smiled at her indignation. 'She always does, Rosie. I know what she's doing, but it seems she just can't help it. I've spoken to the doctor about her, and he thinks that some day there may be something to trigger off the need to speak, and then she'll do it. But until that happens, why should she bother? It's almost as if her small mind has managed to compensate for the wrong done to her mother over the child's birth. You'll no doubt have heard about it by now? Village gossip being what it is.'

Rosie nodded. Bennett was so interesting to talk to. He thought things out to their logical conclusion, and Rosie doubted whether he ever did anything purely on impulse. Far from being dull, she found the fact oddly reassuring, at a time when she was in need of reassurance. Bennett was a man to lean on in times of trouble. She thought about her father in the same way, only there were always some things about which a daughter couldn't confide to a father...

'Well,' Bennett went on, 'my theory is that way back in the past, perhaps when Jess Lawrence was nursing the child and talking to it the way a mother does, crooning and distressed at the same time by her circumstances, the hurt and disgrace in that poor young woman's soul penetrated the child's mind. Jess was shut out by the village, and in return Daisy has shut herself off from them in the only way she knows, by refusing to communicate with them or anyone else.'

'Even with her own mother?'

'She doesn't need to communicate with Jess. The bond between them transcends the need for words. That's my belief, for what it's worth, Rosie. It's probably all nonsense.'

'Oh no! I'm just astounded at the way you've considered it all, Bennett, and full of admiration!'

The school teacher laughed, a little embarrassed. A man could easily have his head turned by having a young woman half his age look up at him with those startling blue eyes with such an expression of awe in them. And he knew he cut a good figure. He was still trim, unlike some of the cider drinkers who frequented the Moule Inn too often. He took pride in his appearance without undue vanity, and he knew his sister Alice mourned the fact that at thirty-five he was still unmarried, and unlikely to find anyone suitable while he continued this ridiculous urge to teach in the wilds of Somerset, instead of remaining in the fashionable part of the city near to Hyde Park at the family home. Alice had long since despaired of him, and Bennett knew it, but his eyes became slightly glazed as he thought of her amazement if he produced a beautiful young wife such as little Rose Nash, like a rabbit out of a magician's hat! It would be enough to get Alice's set talking non-stop...

He realised Rosie was looking at him now in slight alarm, and that he had been staring intently at her. It was Bennett's turn to feel his face grow hot, for of course such an idea was out of the question. At least, until he had considered it from every angle... He cleared his throat and offered her a water biscuit.

'Can I speak freely to you, Bennett?' Rosie said quickly, before her nerve failed her. 'It's on a matter of some delicacy that affects my family. Or so I believe. I'm not sure if I'm being too sensitive about it all.'

At once he reverted to the understanding friend, with some relief. Those other feelings were altogether too conflicting to his tidy mind for the moment.

'Tell me from the beginning, my dear,' he said gently. 'A tale is never as bad when it's shared.'

She poured it all out, hoping it didn't sound altogether inane, and he listened gravely. It wasn't entirely new to him. Bennett knew the history of these parts well, and how the superstitious country man's mind worked, and a whisper of the unease surrounding the Nash family had already reached his ears. Her heart beat with a steady thud as Bennett nodded slowly, and she knew immediately that her anxiety hadn't been unfounded.

'I had hoped it would blow over as soon as the village folk got to know you all, but it was unfortunate that your father had influenza as soon as you arrived here, and that none of you was seen for a few weeks. Especially that you weren't seen in church, Rosie! I don't need to tell you that the vicar reigns supreme at Moule, do I? You were strangers, and a stranger is always suspect. Believe me, I know! And then there were the other things.'

When he paused, Rosie swallowed dryly, guessing some of what was to come. 'You mean because of our name?' she inquired indignantly.

'Not only that. The battle of Sedgemoor —what they call the Duking Days around here—took place in the month of July when you arrived out of nowhere. Your cottage is near to the site, though it's so widespread none but a superstitious community would give credence to any significance in that. Unfortunately, Moule is exactly that—a superstitious community. And a martyr of this parish, one Henry Nash, was hanged on the gallows known as Beech Cross. It's almost fallen into complete decay now, but nobody around here would dare to chop it up for firewood if they froze in their beds! That's what you're up against, Rosie.'

'It's nonsense...' Fearful shivers up and down her spine made her voice angrier than she intended.

'Of course it is, but try telling them that. Have you seen the large rhine near to where the centre of the battlefield is said to be? There's a great mound of sandy soil near it which was a common grave of several hundred West Country men who died in the Duking Days. The people from the parishes of Westonzoyland and Chedzoy nearby carted the sand there to cover up the stench, and the people around here hit on the idea of opening the ground at times of the local fairs for visitors to see the remains. I found the custom in odd conflict with their superstitious nature...

'I think I could have done without knowing all that, Bennett!' Rosie's voice was a little shaky as she imagined the scene. 'It doesn't happen now, does it?'

'Oh no—and I'm sorry, Rosie. I didn't mean to upset you. It was thoughtless of me. When I get interested in any local research, I'm afraid I get a little carried away.'

He suddenly registerd the fact that her lovely face was pinched and white, and cursed his tongue for revelling in the historical facts he had uncovered. This poor child was obviously affected by his gory tale, and he sought to brighten her mood before he let her go home. If she went back to Briar Cottage in this agitated frame of mind, her father would be reluctant to let her work in the school again. And she had definitely been an asset. As he had expected the children were taken with her, and he found her a naturally accomplished tutor.

'I told you I lived in London before I came to Moule, didn't I?' he asked suddenly.

'Yes,' she answered, but her thoughts were still far from easy, still somewhere in that distant bloody era he had evoked for her receptive mind. She half-wished she had never asked, but in any battle it was better to be armed with all the facts, and Rosie hardly noticed that she had used the word battle to describe the conflict between her family and the Moule community.

Bennett was opening a bureau and bringing out several letters and opening the envelopes. She saw some newspaper cuttings along with a closely-written letter in each one. Bennett smiled as he saw faint curiosity replace some of the wanness in her face.

'My sister still lives in our family house near Hyde Park in London,' Bennett told her. He saw at once that the name meant nothing to her, and elaborated. 'It's a very large park quite near to the royal palace,' he explained, and this time he knew he had caught her interest. He opened up one of the newspaper cuttings.

'I wonder if you'll have heard anything of the exhibition that's to open in May of next year, if all goes well?' he asked.

Rosie shook her head. She knew nothing of happenings in a city that was little more than a name to her, and the capital of England where the Queen and Prince Albert resided.

'If you wish, you may borrow these newspaper cuttings that my sister recently sent to me,' Bennett went on. 'They were published in *The Times* newspaper, and are about the proposed site for the exhibition, the largest of its kind, that therefore needs a huge space for the building. The Prince has agreed to Hyde Park being the venue, but there is strong opposition to what many townspeople see as a desecration of one of London's most popular open spaces. My sister is opposed to it too, but I doubt that a single voice will be heard against the weight of politicians and the royal decree! I think you'll find it all extremely interesting, Rosie. Exhibitors from all over the world are to show off their products, including those from

Britain, naturally, and it can only be advantageous to the exhibitors in terms of future orders.'

Rosie's quick brain saw the possibilities at once. The present fashion for basketware was growing daily, and the townspeople had begun calling at the Nash workshop in Minehead in increasing numbers of late. In a way, she had wondered if it was such a clever move to leave a prospering business, but Edwin was adamant that the business would prosper anywhere, even in an area awash with basket-makers already. The Nash name was becoming known for good craftsmanship... Her eyes were shining as she glanced at the cuttings, needing to peruse them properly and digest all that they contained.

'I'm sure my father and brother will be interested too,' she spoke excitedly. If indeed they found it worthwhile to exhibit at this exhibition of the Prince's, then perhaps they would all go to London for a time. The prospect had never entered Rosie's head until this moment, but now that it had, she found the idea dazzling. It was a thought so exciting she couldn't share it with anyone but her menfolk. She guessed unerringly that Edwin would be fired with her own kind of enthusiasm, but whether Dunstan would agree or think any scheme to show the Nash basketware in London was ludicrous remained to be seen.

London...the very name was as remote to Rosie as the land of America. What kind of people lived there? Were they terribly rich...walking on streets paved with old? She laughed at her own fancies, hurrying home to Briar Cottage with barely a limp to remind her that she had a wrenched ankle. The cold compress had improved it so much that she could ignore it, except when she completely forgot about it and came down a little heavily on her right foot. To protect it she had been careful to wear high lace-up boots that day, and was thankful that the beginning of August was not unbearably hot.

Rosie neared the workshop with a little glow inside. Suddenly everything was beginning to feel right in her world. From the direction of the cottage there was an aroma of meat and pastry, and though she knew it would be Mrs Guppey's work, she could almost imagine it was Ma preparing their supper. And outside the workshop the men had hung out the baskets already made and brought with them, advertising the fact that here were experts at their craft and inviting folk to come and buy.

Rosie stepped inside the workshop, and

was enveloped in the familiar scenes. The smell of the withies, damp from their preparatory soaking so that they could be worked, was as welcoming as a June rose, for it meant her father was fully recovered and eager to be at his plank. Rosie smiled at him now, his lap-board across his knees, his eyes and hands aligning the shape of the basket he worked with more expertise than all the fine measuring instruments others might use.

Dunstan was absorbed in his task, and barely spoke to his daughter for some minutes. Rosie didn't mind. It was magical to watch the way his strong fingers caressed the rods into shape, with all the finesse of a lover. The basket was half made, the bottom shaped and the upward stakes in place, and Dunstan had it all pinned to his lap-board with a bradawl so that it could revolve as he worked. The result would be a deep, strong, wood basket, the base weave in the darker brown rods, the main section randed with buff rods, and the brown again at the top for the distinctive three-pair plait border that the Nash men favoured.

'I'll be in the house later, Rosie,' Dunstan said absently, and she knew he was too intent on his work to bother with food just yet. And now was not the time to suggest any gadding off to London! She asked quickly after Edwin.

'He's sorting the stock,' Dunstan said vaguely. 'You can tell us about your day over supper, Rosie.'

There was no use being irritated. They had always discussed the day's doings over a leisurely meal, all of them together. But tonight she was full of impatience, wanting to tell them about the exhibition and show them the cuttings from *The Times* newspaper. Bennett's sister must be very important indeed to read such a newspaper, Rosie thought.

She heard Edwin whistling in the stockroom, the grand name he had given to one of the outhouses for the sale of their basketware. Another would be prepared for the boiling and stripping of the withies soon after they were cut in the early winter season. The Nash men had experimented on it before, but it had never been really practicable in Minehead. Now they had space and opportunity to take the raw withies and prepare them themselves, which would give them great satisfaction.

Even Will couldn't deny the fact that there was something fascinating about plunging the rods into boiling tanks and smelling the aromatic scents thrown off as the bark juices stained the wood. He had told Rosie loftily that he knew all about the process of preparation, even if he was no basket-maker.

Edwin glanced up and smiled briefly. 'Tell Mrs Guppey to leave the supper on the stove, Rosie. She'll want to be getting off home, and Pa and I want to finish out here before we eat. There's time enough for that later. How was Daisy, by the way?'

His question confirmed her thoughts that Edwin's head was full of the milk girl and her daughter, and Rosie was sure he would be making the basket chair for the child at the first opportunity. She felt momentarily at a loss. There was no point in telling Edwin what little she knew about the London exhibition right now. He wouldn't be listening properly, and she needed his whole attention. Besides, she hadn't read the cuttings herself yet, merely skimmed them. She turned to go into the cottage, where the buxom grey-haired woman was setting three places at the table.

'That smells lovely,' Rosie smiled at her. 'If you want to go now, Mrs Guppey, I'll see to the rest. The men won't be in for a while yet.'

'Don't 'ee let it spoil then, Miss Rosie! I know what menfolk be like when they'm in the thick o' summat, and 'twould be a pity to let good food go to waste.'

'I won't let them stay out there too long,' Rosie promised. 'We'll see you tomorrow morning then.'

'Aye, if the Lord be willin',' the woman said absently. She skewered the black hat on top of her head with an evil-looking hat-pin, and pulled her black shawl round her shoulders, looking at Rosie thoughtfully for a moment. Then she nodded sagely, as if coming to a decision.

'I'm agreein' wi' my Perce, me dear,' she announced. 'A pretty maid wi' a pretty name can't be a bad 'un, and them that say different be missin' out in human charity. Vicar welcomes 'ee, and so do Perce and me. So good-day to 'ee now.'

She marched out of the cottage as if delivering as good a sermon as Vicar Washbourne himself. Rosie wasn't too sure if she should laugh or cry at the dubious compliment Mrs Guppey had delivered. She decided to forget it, and drew out the cuttings from her pocket, spread them on the scrubbed kitchen table and began to read.

By the time the men came in for supper she was near to bursting with excitement. When they had washed their hands and faces and were sitting round the table with the succulent pie and potatoes in front of them, Rosie couldn't keep it to herself any longer. She had answered their queries as to the school and the children and was impatient to inform them of her news.

'Pa, there's to be a great exhibition in London next year, and all the finest craftsmen in the world are to show their work, and it would be wonderful if you and Edwin were to have your baskets there too! Say you'll think about it, Pa. You tell him, Edwin! It's far too exciting a chance to miss.'

'Hold on, Rosie!' Edwin broke in to her torrent of words with a laugh. 'Have you been at the wine bottle?'

'Of course not,' she said, too excited to be cross with him. 'Only listen, will you? Bennett says that anyone can display their work on application, so why not Nash and Son? Bennett's sister lives in London and has been telling him all about it, and here are some cuttings from *The Times,* and one from the *Illustrated London News* that she sent him. There's such a fuss about the building, which is to be so large that the people in London fear they will have no park left for their walks on Sunday afternoons.'

'You'd better read out then, for I can see you won't have the patience to hand them to your brother and me to read for ourselves,' Dunstan said indulgently. 'And we intend to eat our supper if you do not, Rosie!'

'Oh, supper can wait! Oh, *listen*, please!' She opened out the first cutting that Bennett had lent her.

'This is from *The Times* newspaper, dated June 25th. The exhibition is to be shown in Hyde Park, and Bennett's family home is nearby. You'll see that people like her and many others are unhappy about the proposed site,' Rosie paused, and seeing that she had their attention she began to read.

'"The whole of the Park, and, we venture to predict, the whole of Kensington Gardens, will be turned into a bivouac of all the vagabonds of London so long as the Exhibition shall continue."'

'And this is the place you want us to take our work?' Dunstan queried mildly. Rosie sighed and begged him to listen.

'Alice Naylor has added a few comments alongside the cutting, complaining about the noise and so on, but the next cutting goes into more detail—it's dated June 27th. "In fact a building is to be erected in Hyde Park to be fully as substantial as Buckingham Palace!" Can you imagine that, Pa?'

'Well, never having seen the royal palace, I can't really say that I can,' he said dryly.

'*Oh!* Listen to this piece. "Not only is a vast pile of masonry to be heaped up in the Park, but one feature of the plan is that there shall be a dome 200 feet in diameter, considerably larger than the dome of St Paul's"... It goes on to say that "by a stroke of the pen our pleasant Park, nearly the only place where Londoners can get a breath of fresh air, is to be turned into something between Wolverhampton and Greenwich Fair."'

The names didn't matter. Rosie had never heard of them. It was the magnitude of the exhibition that held her enthralled. There would be many influential business-men there. Her family's work, of which she was so proud, could stand among the finest in Europe and the world! Even now, the two of them didn't seem to appreciate the potential of the occasion. Was she the only one looking far enough ahead to know what it might mean to all of them to interest the fashionable London gentry in their craftsmanship? A commission from a noted London establishment could put the seal on Nash and Son as basket-makers of quality.

She realised that the two men were finding it hard to hide their amusement at her impatience with them. They were teasing her all the time. She caught the gleam in Edwin's eyes, and knew he was really as interested as Rosie. Well, she would pay them back for it. She sighed, and folded the cuttings carefully.

'Oh well, I won't bother to read you the next one from the *Illustrated London News* dated a week or so after the others. I can see you wouldn't want to know about the plans for the building.'

'All right, Rosie, let's see it,' Dunstan said at once. 'Of course we're interested, but so much enthusiasm from one person seemed to be enough for all of us!'

'And you'll consider the idea of exhibiting?' She held on to the last cutting teasingly.

'Of course we will, if it's possible!' Edwin said impatiently. 'Now stop being so superior and share the news with us or I shall set the dog on you.'

Rosie grinned as Boy lifted his head from his place in front of the stove, gave a token bark and sighed into oblivion once more. His size belied his softness, and he didn't care which part of the world he lived in, as long as there was grass to play in and the occasional rabbit to catch.

Rosie spread out the cutting, and this time three suppers were left to get cold as they each silently took in the details of the exhibition building.

'It's to be made of glass!' Dunstan exclaimed disbelievingly. 'But what of the effects of rain or thunder, or thousands of people walking through it, if it's to be as large as it says! It's madness!'

'No, it's not,' Edwin said slowly, his keen mind taking in the dimensions and proportions and the technically perfect design of the great glittering palace. For it could be described as nothing less than a palace, surely!

'Whoever this Joseph Paxton is, he must be something of a genius to have conceived such a design as this, Pa,' Edwin went on. 'And it seems the school teacher's sister knows something about him. She's written some brief notes for her brother alongside, if I can read them.'

As he squinted at Alice Naylor's closely-written script, Rosie helped him out, having already read the information.

'It says he's the protégé of the Duke of Devonshire, and designed the great conservatory at Chatsworth, the Duke's seat in Derbyshire.' Rosie spoke as if she was totally conversant with such places, and rushed on, on seeing her brother's raised eyebrows. 'Alice Naylor also comments that discussions to decide on the final design of the building are running at fever-pitch, and that more than 13,000 applications for space to exhibit have already been submitted! So if you want to be included, it had better be soon, Pa!'

'I'm not sure whether the attraction is in furthering the business, or in seeing the sight of London, young Rosie,' Edwin said suddenly, seeing the hopeful lights in her eyes.

She squirmed, hating it when he referred to her that way, when she was already a grown woman, even if it was left to young men other than her brother to notice the fact!

'It's both,' she said crossly. 'And you wouldn't think of leaving me here while you two went there, would you? Not after I had put the idea in your heads!'

'No, we would not,' Dunstan saw her sudden panic. 'But London...' He ruminated for a moment. 'We would need to find out how to apply for space, and be sure we did our very best work in good time to deliver it there.'

'Let me take the cuttings back to Bennett this evening and ask him to write to his sister for the information, Pa,' Rosie begged him eagerly. Her impatience was infectious. And Dunstan was in a mellow mood. He was back at his plank in the workshop and there was a feeling of optimism in his veins that he hadn't felt in a long time. Edwin seemed more than content to be in the heart of Somerset, and his darling girl-child positively glowed tonight. What harm could it do to indulge her? The school teacher was a respected member of the community, and he too was highly intrigued to know more about this exhibition instigated by a royal prince.

'Well, all right,' he smiled at Rosie. 'Edwin can walk with you to the village, since he feels the need for a walk this evening, and I feel the need for a read and a doze after my first day back at work. So don't stay out too late, Rosie. We don't want to start any gossip in the village. If you two can arrange to meet later to come back together, it will be as well.'

Rosie nodded, but she didn't miss the way Edwin avoided looking at her when their father spoke of his evening arrangements. And she knew instantly where Edwin was going, and it wouldn't be in the direction of the village, but halfway between here and the Merrick farm. To Jess Lawrence's cottage...

When Rosie had cleared away the supper table and given the three half-eaten meals to the dog, thanking heaven that Boy couldn't speak and tell Mrs Guppey what had happened to her lovely pie, she put a warm shawl around her shoulders. By the time she came back to Briar Cottage it would have grown chilly. Outside, she waited for Edwin to start walking beside her, his long loping stride covering two of hers.

'You needn't come all the way with me, Edwin,' she smiled knowingly. 'I'm quite sure this isn't the direction you're intending to go in, and I won't tell Pa!'

He hesitated. 'You're sure you'll be all right? I can arrange to meet you later.'

'And cut short your precious time with a certain person?' she teased him. 'Don't be silly, Edwin. If you're to meet me to go home again, you'd barely reach Jess's cottage before you had to come back, and I don't want to be called a spoilsport! Is she expecting you?'

Edwin nodded. 'I spoke with her this morning when she came with the milk. Rosie—do you think I'm being feckless?'

She had that odd feeling of being older and wiser than he once more.

'Of course I don't. We can't help falling in love, can we? Even if it is with the wrong person—and I don't mean that Jess *is* the wrong person for you Edwin. Only—be sure, that's all. I like her—and she doesn't deserve to be hurt a second time, and I care about you too.'

He gave her a quick hug and she watched him go in the opposite direction, a jaunty lift to his shoulders. Lucky Edwin, to know what he wanted, the thought flitted through her mind.

She thought of Will. The image of him was so real at that moment that she could almost feel his presence beside her as she walked, but it was nothing but the soft breeze merging summer into autumn. Was he what she wanted? She had thought so, with a spectacular reaching out of mind and senses...but she had thought Cory was the one too. And now she was almost dazed by the new and exciting prospect of visiting London that Bennett Naylor's words had brought her. Bennett...there was an attractive man with whom she had an instant rapport, sharing a vocation and a love of learning and imparting knowledge. Was it any wonder if her head was turned just a little away from Will Merrick and his earthy passion, in favour of a man who breathed elegance and a vastly different life style from anyone she had ever known?

And was she doomed after all to flit from one man to another like some frivolous butterfly, Rosie thought shamefacedly? When what she really wanted and yearned for was a steadfast love to last a lifetime, such as her parents had known. Perhaps she hadn't even met him yet. Perhaps the best was yet to come...

Chapter 7

'I tell 'ee I seen 'er going into the schoolhouse, you buggers,' Cyrus Hale insisted angrily. He and his two cronies were restless and looking for mischief, and the sight of Rosie Nash tripping daintily along the village street at dusk had sent the blood fair skittering through his veins.

'What would she be doin' in the schoolhouse at this time o' day?' Seth Weaver scoffed as the three of them swaggered along the street, where the cottages were so ill lit it was hard to see whether their inhabitants were inside or not.

Hubert Pond sniggered. 'Mebbe there's a bit o' extra learnin' that poncey school teacher wants to give her! Reckon as how he's stole a march on 'ee, Cyrus. Rosie Nash'll have her sights set higher than a village blacksmith, I'm thinkin'.'

His thanks was a swipe around the head from Cyrus. The blow sent his senses reeling for a minute, and the stars in the sky were suddenly dancing in front of his eyes. He was no match for Cy when he was in a dangerous mood. Hubert worked with his father in the village bakery, and the fact that he was thin and puny was attributed to constant steam from the ovens threatening to waste him away. The doctor had once told his parents he wouldn't make fifteen years, but here he was nearing twenty, and still snuffing his way about the village and looking as though one more damp winter would see the end of him.

'At least I'd give 'er more'n you could, you bag of bones,' Cy snapped. ' 'Ave 'ee seen the tackle this turd's got in his breeches, Seth? A penny whistle and a pair o' gnat's knackers! No wonder the village maids look right through him when he passes 'em by. They'd get more stuffing from a Christmas cock than from Doughey here!'

The other two roared with laughter, while Hubert glared at them furiously.

'You know my Pa don't like me to be called Doughey.'

'He ought to set up in chicken farming then,' Seth chortled, 'then we could call him Cocky.'

'Nay. 'Twould be a waste of a good name on him.' Cyrus was tiring of this game. Baiting Hubert was a nightly ritual, but tonight there were better things to think of. 'The point is, me buggers, what are we goin' to do about Rosie Nash?'

The other two stared at him. Their

159

footsteps slowed as if by mutual accord, and they lounged against the small humped stone bridge that crossed the stream running through the village.

'I don't 'specially want to do anythin' about her,' Hubert muttered. 'You know what they'm sayin' about her. She'm best left alone to my way o' thinkin'.'

Cyrus ignored him. He looked inquiringly at Seth, who was more of his own build and a brawny farm labourer working nearer Bridgwater way. Sometimes Cy wondered why the hell they tolerated Hubert's company at all, except that the poor sod didn't have so long to live. Though they'd all been told that for so many years now, that Cy suspected the baker's boy led a charmed life. He swilled so much cider some nights, and lurched off with arms and legs flying in all directions, that Cy swore that without him and Seth to see him right back to his home he'd disappear without a trace under some farm cart, trampled into the mud, and hardly nobody would miss him.

'What do you want to do about 'er?' Seth grinned back. 'As if I didn't already know!'

For a moment Cyrus let the idea of what he'd like to do to Rosie Nash send a glow of heat around his body. He recognised the earthiness in her full red lips and wide

160

blue eyes and the luscious tempting shape of her, but there was a haughtiness about her too that the village maids didn't share. Rosie Nash needed to be taken down a peg or two, and he was just the one to do it. If he was a little wary of the reputation her family had brought with them, he wasn't bloody well going to show it, especially not in front of a snivelling turd like Doughey Pond!

'I reckon we ought to sit it out an' see how long she stays with the school teacher,' Cyrus stated. 'Then we'll guess if he's had his share or not, and whether it's time we had ours. Agreed?'

The other two weren't sharp enough to see that, as usual, Cyrus neatly side-stepped any positive action. More often than not, he set up the situation, but didn't know what to do with it afterwards, relying on the momentum of his companions to carry the thing through. As yet, nobody had challenged him on it, for if all else failed Cyrus Hale's fists had always been a match for anybody in the village. That, and his bluster.

Bennett Naylor opened the door of the schoolhouse that evening, half expecting it to be some parent with a query about his child's progress in the village school. His eyes widened with a mixture of astonishment and delight when he saw Rosie standing there, her expressive face softened in the shadowy dusk, yet still portraying the excitement she was feeling. Around her shoulders she clutched a warm shawl, and behind her head the pale full moon rising in the evening sky glinted like silver on the dark gloss of her hair. Bennett's mouth widened into a delighted smile.

'Rosie! I never expected to see you. Is anything wrong?'

And if there was, why should she come to him? Even as he said the words, he knew it could be nothing like that. If it had been he would have felt honoured that she should turn to him... He stopped the flow of thoughts that so often stilted his conversation, while he tried to get them in proper order. This was no time to be cautious. He opened the door wider as Rosie gave a slightly self-conscious laugh, suddenly aware that Bennett might find her impulsive arrival unseemly.

'I'm so sorry to bother you like this, Bennett,' her voice was oddly breathless, holding a charm for him he found quite unexpected. 'It's just that my father and brother were so interested in the information about the exhibition, and I wanted to ask you more.'

'Then please do come inside, and don't

let us alert all the village to our meeting, dear young lady,' he smiled at her. Rosie stepped inside, familiar at once with the scene of her day's activities. But now Bennett ushered her through, up a small flight of stairs to his living quarters, and if he hadn't been such an eminently respectable gentleman in a blameworthy profession, she might have questioned her sense in coming here like this. As it was, she sat primly on the edge of a chair, while Bennett offered her a glass of wine from a decanter.

The very elegance of it was reassuring. Bennett's world was clearly very different from hers, and despite what he had said earlier, Rosie thought he must truly have a vocation in teaching to bring him to the wilds of Somerset from fashionable London. The thought lulled her slight nervousness, and as she accepted the wine, she blurted out her reasons for coming at once.

Bennett let her ramble on, thinking that never before had there been a prettier picture in his small living-room than Rosie Nash, with her cheeks all flushed and animated, and her eyes glowing like sparkling sapphires. It should be a man who put such lights into her eyes, he was thinking, not a sheaf of letters and newspaper cuttings... But at least he had been the catalyst to arouse such interest. He forced himself to listen to what she was saying, instead of letting his eyes feast on the pleasure of seeing her here in his domain.

'So you see, Bennett, it would make us all so grateful if you could write to your sister and enquire how we may apply for space to exhibit.' She clenched her small hands together in her lap, entirely taken up with the excitement of it all. 'You won't have seen samples of Nash Baskets yet, but I assure you they are of the very best, and—perhaps you would care to come to Briar Cottage next Sunday to take some tea with us all, and you may inspect the work for yourself.'

'Rosie, Rosie, please stop!' He broke in with a laugh. 'You don't have to sell Nash Baskets to me, nor explain their virtues! If as much enthusiasm goes into the craft as I see in you, then I'm sure they must be superb examples! And of course I will write to my sister on your behalf. And I accept with much pleasure your invitation to Sunday tea. I wouldn't presume to "examine the work" in the way you suggest, but I would be most interested to see how a basket-maker works. It is most kind of your father to make the offer.'

Rosie felt herself blush at his rather

ponderous reply. Her father had no notion yet that they were to have a guest for Sunday tea, and it had been said on the spur of the moment. She was sure he would be unperturbed when she told him, but just for a moment Rosie wished she had a little more of Bennett's own dignity, and less of her own impulsiveness. Of course he had the advantage of years on his side, and the respect that came with his profession. She was part of that profession now too, Rosie told herself, and should try to behave accordingly...

'I had better go, Bennett,' she was suddenly awkward, rising to her feet, and very aware that she was a young girl unchaperoned in a gentleman's establishment. What would his elegant sister have said to such a situation? The less formal ways of the countryfolk would probably scandalise the city dwellers. 'I apologise at my sudden arrival like this, and for intruding on you.'

'Please don't apologise.' He was aware of something too. There was a lack in his life he hadn't even noticed until Rosie Nash appeared to fill it. She gave an added grace and lightness to the sombre rooms he occupied, and when she left them he would once more see the shabbiness he hadn't really bothered to change. His sister would be appalled at the way he lived, but he had come here with the firm belief that he shouldn't appear to be above the station of those already in the community. If a parent called to see him he wanted his home to be a reflection of theirs, and not a rich man's showplace. Suddenly, he wished it had looked smarter for Rosie Nash. He cleared his throat in embarrassment, knowing he was staring at her again in that absent-minded yet intense manner of his.

'And you will write to your sister on our behalf?' She couldn't resist asking eagerly once more, since that had been her mission here this evening.

Bennett laughed again, as the impatient child in her reasserted itself. He held out his hand to shake hers in a sealing of the bargain, knowing that the warmth of the contact would stay with him long after she had gone. He was beginning to feel alarmed at the way his reactions could be likened to those of a love-sick fool.

'I promise, Rosie. I'll do it this very night. And I'll do even more,' he said, as a thought struck him. 'If you should think of attending the exhibition yourself, I will ask my sister to give you hospitality at our family home, which would be so much more comfortable than an hotel. Would you like that?'

He hardly needed to ask. Rosie's eyes

166

shone even brighter, dazzling him. At that moment Bennett wished he could have offered her the royal palace itself, if it prompted such a reaction! It was so much more than she had ever expected and she found herself stammering a reply.

'Oh, it would be wonderful, Bennett. But I couldn't presume so much—your sister would think it an intrusion. I don't even know if I should go to London—or if my father would let me...'

'Let's wait and see then, shall we?' Bennett said kindly, suddenly the bene-volent benefactor and liking the role. 'I shall mention it to your father on Sunday next, and there is plenty of time for you to decide. It's almost a year away, after all.'

'It seems an eternity now that I know all about it,' Rosie sighed wistfully.

'That's because you're young,' Bennett observed. 'A year to an infant can be double its life-span, while to an adult it's hardly more than a twinkling of an eye. Patience is largely a matter of maturity, Rosie, but don't ever wish your time away. A moment lost can never come again, so savour every experience life has to offer you. That way you'll sort out the dross from the consequential. But please forgive the little lecture, my dear! It's not often that I have such a receptive audience, and

I'm afraid my tongue rather runs away with me.'

'Oh, but I love to hear you talk so,' Rosie burst out. 'My mother used to philosophise sometimes, and I always loved to hear her talk that way. I do admire anyone who uses their mind to the full.'

She blushed again and hoped she didn't sound ridiculously fatuous, but Bennett seemed pleased at her remarks. She had meant what she said. It was a pleasure to be able to converse with someone of his intelligence, and the thought of meeting his sister in London was at once unnerving and exhilarating. Who knew what kind of contacts she might make there? Her thoughts rushed on as she left the schoolhouse, assuring Bennett that she could find her own way back easily enough. Truth to tell, she didn't want company at all. She just wanted to absorb all his interesting words, and let the prospect of a visit to his family home in London seep into her mind. She pulled the shawl a little tighter around her as the cooler night air added to the delicious little shivery feelings that the thought of the visit evoked.

She was so deep in her own thoughts that the sound of another voice brought her up with a little shock. She had crossed the humped stone bridge over the stream and was walking quickly past the church and the churchyard, where the headstones loomed like grey-white sentinels in the gloom. There was a soft gossamer misting on the meadows surrounding the village, like the sea-foam Rosie remembered with occasional nostalgia. For a heart-stopping second she thought the voice came directly from one of the headstones, until she saw the dark shape move out from behind it, a very human shape, followed by a second and then a third. White moon-sharpened faces with leering grins and glittering eyes came nearer, and she wasn't so much frightened as annoyed at being woken out of her reverie and the stimulating ideas that Bennett Naylor had stirred in her.

'So here you be at last, my pretty,' Cyrus Hale's voice jeered at her. 'Do 'ee reckon as master school teacher 'ad time to dip 'is wick, me boys?' He spoke to his friends now, instead of Rosie. They took the bait at once.

'There's only one way to find out,' Seth sniggered. 'I daresay it'd still be warm...'

'So long as 'ee don't mind another's leavings,' Cyrus grunted.

'We never 'ave afore, 'ave us?' Seth and the thin one were stalking quietly around her now, so that the three of them encircled her, and Rosie's flesh began to crawl as the full meaning of their words sank in. She could scream, but the churchyard was a distance away from the village, and no one was likely to hear her. Folk kept inside their cottages at night except those who frequented the Moule Inn, and the drinkers would be too well in their cups to heed a scream in the night. Apart from that, her mouth had become so dry Rosie doubted if her voice would carry that far.

All the same, she wasn't going to be intimidated by these oafs. Her pointed little chin came up, as she pulled the shawl tighter around her in self-defence.

'You'd better let me pass,' she added icily. 'My brother will be out looking for me, and he's already got the better of you once.' She glared witheringly at Cyrus Hale, whose face darkened with rage at the reminder.

'Your brother!' he mimicked in a pseudo-feminine voice. 'He ain't here now, is he? Unless he's skulking among the stones with a wench of his own, and I'm thinking he ain't gonna be tryin' that lark on for a night or two since I put the fist in his tackle!'

The other two hooted with laughter at the memory, and Rosie saw it would take more than the mention of Edwin or Dunstan or even Bennett to deter these three. Cyrus Hale had come closer, and she

170

was hemmed in by his companions, and the sense of being sucked into a whirlpool, from which there was no escape other than drowning, was searingly strong.

She saw the blacksmith run his tongue over his slack lips, and they gleamed wetly in the moonlight. 'I reckon 'tis my call for bein' first,' he said importantly. 'So you two buggers can do the holdin' down.'

Rosie's eyes dilated as she felt her arms grasped at once. Now that Cyrus's plan was moving swiftly into action, he wouldn't turn back. Goaded on by his cronies, it was more than his status in the village was worth to back down now.

Besides, there was a throbbing in his loins that said this was going to be a night to remember. Little Rosie Nash was due for the best of him, and he was going to relish the spreadin' of her. He reached out one hand and fondled the swell of her breasts, made taut with fear, and adding to his enjoyment as she squirmed with revulsion.

'You bastards!' She used words they would understand. 'Pigs! If you don't let me go, I'll tell the whole village what you did. And if you think I'll make it easy for you—'

'You won't tell nobody,' Seth Weaver's voice in her ear was suddenly menacing. Rosie felt her head jerked back by his fingers entangling in her hair. 'You know what happens to wenches who tell? They just get branded as whores! And them that don't, like Jess Lawrence, gets away with it!'

Rosie felt as mute as Daisy at that moment. The great mindless oaf, too stupid to imagine the pain and humiliation that Jess had suffered from the village all these years... But this bully would have been too young to know the full horror of it at the time... Her thoughts veered away from Jess. She had problems of her own that were too immediate.

She could feel Cyrus Hale's body writhing against hers in a mock love-act. The smell of him sickened her. The thin one, who somehow made her flesh creep even more than the others, was behind her, his scrawny fingers lifting her skirt and touching her leg. She could feel their slow progress upwards like the crawl of some slimy creature on her skin. Wild hysteria took hold of her as the menacing one, Seth Weaver, clamped his hand over her mouth and rapped out instructions.

'Over in the corner, Cy. There's a flat patch of ground there the vicar ain't used for buryin' yet. 'Twon't be as fine as a mattress, but I daresay you've enough spring in yer arse for what's needed, and the wench has got a fine rump on 'er.'

Rosie kicked out with her feet until the pain from her wrenched ankle made that impossible. She tried to fight back, but they held on fast to her arms, until it felt as if they would be pulled from their sockets. The three of them were too strong for her, and she couldn't believe this was happening. It was all some hideous nightmare, and the hand that was clamped across her mouth was no more than a fold in the bedcovers, despite the fact that it was clammy with excitement and she could taste the sweat in it with a revulsion that almost made her vomit.

Maybe if she forced herself she could actually vomit all over them, and surely that would put them off their plan! But although the bile stuck in her throat it stayed exactly where it was, and it was becoming difficult even to breathe as she was hauled across the stony ground among the headstones to the flat grassy patch among the trees. Rosie's heart pounded with sick fear, all the earlier joy of the evening vanished. It was all going to happen, and there wasn't a single thing she could do to stop it...

She gave a sudden bite at the fingers across her mouth, distasteful though it was, and Seth let go of her for a moment with a yelp of anger. He lashed at her face, but with a great effort Rosie suddenly found her voice, and let forth with a burst of inspiration.

'You're not afraid to seduce a witch then, Cyrus Hale?' she said, her voice ringing out in the stillness of the night.

For a few seconds there was no reply, only the rasping noises of the three as they breathed heavily, and the rustling of the night breezes. In the distance a cow coughed, and a fluttering of wings told of a bird's disturbance.

In the same instant she realised the thin one's hand had stopped stroking her skin and that he had removed it from her skirt. Seth Weaver made a little sucking noise in his throat.

'Mebbe this ain't such a good idea, Cy,' he growled. One hand still held her arm, but his voice was unsure, a query in it, and Rosie felt a quiver of hope, even if she'd had to go to appalling lengths to find it. They'd know it was only bravado by this time tomorrow, but if it made them let her go tonight she hardly stopped to think of the far-reaching effects of her words.

'If she were a witch, she 'ouldn't be wantin' to step inside the churchyard, 'ould she?' Cyrus was reluctant to let her go now that he had her here, and the throb in his loins was getting more urgent.

'I didn't want to step in here, did I?' Rosie shouted, the dryness in her throat lessening now. 'You had to drag me here, didn't you?'

'Hey, hey, that's right, Cy,' Hubert Pond muttered. 'She didn't want to come in 'ere with we, did she?'

'Well, of course she didn't, but only because she didn't want what was coming to 'er,' he snapped. Then his voice changed to a more triumphant note. 'Anyway, if she were a witch, she 'ouldn't have come to church so readily on Sunday, 'ould she? 'Tis well known that witches be afeared to put foot inside a church, so how do 'ee answer that one, me beauty?'

The dryness was returning to her throat again. Oh God, couldn't they let her go? Where was God, if He could let this happen to her! She shared her father's disbelief at that moment.

'Witches can do as they please,' she heard herself say in a cracked voice, because she suddenly knew she was playing a dangerous game in this pretence. 'They go where they like, and if that includes a church for their own reasons, then that's what they do. So you just let me go, or I'll see that you don't get the chance to seduce any more girls for the rest of your lives. I'll—I'll make your—your parts burn like they've been scalded!'

She heard Hubert Pond draw in his

175

breath, and knew that at least she'd got him well and truly scared. Something in her voice was fast reassuring Cyrus, all the same.

'Well, my guess is that you'm just bluffing, my maid,' he taunted. 'An' my Granpappy reckons that a true witch will have a witch's mark on 'er. So before we decide one way or another, we'd better just find out whether you've got the mark or not. Right, boys? I'd say that was fair arguing, what say 'ee both?'

'Sounds fair,' Seth nodded in agreement. 'An' there's a bright enough moon shinin' for us to see. We'd best have the skirt off her to find out.'

'And the rest on it,' Cy grinned. ' 'Tis only fair to give 'er the benefit of the doubt, boys. And if we don't find what we'm looking for, then you can pin 'er down for me to get me leg across. Can't say no fairer than that, can us?'

Too late, Rosie saw that she had fallen into her own trap. But even as the clawing hands reached to pull the clothes from her, she found her voice and screamed, and screamed, and screamed again...

'Bloody tulips, she'll wake the dead,' Seth gasped out.

'There's only the dead around here to worry about, so forget it,' Cy snarled as the others looked fearfully around them, loosening their hold on Rosie for an instant. He lunged for her as she took advantage of the momentary chance of escape, and twisted out of their grasp. Her ankle pained her more than it had done since she had wrenched it, in what seemed like another life, back in the withy fields with Will Merrick... A sob welled up in her throat as she dodged among the headstones, knowing the three louts panted behind her, not done with her yet. She was still screaming, uncaring of what folk might think, when suddenly her screaming changed to a shout of terror, as a black shape seemed to surge up in front of her eyes and envelop her, and she was being shaken so hard her eyeballs seemed to spin in their sockets.

'What devil's work is going on here in this sacred place?' Vicar Washbourne's voice thundered out in the darkness, vibrating among the headstones and re-ducing Rosie to a violent sobbing with mingled fright and relief.

Instinctively his arm closed around her, feeling the shivering body in his arms without yet knowing who she was. There was time enough to deal with her later. For now the vicar was more concerned with roaring a dire warning to the three shadowy figures dispersing in all directions, to be fast swallowed up in the darkness and the mist. Rosie shook all over, thankful beyond words to her unlikely rescuer.

'Now then, what have we here?' She heard the accusing sound of the vicar's voice as he loosened his hold on her and inched her away from him. His fingers remained on her shoulders so that she had to endure his inspection, and when he saw her dishevelled appearance, she saw his tight lips disappear into his cheeks in a disapproving line.

'They—they set upon me, Vicar,' she stammered. 'I could do nothing to stop them! I was merely on my way home, and they grabbed hold of me. They—they tried to—to—'

'Silence, girl!' The voice rose once more, echoing around the headstones. As it did so, a little flurry of a breeze sprang up, seeming to moan among the leaning stones like murmuring voices, all disapproving of Rosie Nash's presence here. She shook visibly, but he showed no mercy, his eyes boring down into hers.

'Have you no shame, for daring to mention fornication on hallowed ground?'

The outrage of his words stunned her. 'But I didn't, Vicar. I haven't...' It was he who had said the word, not her!

'I'll hear no more of it. Nor will I have such wanton behaviour in the village.

Young girls who walk the streets after dark can have only one thought attributed to them. What is your father thinking about? I am beginning to reverse my opinion of him, and thinking my first one was correct after all.'

It was too much. 'My father is a good man, Vicar Washbourne,' Rosie's voice shook with indignation, now that her immediate fear was subsiding. 'And I have been out on a business matter to the school teacher's.'

'You should not be out at all.' There was no swaying him when his mind was set on a thing. 'I shall make it my business now to see you safely indoors, and you will pray to our good Lord to make you see the folly of your ways. Follow me, girl.'

For a second Rosie was tempted to turn and flee, but if she did, there was no knowing what may be out there waiting for her in the darkness. She scurried behind the vicar as he strode ahead of her to the small vicarage behind the church, and as he motioned her silently to sit beside him in the dog-cart, she felt as if she was being blamed for the entire episode that evening, though none of it was her fault at all. It was so unfair...but that was just how Jess Lawrence must have felt, when the whole village blamed her for bringing an illegitimate child into the world. For the first time Rosie knew exactly how Jess must have felt.

The vicar stopped outside Briar Cottage, waiting stiffly for Rosie to dismount. There wasn't a single thing she could say to the granite-faced man, so she simply sighed and said nothing but a quiet thank you.

'The Lord gives us all our cross to bear, Rosie Nash,' he said sternly. 'It seems that you are destined to be mine.'

She fought back the tears for several minutes as the sound of the dog-cart receded into the distance, before she felt composed enough to go indoors and tell her father that all was well, and Bennett Naylor was writing off to his sister for more news of the exhibition entries that very night. It all seemed like centuries ago since she had left here so eagerly and lightly. Now, her ankle throbbed unbearably, and she felt oddly light-headed, as if she was to be the next victim of influenza, and she seized on the fact as an excuse to say goodnight to Dunstan and have an early night. Her father may not notice anything amiss, but Edwin certainly would, and she wanted to be safely in her bed before he came home. Once there, she buried her head beneath the covers and tried to blot the entire evening from her mind.

Chapter 8

All that week Rosie awoke in the middle of the night, her body drenched in perspiration as the nightmares tormented her. She would see Cyrus Hale's leering face, grotesquely distorted, swimming in front of her glazed eyes... She would feel herself pinned and spread-eagled by a dozen hands, while the whole village laughed demoniacally at her nakedness. She would see Will Merrick's disgusted face on learning that she was a witch after all...and Bennett Naylor would turn away and bar the schoolhouse door from her, telling her in that ponderous way of his that his sister no longer wanted her to visit her in London.

But worst of all among the churning mêlée of the nightmares was the image of Vicar Washbourne in the pulpit on Sunday morning. Rosie saw herself rising slowly from the Nash pew, while all faces turned away from her as the vicar's resonant tones condemned her...

'Let us all beware of that which is born of the darkness in man. Let us cleanse it from our midst, that we may all be the purer for being rid of it. Let us cut it out from our hearts and bury it with our dead.'

By the end of the week Rosie was in such a state of fright, expecting to hear the vicar say the actual words that filled her head in her sleeping hours, that she knew she had to deal with it in the only way she could.

There had been such a temptation to confide in someone about her ordeal in the churchyard, and the first person she had thought of had been Jess. Surely Jess would understand, and sympathise, calm her anxieties... But the more she thought about it, the more she knew she couldn't go to Jess. If she did it would only stir up all the bad memories the other girl had fought to suppress. And that in turn might jeopardise the growing tenderness between Jess and her brother. She remembered Mrs Merrick's words of the effect Jess's seduction had had on her, in turning her so afraid of men that she couldn't bear their touch...and knowing that Edwin had broken through that barrier in a small way so far, Rosie knew she couldn't be the one to close it once more.

She couldn't confide in anyone else. The knowledge of how foolish she had been, in taunting Cyrus and the others that she was a witch, was making her extra sensitive.

Was it her imagination that folk stopped what they were doing as she passed, only to whisper together when she had gone by? Did several pupils, who were there in the schoolhouse on Monday, stay away for the rest of the week for any sinister reason? Did the fact that folk weren't quick to call at Nash Baskets in the same way they had in Minehead have anything to do with her actions. Whatever the cause, Rosie couldn't stand the uncertainty one minute longer, and on Friday afternoon, when school was over, she went straight to the vicarage and asked to see the vicar.

A silent housekeeper showed her into the front parlour, where the vicar sat at a desk, his back to the window so that Rosie couldn't see his face too clearly. He motioned for her to sit down, and she wiped her clammy hands on her skirt, feeling the damp beads of perspiration on her forehead and upper lip.

'Vicar, I know I'm right in believing you to be a fair and just man.' She had rehearsed her words carefully, and saw him nod at once. 'You do the Lord's work, and admirably so, by the size of your congregation each Sunday.'

'And at last you have seen fit to join it,' he couldn't resist commenting.

'I think you know the reason why my family couldn't do so as soon as we came to Moule, Vicar. My father was ill, but now we want to be accepted into the community like everyone else. Is that so wrong of us?'

He studied her thoughtfully, his face still stern. She was too comely, too shapely, too alluring a young woman. There was nothing humble about the girl, and Vicar Washbourne realised that was what irked him most about Rosie Nash. She sat in front of him now, as defiant as her ancient namesake who had gone to the gallows for his pains, and he didn't like defiance in any shape or form, nor to have questions thrown at him...

'What have you come here for, girl? I have my work to do, and my sermon to compose.'

He saw her flinch. It was that very sermon Rosie feared. This man had the power to drive her family out of Moule, and with the realisation came the knowledge that she liked it here, and so did her father and brother. She couldn't let it happen because of her foolishness, and the only way to avoid it was to confess everything to Vicar Washbourne and let him see what trouble she had inadvertently caused.

'Vicar, I'm sorry about the other evening,' she burst out, taking him by surprise. 'It seems that if I'm your cross, then the blacksmith is mine! He has entirely the wrong idea about me, and I beg you to help me put things right! I did such a foolish thing in trying to save my honour, and now I am desperate to save my family any more embarrassment. Will you help me, please?'

She could be artless when she tried. She could be downcast, her head lowered as if in shame, yet still preserving her young dignity. Vicar Washbourne was grudgingly impressed, relenting just a little to ask again what she wanted of him.

Rosie raised her eyes to look at him across the desk, slightly blurred by her tears. 'You're a good man, Vicar,' she said chokingly. 'They listen to you, and rightly so. If you could find it in your heart to condemn those who still believe in witchcraft and point the finger at innocent folk, I know they would follow your lead. And this tale of our being some kind of reincarnation of that other Nash is just foolishness. You must know it, Vicar. You are not so uneducated as to believe such nonsense.'

She knew she had won by appealing to his scholastic background. She saw him nod slowly in agreement.

'Of course such pagan foolishness must be stamped out. But first I must have your own word on it.'

He moved so swiftly Rosie could hardly

believe it. One minute she was sitting tensely, wondering what his reaction would be. The next, he had reached for a copy of the Bible, grasped her hand and placed it above it, holding it there with his own hand.

'You will repeat after me,' he said sternly. 'I, Rosie Nash, have never and never will have aught to do with the black arts, so help me God!'

'I, Rosie Nash, have never and never will have aught to do with the black arts, so help me God,' she repeated steadily, her gaze unwavering from his penetrating stare. She suspected he had just made up the incantation for her benefit, but that didn't matter. It was better so. Surely one who was a witch would have snatched her hand away as if it had been burned, and would have been unable to voice the avowal he demanded.

Apparently it was so, for he seemed quite satisfied with her reaction, and intoned his approval.

'I welcome you into the church, Rosie Nash, and on Sunday you may rest assured that others will welcome you also. If the house of God admits you, then so shall the houses of lesser men.'

Rosie felt utterly drained when he showed her out of the vicarage, but as she made her way home in the late afternoon sunlight it was as if all the strength was beginning to come back into her limbs once more. There was no need to tell Edwin or her father what she had done. Maybe one day she would tell them, when all this was long behind them...

Will had made up his mind. His Ma had been nagging him for months that it was time he went a'courting, but he wasn't getting himself tied up with any girl except the one of his choice. Not to please his Ma or to provide her with grandchildren to dandle on her knee. Not until he met one who was right for him, and there hadn't been one even remotely like that until now.

He was starting to think in terms of before Rosie and after Rosie. Though he didn't even want to think of after Rosie. He wanted Rosie to be here and now and always. Will was surprising himself lately. He was thinking of her in poetic terms, likening her hair to the blackness of ebony, and her mouth to the ripeness of cherries...and the softness of her to summer nights that were heavy and drowsy and fragrant... The feel of her in his arms when he had kissed her in the withy beds still came to him in the night, and all the lusty young urges of manhood were tempered by a tenderness he couldn't rightly explain. He wanted her rightly enough, but he also wanted to do right *by* her, and the sense of it all didn't come so easily to him.

He wasn't ready yet to admit that what he felt could be love. Love meant giving yourself to another person, body and soul, and Will Merrick was his own man, and nobody else's. He may not have all the finesse of the school teacher, nor the learning, but his was a heritage that went back generations, and this had been Merrick land as long as the Somerset Levels had been a farming community. He belonged to it and it was part of him, and he couldn't deny the intriguing thought that Rosie's own family business and his were greatly interdependent on each other. The withies and the basket-making...made for each other.

And on Sunday afternoon he had made up his mind he was going to stay in his Sunday best clobber, and ride over to Briar Cottage to ask Rosie Nash to come a'courting with him.

He eyed Jess Lawrence with a mild curiosity on Sunday morning as she and Daisy climbed into the calling-cart. There was something different about Jess lately. Will couldn't tell just what it was, though his Ma had said the certain bloom about a woman only came from one cause, and that was to do with a man! But everybody knew that Jess hated men, except those with whom she came into contact in her working day.

Will was feeling oddly perceptive, as if the new emotions stirring in himself were opening his eyes and mind to things hitherto unsuspected. And that morning he was astonished to see the faint blush on Jess's cheeks and the smile on the silent Daisy's face as they exchanged brief glances with the basket-maker's son. Jess and Edwin Nash...it was a combination that had never occurred to Will, but in that instant he could see that it might very well have occurred to the two of them.

He switched his thoughts almost immediately to Rosie, by whom they were so often occupied. And the reaction he experienced was the same as before, only this time he managed to control it without the fierce glare on his face, so that when she turned and glanced his way he was able to smile at her, and see the warm colour rise in her velvety cheeks. She turned her head quickly as Vicar Washbourne entered the church, but Will's spirits lifted, knowing instinctively that Rosie's eyes had been searching for him too.

From then on he knew he had better concentrate on what Vicar Washbourne was saying, particularly since he seemed to be more ferocious than usual that day. He glowered down at the entire congregation from the height of the pulpit and more than one there cowered back in the hard pew, wondering if he was the one to feel those piercing eyes fixed upon him for all to see.

'God's word is love,' the vicar suddenly roared out into the uneasy silence. 'And love is lacking in Moule, my friends! Love for your fellow man—or woman, as the case may be! The man who does not love, who is not tolerant, who cannot see the innocence in a newcomer's face, is not following God's word, and is himself not worthy to enter His house!'

He paused to let these words sink in before he began his next tirade. If they dared, they would have avoided his eye, glancing shiftily at each other and hoping each one wasn't the cause of Vicar Washbourne's displeasure. But they didn't dare, and each one in turn had that icy glare centred on him for an interminable moment before it moved on. Only three people escaped the glare, which in itself made it very clear to the congregation that the Nash family was blameless in his eyes, and to be welcomed by the rest of them in no uncertain manner.

'Suffer the little children to come unto me!' Vicar Washbourne thundered. 'We are all God's children! And all those who enter this holy place should have shown their belief and their wish to follow Him. But not all of *you!*'

Rosie felt her heart hammering in her chest. She prayed that the vicar wouldn't reveal the cause of this sermon in any detail. She would feel doubly humiliated if he condemned Cyrus Hale and his friends from the pulpit. Even if he didn't know their identities, they would know she had told on them, and she feared for the consequences. But Vicar Washbourne was too old a hand for that. He knew just how to make his congregation squirm with a mixture of subtlety and brashness.

'You profess yourself Christians! Is it an act of Christian charity to kick a dog in the street? Or to walk past a blind man and not to offer help? Would you turn your back on a dying man? Unless you are the most miserable sinners on earth, I trust you would not, and therefore I say unto you, do not let your minds be corrupted by the sins of others! Let each one examine his conscience and see which is lacking in human charity. I repeat *human* charity, for there is nothing here that is not as human as you or I, and the Almighty *alone* sees all, and knows all! And be well assured that He sees all of *you*, and knows what is in each and every heart. Beware the day of judgment, if you have not been as He would wish you to be to the stranger in our midst!'

By the time they poured out of the church that morning, each one felt as if he had been personally wrung through the vicar's mangle. Each felt an overwhelming urge to speak with one or more of the Nash family, and Rosie found herself offered invitations to come calling and for afternoon tea, and her menfolk were promised the village custom...and it was just as if the vicar had somehow waved a magic wand and turned these suspicious villagers into effusive admirers. Despite the relief, Rosie had a deep suspicion that it couldn't last, and that this day might well result in a divided village, some stoutly backing the vicar while others hid their innermost distrust of the strangers.

But for now she revelled in the sudden burst of well-being extended to them all. And the Merricks decided they wouldn't wait to chinwag with the popular Nashes that morning after all, and since it was well-known the two families were already business-dealing, it would be seen as no slight.

It took a long while before Rosie and her menfolk finally made their way back to Briar Cottage, after reminding Bennett that he was expected around four o'clock.

'Come earlier, since Rosie says you're interested in our work,' Edwin said suddenly. 'I'm making a child's chair and wanting to finish it today, though not a word to the vicar! You may like to see how it's progressing, so come about three o'clock if you wish, Mr Naylor.'

'Thank you, then I will, providing you will call me Bennett. I can probably answer more of your questions about the exhibition. Since Rosie showed such interest I have looked out every reference my sister made to it in her letters that may be useful for you to know,' he smiled.

He walked off in one direction, while Rosie linked arms with her father and brother, feeling lighter in her heart than at any time since coming to Moule. Behind them, dawdling about in the churchyard, Cyrus Hale tugged at the confining neckcloth he only wore on Sundays, and scowled at his two cronies.

'That were meant for we,' he announced. 'The wench went blabbing to the vicar that night, boys, and we had to sit through an extra hour of sermonising because of it!'

'It might have been worse, Cy,' Hubert Pond said uneasily. 'Vicar might have said all our names in public, instead of going all round the bush on it. It proves she kept 'er mouth shut a bit, don't it?'

'Aye, I s'pose it does,' Cyrus said

thoughtfully. 'Mebbe that's the only thing in her favour. She can keep 'er mouth shut when she wants to. We'll remember that.'

And he wasn't done with Rosie Nash yet either, Cyrus was thinking to himself. Not by a long chalk...

Rosie had changed her dress for a soft violet afternoon voile by the time Bennett was expected. It was ruched across the bust and was frilled and ribboned, and the colour of it deepened her eyes and made them glow like wood violets. She knew she was looking her best, and when she heard footsteps outside, she called to her father that she would answer it. Edwin was already in the workshop, fashioning the basket chair for Daisy Lawrence. Rosie opened the cottage door, a ready smile on her lips.

'Well, good afternoon, Rosie,' Will cleared his throat awkwardly at the unexpected vision standing in front of him. A swift embarrassment made him tongue-tied. He hadn't dreamed she would look like this, almost as if she had known he was coming. If he had ever given credence to the ridiculous talk going around about her family, he might almost have believed she had second sight! He saw the welcoming smile on her lips die a little, and she seemed to be looking past him, but then she remembered her manners.

'It's good to see you, Will. Do you want to see my father, or Edwin?'

He was suddenly angry. Didn't she know he had come to see *her?* Wasn't it written all over him that he was here for one purpose only, and that to come a'courting her? He stemmed his quick temper. This was no way to begin.

'It's you I came to see, though maybe I should be seeing your father as well,' the thought struck him. 'I wondered if you'd care to go walking with me this afternoon. We could go over Bridgwater way.'

'Walking-out, you mean?' Rosie's mouth curved into a smile Almost as soon as she had said the words the approach of the school teacher caught her attention, and she spoke to Will all in a rush. 'Oh, I'm sorry, Will, but not today. We have company—but why don't you stay and have some tea as well, now that you're here? Edwin is going to show Mr Naylor how he works, and maybe you'd be interested too?'

Will's first reaction was to tell her to go to blazes, and he didn't need a spur of the moment invitation to tea, like crumbs thrown to a dog. Nor did he need to see the way she smiled so prettily at the school teacher, and the extra little flush in her cheeks at his arrival. He didn't need to know he had a rival, nor to know the first pangs of jealousy he had ever felt in his life, on Rosie Nash's account!

His shoulders involuntarily squared. It was also the first time he had spoken to the school teacher, to whom Rosie was now introducing him. Will was by no means illiterate, but he felt out of his depth with these two, who were obviously more intellectually suited to Will's simple way of thinking, and the realisation left him both frustrated and angry. But he was also one for digging in his heels, and he'd come here today with a purpose. Until he saw just which way things were going with the school teacher he was bloody well going to stay, since Rosie had asked him.

The small embarrassed silence between the three of them was covered by Bennett's smooth manners.

'I realised this morning that there would be fierce competition for your company, Rosie,' he smiled gallantly. 'And it's a pleasure for me to meet you too, Will.'

'Likewise,' Will grunted. He looked directly at Rosie's uncertain face. 'Didn't you say something about showing us the workshop?'

'Oh yes!' She seized the idea gratefully, and the two men followed her silently out to where Edwin sat at his plank, neither quite sure of the other's standing with Rosie.

Each concentrated ridiculously hard on Edwin's explanation of his work, as if it was a test for Rosie's approval. Bennett watched intently, as Edwin's strong hands thudded the withies into place, making the child's chair as comfortable as the material would allow.

'It seems to be truly a labour of love,' he commented, as Edwin took such obvious pains over the task. And surprised a secret glance between brother and sister that made him wonder idly just who the chair was intended for.

Will was looking round the workshop, his interest taken up with the withies stacked in sheaves around the place, and looking vastly different from the way they grew in sturdy rows at the Merrick farm. Stripped of their leaves and bark, and in various shades from white to buff to brown, they had become a craftsman's working material, instead of the living plant he tended in its growing state. The continuity of their two livelihoods struck him anew, and the thought gave him renewed confidence.

He fingered one of the rods in the sheaves remembering Rosie's haughty words. 'The butt and the tip, right?' He smiled at her, touching the thick and thin ends of the rod.

'Right!' She smiled back, and it was a small link between them as each remembered the climax of that afternoon, when Will had held her in his arms and kissed her. Her heartbeat quickened as if everyone else in the workshop could read her mind, and know how sensational a moment it had been...

'I'll bet you don't know what this is for.' She averted her eyes as Bennett glanced from her to Will, challenging them both as she pointed to the cow's horn hung on a nail near where Edwin worked.

'All right, I give in,' Bennett indulged her. Rosie glanced at Will, who shrugged. He wasn't in the mood for guessing games anyway.

'It's to keep the grease in so the bodkin is kept ready for making the holes in the basket base,' Edwin informed them.

'I wanted to tell them,' Rosie pouted a little, but by now Bennett was becoming very interested in the whole procedure and the brief history Edwin had told him.

'How do the withy rods become the rich chocolate colour?' he asked now. 'I understand about the stripping and boiling, but this colour is so very deep. Do you use a dye?'

Edwin shook his head. 'The only dye is in the rod itself. To produce the dark brown, the rods we select aren't stripped, but boiled in water already used in previous boilings. The rod itself releases an acid into the boiling and the dye is quite fast and needs no colouring material. Much of the fascination of the work is in the pure natural processes.'

Bennett was full of admiration as Edwin put the last touches to Daisy's chair and tested its strength and symmetry with a practised eye.

'You absolutely must attach an outline of your work methods when you exhibit in London, Edwin,' he went on. 'I guarantee the vast majority of people, particularly the city dwellers, have no idea at all how the products are made. To learn such details from the craftsman himself will add enormously to the interest shown in Nash Baskets, I promise you. Rosie can compose the lines once you've got your application accepted, and I have a friend in London who is an expert at copper-plate hand-writing. I am sure I can persuade him to make a splendid advertising outline to stand with your exhibits, Edwin!'

'Oh, Bennett, it sounds so exciting.' Rosie's eyes shone at the prospect. 'We'll have to get together with Pa and see what he thinks, but I'm sure he'll be as keen on the idea as the rest of us!'

Bennett laughed at her enthusiasm. 'I'm sure the London folk will only need to take one look at Rosie Nash's sparkling eyes and the excellence of Nash Baskets, and the exhibits will be a great success.' He didn't bother to hide the admiration in his eyes, and Rosie couldn't help a moment's preening at such a look from an elegant gentleman.

It was only then that she registered Will's glower, and the way his hands were clenched tightly at his sides. For a few moments Will had been entirely forgotten, and she knew it now with a feeling of embarrassment.

'What's all this about London then?' He didn't wait for her explanation, if any was coming. He felt full of resentment at being shut out of the conversation that seemed to have these three—and Dunstan Nash as well—in the grip of some fever. 'Don't tell me you're moving to London as soon as folk have got used to seeing you in Moule!'

He spoke with a flatness in his voice that betrayed him. Rosie couldn't resist a teasing laugh.

'Would it worry you if we did, Will? Would you miss us?'

He gave a snort. 'I daresay we'd soon find another buyer for our withies,' he said scornfully, as if that was the only reason he'd regret the departure of the Nash family.

'Oh Will, what a sourface you are at times!' Rosie still teased him, knowing full well he was hitting back at her in the only way he could for the moment. If she dared she'd thread her hand through Bennett's arm, just to see Will's reaction, only she certainly didn't dare! And she knew Edwin wouldn't be too pleased to see her playing one man off against the other... Seeing his sudden frown, she guessed that he was already aware of it, and spoke hurriedly.

'It's just that Bennett's told us of an exhibition in London next year, Will, and Pa and Edwin are thinking of putting Nash Baskets into it, that's all!'

That was all...just as if it wasn't one of the most important things in her mind right now, and had been ever since she heard about it!

'And you'd go to London as well, would you?' Will knew he sounded surly and couldn't seem to stop himself. His eyes brooded, and he felt himself to be a poorly turned out farm fellow, despite his Sunday garb, beside the amused look of Mr Fancy-Boy school teacher. His confidence seemed to ebb away as Rosie laughed with impatience at him.

'Haven't you been listening at all, Will? Of course I'll go to London for a while. Wouldn't you, if you got the chance?'

She looked at him coolly, challenging him. He glared back.

'What would I want to go there for?' he snapped. 'They say there's no clean air to breathe, and you get near trampled to death by all the carriages on the streets. Folks must be mad to want to go there, if you ask me!'

Rosie took a deep breath. 'Well, nobody need bother asking you again! I think we'd better all go and have some tea before Pa thinks we're starting to fight out here!'

She stalked out of the workshop, all her feathers ruffled, and all her pleasure in the exhibition suddenly dimmed a little by Will's rudeness. He could learn a lot from Bennett's bearing, she thought, smarting a little. While Will himself followed behind the others, wishing himself anywhere but having to sit down to Sunday tea in the Nash house while the school teacher was so much in favour. And very conscious of the gnawing fact that having only just found his love, he was already losing her...

Chapter 9

As usual, the gypsy caravans trundled across the Somerset Levels in late September. Seth Weaver spotted them first, while labouring in the fields north of Moule. That night he reported it to his cronies in the Moule Inn.

'Aye, 'tis time for the autumn fair,' Cyrus said with satisfaction. 'A bit o' sport to brighten up the days, me boys.'

'We ain't had much of it lately,' Seth agreed gloomily. ' 'Tis all the fault of they Nashes, since the vicar went all pious about 'em. I notice you ain't had much to say to young Rosie of late, Cy.'

'Just bidin' me time, boy.' The blacksmith tapped one finger on the side of his nose mysteriously. 'I been hearin' things lately, see? Seems like her father and brother be taking their goods up to Lunnon in the spring to some show or other, and our little Rosie might be stayin' by herself in Briar Cot!'

'That's not the way I heard it,' Hubert Pond put his penn'orth in. 'She be goin' with 'em to stay at some fine lady's house.'

Cyrus cuffed the side of his head to remind him who was leader of the group and had got the tale right.

'That be later on. First off, the men be takin' the goods in a waggon, and the school teacher's sayin' summat about formin' a club for any folk who wants to go up Lunnon to see this here show.'

Seth gave a derisive fart. 'Who'd want to go there?'

'Well, some folks might,' Cy farted back, and had the landlord bawling at the two of them for fouling the air, when good honest folk had come in to enjoy a jaw and a jar.

'How'd you know all this anyway, Cy?' Hubert fought hard to stifle the cough that would have the landlord sending him packing, though his eyes bulged with the effort and roused the only colour in his pallid face. Cy studied him thoughtfully, wondering how long it would be before they carted him off to Moule churchyard, and smothered his momentary pity.

'I know it all, stick insect, the way I get to know everything round here, by keepin' my eyes an' ears open!' he said aggressively, and then he relented, hearing the poor sod's chest wheezing like an old squeeze-box. 'My Granpappy got it from old Perce Guppey, who got it from his missus, who works for they Nashes, see?' There was no disputing the trail the information had followed.

'So what be 'ee doin' about it then, Cy?' Seth said lazily. 'Thinkin' of goin' up to Lunnon, or summat? A right fish out of water you'd be.'

'No, I ain't thinkin of goin' up to Lunnon, stupid,' he snapped. He might as well think of going to the moon for all it meant to him. 'If you'd use your loaf a bit, you'd know that little Rosie's goin' to be on her own in the cottage while her men be away, like I told 'ee, only I'm aimin' to see she ain't lonely!'

Hubert grinned. 'You'm riskin' it then, Cy. You don't reckon as how there's a witch's mark on her, after the way the vicar's been carryin' on lately?'

'I never thought there was,' Cy growled. 'She only said she was a witch to put the wind up us, but it'd take more'n that to frighten me!'

The other two hollered with laughter until Hubert couldn't stop the coughing a minute longer. The next instant the landlord poked his head through from the taproom.

'Out of it, young Pond.' He spoke kindly but firmly. 'We can't have you spitting and frothing while decent folk are enjoying their ale.'

Cyrus began a loud protest, but Seth

pulled at his sleeve. An argument would get them nowhere. It never did.

'Come on, let's take a look round the gypsy camp. There was a wench with 'em last year who knew a trick or two. If old Doughey can walk that far, we might find us summat more lively than old men's gossip anyway.'

'I'm all right,' Hubert gasped, the tears streaming down his cheeks from his exertions. But the paroxysm had stopped now, and the countryside was flat and open until it rose gradually to where the gypsy encampment always appeared at this time of year. They set out at a steady walk, though Hubert knew he'd have his father's wrath on him when he found out. The nights were nippy now, crisp and mist-laden, with the rhines stretching out like silver ribbons in the frosty moonlight. The meadow-grass was springy with damp and the Parrett river would be threatening to flood before long. It wasn't the best of times for Hubert Pond to be walking the Levels, but he had been told so often that each winter would be his last that he virtually ignored the doctor's warnings and trusted in the good Lord to make the end of it all as easy as He saw fit. Meanwhile, Hubert made the best of it and tried not to be too much of a trial to his companions by complaining, knowing that such a failure as himself was lucky to have friends at all.

The sight and smell of the gypsy encampment held a strange excitement for Cyrus Hale. The wood smoke and earthy tang of horse flesh, and the air of mystery the broom squires brought with them, always enlivened the dull end of the year. If he didn't have his Granpappy to mind out for, and the blacksmith's trade, he'd be for upping stakes and roaming round the countryside alongside them... The thought of all the wenches that a lusty black-eyed feller like Cory Pendle must have got his leg over on his travels was enough to make Cy green with envy.

It was Cory he looked out for as the three of them made their way through the cluster of painted caravans and snorting horses. Some of the older gypsies looked at them darkly, and would have sent them packing, but for the fact that Cy had mended a bit of ironmongery for them more than once.

The old crone who normally did the fortune telling at the fair was sitting outside a caravan, a kerchief tied round her scanty black hair, an evil-smelling pipe between her scrawny lips. She removed it, and squirted a jet of brown spittle in their direction as Cy asked about Cory.

'Cross me palm with silver and I might

be tellin' 'ee,' she cackled. 'I'm paid for tellin' secrets.'

'There ain't no secret in finding Cory, you old crone,' Cy snapped. ' 'Tis all a'fairyin' anyway. There ain't no truth in the things you say—everybody knows that.'

She suddenly pointed a horny hand towards Hubert. 'I'm sayin' this one won't be lastin' another winter, and you, me fine feller, be movin' in dangerous waters. You mind an' keep an eye behind you.'

'Come on, Cy,' Seth muttered, before the old crone's eyes turned on him with her prophesies. If Cy was scathing of her powers, he was not, and he'd just as soon not know what fate had in store for him. Cyrus shook him off.

'She ain't no real crystal gazer,' he snorted. 'And it don't need a prophet to tell old Doughey's on his last legs, do it? Come on, let's find Cory ourselves.'

'He'll be chopping wood, or tending the horses,' the old woman growled. 'I'd ask 'un to make 'ee a wooden cross while he's at it, for 'tis anybody's guess which one of 'ee will need it first, the consumptive one or the blackie...'

'Let's get away from here.' Seth was already moving away, not liking the turn of this conversation one bit. Cy might scoff at the gypsy's foreboding, but he didn't.

As for Doughey, he'd heard the tale of his own forthcoming demise so often that he no longer bothered to listen. It was a relief to all three when they spied Cory Pendle, stripped to the waist and with his powerful brown body glistening with sweat at the exertion of wielding a large axe to split the huge logs for the cooking fire.

Hubert Pond felt a brief, sharp, futile envy for a healthy body like Cory's, broad of shoulder and deep of chest, the tangled black hair that told of strength and masculinity running from the dark mat across his torso to a fine line that appeared in the waist of his breeches. Cory's brown skin rippled with muscles, the like of which God seemed to have forgotten to give Hubert, and added to that the gypsy boy had a handsome, strong face, and an arrogant look about him that was inborn in his race. As Cory saw the three of them approach he paused in his chopping, a wide grin on his mouth.

'Still here then, Doughey?' Cory greeted him. 'My bet is you'll outlive the lot of us.'

'Not according to your old faggot who does the crystal gazing,' Cyrus snorted. Seth didn't miss the way Cory's grin faded a little, and the look he gave Doughey at that instant was like a glance of farewell. Seth was angry for noting it, and for letting himself get so fanciful. It was all to do with Rosie Nash and her witch nonsense, he decided, putting all the blame on her and her family.

'There's some new folk hereabouts,' Seth said quickly, knowing Cy would take up the tale and switch the conversation from things that were making him increasingly uneasy.

Cory swung the axe over his head in an easy circular movement before it crashed down on the hefty log, splitting it cleanly in two. In the soft evening light the glint of the blade was echoed in the glow of Cory's skin. He'd almost come to the end of his task, but Cyrus knew the gypsy wouldn't make a move from the spot until it was finished.

'Oh?' Cory said. New folk didn't interest him too much. He saw plenty of them, every day of his life. They were no novelty, as they obviously were to these feller-me-lads.

'Cy's got his eye on the wench,' Hubert sniggered, and then had to stem the coughing bout that racked him again.

'It's just as well 'tis me and not you then,' Cyrus crowed. 'A fat lot of good you'd be to Rosie Nash wi' your coughing and wheezing! Your tackle 'ould shrivel up afore you even got aboard.'

'Did you say Rosie Nash?'

The three of them were suddenly aware that Cory had put the axe down for a moment, and Cy looked at him curiously. It wasn't too often that anybody put one over on Cory, or even surprised him. Living on their wits half the time as the broom squires did, they liked to think they knew everything, and usually did, but this time there was a look of astonishment on Cory Pendle's face.

'Know er, do 'ee, Cory? Fine bit o' skirt with a shape all primed up for fittin' into a man's, if you get my meanin'.'

'What's she doing here then? You say she's living in Moule now? If 'tis the same Rosie Nash I'm thinking of, she lived in Minehead with her father and brother. Basket-makers, I think they were, though I never took that much notice of what she told me about them. I was more interested in Rosie.'

The memory of her was suddenly sharp in his mind. And these louts knew her... He caught the gleam of lust in Cyrus Hale's eyes, and disliked him as much as ever. For all that the village folk thought they were vastly superior to the gypsies, Cory and his kin were lords of the road, and their travellers' knowledge was more widespread than these close-minded villagers would ever have. Why he tolerated the likes of the blacksmith, Cory didn't know, except that he was a mite sorry for the weedy one, and the farm-boy was a smidgin' less objectionable...

'You've got the right family, then,' Cy was saying with satisfaction. His mind was working sideways to think how he could turn this situation to his advantage. The gypsies weren't welcome in the village, and Vicar Washbourne had put his foot down on that score long ago. They could use the site for the fair, and they could stay for three days and no more, but they weren't to set foot in the village, not even to sell their wares. If folk wanted to buy clothes-pegs and paper flowers and brooms, they could do it at the fair...

'I could arrange a meeting between you and her,' Cy said slyly. 'You name the place and I'd pass the message on for her to meet you. That is, if you know her as well as you say you do! Mebbe she 'ouldn't want to go cavortin' with a broom squire.'

'She knows me all right,' Cory's hand-some face darkened with anger at the oaf's taunt. 'She'll remember me too. I told her we'd meet up again, but 'tis sooner than I thought.'

'Well then, do I fix it or not!' Cy was getting impatient. It was a mission he hadn't expected, and he wasn't sure how it was going to do himself any good, but to deliver Miss Rosie Nash a message was something to be going on with. He was curious to see how the news of Cory Pendle's arrival affected her. Miss High-and-Mighty, who thought herself too good for the village blacksmith, but apparently wasn't above a rough and tumble with a broom squire! From the tales Cory had told him of the wenches he'd met on his travels, Cyrus was in no doubt now that Rosie wasn't as pure as she appeared. A pity, he thought mildly. He'd have liked to be the first...but at least now he knew she'd be ripe and ready, for if Cory had given her a layin', she'd know what it was all about! And the gypsy obviously hadn't been scared off by all this talk about witchcraft either.

'Was it good, boy?' Cy couldn't resist slurring. 'Did 'ee find a mark, or didn't 'ee bother looking?'

'Cory, bring them logs and stop that jawing!' A great bellow from the direction of the caravans stopped Cory asking what the hell Cyrus was on about, and he told him swiftly to arrange with Rosie that he'd see her by Beech Cross gallows after dark the following evening. He had gathered up his bundle of logs in his strong arms, told Hubert to take care of that hawking cough and get indoors out of the night air, and was striding away with his burden while Cyrus was still pondering over the wisdom of the meeting place between Cory Pendle and Rosie Nash. Then he shrugged, because it didn't matter a damn to him anyway, and if she didn't see the association between one ancient Henry Nash who'd been strung up at Beech Cross gallows and herself, then why the hell should it concern him? If she did see the significance of it, it would just prove something, wouldn't it? Though Cyrus wasn't quite sure what.

'We'd best get this poor sod back home,' Seth muttered, as Hubert racked painfully. The three of them struck out, having to stop every few yards for Hubert to catch his breath. Seth was feeling disgruntled, thinking the whole journey to the gypsy encampment that evening had been a waste of time. Nothing was happening up there as yet, nor would it until tomorrow when the travelling performers joined up with them, and the stalls were set up in readiness for the next day's fair. The day after that it would all be dismantled again, and apart from the churned-up fields and the gypsies' rubbish everything would be the way it was before. Seth wasn't much interested in churning up the land for folks' enjoyment, and the only feet that had any right to scuff the fields belonged to cattle and farmers, but his was only one voice against a community that welcomed a bit of frivolity. Especially since their vicar didn't wholly approve of it, but allowed it grudgingly because of its ancient origins.

'How you goin' to pass on the message to Rosie Nash, Cy?' Hubert managed to wheeze out, his eyes streaming with the exertion of the coughing fit, and the cold night air hitting his skin with an almost icy blast. To a healthy body like Cory's it was no more than a cool September blow, but to Hubert Pond it was like the chill clutch of death.

'I dunno yet,' Cy grunted back. 'I can catch her on her way to the schoolhouse in the morning, I s'pose. That'll be best, for sure.'

'I'm surprised at you fixin' up for her to meet another feller, Cy,' Seth mocked. 'Givin' up on her now Cory's in the runnin'?'

His answer was a cuff around the head. Hubert stumbled, and the other two had to support his crumbling legs for the last mile back to the village. They paused on the stone bridge for the boy to get his breath. There was still time for a jar at the Inn, and old Isaac Hale would be there an hour or so yet. Cy wondered if it was worth his while meeting up with his Granpappy there, since Hubert was clearly ready for bed, and Seth was in no fit mood for company for some reason, and clearing off as soon as they got Doughey safely indoors.

'Come on, me old doughboy, let's get you back home.' Cy hauled him off the bridge, but Hubert seemed to cling to his arm for a minute with leech-like fingers.

'You know me Pa don't like me to be called Doughey,' he complained in a mawkish whine. And then he gave one great racking hack, spewing up a gush of blood and mucus right into Cyrus Hale's face, before he slithered to the ground as if every bone in his body had been turned to water by a magician's stroke.

'Bloody hell!' Cyrus wrenched the back of his hand across his face to rid himself of the taste and stench of the muck in a furious gesture. The stupid bugger didn't have enough sense to turn his head away before throwing up his guts...

Through a haze of fury and vomit Cyrus realised that Seth was kneeling over Hubert and trying to pull him to his feet. Only the silly sod was acting more like a rag doll than a real human being. He'd be mortified at his puking, that was it, and so he should be, Cy thought savagely. It would take days to rid himself of the smell...

'He's dead,' Seth looked up quickly, his voice hoarse with fear, his face white and disbelieving in the pale moonlight. 'I can't get no movement from 'un, Cy, and he's not breathing no more. Listen to 'un a minute.'

They could only hear the sound of their own breathing, uneven and short now, and the contrast with minutes ago, when it had been accompanied by the familiar rasping of Hubert's chest, made the moment doubly uncanny.

'He can't be dead,' Cy said roughly. 'Cory Pendle said he'd outlive the lot on us.'

'And the gypsy woman said he wouldn't last another winter.' Seth was still hoarse, his eyes suddenly glazing. 'She put a curse on 'un, Cy, and what's more, she said as how you'd be next!'

'Shut up, you bloody fool,' Cy shouted. 'Is that all you can think about, you snivelling cow-turd? Anybody with half an eye could see old Doughey wouldn't last much longer, and you'd best go and fetch the doctor while I carry 'un back to the bakery. And get the vicar too,' he added for good measure. 'Neither of 'em are of any use to poor Doughey now, but 'tis their job to be in on the dyin', so go to it afore I give you the job of lifting him instead.'

Seth sped off, as Cyrus knew he would, and then he scooped up the limp frail remains of poor Doughey Pond and carried them back to the bakery. He'd be glad to be done with this night, he thought feverishly. All he wanted was to dump Doughey Pond in his father's care and get off home and scrub himself clean. Any thoughts of enjoying a jar at the Moule Inn were quickly vanishing.

It seemed an eternity that he lugged the inert body to the bakery. Heavier in death than he'd ever appeared in life, Hubert still seemed to cling to him with a phantom attachment, even though the stick arms swung lifelessly at his sides. Cyrus gritted his teeth while he delivered the baker's son to him and heard the low wailing begin. Then he was forced to explain the circumstances, and take a tot of spirit with the baker until the doctor and Vicar Washbourne arrived. Seth was nowhere to be seen, and Cy didn't altogether blame him.

At last he could get away, and by the time his Granpappy lumbered home from the Moule Inn a while later, the blacksmith's cottage was steamy with the smell of soap and disinfectant and hot water with which Cy had lathered himself and his clothes. And then the explaining had to begin all over again...

The death of poor Hubert Pond put a

gloom over the village, but in their simple way folk reasoned that if the lad was alive he'd have been enjoying the autumn fair, so they might as well do likewise in his memory. All next day it seemed Cyrus was answering questions from sympathetic matrons, and it wasn't until late that evening that he remembered the message he was supposed to give to Rosie Nash. It was too late now. Cory would have waited until dark and then some, and then he'd have concluded the wench wasn't going to turn up, and he'd have pleasured himself with another if he was in that frame of mind. It wasn't Cyrus Hale's fault that Doughey Pond had convulsed and died and thrown the whole village out of step for a time.

The death of the baker's son meant little to the Nash family, having been acquainted with him so slightly. Although Rosie still remembered that night in the churchyard, when the claw-like fingers had stroked her skin and tried to get their fill of her, and she could only spare him a token pity. Truth to tell, he had truly repulsed her, but now he was dead and no longer a person to be feared.

More important to her mind was the idea of the autumn fair. Edwin announced that they would all go in the family cart, and that he understood the Merricks were also going to be there and bringing Jess Lawrence and young Daisy. Now just how did he know that little bit of information, Rosie wondered!

She had watched her brother use his picking knife in-the workshop to trim off the rough ends of withy from Daisy's chair, and noted how lovingly he fashioned it. And all because it was for Jess's child... In a sudden burst of inspiration Edwin had tested the deftness of his fingers and made a tiny doll's chair in an exact copy of Daisy's own, as an added gift, and when he had delivered both items he had come back to Briar Cottage with an extra lift in his bearing. He had made little comment about the reaction to the chairs, but Rosie guessed her brother was now a regular visitor to the modest little cottage.

And she would be seeing Will at the fair! Since the day he and Bennett had chanced to be at Briar Cottage together, Will had been decidedly cool towards her on the few times Rosie had seen him alone. She brooded on the fact. It wasn't that she expected or wanted everyone in the world to love her...but she certainly wanted Will Merrick to do so.

She knew how insensitive she had been on that Sunday, in teasing Will about walking-out with her, and then practically ignoring him in favour of Bennett Naylor!

She didn't blame Will for getting huffy. It was as if some perverse little devil inside her wanted to see the look of jealousy come into his eyes at that moment. It was a piquant situation to know she had two men interested in her, and that they were as unlike as chalk and cheese made it even more intriguing.

But Will wasn't a man to push too far. Rosie knew it with an instinctive certainty. And knowing by now the general times Will walked into the village, she had made sure she happened to chance his way a week or so before the fair arrived on the Levels. She had faced him squarely, seeing how his eyebrows almost met in the black frown he gave her.

'Don't be so stuffy with me, Will,' she began at once, her pretty mouth pouting at him. 'I thought you came to ask me to walk-out with you a few weeks back, and now you hardly speak to me!'

She saw his face go a dull red colour. 'I'd have thought you get all the talking you want from the school teacher! He's got far more words than a farmer's son! If it's talking you want, then you know where to go for it.'

Rosie moved a little closer. The soft September breeze lifted her dark hair into gleaming strands, caressing her smooth shoulders. Her blue eyes were as lustrous as jewels, her mouth moist and inviting and full.

'What if it's not talking I want, Will?' She was being provocative and she knew it, and she saw his eyes narrow a little.

'You want talking from a school teacher and kissing from me, is that it?' he inquired brutally. 'One of us is not enough for Miss Rosie Nash, it seems.'

'I didn't say that, and you're hateful to suggest such a thing,' she snapped, her mood changing with lightning speed. 'You make me sound like some kind of—of—Jezebel.'

'Well, you said it, not me. Didn't your mother ever teach you a man likes a lady to be modest and not to throw herself at every man in sight?'

Rosie gasped at the arrogance of him. 'My mother taught me that there's a time for a lady to be a lady, and a time when she needs to be a woman,' she said, her voice shaking. 'Not that I expect you to understand what that means!'

She hadn't fully understood it herself at the time, but now she did. Oh, *now* she did, when she wanted so desperately for Will to stop looking at her as if she was one of God's lowest creatures! She suddenly realised Will was laughing at her, and after a quick look round he saw there was no one but themselves in the secluded lane, and he caught her to him with breath-catching suddenness.

'Oh, I understand, Rosie,' he said huskily. 'And you think the time has come for you to be a woman, do you?'

She could feel the warmth of his breath on her eyelids as he held her captive in his arms. Against the hardness of his chest the softness of her breasts yielded gladly, their tips aroused and tingling.

'Do you doubt it, Will?' Her voice was caught on a breath. 'Don't you feel it?'

'Don't you?' he answered softly, moving slightly against her so that she registered fully the hardness of him, and the flame that had burned gently between them became fever-bright.

His mouth touched hers, softly at first, and then with a wild consuming passion. She could feel the warmth of his hand curving over her spine to reach the slender dip of her waist, and then it moved gently round to the front of her, to cup the globe of her breast. He gently squeezed the peaked nipple in an exploratory caress, and Rosie was aware of shooting shafts of desire running through every part of her.

The moment was so exquisite she could hardly breathe. She wanted to hold the sensation for ever. She wanted to tell Will how beautiful it was, this flowering of love, but somehow the words wouldn't come, and she couldn't bear it if he laughed at her again. Not now, when he was all man to her, and she all woman to him... It was no more than a fleeting moment, but in that time Rosie had pledged herself to Will for ever, no matter what or whom came between them. The thought was as perfect and binding as a prayer.

'Rosie, you're so beautiful,' his voice was deep and thickened in her ear as he held her close. 'I can hardly look at you without wanting to—to—'

She looked up at him, her love for him mirrored in her eyes. She was so stunning that she took his breath away. He couldn't really believe that she truly loved him. It had happened too fast, and Will was too used to the ways of the country, where things happened slowly and in an orderly cycle. He didn't quite trust the meteoric way that Rosie Nash had taken over his waking and sleeping fantasies...nor was he always too easy at sometimes waking in the middle of the night with a raging need for her, and having to find relief in only one way or go mad with the ache in his loins.

'Without wanting to what, Will?' Rosie whispered, wanting to hear him say it, wanting to know, wanting, wanting...

'To hold you and kiss you,' he said, folding his arms around her once more, partly because she felt so good there, and partly because he was afraid to look into those lovely blue eyes and betray his lust for her. She couldn't know what she did to a man with that mixture of wordliness and innocence that she exuded...

As if she somehow understood the effect she was having on him, and the impropriety of the two of them standing there locked in a close embrace, she moved slightly out of his arms.

'Then why don't you ask my father if you can come courting?' she said softly. 'Once we're officially walking-out, folk will expect you to be a little tender towards me, won't they?'

She put her head on one side, for all the world like a lovely, inquisitive little bird, her bright eyes glowing and teasing, and this time Will didn't disguise the laughter. Rosie laughed too, because the day was suddenly beautiful, and so was he...

'Rosie, I'm not sure that's the right word to use for the way I feel about you,' he teased her, 'but if you think your Pa will have no objection to me courting you, let's go and ask him right now. You don't think the school teacher will have any objection either, I suppose? We don't have to get his permission, do we?'

'Of course not! You are silly sometimes, Will!'

She felt his fingers interlace with hers as they walked back towards Briar Cottage. She was happier than she'd ever dreamed she could be, though she just wished Will hadn't made that silly remark about Bennett. She didn't really mind him being a little jealous, because a bit of healthy jealousy never did a relationship any harm, Rosie thought sagely...but in the last delirious minutes with Will, she hadn't thought about Bennett at all. Nor of the notions he'd put into her head about going to London and all that such a different life might have to offer.

Chapter 10

To Rosie's dismay and astonishment Dunstan was totally against the idea of Will coming courting. The two of them faced him in the workshop where he sat at his plank, his hands never stopping work as Will made his request, the current basket half-finished, the long supple withy stakes flailing about as the work turned on its pivot and Dunstan rammed the weave down with his iron.

'You're always welcome here, Will, and I've no doubt that in time Rosie might choose to wed you, but not yet. You can go walking-out, but on a friendly basis, with no commitments on either side. I mean it for Rosie's good, Will, and if you've any regard for her you'll agree to it.'

'Pa, how can you say it's for my own good, when I've no wish to go courting with anyone but Will?' Rosie burst out, all other considerations gone from her mind.

Dunstan eyed his daughter, unflustered, knowing her ways too well. She did everything too intensely, which came from the child in her. For all her womanly shape, she wasn't yet a woman, and he sensed that if Marjorie were here she would have said the same. Will Merrick was a fine young man, and it would do neither of them any harm to take things slowly. If they were really suited, then time would make no difference.

'I haven't said you can't see him, have I?' Dunstan said reasonably, in a manner that infuriated her. 'Be good friends, by all means, but leave the courting until you're a little older, that's all I'm saying. You understand me, I hope, Will? I've certainly got nothing against you. It's both of you I'm thinking about. Better to take it slowly now than to make a mistake you'll both regret.'

'Aye, you're probably right, Mr Nash.' Will respected the comment, for in essence it matched his own way of thinking. That it incensed Rosie he didn't yet register, but it was obvious her stampings and pleadings weren't going to do any good, and finally she went outside the workshop into the sunlight with Will, smarting at her father's injustice.

Inevitably she turned on Will when he tried to reason with her. 'You don't really want to come courting, do you? It was all a pretence, wasn't it? You didn't take much persuading when Pa put his word in! You weren't so slow back in the lane, nor in the withy field if I remember rightly.'

'Rosie, let's be sensible.' He gripped her hands, his voice firm and strong. He followed her inside the cottage, where she glared sulkily at him. 'God knows I don't understand women any more than the next man, but if you're unhappy about the waiting, then at least believe that it's the same for me. We're not that different in our feelings.'

'Why didn't you object then?' she cried, smarting. 'At least let me think you cared that much!'

He put his arms around her. Even through his strength, she could feel the trembling in him.

'Rosie, I care so much it scares me sometimes,' he spoke in a low voice. 'So much that I wonder if it's right for a woman to have such power over a man. Every night I dream of you, did you know that?'

In the small silence, Rosie's mouth suddenly curved into a smile. She touched his cheek with her soft finger, letting it run around the shape of his mouth.

'That's all right then. Even if I'm not there with you in person at night, I shall like to think of you holding the dream-me. What do we do together, you and the dream-me?'

Will groaned. 'For God's sake, Rosie, if we're to go on seeing each other at all, you've got to stop teasing me. I can't stand it, and one of these days you'll know enough about a man's body to know what I mean.'

'Is that why you glared at me in church? Was I doing something to you without knowing it?' The thought suddenly made some kind of sense, though she was too innocent of the full meaning of his words.

'That's it,' he said grimly. 'It wasn't that I didn't want you—just the opposite, in fact.'

'Really? Then if a man glares at me, does that mean he wants me?' She gave a sudden giggle. 'My goodness, you don't mean Vicar Washbourne secretly desires me, do you? He glares at me enough, and at everybody else, come to that!'

'That's not what I mean, but I'm not going to explain any more. Let's just be good friends like your father wants, shall we? You and I will know we belong, Rosie.'

Her eyes were bluer than ever as she looked up into his. 'We do belong, don't we, Will? Tell me that we do, and then I'll agree to anything. We'll be patient, and I'll be good and try not to make you glare at me again—only just tell me that we belong together.'

'Always,' he said simply. 'Till the end of time and back again.'

'Why, Will Merrick,' Rosie said softly, 'that was almost poetic, and worthy of Bennett Naylor's wordiness!'

They were in the lee of the second outhouse in which the Nash baskets were displayed for sale, and Will caught her around the waist, his face darkening.

'Are you saying I have to paint pretty word pictures to make you know the way I feel about you?' he demanded arrogantly. 'Because if so, you'll wait a long time for me to mimic that one! If that's what you want, say so now, and we'll end this.'

'You're the touchiest person I've ever met,' Rosie stopped him, her arms reaching to pull him closer. 'Don't you know by now it doesn't matter about words, Will? Or are

230

all men so stupid? You and I don't need words.'

He bent his head and tasted her lips, hoping desperately that no one would see them, or it would be all round the village in no time that Rosie Nash was quite ready to cavort with a young man in broad daylight. She seemed oblivious to the gossip that could spread with the speed of a forest fire and ruin a reputation quicker than blinking. Or if she knew, she didn't heed it. She was the most reckless and adorable and unique person Will had ever known, but she needed to be more careful... He shifted his head away to tell her so, and her soft lips moved against his.

'Kiss me again, Will,' she breathed. 'Just so I can remember the way it feels, and perhaps I can dream of you tonight as well. We'll be together in a dream.'

He gave a small groan, losing himself in her embrace and the ecstatic feelings she awoke in him, and the thought of warning her against her own passionate nature was forgotten. It could hardly be otherwise, when Will was discovering a delight in her that was hitherto unknown to him. By the time he left there was a glow about him, and a self-satisfied smile on Rosie's mouth. He still hadn't said he loved her in words, but she knew she had spoken the truth to him. They didn't need words to know there was love between them.

On the day of the autumn fair it seemed the village was a sudden mass of walking feet and creaking cart wheels, as folk shut up cottages and work-places and made their way to where the gypsy caravans made a colourful welcome to all comers. The travelling performers had arrived and set up stalls and arenas, and there were conjurors and stilt-men and hot potato stands, and a stall doing brisk trade with its paper twists of lusciously aromatic sweets, scented satins and fairy cushions, cachous in the shape of alphabet letters, chocolate limes and sugar mice, liquorice twists and marzipan mixtures. Rosie saw most of her little class milling around the sweet stall, including Daisy Lawrence's bobbing fair head.

Will must be here then, the thought ran through her mind. She had left her father enjoying the sight of the horse-dealing and the wagers being done on the races. Edwin had probably gone off to seek Jess, and she looked around eagerly for Will. The next minute her heart seemed to leap in her chest as she came face to face with someone she'd hardly thought to see again, and encountered his dark glare.

'Cory!' Rosie stammered. 'What are you doing here!'

In the first confused seconds she was conscious of several things at once. That it had been merely the surprise of seeing Cory that had made her heart react, and that she was no longer seeing him with the eyes of a besotted young girl as she had done six months ago. She was aware of his uncouth appearance and his black fingernails, compared with Bennett's neatly manicured hands, and even Will's healthily square ones that responded to an enforced scrubbing on his mother's insistence. She was aware of embarrassment, remembering those stolen nights on the moorland bracken with the scent of the sea romanticising the whole affair...and she saw that Cory was suddenly seeing her for a fine young lady after all, and that he was very put out over something.

'Why didn't you come?' he asked abruptly. 'Am I so low a fellow to you now, Rosie, that you can forget me so easily?'

His eyes took in the dark satin gleam of her hair, and she remembered in an instant the way he had twisted it around his hand as if to trap something of herself in his grasp for ever, and she gave a small shiver.

'I don't know what you mean,' she muttered quickly, seeing Bennett approach smilingly, nodding to one and another of the schoolchildren, and obviously assuming he had best come and rescue Rosie from the gypsy boy who might be accosting her.

'You were to meet me by Beech Cross gallows,' Cory went on. She had forgotten how guttural his voice could be when he was at his surliest. 'The blacksmith said he'd tell you.'

Rosie felt the wild colour in her face. 'I have nothing to do with the blacksmith! I'm sorry, Cory. There must have been some mistake. I got no message to meet you.'

'And if you had, would you have been there?' His brown face was glowering and coarse, all its handsomeness gone. He looked what he was at that moment, swarthy and foreign, a race apart with whom honest folk had little dealings except on these occasions, or when the broom squires came knocking on cottage doors to sell paper flowers or clothes-pegs. It was wiser to buy than refuse, to avoid any gypsy curse, but otherwise they were best left to themselves. Rosie flinched a little as she felt the touch of Cory's fingers on her arm, the nails digging into her flesh.

'I'm sorry, Cory,' she gasped, turning

quickly away from him into the crowd, filled with a panic she couldn't explain. And if she looked into those black devil-eyes much longer, she'd feel renewed shame and humiliation at what had so nearly happened between them.

Bennett was nowhere to be seen now, but she almost stumbled into Will's arms.

'I've been looking for you,' he said. 'Do you dare to have your fortune told?'

'Do I need to?' she countered. She tried to appear at ease, though her heart was thudding at the unexpected meeting with Cory and her shivering realisation that she had fallen out of love with him as quickly as falling in. She smiled up into Will's face, her blue eyes brilliant, hoping he wouldn't guess at the way her insides were churning at her own shallowness.

Since she and Will were walking-out it was permissible to hug his arm, and she did so with a feeling akin to desperation at that moment. It was noted furiously by the black-eyed gypsy who was scowling after her.

Cory had thought Rosie was eyeing up the elegant man who'd been surrounded earlier by children as if he was some dandified Pied Piper. Now he saw it was the farmer who was taking up all her attention. He still seethed at Cyrus Hale for not passing on his message to Rosie to meet him, but Cyrus wasn't around, nor any of his cronies, and it was at Will that Cory directed his present hatred. Will, who needed to be told a few things about Miss Rosie Nash...

'The fortune telling's only a bit o' nonsense,' Will was saying as they neared the decked-out tent. 'She'll say you'll meet a dark-haired man and marry him and live happy ever after—and we know all that, don't we?'

'Do we?' she teased him. 'Perhaps I'd best cross her palm with a coin in case the gypsy thinks otherwise then!'

He knew she was provoking him again, and told her he'd come back for her later if she wanted him to hear what she already knew! Rosie hesitated, then tentatively entered the tent, which was fusty and dim, with all the raucous sounds of the outside throng oddly muffled and distant through the heavy canvas. She saw an old crone with a kerchief tied around her head, wisps of untidy grey hair escaping from it like rats' tails. She wore a dark shawl and tawdry jewellery that clanked about her as she motioned Rosie to sit down. Rosie perched on the very edge of the rickety chair. Her heart was beating very fast and she wished she hadn't come in here. She hadn't intended to...

The old crone put both hands around

the crystal ball in front of her, and Rosie felt her eyes drawn to it as if she was mesmerised by its presence. It seemed like a vortex—a focal point between the two of them, uniting them in a way that was both indefinable and unwelcome. Rosie felt as if all her soul was exposed in that orb, and she seemed to hear the old gypsy mumbling unintelligibly as if from a very great distance. There was a strange smell in the tent that was both relaxing and stifling, and Rosie felt a deep lethargy creeping over her.

It completely arrested the feeling she'd had moments before. Then, Cory had looked fit to strike her when it was obvious she'd wanted to get away from him, and an odd fear had gripped her. He saw instantly that to Rosie he was an episode in her life that was over. She wondered uneasily if he accepted the fact as readily.

'There's a troubled heart in you, missie.' The old crone's droning voice made Rosie jump. The hallucinatory mood receded, leaving her suddenly alert as she concentrated. There was nothing here to fear. Old gypsy women spoke these dark and mysterious words to coax another coin for more information, and perhaps to sell a sprig of herbs to ward off evil...

'You've a cross to bear.' This time, Rosie's heart jumped harder, for it was the same phrase she had used to the vicar regarding Cyrus Hale. She ran her tongue over her dry lips as the crone peered intently into the crystal.

'What do you see?' Rosie's voice was thin and scratched.

'There's a dark man who means you harm, and another who'll be the savin' of 'ee. There's a long road for 'ee to travel before you find what's right under your nose, and your own nature will lead 'ee into perilous waters. Beware the dawn, pretty maid.' She paused for her words to sink in. 'You're a wilful one, for all your pretty ways and soft white flesh and red mouth.'

Rosie leapt to her feet. 'I don't want to hear any more,' she said jerkily. Her hands were clammy, yet she was icy cold.

The old woman gave a sudden cackle. The sound was like tin cans rolled along the cobbles. 'Ah well. If 'tis happy endings you're wanting to know about, I can't give 'ee none of they, missie! They be in your own hands, so use them well—and you mind what I said. A dark-haired man who means you harm!'

Rosie flung the coin on the table and thrust her way out of the confining canvas of the tent into the clean autumn air, feeling the need to breathe in deeply and rid herself of the aromatic fragrance still clinging in her nostrils. The old crone must have mixed up a potion to scent the air in the tent, Rosie thought, just to add to the mysterious atmosphere she tried to create. It was all a lot of mumbo-jumbo. A dark man meaning her harm indeed...

It was a remark that could be applied to anyone. A body would be fortunate indeed not to have at least one enemy, and Rosie wouldn't heed it as a warning. To do so only gave credence to the old woman's mumblings, even though Cyrus Hale undoubtedly came to her mind as she looked about for Will. Cyrus was dark...but so was just about every other man Rosie knew...where *was* Will! She wanted to tell him what she'd heard, and tease him about meaning her harm, and hearing him put it all into perspective while they laughed over it together...

Cory had followed Will to where the fine-maned gypsy horses were being groomed for sale to the highest bidder, their brasses gleaming like gold in the late afternoon sunlight.

'Buy one for your lady,' Cory said abruptly, his black eyes suddenly vicious. 'One with a good wide back. 'Twon't be the first time she's spread 'er legs.'

It took a few seconds before the gypsy's meaning sank into Will's brain. It was such an outrageous statement that Will didn't really believe he'd heard aright. The gypsy couldn't be referring to Rosie... Although the two of them had been standing very close together when Will had found them, and Rosie's cheeks had been burningly bright, now he came to think of it...

'I hope you're not meaning Miss Rosie Nash,' he snapped, thankful there were no others about at that moment. He saw the leer in the other's eyes. Cory threw back his handsome black head, his hands on his hips beneath the flamboyant waistcoat he wore over his breeches. For a woman who liked a bit of rough and tumble, Will thought grudgingly, there was something raw and exciting in the lout's manner, but he was more concerned with the slight to Rosie than considering the gypsy's appeal to women.

'Miss Rosie Nash,' Cory dropped his voice to a softly sensual utterance, as if remembering... 'Mebbe she never told you of the nights we shared under the stars on the moors above Minehead! The young spring bracken makes a fine bed for a wench with a mind for it, and pretty Rosie's a quick learner.'

He said no more, the breath strangling in his throat as Will leapt at him, his strong farmer's hands closing round in a vice-like grip. Cory's black eyes bulged, knowing there was murder in Will's heart at that moment. He swung his arms into Will's stomach as though they were battering rams, and it forced Will to let go of his hold on the gypsy and go staggering backwards for an instant. He recovered almost immediately and head-butted Cory while he was still choking and rubbing at his throat.

'You bastard,' Will snarled. 'Taking advantage of a young innocent girl.'

'There's nothin' innocent about sweet little Rosie,' Cory hissed back, his throat too bruised to do otherwise. 'Ripe as a juicy red apple for the plucking, an' if you don't want the poncey school teacher to get under her skirts afore you, you'd best stop wasting time, farm-boy! I seen the way she eyed 'im up. I seen that look in 'er eyes afore now! Made for it, she is, and wantin' it bad, I'd say.'

He gave a loud holler as Will shoved him into the horses where he went staggering among the frightened beasts. Will left him, uncaring whether they trampled him or not, and strode off without seeing where he went. If he went headlong into a rhine and was sucked beneath the treacherous green carpet of weeds to the dank waters below, it hardly mattered right then.

He couldn't believe it. He'd have staked his life on Rosie being as pure and innocent

241

as a new day, yet to hear that black broom squire describe the scene so vividly, in a place where Rosie herself had told him about, left Will with no doubts in his mind that it must be true. She was a whore. A rotten, trolloping piss-pot of a whore.

He thought of the times he'd fought to restrain himself from his lustful thoughts and dreams about her, even to waking in the night with his nightshirt tacky between his legs and knowing shame because of it. While all the while his so-called virginal Rosie had been laughing up her sleeve, no doubt wondering how long she could keep him dangling on a string and teasing him. Maybe she didn't even think he'd come up to expectations after laying with a gypsy with their reputed virility...

He'd show her, Will thought savagely. If that was what she wanted, then by God she'd get it, hot and strong!

It was dusk before he stopped tramping about the fields and lanes, and realised he was parched. He had come a long way from the fair, and the noises had receded in the distance. Soon every man there would be making his way to the Moule Inn to drink himself silly until long after normal closing hours. Normally Will might be there too. It was a safe bet the Nash men would be there, in the new spirit of cameraderie towards them since Vicar Washbourne's sermon. Will's eyes narrowed. Rosie would be alone at Briar Cottage.

He called in at a farm for a drink of milk and was offered a bite of food and a jug of cider to go with it. It went down well. The folk at the farm knew his father slightly and were hospitable and friendly, and might have put him in a mellower mood if his mind hadn't been made up, and set on the only course of action he felt would restore his pride in his manhood. If Rosie could open her legs for a broom squire, she could do the same for him...and he wouldn't let his thoughts revert to how different the coupling would be from that which he had imagined.

What a gullible, romantic idiot he had been, Will thought murderously. Like a reader of tear-wringing slush papers for young women, instead of the man that he was. But no more. Tonight Rosie Nash would discover he had a ramrod worthy of the name in his breeches.

By the time he reached Briar Cottage it was quite dark. He'd peered into the windows of the Moule Inn on the way and seen it full to bursting with menfolk, including Rosie's father and brother, singing and cavorting with the rest of them. Just as if no man had ever said a word wrong about the Nash family, Will thought grimly. But opinions could change in the twinkling of an eye, and they had best enjoy their brief popularity in Moule. With a prophetic thought to match any the old gypsy crone could deliver, he knew it couldn't last.

The cottage was in darkness, and he guessed Rosie would be in bed. So much the better. Will spoke in a low voice to the dog, who lifted his head briefly, then recognised a familiar voice and settled back in his kennel. Will opened the cottage door stealthily. This was no time for niceties and knocking for admittance. He hardly recognised himself...but he felt he didn't know anyone any more, least of all Rosie.

He crept carefully up the stairs and found her room. The door opened, making hardly a creak as he lifted the latch, and he could see her sleeping form beneath the covers, her face pale in a shaft of moonlight from the window. Her hair was spread all about her on the pillow. She was like a pale goddess. If he didn't know so well that, despite how she appeared, she was a fornicator, he'd have hated himself for what he intended to do.

As it was, he felt the stirring in his loins for her, and without a sound he stripped off his clothes until he stood naked beside her bed. Still she didn't waken, and with an oath Will pulled the bedcovers from her body in its cambric nightgown.

Her eyes flew open, and she gasped with fear and horror at the sight of a man's body looming over her. For a second she didn't register who it was, and Will clamped his hand over her mouth, so that her wild dilated eyes peered over the top of his fingers as she tried to croak his name.

'Shut up, whore,' Will ground out. He eased himself over her, pulling the nightgown out of the way of her soft white thighs. God, but she was beautiful, he thought, as he let his eyes flick downwards for a moment to where the luxuriant dark hair tangled at her groin in a tempting triangle. He forced her legs apart with his knees, and the warm secret part of her opened to welcome him in.

Or so he thought. Crazed now with desire for her, he didn't even register the sobbing noises coming deep in Rosie's throat, nor the fact that she was too numb with shock to resist, thinking with stunned horror that this couldn't be Will, not her dearest Will... This was some fiend smelling of cider who'd come to ravish her, disguised as her love...

Will caught hold of the hard bone between his legs and positioned it for a final exquisite moment at the edge of her moistness, before he rammed it into her with all his strength. It was tight for a moment, and then it was like sailing into a warm velvet ocean that rippled pleasurably all around him.

Rosie's scream beneath his free hand gurgled in her throat and was lost to him as he panted furiously to give her his best. He didn't care how many had gone before. Not now, when every nerve in his body told him this was perfection, and if he died a thousand deaths tomorrow because of enjoying a whore, then he didn't care. Whores were meant to be enjoyed. They knew how to pleasure a man...

Will suddenly realised that although he thrust vigorously again and again into her, Rosie didn't move a muscle. She lay like a dead thing, her blue eyes dark and enormous above his hand. Will didn't like to see them, accusing him like that. He took his hand away from her mouth and pushed both of them under her nightgown to fondle the lush ripe breasts with their taut nipples, needing her response.

'Come on, damn you,' he said hoarsely. '*Give!* Arch your back. Push with me. *Move* with me!'

Rosie's breath suddenly gathered in her throat in a great choking gasp. The words came slowly, painfully.

'I can't—I don't know how. Will—please

don't—I hurt, Will. You hurt me—please don't.'

His eyes glittered down at her in the white moonlight. He had lifted her nightgown to take his fill of her lovely body for the first time, the breasts like carved marble domes with their tantalising pink pearls. Will bent his head and circled each one sensuously with the tip of his tongue, feeling a stab of pleasure run through him like molten fire as he did so.

He just didn't believe that what she was mumbling was the truth of it. It must be her particular way with a man. He'd heard that whores had their own specialities. Rosie's was evidently to pretend an innocence she had long lost. And yes, Will thought grudgingly, it had the desired effect...it was exciting in its way...

'It's a long while since you've been hurt by this game, my sweet whore,' he said roughly. 'Though mebbe it's not so often you've performed in your own bed. More likely to be beneath the stars in the moorland bracken, from what I've heard!'

The thought of the gypsy taking his pleasure of her like this made him thrust into her more cruelly for a few minutes, as if to emphasise his words. He had been wrong before. Now he knew that it incensed him to know someone had gone before him, when he had thought her so pure.

'I don't know what you're talking about,' Rosie sobbed, the words trembling on her soft lips.

This was not the Will she knew. Not this fiend who seemed intent on splitting her in two before the night was out. There was still pain at his onslaught. The rupture of her maidenhead had been done with such ruthlessness it could hardly be otherwise, and her body had been totally unready to receive him. She saw the mocking look in his dark eyes.

'Mebbe you prefer a change of pace now and then,' he taunted her, slowing down the fury of his driving body. The new sensations were hot and languorous, as each sensual penetration began to awaken the dormant womanly responses in Rosie that she had never known existed until now.

Without realising that it did so, her body reacted in small rhythmic movements to match Will's. Her hands, that had been clenched tightly at her sides, now relaxed, her arms reaching around him, her fingers entwining in the thickness of his hair. Small whimpering sounds still escaped her lips, for the shock of Will's attack was still searing, and she still didn't understand what had provoked it.

Instead of pleasing him, her seeming capitulation seemed to anger him more, and he stopped moving altogether for a moment, and looked down at her contemptuously. His breath came harshly in his throat, for it was difficult for him to remain apparently unmoved by her, and to treat her as he thought she deserved.

'Well?' he demanded. 'Do I match up to the gypsy?'

Total shock drained all the warm colour out of her face, and for a moment she looked as pale as death. Realisation came to her immediately, and there was a physical ache in her throat as she fought to keep back the tears at the wrong Cory had done her. And Will too...the brief pleasure she had felt was swiftly turning to bitterness.

'How could you believe anything he told you?' she said in a ragged whisper. 'Or that I had done—*this* before. Didn't you *know* this was the first time?'

For a second the only sound in the tiny room was the noise of breathing—Rosie's, thin and choked; Will's, rasping and suddenly appalled. His eyes moved downwards to where his body still covered her, and as he slowly withdrew from her he saw the telltale red stain on his own skin as well as hers.

She pulled her nightgown down over her nakedness quickly, and the sight of

249

her silent tears gleaming on her cheeks like diamonds sent a burning shame right through him. He tried to gather her up in his arms, but she remained motionless and rigid.

'God forgive me, Rosie,' he said, his voice gritty. 'I swear to you it would never have happened like this but for the thought of the gypsy.'

'God may forgive you, but I never will,' Rosie said tightly. 'Get out of here, Will, and don't come back. I don't ever want to see you again.'

She turned her face to the side, as if the very sight of him was abhorrent to her. For a moment more he tried to placate her, though it was as if he held a stone statue to his chest instead of the warm, loving woman he wanted her to be.

'Rosie, please.'

'Get out, Will!' she suddenly screamed. 'I hate you for this. Don't you understand? I hate you—*hate* you!'

He moved away from her, dressing quickly without another word. In her present state she was likely to say and do anything, and it was best to do as she wanted and get away from here. In a day or so he could find some way to prove his remorse. He hesitated at the bedroom door, but not by a flicker did she make any response to his pleas or his leaving her. Will gave a brief word of goodbye and closed her door quietly behind him, letting himself out into the chill night air.

He was truly appalled at what he had done, not knowing how he could put it right. There was no way of putting it right. He had raped her...the ugly word swam in and out of his senses, and the throbbing, unfulfilled ache in his loins was a bitter reminder of how he had besmirched their young love, however unintentionally. At that moment Will had never hated himself more.

Only when she heard him leave did Rosie let out her breath in a long drawn-out moan. She would never trust any man again. First Cory and now Will...who was the dark man who meant her harm? In her tortured mind that night it was all men, and if her own apparent sensuality was the trigger that roused their base urges, then Rosie would do her best to smother it.

In the darkness she touched herself where Will had touched her, wincing at the tenderness there. In that instant she could identify so well with Jess Lawrence, brutally used by a man in a world dominated by men. Rosie hated them all.

Chapter 11

Autumn was the time for the withy auctions. Moule Inn had become the accepted auction room for farmers for some distance around. Each farmer made his own arrangements with his buyer. Some basket-makers would arrange to go to the withy fields and do their own cutting after the fall of the leaf when the rods were in prime condition. Others paid the farmer to do the cutting. Some farmers undertook to do the boiling and stripping of the withies after the cheerless, hard labour of the cutting. Others left it to the basket-makers to take on this part of the work, preferring to be growers only. Whichever faction took on the boiling and stripping, the resulting swatches of withy rods, boiled and stripped and propped up to dry against the hedgerows, added an almost frivolous gaiety to the sombre wintry Sedgemoor scene, turning from honey colour to a warm golden brown.

Dunstan and Edwin Nash had already made their arrangements with Farmer Merrick for the buying of one withy field, with the option on another. There were vast acres of the crop coming to readiness for cutting in a few weeks' time now. And the scene at Moule Inn on auction night was of great jollity and bargaining, as one of the country man's seasonable tableaux was enacted.

The landlord acted as auctioneer, as farmer after farmer quoted his particular crop's qualities, according to location and yearly growth, and waited for the hammer to fall as each basket-maker nodded in agreement. The right to each field was held by tradition for one winter only, and the following year the auction would take place all over again to the highest bidder. Only a portion of the price agreed was paid out at the time of auction, with the balance due at the end of the season. The auction was a time for withy growers and basket-makers to jaw together over mutual interests, comparing prices and crops and the changing nature of the craft. Where once it had been more of a functional craft, with a constant need for fish baskets and homely carrying articles and the like, the great upsurge in basketware as a city fashion was turning the work into a skill of far more importance than the old country craftsmen had ever dreamed of.

The business end of it all done, the men were content to jaw on into the night, and the landlord was kept happy filling cider jugs and his coffers at the same time.

'We haven't seen you around for quite a time, Will,' Dunstan Nash said companionably, as he and his son joined the Merrick men on more social than business terms.

Edwin didn't miss the dark flush on Will's face, and wondered anew what had gone wrong between him and his sister. That it was something serious was obvious to Edwin, if not to his father. Dunstan by now was full of enthusiasm for the exhibition in London the following year, and making and discarding plan after plan as to which items to exhibit. Dunstan, at least, was back on an even keel once more. The same couldn't be said for Rosie, Edwin thought with a frown.

'I keep busy, Mr Nash.' Will's voice was almost grudging, as if he'd prefer not to speak at all. Edwin hoped keenly that all that superstitious nonsense hadn't finally affected Will, especially since it seemed to have died down in the village for the moment. He wouldn't have thought Will was so short-sighted as to give it credence anyway.

'I keep tellin' 'un 'tis time he found himself a maid to court,' Farmer Merrick said, lazy with cider and a good night's work. 'But he don't seem in no hurry.'

'I thought he'd found one,' Edwin spoke

under his breath, so that only Will could hear him. 'What happened, Will?'

He didn't miss the way the other man flinched. If it hadn't been for the way Rosie seemed to have changed lately, Edwin might have thought she'd been teasing the boy and leading him a pretty maid's dance; but from the dark shadows beneath Rosie's eyes, and the way she'd started to drag her hair into an unbecoming matronly style and wear her clothes buttoned to the neck as if she didn't like the very air on her skin, Edwin doubted it.

'Nothing happened,' Will snapped. 'We made a mistake, that's all. Your Pa was the one who said he didn't want us to treat it as too serious, didn't he? Well, we just decided he was right, and we chose not to go walking-out after all.'

Edwin looked at him thoughtfully. It might have convinced some people, but it didn't convince him. He'd have gone to the old Rosie and asked her what was wrong. They had never made a practice of covering up secrets from each other. 'Better to get things out in the open,' their mother used to say. 'Troubles are never half as bad when they're given the light of day and shared with a sympathetic listener.' But this new Rosie prickled every time Edwin made any attempt to coax her out of the strange moods in which she existed lately. Sometimes lethargic, with a lost blank look in her eyes that alarmed him, at other times as pithy and aggressive as a man.

The only time she came to life was when she spoke of the school teacher and her work with the children. Maybe that was the reason for the distance between her and Will Merrick. Maybe it was the school teacher who had captured her heart... Edwin didn't think so. Whatever Rosie had on her mind, Edwin was certain she wasn't acting like a young girl in love. She didn't act like a young girl any more, in fact.

'You'll have heard that the school teacher's organising a club outing to London to see the exhibition next year, Will?'

Will scowled fiercely. 'Aye, I've heard. It won't interest me. Farmers can't take time off whenever they please to go gallivanting like some folks.'

'I thought you might have liked seeing our goods exhibited. After all, you'll have an interest in it, whether you like it or not. It'll be your withies that go into our baskets. Don't you want to see how the fine ladies and gentlemen react to them?'

'No!' Will growled. ' 'Tis nothing to me.'

'Rosie plans to go,' Edwin went on

relentlessly. 'We shall all attend, and Bennett Naylor is starting a savings fund for those interested. We're to go on the train from Bridgwater to Paddington.'

Will snorted. 'How many folks around here do you think can afford that kind of caper?'

'Not many,' Edwin admitted. 'But if they start putting little bits of money into the savings fund now, they've got more than eight months till the end of June, when Bennett plans to take the Moule club.'

Will's scowl said all he felt about the school teacher taking charge of the village in this way. He felt a sudden nudge from his father behind him. Farmer Merrick was adept at carrying on one conversation while keeping half an ear cocked for what was going on all around him.

'I think 'ee should represent us, Will. One on us can go, and 'tis for young 'uns to go up to Lunnon, to my mind. We old 'uns can hear all about it later on. You put your name down, me boy, and don't let it be said that we Merricks can't afford no treats. 'Tis right what Mr Edwin says an' all. Our withies be the finest for miles, and let's be hearing what the city folks think about 'un!'

His words were greeted with jeers and friendly catcalls from the other growers in the Inn, and Will groaned, knowing now that he'd get no peace from his Pa unless he agreed to go on this club outing to London. He said he'd think about it, knowing that the last thing he wanted was to be in the company of Rosie Nash for any length of time.

Though that wasn't strictly true. Since that night of the fair when he'd gone to Briar Cottage and treated her like the whore he'd thought her to be, Will had been struck by the most terrible remorse. He despised himself for what he'd done, and he knew Rosie was shunning him, and he couldn't do a bloody thing to put things right. Any attempt to explain to her just stuck in his gullet, and anyway, he sensed that she wouldn't listen. Not since she'd seemed to shut herself up inside herself these days.

Yet, in the stillness of the night at Merrick Farm, he was unable to resist the sweet memories taking him unawares. For all that it was rape that he had done, the man in him remembered the softness of her and the way she had felt in his arms, and the need to love and cherish her again could still become a raging desire within him at times when he least expected it. Because of the futility of it all he had become surly and morose, and his mother was beginning to despair of him ever finding a wife and providing her with grandchildren to dandle on her knee.

'All right, I suppose I'll get no peace from this one unless I agree,' Will grunted at Edwin, jerking his head towards his jovial father. 'If you're seeing the school teacher you can put my name down for the outing, though 'tis not going to be for too long, I hope. Farm work can't wait for fancy outings.'

'Stop being such a grouch, Will.' Edwin was well pleased with what he thought might be a way of bringing Rosie and Will back together, even if it was some time ahead. Hopefully by then, whatever had crossed them would be muted by time, and they would see what he so clearly saw, that they were made for each other. He and Jess had remarked on it more than enough times.

'The train gets us to London in the space of a morning! We'll have the next day and one after to see the exhibition, and then come home again. Four days in all! The farm can spare you that long, can't it? And folk around here won't want to spend any more on hostelries than they need to, so Bennett reckons it's just about the right amount of time.'

Bennett this and Bennett that... Will was irritated by the man's very name. Particularly since he knew Rosie worked with him each day at the schoolhouse. He'd taken some work into the blacksmith's one afternoon, and seen her walking back down the main street on her way home. He'd been shocked at the change in her appearance, and as his eyes followed her as she looked neither to left nor to right, he heard the sniggering from the burly blacksmith.

Cyrus wiped the back of a grimy sleeve across his forehead to soak up some of the sweat. Other folks might be complaining of the autumn nip in the air, but in here where it was furnace-hot he sometimes felt he'd melt clean away like candle wax left in the sun. He thrust Will's piece of ironware into cold water to sizzle and cool before handing it to him, and looked at him speculatively.

'Not quite as pretty a maid as when she come 'ere, be she, Will Merrick? Flauntin' herself like that were bound to come to no good. Vicar must 'ave had words wi' her, unless 'tis t'other thing, o' course.'

'What other thing?' Will snapped. He wanted to be out of there. God knew how the blacksmith could work in such cloying heat, and he didn't want to discuss Rosie with him either, but his interest was caught.

'The witch talk,' Cy's little eyes glittered. 'They say a witch can turn 'erself into anything she fancies, don't they? An' I reckon there be a bit o' mischief involved to turn a pretty, luscious little piece into a drudge-mop! 'Ouldn't 'ee say so, Will Merrick?'

Will threw the coins for the work at him and stomped out without answering. It infuriated him to hear such talk, especially since it was clear on Sundays that most folk, from the vicar down, approved of the new, demure Rosie Nash and failed to see the bleakness in her lovely blue eyes.

At least the blacksmith was showing little interest in her now, which was a brief consolation to Will, knowing of old of his lechery. Though Will himself was a fine one to talk, he told himself bitterly as he made his way home from the village...and tried to put Rosie from his mind.

Cyrus Hale watched him go, pondering. He'd seen the way Will Merrick ogled Rosie Nash at the fair, and he'd heard vague stories of their walking-out together. Couldn't be any truth in it, Cy decided. They were never seen together, not even talking on Sunday mornings after church. Cy didn't want to think too much about Rosie Nash now either. Not since things had started to happen.

At first he hadn't thought too much about them. Poor Doughey Pond had outlived his expected time, so there was nothing untoward in the fact of his dying, even though it had taken time before Cyrus could forget the manner of it in his arms.

What was more disturbing was to wonder what in devil's name had happened to Seth Weaver a few weeks later when he failed to turn up at the Moule Inn. And when Cyrus had gone marching to the farm over Bridgwater way where Seth worked and lived, it was to be told the poor lad had died from eating a poison mushroom he'd fried himself. One bad one among a dish of his favourites... Cy had got a cold bad feeling in his gut listening to the farmer's wife sorrowing over Seth. How could a country man born and bred be so foolish as to mistake the poison fungus for the breakfast tasties?

The answer had come to him like a thunderbolt. Rosie Nash had done this. First Hubert Pond and now Seth...two out of three. It was her revenge for that night in the churchyard when the three of them had tried to spread her and find the witch's mark...and since nobody but Cyrus himself knew the truth of that night, except for Rosie of course, there was no one in whom he could confide. Especially not Vicar Washbourne, who would flay him alive for what he'd tried to do, either physically or verbally in his sermonising, or both.

There wasn't a damn thing he could do except be extra wary of Rosie Nash, and drop his own little bit of poison into any receptive ears when he got the chance, as had happened when Will Merrick came into the smithy. She had a lot to answer for, Cyrus thought viciously. If it was all true what they said, then she was responsible for the deaths of Doughey and Seth...two out of three, the startling thought caught him...and for his getting a rollicking and a pasting from his gypsy friend, Cory Pendle, for making him wait on a fool's errand for a wench who didn't turn up. Oh yes, Cy owed Rosie Nash quite a lot, he thought grimly, and never had he turned his little trick of dropping a word in an ear, and sitting back while it took effect, to such advantage as he did now.

If he only knew it, he wasn't the only one who was beginning to wonder about Rosie Nash's powers, though that wasn't the way she was considering it personally. Rosie was bothered by her own insecurity. Will's attack had affected her more deeply than she would ever have imagined it could. She ached to confide in someone, but again she felt unable to tell Jess, and there was no one else. She missed her mother with a sharpness that almost amounted to anguish, as if the grief that had mellowed was starting all over again. She felt as if she had grown to maturity in a single night because of what Will Merrick had done, but it wasn't a lovely flowering of womanhood that she felt. Instead, she felt she knew all the sins and ugliness of the world, as if a door had been opened to her, and she knew at last how beautiful it was to cling to childhood as long as possible. It was a revelation that came to everyone too late, Rosie thought, with a wisdom that was almost tragic.

In some frightening way, too, she began to think she had taken on the outcast role that had once belonged to Jess Lawrence. Jess was accepted into the community now, after serving her time of penance. And although Rosie couldn't honestly say that she and her family were treated with the same suspicion as when they first arrived in Moule, the first flush of approval brought on by Vicar Washbourne's sermon had waned. And then too, she felt surrounded by secrets...

How could she ever tell her father and brother what had happened on the night of the fair? To admit to being seduced was shaming for a woman, as if she was the guilty one merely for being the receptacle of a man's lust. Her menfolk liked Will Merrick, and the Merricks were important to them, supplying their withies and counting themselves as friends of the Nashes. For Rosie to start a rift between them all was more than she could do.

It was far better to concentrate on her school work in the village than on young men for the present. At least with the small children, and with Bennett Naylor, she could behave in a reasonable, natural way.

In an eerie way, Rosie couldn't quite rid herself of the ancient tale of the sin-eater. After a death he would come and stand over the body with a handful of herbs, mumbling an incantation that ended with the words, 'I eat thy sins.. I eat thy sins...' upon which he would stuff the herbs into his mouth gobbling them down at a fierce rate as if gobbling up the very flesh of the deceased and absorbing all that was evil in him...

Rosie would awaken burning and sweating in the middle of the night, fearful that in truth she was touched by the black arts. That all her fears were a sign. That the old custom was being enacted in her, by this feeling of taking on Jess's role. For a time it seemed as if the whole world had shifted beneath her feet, the way it had done when her mother and then little Dorcas had perished. It was a long road back to normality when it was travelled alone, and only with Bennett did Rosie feel able to relax fully.

He was aware of the fact, though not the reason. If he was surprised at the way Rosie had changed her appearance lately, he thought it was only to the good. She looked and acted more mature, which could only command more respect from the children. And when he introduced her to his sister in London, Alice would not think him such a nonce for being attracted to such a young and comely woman at his age.

Bennett's thoughts on the subject of Rosie and marriage were still only in the ethereal romantic stages. He had been his own man for too long to rush into anything without full consideration and weighing up every advantage and disadvantage with precision-like thought. Right now it was his very stability and calmness that did much to restore Rosie's troubled mind to its former nature.

She couldn't totally avoid Will, of course. At the first cutting of the withies he delivered a cartload of them to Briar Cottage, all stacked into bundles and tied round with a whipping of withy rods. He was unloading them into one of the outhouses where Edwin was preparing the tanks for the boiling and stripping of the rods. Rosie felt her face flame as she came into the yard from her day at the schoolhouse, and was face to face with Will. It was the first time she had seen him since the night of the fair, apart from the cursory glances at church.

'How are you, Rosie?' Will asked abruptly, his voice as stilted as if he had never held her in his arms and kissed her full soft lips. As if he had never known her more intimately than any other man, nor ached with the desire to have her in his arms again... The thought of her was like a piercing dart of pleasure.

'I'm well enough,' she said coldly. 'And you, I trust.'

Oh Will, Will...the weak, vulnerable, womanly part of her could still reach out to him in spirit, even while the stubborn resistance in her said that this was her seducer...her enemy.

Edwin looked from one to the other of them in exasperation.

'I hope you'll be on better terms with each other by the time we go to London for the exhibition,' he commented. 'It might be embarrassing if we're all to sit in the same railway carriage with you two glaring at each other!'

'I didn't know you were going to London,' Rosie spoke quickly, ignoring her brother and looking straight at Will.

'I might,' he hedged away from acknowledging it right off. 'Then again I might not.'

Rosie flounced out of the shed, bright spots of colour burning her cheeks. 'Well, don't put yourself out to go there on my account!'

'I won't,' his voice followed her. 'A farmer's got better things to do with his time than wasting it looking at fripperies.'

This time Edwin looked at him in annoyance. 'It's clear you don't know what's going on in London, Will. Rosie's got some pictures from the newspapers that Bennett's sister sent him, showing the scale of the exhibition building. Folk from all over the world are sending goods there, and they say it will be opened by the Queen herself. I'm thinking plenty of folk will find it a good platform to sell their goods!'

'I daresay,' Will muttered, knowing he'd sounded a boorish fellow and hardly knowing how to put things right. He had no quarrel with Edwin Nash...

'Are you starting on those rods now?' he asked directly. 'I can give 'ee a hand, if you like. It's tedious work, and you won't be too used to it.'

'If you like. A lad from the village is coming along soon as well, to help stack them out to dry. You probably know him—Hal Stone. He tells me he helps with the withy stripping around the farms at this time of year.'

'Aye, I know Hal Stone,' Will nodded. 'Let's get to it then.'

He rolled up his sleeves. The atmosphere in the outhouse was heavy with steam from the boiling water, and the first batch of withies were plunged in before peeling, so that the bark juices stained the wood brown. The boy, Hal Stone, arrived soon afterwards as they worked on. The scent from the rods was vaguely herby and aromatic, the steam billowing out through the glassless windows. In the tanks the boiling water was turning a rich earthy colour. If the rods were used green as soon as they were cut, they would shrink and the basketwork would become loose. Some penny-quick basket-makers were less ethical in the preparation, and it showed in the shoddiness of their workmanship. But not so the Nash men.

Rosie brought them out a drink of lemonade after an hour or so. It was hot work, and she avoided looking at Will's strong bare arms glistening with sweat. She remembered all too well the last time she had seen them like that, and her mind shied away from it. The young boy, Hal, was a chatterbox, and covered up the lack of conversation between the rest of them.

'Will 'ee be watching the funnin' on the fifth o' November, Mister Nash?' the tousle-headed boy inquired eagerly. 'You'll not have seen it in Moule afore, will 'ee? Blacksmith does us proud, pluggin' the holes in the anvil wi' gunpowder and settin' it off! 'Tis guaranteed to scare away the devil hisself,' he sniggered, then darted a sudden nervous glance towards Rosie and Edwin, as if remembering the odd tales that had been spun around these two and their Pa in recent months. Not that there seemed anything odd about them now, Hal Stone thought sensibly, and his young sister was full of the nice Miss Nash who taught at the village school. The smile returned to his ruddy face.

'Sounds pretty dangerous to me.' Edwin was too intent with the second boiling and the stripping of the withy rods through the pair of prongs known as the breaks. Outside in the air there were already rows of stacked rods tied around with another piece of withy and gaily drying in the thin pale sunlight.

'Oh ah, 'tis dangerous all right, but blacksmith don't give a tinker's cuss for danger,' Hal said proudly, as if Cyrus Hale's recklessness was something to be admired. 'We're afeared o' nothing in Moule, 'cepting mebbe for the devil. There be fireballs and tar barrel rolling on the night o' the fifth, and they that stay indoors be old women!'

Edwin looked at the boy, a glimmer of laughter in his eyes. 'Is that what they'll call me if I decided to stay home then?'

'Ah, to be sure they will!' Hal said seriously.

'I'd better join in the fun then,' Edwin laughed aloud now. Jess had already told him of the festivities, and he had promised to take her and Daisy along to the common near Beech Cross where all the fun began...

'Well, I shan't go,' Rosie declared. 'I hate it all—and besides it frightens the animals. I shall stay indoors with Boy.'

Outside the doorway the dog gave a token growl as he heard his name, then he gave a short bark as Will went outside to bring in the last batch of withies from the cart.

'He seems more nervous of Will these days!' Edwin remarked. 'He's taken a dislike to you for some reason, Will. Mebbe it's the smell of blood on you from your rooster kill.'

'Mebbe,' Will's face was scarlet as he caught Rosie's look. They both knew why Boy had turned against him, the silent witness to the ravishing.

'You won't do any tar barrel rolling, will you, Edwin?' Rosie said nervously. She had seen it once, and been terrified by it. It wasn't so bad so long as the men left the barrels on the ground and rolled them with their flaming innards through the village streets. But it nearly always got out of hand, and some cider-happy ones would lug the barrels on their shoulders and race through the onlookers, with the blazing tar shooting flames from each end and frequently catching the spectators alight.

'Don't worry about me, Rosie. I can take care of myself,' Edwin said. 'Do you join in, Will?' he asked as Will returned, and caught the last of the talk.

'I might. The fireworks brighten up the dull end of the year, and the fireballs can be spectacular as long as they're sent off in the right direction, and not among the crowd.'

'What are they?' Rosie couldn't resist asking, though it was to Hal Stone that she looked, not wanting any information from Will Merrick, or for him to think she was encouraging him to speak to her.

'Ain't you seen 'em, miss?' Hal looked at her as if she must have been born on another planet. 'Great fiery things they be, made out o' balls o' hessian soaked in pitch and set alight, then whirled round and round on the end of a wire! Fair set the sky alight, they do.'

'Well, that settles it then. I shall stay indoors on the fifth!' Rosie turned and walked primly away from the outhouse.

On the outskirts of Minehead where they used to live, the celebrations had been distantly observed by the Nash family. It all sounded like dangerous madness to her, and no doubt another excuse to end the night in a drunken stupor at the Moule Inn, she thought cynically. The best place to be was safely inside the cottage.

She had reckoned without Bennett Naylor's unexpected enthusiasm for the night's mischief however. And his little lecture as to the need to remember the treasonable plot in the Houses of Parliament by Guy Fawkes was something she would rather have done without.

'The children have learnt about it from us, Rosie, and will be joining in the fun. How will it look if their teachers decide to stay away like scared rabbits! I'm sure you'll enjoy it, so please come. There's safety in numbers, and it's good to see a united village, for whatever reason.'

She couldn't deny that, when there had been times that she felt herself to be the object of dissent among them. Though the comment about safety in numbers was disputed on the night in question, when the reckless young men hoisted the tar barrels on their shoulders again, and raced through the main street with them, shouting to all to keep their distance. There was many a spectator caught by flying missiles of burning tar who'd wished he wasn't hemmed in by the crush of people behind him, and wished himself safely home in bed before the night was over.

Bennett had decided that the school-house would provide hot mulled punch for the adults and lemonade for the children, as well as home-made fudge and brandy snaps contributed by the local mothers. All in all it was a fairly stable evening, considering the dangers involved, but Rosie couldn't help the thought that she and Bennett must appear a very united couple in their roles as schoolhouse benefactors. She wasn't at all sure whether she liked the idea of it or not.

At least one thing was cheering. No one refused to take a drink or a bite from her, and the old matrons nodded amiably at this new and sensible young woman in the sober beige bonnet and dress. There was none of the fancy piece about young Rosie Nash now. She was scrubbed clean as a new pin, and while nobody fanned the flames of the ancient old tales of Sedgemoor, they were content to accept her for what she was.

Only Rosie herself, and perhaps one other, knew of the change in her, and that in a single night the sweet dreams of a young girl had been tainted and destroyed. Dreams that once lost could never come again.

Chapter 12

Vicar Washbourne fastened his glowering stare on his dwindling congregation, and those attending on the bleak damp Sunday morning sighed briefly, knowing they would get the brunt of his anger because of the non-appearance of the others. The turn of the year was always a bad time for church-going, with the habitual coughs and ailments of the chest brought on by the flat, damp marshlands of the Somerset Levels, where by now the water lay in great gleaming sheets over the fields and rhines and pathways, so that it was hard to tell where one ended and another began. Brief snowfalls had spangled trees and hedgerows, and early morning frosts made walking treacherous. At night few people ventured out of doors, save those bent on mischief or making their way to the Moule Inn, for the January mists were as dense as thick pea soup. February wasn't much better with its biting winds that moaned unchecked across a landscape made more grey than green, when the animals huddled together in miserable attempts to keep warm, and many a human envied them their coats.

'The Lord's work continues in the face of wind, rain and storm,' Vicar Washbourne thundered. 'And unless a man is too ill to put one foot before the other, the rightful place for him to be on Sundays is in God's house. Is there one here who would deny it?'

None would dare, and more than one among the congregation prayed that the vicar wouldn't come calling until it was certain the miscreant was safely tucked up in bed where he was supposed to be.

Cyrus Hale stared back defiantly, knowing his Granpappy's ailment was genuine, and that old Isaac had wheezed himself near to death these last damp weeks. Cyrus had never been one to fear God or the devil, but since Rosie Nash had come to Moule he was more often than not beset with dark wonderings. He'd had a nonsense moment when he'd thought he might be the last of three, after poor Doughey and then Seth died... But mebbe the wench was working out her spell on old Isaac instead, he thought in an odd fearful notion. He tried to brush the idea aside. None but him seemed concerned with the Nashes for the time being. At this time of year the villagers tended to close in on themselves, taken up with the need to keep warm and dry and to eye the rising river Parrett with apprehensive eyes as it brimmed and ebbed with each new high tide gushing in from the Channel, through Bridgwater and out on to the Levels. Worrying about the present was more urgent than pondering on the ghosts of the past.

Cyrus forced himself to concentrate on the vicar's sermon. The old goat was smirking, almost benevolently for him, though it emerged as more of a grimace through those thin straight lips. And he was gazing in the direction of Edwin Nash and Jess Lawrence, Cyrus realised with a dart of surprise. He hadn't noticed that the Merrick's milk girl and her dummy child were sitting in the pew with the Nash family. Cy gave a subdued snort. Once a whore, always a whore, he was thinking, and if Edwin Nash wanted to consort with the likes of that one, he couldn't be over-fussy where he dipped his wick.

It was a strange coincidence, Cyrus went on musing, that both Jess Lawrence and Rosie Nash should have got the vicar's blessing in a way... A sudden clap of the vicar's hand on the lectern reminded him that he had best pay attention, or the next sermon would be composed directly for his benefit!

On the other side of England a more temperate clergyman than Vicar Washbourne ushered his congregation out of his parish church with a benign smile at the elegant ladies and gentlemen who adorned it like pretty peacocks each Sunday. He beamed approvingly and deferentially at Miss Alice Naylor, that stalwart maiden lady with friends in high places, about to enter the waiting carriage of Lady Lydia Fitzgerald, herself an acknowledged leader of fashion in dress and coiffure. It was said that her spacious home echoed all the latest innovations money could buy. The clergyman sighed briefly, turning back to his church, and preparing to return home for his own modest dinner.

In the rocking carriage Lady Fitzgerald turned eagerly to her friend, grey eyes agog above the rouged and crumpled cheeks.

'Now then, Alice, you must tell me everything you know about this little ingénue that dear Bennett has got himself entangled with. Is she a fortune hunter? And does this mean the stupid boy will stay for ever in that dreadful part of the country? I had so hoped he would see the error of it all and come back to town where he belongs!'

Alice spoke as soon as Lady Fitzgerald paused for breath. 'I have the feeling that Bennett means to stay in Somerset for good, Lydia,' she said sorrowfully. 'As for the young woman he mentioned with increasing frequency in his letters, I really don't know what to think. He hints that she is young, but does not say how young. She works with him in this village school, I understand.'

'Then heaven be praised that at least she is not illiterate!' Lydia said tartly. 'But it's all too irritating of Bennett, when there are so many pretty young things in London for him to marry. Lord knows he's waited long enough. One began to wonder. It's one thing for a woman to remain unmarried, and there's a certain dignity in the state of spinsterhood, as long as one is well provided for as you are, my dear. But in a man prolonged bachelorhood is so often misconstrued. Either one is taken for a roué, or—well, one doesn't want to surmise, does one?'

Alice kept the smile on her face. Lydia Fitzgerald was her dearest and oldest friend, and if she was sometimes too outspoken to the point of rudeness, Alice knew full well she would have been astonished to know how often she upset her friends with her caustic tongue. Lydia's dearest wish was for Bennett to come home and marry one of her many nieces, all empty-headed girls who spent hours prettying themselves in front of a mirror for the benefit of the young officers at balls and parties. Most of them had little to offer a man in terms of conversation and intelligence, and Alice could see very well why Rosie Nash had intrigued her brother so much. It ran loud and clear through every letter he sent her.

'Rosie is as fresh and delightful as her name, Alice,' Bennett had written in his last letter to her. 'You will find her so interesting to talk to, with none of the simpering ways of certain young ladies we know! I do hope you will agree to let her stay with you while she is in London for the exhibition. I shall be there too, of course, though I expect her father and brother will prefer to stay in a hostelry. Rosie has intimated as much.'

Well, thank goodness for that, Alice had thought instantly. For a second she had feared her brother meant to have the whole Nash family invading their London home, where they would obviously be sorely out of their depth in fashionable society. Alice was far from being the social snob that she had to admit her dear friend Lydia was, but there were standards to uphold all the same. And the unwilling thought, that she wanted no clodhopping country-folk soiling her lovely carpets and embarrassing her guests, filled her with an uneasy guilt; with the consequence that she had written straight back to Bennett, assuring him that Rosie would be welcome to stay with her while she was in London, and that she looked forward to meeting her. And until today she had said nothing of it to Lydia. Now that she had, she expected the inevitable quizzing.

It wasn't until the carriage arrived at Lady Fitzgerald's residence and the two ladies had been handed down by the footman, entered the drawing-room for their pre-luncheon glass of sherry and been relieved of their outer garments by Lydia's efficient personal maid, that the matron settled herself in an easy chair with a rustle of petticoats and looked across at Alice.

'Now then, you must tell me all,' Lydia said imperiously. 'My nose tells me you know more than you've let on, Alice. The foolish boy isn't thinking of marrying the little country gel, is he?'

Alice felt her heart jolt. Truth to tell, she wasn't sure, nor even if she minded if it were so. She had nagged Bennett to get himself a wife...but in Alice's own mind it had always been one of their genteel friends, and Bennett would come back to town and bring his dutiful wife back into the family home. It had never been a frivolous young girl with the flower-like name sometimes given to a skivvy! Alice was more disturbed than she admitted, and at Lydia's questioning remark, she finally confided in her friend.

'You'll see her for yourself in June, Lydia. Bennett is arranging for a party of people to come to town for the exhibition. It's in the form of a club, I understand. I don't suppose any of these people have the remotest idea of what London society is like, to be honest, and Bennett says they'll only stay for several days in some hostelry that's doing cheap rates. He's asked that the girl stays here, so if you think there's anything to be read in that...'

'Bless my soul!' Lydia stared. 'You mean there will be rogues and ragamuffins invading the city because of this wretched exhibition?'

Alice looked at her mildly. Lydia might be more affected than herself, and vastly more wealthy, but sometimes Alice suspected her head was as empty as that of her silly nieces. Did she never read the newspapers or take an interest in things outside her own twittering circle! Alice felt a vague irritation towards her too on account of these country visitors who were apparently all known to her brother, and spoken of so disparagingly by Lady Fitzgerald.

'I daresay there are as many rogues and cut-throats roaming the filthy London back alleys and waterfront as there are in the country, Lydia.' Alice came as near to snapping to her friend as she had ever done.

'Well, maybe so. And this girl will stay with you, dear?' Lydia's sculptured eyebrows rose to pantomime exaggeration. 'It sounds as if Bennett is definitely serious about her. What's her family background, Alice? I don't know any Somerset gentry, though I suppose there may be one or two that Vivian knows through his club, what?'

Alice felt herself flush. She doubted whether Lord Vivian Fitzgerald, Lydia's portly and aristocratic husband, would know any of the kind of people her brother had described in the wilds of Somerset! She cleared her throat delicately.

'Actually, Rosie's father and brother are craftsmen, Lydia. They make basketware, I understand. Why, some of their work might grace your conservatory, for all we know!' She spoke with studied amusement, as if it was perfectly natural for Miss Naylor and Lady Fitzgerald to be on nodding terms with such people...there was a stunned silence in the room.

'My dear Alice, this is a real turnaround! Bless my soul if you haven't almost taken my breath away. Basket-makers, you say! Dear me, oh dear, dear me. I'm quite bemused at the thought of it! We don't know any people in such work, and nor do any of our acquaintances. Oh dear, this will need some thinking out!'

Lady Fitzgerald stood up and began pacing the room. When she was in this mood, Alice knew there was no use interrupting her thought process. Lydia was as disturbed as Alice herself now, and her tiny slippered feet made a small trail back and forth over the soft pale carpet, until her face cleared a little and she looked at Alice with all the eagerness of a bright little bird finding a tasty titbit.

'We must introduce this gel of Bennett's as the daughter of a country squire with business interests in the basket trade,' Lydia announced. 'I shall give a soirée for her here, and we will invite some officers and my nieces, and some of Vivian's influential friends. Bennett's young friend must be seen to be respectable, whether he marries her or not.'

'Oh, but Lydia dear, that won't do!' Alice said in some distress. 'It's very kind of you, but have you forgotten that Rosie's father and brother will be here for the exhibition as well? I did mention it.'

Lydia brushed them aside effortlessly. 'You also said they would be staying at a hostelry, didn't you? Let them stay there then! My soirée will be for the gel's benefit, not theirs. I daresay the fellows can find their own amusement in the city.'

Alice ran her tongue around her mouth. 'I don't think you quite understand, Lydia,' she went on carefully. 'The reason the Nash family is coming to London at all is because they are to exhibit their goods at the Crystal Palace. The club outing that Bennett will accompany here is something quite apart. I gather that the Nash baskets will be brought here before the exhibition opens, as they already have their applications approved.'

Lady Fitzgerald's breath exploded in a heavy sigh of impatience. 'Do you mean to tell me you have known of this all along and haven't told me?' she demanded. 'And this—this Rosie person who has obviously twisted herself round your brother's gullible heart is quite low-born!'

'I never pretended otherwise, Lydia,' Alice protested.

'You never said anything at all, did you, you oyster-mouth?' Lydia said disapprovingly. She tapped the edge of her fan against her teeth for a moment, and then snapped it shut as Lord Vivian came into the room rubbing his hands against the February cold.

'We have a pretty tale here, my dear,' Lydia greeted him as he nodded at the two ladies and held out his arms for them to take as the luncheon bell sounded.

'And from the looks of you, there's some pretty scheming afoot in that head of yours, my love,' Lord Vivian growled amiably. Lydia laughed prettily at him, as coquettish in her fiftieth year as she had been on the day she set out to be Lady Fitzgerald three decades before.

The three of them seated themselves in the beautiful dining-room, attended by the Fitzgerald staff, and awaited the soup course. Lydia's eyes sparkled into her husband's.

'It will be a bit of a lark, Vivian. There's this little country gel who seems to have captured dear Bennett's heart, and her family are basket-makers of all things!'

'Good God! Begging your pardon, my dears, but well, I mean to say. What does Bennett mean by it?' he said indignantly.

'Oh, shush, my love, and let me finish,' Lydia said indulgently, her own indignation lessened by now. 'And please don't alarm the servants by blaspheming on the Sabbath! Well, it seems that the gel's family is to exhibit at the Crystal Palace. I'm sure that if Bennett has taken a fancy to her she must be pretty enough, and I've already promised Alice to give a soirée for her, so I shan't go back on my word.'

Vivian Fitzgerald spluttered into his

soup, but knew better than to try and stop his wife when she had that determined campaigning look in her eyes.

'Wouldn't it be tremendous fun to get our friends to patronise their little stand, Vivian? I mean, how many basket-makers do any of them know? They all live in the marshes or somewhere.'

'I daresay the fellows have all got webbed feet,' Lord Vivian snorted inelegantly, but Alice could see that he was listening, despite his mockery.

'Oh well, if you don't want to take me seriously, I shall just have all the basketware cleared out of the conservatory and order some new from these new people,' Lydia declared. 'If they are to exhibit in London, they may be patronised by *very* special people, if you get my meaning—and why shouldn't the Fitzgeralds be in the forefront of fashion?'

'No reason at all, my love. *You* always are,' Lord Vivian said dryly. 'And you must do as you wish, of course. If it makes you happy, then it will make me happy.'

Lydia darted a look of triumph at her friend. It never failed. She knew her husband too well. He was as much of a social-climber as she was, though she never put it quite as baldly as that, and her hint that even royalty might be interested in the exhibits of the fashionable basketware was enough to make Lord Fitzgerald more than interested to have some of it in his own house.

She left the subject alone for the time being, but while Lord Vivian was taking his Sunday afternoon nap in a shaded room upstairs, Lydia and Alice retired to the drawing-room once more after a sumptuous lunch, and Lydia smiled gleefully.

'There you are, my dear, we'll arrange something splendid so that Bennett's little gel won't be looked down on by London society. We can't have that, can we? Vivian has some very important friends at his club in town, and I'll make sure he recommends these Nash Baskets to them in good time. The fellows won't know what's happening when they reach London! But it will be good for Bennett, and that's the important thing. And if the young gel is a pretty piece and nicely mannered, then I daresay we'll overcome all the obstacles, Alice, never you fear.'

By the time Alice left the Fitzgerald house in Lydia's carriage, which she insisted on putting at her friend's disposal, Alice felt wilted as always. Lydia's energy seemed to drain her, and now that she was over the initial shock at learning more about Rosie Nash and her connections, Lydia clearly saw the whole matter of establishing Nash Baskets as a respectable business, as something of a cause.

The carriage bumped over the cobbles, and Alice clutched at the hand-grips to steady herself. They were passing Hyde Park, and she peered out with renewed interest at the great, half-built structure so aptly named the Crystal Palace. A poem of glittering light, as one exuberant columnist had put it in one newspaper... Public interest in the whole project was becoming immense. Daily the whole area teemed with people coming from all quarters to watch the progress of the building. Regular visits from the little Queen and Prince Albert, and their total commitment to the entire exhibition, ensured its success.

For the first time Alice Naylor began to appreciate the value of such an exhibition in terms of a small businessman, whose future had never even touched her life before now. Although she still couldn't quite bring herself to imagine Bennett actually marrying the daughter of a basket-maker, nor even a country girl, and Lydia Fitzgerald's reaction had frankly astounded her.

Lydia was a woman of great enthusiasms, although she could be extremely fickle as well when she tired of one of her causes. She never went back on a promise however, and the soirée for Rosie's benefit would undoubtedly take place during the girl's visit to London.

Alice supposed she had better write to Bennett to tell him of these latest developments, and to suggest delicately that Rosie might need to look to her wardrobe. Finally, Alice thought reluctantly that it would be only courteous to write to Rosie herself and invite her formally to stay with her while in the city. It wasn't an easy letter, and Alice knew she was trying over-hard to avoid being condescending. It ended up a little stilted, but as she sealed it Alice tried to remember Lydia's words. It would be good for Bennett, and that was the important thing. And Alice was doing this with her brother's interests at heart, whether they conflicted with her own or not.

A few days later, unaware that people unknown to her were shaping her destiny, Rosie hurried home from her day at the village schoolhouse, wishing that summer would hurry up and come. The earliest signs of spring were evident here and there, even through the frosts and mists that shrouded the mornings and enveloped the nights. It seemed to Rosie that the days had shrunk to a few middling hours of clear daylight, when the children gathered sprigs from the hedgerows and leapt on the first primroses and snowdrops, and the occasional vivid gleam of wood violets. Rosie encouraged them to bring them to the classroom, both for nature study and for the practical drawing lessons she was so keen to include. Her own talent in that direction was only slowly being discovered, and Bennett gave her a free hand to choose her own way of teaching the children.

She had made a game of it at first, drawing roughly around her own hand and letting the children do the same. Then it was the shapes of ordinary familiar objects, flowers and twigs and buttons. Then Rosie had tried encouraging them to draw a silhouette of the child sitting next to them, and in showing them had found she could draw an extraordinary likeness of any one of them.

Bennett had been charmed by her talent, and had suggested that she might like to draw a silhouette likeness of himself to give to his sister when she stayed at Alice's house in London. Rosie agreed gladly, for it saved her the embarrassment of not knowing whether to offer payment or not, and made it easy on her pocket as well as being a personal gift.

She was still enjoying the delight of knowing she had such a gift, and thinking about it on her way home to Briar Cottage. She hardly registered the sound of a small cart coming her way, until she heard her name called, and gave a start at seeing Farmer Merrick and his wife in the farm cart. Mrs Merrick beamed down at her while the farmer calmed the restless horse.

'Well now, it's a real pleasure to see 'ee, Rosie. I were only saying to our Will that we ain't seen 'ee for many a week, 'cepting for church morning, and it don't seem the weather for lingerin', do it, my dear?'

Rosie said it didn't. She felt vaguely uncomfortable with the Merricks. They had been so kind to her when she had first come to Moule, and now it must seem as if she was avoiding them. Only it wasn't them, of course. It was Will she didn't want to see. Will that she *couldn't* see, without all the panic starting up in her again as if she ailed with a breath-catching fever.

'We've just called in to see your Pa, Rosie,' Mrs Merrick was saying easily now. 'Ever since our Will mentioned about this going up to Lunnon and we learned the ins and outs on it, I been meanin' to call on your Pa, and now I've done it.'

'That's good,' Rosie murmured, not too sure what Mrs Merrick was getting at. She didn't want to stand here discussing London, nor Will, nor anything. She had had a tiring day and she wanted to get home and relax for a little while before she attended to some of the family clothes washing that evening.

'Missus 'ouldn't be satisfied until she got it all sorted out,' Farmer Merrick said jovially. Rosie looked at him blankly.

'I'm sorry—should I know what you're talking about?' she asked quickly.

Mrs Merrick tut-tutted. 'O' course not, my dear, and 'ere we are going on about it, and you're all in the dark! No, 'tis this business of your menfolk takin' their goods up to Lunnon before this grand exhibition starts. Will tells me they'll be gone for nigh on a week, about a month afore the time o' the opening.'

'Maybe nearer the time than that.'

'An' that's too long for a young maid to stay in a house alone,' Mrs Merrick said firmly. 'So 'tis all arranged, my love. You're to come an' stay wi' us for the time your menfolk are away. You look as if you need some good farm cookin' lately. An' I shall enjoy havin' another woman in the place!'

Rosie couldn't find her voice for a minute. When she did, the words all came out in a rush. 'It's very kind of you, Mrs Merrick, but I couldn't possibly, and anyway it's not necessary! I'll have the dog at the cottage, and it's too far for me to get to the village every day for my work!' She hoped she didn't sound as panicky as she felt. Stay at Will's farm? It was unthinkable. The tension would be unbearable...

'Now then, love, your Pa said you'd be stubborn about it, but 'tis all arranged,' Mrs Merrick said soothingly. 'He said that if 'ee won't agree to stay wi' we, then he and your brother won't put their baskets in the exhibition, so there'd be an end to it! An' you 'ouldn't want 'em missin' their chance to make a few shillin', I know!'

Rosie looked at her helplessly, at the round, ruddy face beaming down at her, echoed by Farmer Merrick's alongside her. Thinking they were doing their best to help out a neighbour, when they fondly hoped Rosie Nash would eventually marry their Will, whatever the cause of their upset recently!

'Don't 'ee worry none about gettin' to Moule for your teachin' neither, Rosie,' Farmer Merrick put his spoke in. 'Will can take 'ee, or else Jess can along wi' the milk churns when she takes in young Daisy. As for the dog, well, when did 'ee ever hear of a farmer who 'ouldn't take in a neighbour's dog for a day or two!'

It was all cut and dried as far as they were concerned, and Rosie had no doubt her father had been relieved when the Merricks had made the suggestion. It hadn't occurred to her that she'd be all alone in the cottage when the men delivered the basketware to London. If it had, she might have suggested staying with Jess and Daisy...maybe she still could. But seeing the expectation on the two homely country faces, she swallowed, knowing she couldn't do it. They would feel very hurt, and she found herself thanking them for their hospitality, and walking on home as if she was in a dream. Or was it a nightmare?

For the briefest moment Rosie found herself wishing she had some of those magical powers Cyrus Hale attributed her with. If she did, she would surely be able to do something about this situation. She would turn back the clock to yesterday, and make sure she made her own arrangements to stay with Jess before Will's mother came to Briar Cottage with her generous offer.

As it was, she had to accept it. Though obviously she would make sure that it was Jess who took her into Moule each morning and not Will. She had no wish to sit beside him in the farm cart and make pointless small talk or, worse still, sit there in total embarrassed silence. Rosie felt a lump fill her throat.

Things might have been so different. *Should* have been... The gulf between her and Will right now was as wide as the ocean. They had once been so close...belonging together in a way that was right and natural, and in time that closeness would have grown and matured and been so beautiful...

As it was, Will had ruined all that. He had listened to Cory, who had betrayed her, and in the listening had given way to lust. Will had spoiled their lovely, fresh young dream because of a gypsy's lewd untruths about her. She hadn't forgotten either of them yet. She doubted if she ever would.

Chapter 13

Bennett Naylor was seriously asking himself what he should do about Rosie Nash. That he felt warmly towards her was without question, and they certainly shared a common love of teaching. Rosie had a freshness about her that appealed mightily to Bennett, and a mind that was keen and intelligent, contrasting sharply with some of the young women he knew in the debutante circles in London. Not all of whom were dunces, of course, but those with whom Bennett had come into contact seemed unbelievably flippant, their heads filled with nothing more relevant than the next party or ball. In a moment of perception, too, Bennett guessed that any of those London debs would run through his money like sand through a sieve. He was comfortably off, but not to the extent of living the way they would require.

And now there was this odd communication from his sister, Alice. Almost encouraging him to present Rosie at her best and most attractive, because Lady Lydia Fitzgerald intended giving a soirée for the girl while she was in London. Alice phrased it delicately enough, but Bennett realised the Nash men weren't to be included in the invitation, and he couldn't resist a smile at his knowledge of Lady Fitzgerald.

But why invite her at all, unless Alice had been talking, and putting ideas of marriage between him and Rosie into Lydia's fertile brain! The idea wasn't unpleasant to Bennett. It was just that he preferred to decide for himself, and not be manipulated by the way so many of the London matrons liked to behave. He would do things in his own good time and not before. But lately, he had to admit, he had begun to think the time may be right. With spring fast approaching, and certain feelings stirring in him, the thought gave Bennett a strangely dreamy pleasure.

And what would be more enjoyable than accompanying Rosie to London on the special excursion train as her intended husband? It would give them both a new status, for one thing. And it would dignify them still further in the village. Bennett's suggested club had met with surprising enthusiasm, and more than a dozen had put their names down and were subscribing weekly. He suspected there might even be several more as the time drew near. He had decided on a week in June to be the best. The schoolhouse would be closed for a time during the summer, and the first hectic excitement at the exhibition itself, to be opened in May by Her Majesty and the Prince, would be over. With foresight, Bennett thought the country folk would be completely overwhelmed at the sight of the royal procession and the hordes of people, but he had been diplomatic about it and taken a vote among those attending. To his satisfaction he had been right, and the thought of glimpsing the Queen was still there, since it was intended she would visit the site frequently.

So now there was only the question of Rosie. Bennett sometimes wished he didn't have this accursed analytical mind that prevented him from acting impulsively. In his work it was an admirable trait, but he sometimes suspected that it made others around him impatient. He had thought about her in more intimate terms for several months now, unknown to her, of course. Now it was almost April, and he was still as undecided as ever whether to say anything and make his feelings known.

He watched her dealing with the last of the children on one of the milder afternoons they had had for some time. The warmth of so many small bodies still pervaded the schoolhouse, and Rosie's face was flushed and glowing. The dark hair spilled out of its confining pins despite her attempts to keep it under control, and her body was taut against her dress. She looked more like the Rosie who had come to Moule than she had done for a long time, Bennett thought swiftly. And much as he admired the new Rosie with her talent with the children, this was the womanly Rosie who had stirred his blood...

Little Daisy Lawrence was the last of the children to remain. Rosie usually took her as far as Briar Cottage now, and the child's mother would collect her from there, which seemed to suit them. Bennett glanced towards them now, where Rosie's dark head contrasted with Daisy's shining fair one, both poring over the pressed flowers from last summer that Rosie had been teaching the children to draw that day.

'You see, Daisy?' Rosie said cheerfully. 'This is a rose, the same as my name. A dog rose that grows in the hedgerows. Do you remember when we walked in the fields and collected them, and you had to be careful not to prick your fingers?'

Daisy nodded silently, her small fingers tracing the five pink petals of the rose. Beside the pressed flower was Rosie's pencil drawing of it, simplified for the children to copy. She pointed to the flower and then to Rosie, who laughed delightedly.

'There's nothing stupid about you, is there, sweetheart?' Rosie said lightly.

Daisy suddenly scrambled to her feet, her eyes moving quickly around the room, to alight on a jug of wild spring flowers on the window-sill. She pulled one out and ran across to Rosie, her eyes suddenly shining with excitement, stabbing at her thin chest with her finger. From then the child's fingers worked like quicksilver, pointing first to the drawing of the rose and then to Rosie, then to the flower in her hand and herself. Rosie caught her breath, feeling her heart begin to beat faster.

'That's right, darling,' she breathed. 'You and I have something in common, don't we? I should have made more of it before.'

Daisy was staring at the small white

flower in her hand now, the petals beginning to wilt a little. Her mouth curved into a smile, her eyes large and intent.

'Daisy,' she mouthed the word slowly, with just a whisper of sound.

Rosie heard Bennett breathe sharply, and motioned him to be quiet. This was too important a moment to spoil by urging Daisy to say more unless she was ready. She felt him move beside her as she spoke softly to Daisy. She picked up a scrap of paper and quickly drew the shape of the tiny flower, laying the real thing against it and handing it to the child.

'For you, Daisy. Especially for you. Take it home and show your mother.'

For a moment there was no response, and Rosie's heart sank as the child merely pointed to the rose drawing beside the pressed flower.

'She wants that one too,' Bennett said swiftly. 'To show her mother what you've explained about your names.'

'Is that what you want, Daisy? I don't understand.' Rosie looked at her steadily, challenging her as Daisy had played with her so many times in recent months. Hadn't the doctor said the speech was there, as soon as Daisy was willing to use it? Daisy's eyelids flickered for a moment.

'Daisy's picture,' the words came haltingly, as if unwilling to be spoken, but the voice was there, soft and firm, wanting the drawing for herself. 'For Ma. And—Rose's picture.'

Rosie felt a great surge of emotion inside. A lump as big as an egg threatened to choke her as she ripped the page out of the pressed flower scrapbook and handed it to Daisy. She held on to it for an instant, waiting expectantly.

'What do you say for it, Daisy?' she breathed. She willed her to respond, and prove that this wasn't merely a token step forward.

'Thank you, miss,' the slow reply came, and then all Daisy's attention was taken up in studying the two pieces of paper in front of her, heedless of the two people in the room who were suddenly wild with excitement.

Rosie leapt to her feet, her hands automatically outstretched towards Bennett in a gesture of delight. Bennett took them in his, as moved as Rosie, and in doing so he could feel the trembling joy in her, and a deep humility that she had been the unwitting instrument in bringing about something almost miraculous. A mixture of ecstatic and thankful tears spiked Rosie's eyes, at that moment as blue as brilliant sapphires, and it was at that moment that

Bennett made the first impulsive statement of his life. Looking down into those liquid eyes, so close to him, and sharing an occasion so emotive, tipped the balance of all he had been so hesitant to say. As if Daisy Lawrence's own unsteady speech had somehow unlocked all his own...

He seized Rosie's hands more tightly in his, his strong face blotting out everything else from her gaze. 'Marry me, Rosie! Say that you will, please! Let's make it official before we go to London. It would give me the greatest happiness in the world to present you as my intended bride. You must see how well we suit each other, Rosie. We belong together!'

He felt a different kind of trembling run through her as he finished speaking, that he didn't altogether understand. Unless she was a little frightened that he was being so ardent, so unlike the Bennett she knew and trusted! He moved back from her a fraction, still keeping hold of her hands, but less urgently now. He had no idea that it was Will's voice she was hearing over and over in her mind, telling her that they belonged together for always, to the end of time and back again... Will, whose strong country voice hadn't made facile comments about how well they would suit one another, because the feeling between them had said it all...

Will, who had spoiled their love... The turmoil of Rosie's emotions wouldn't let her say a word for a moment. She felt as dumb as Daisy had always been, and Bennett completely misread her reaction to his proposal.

'Forgive me, Rosie, for acting hastily,' his voice was awkward, his face darkly red. He rarely made a move without being certain of the consequences, and this was the result. He had made a fool of himself, and his stupidity could even end with Rosie refusing to work with him any more. The thought of losing her valuable assistance vied with his dismay at losing any affection she might have for him.

'At least think it over, please,' he went on. 'Don't feel that I'm an impatient man, or that I will feel in any way slighted if your answer is no, though naturally I hope it will be yes! I've come to hold you in very great esteem in the past months, as you must realise, Rosie, and it would be a great honour for me if you would consent to be my wife. But please take your time, my dear.'

He let her go, turning away as if in embarrassment at her silence. Rosie knew she must say something, but she felt almost hunted at the unexpected declaration. Acceptance never entered her head. How could it when she didn't love him? How could she love anyone when she already loved Will Merrick, even while she despised him? Bennett's ponderous words dug their own grave as far as Rosie was concerned, but he still meant something to her in terms of friendship and mutual respect, and she felt the need to let him down lightly. She touched his arm.

'I feel honoured that you have asked me, Bennett,' she said huskily. 'But just now I don't want to marry anyone, nor to feel committed to anyone. I don't want anything to change between us, because I think we have something very special here in our work. For the time being I would much rather it continued exactly the same. Please understand, Bennett.'

'Of course.' If she thought he answered a mite too readily, it didn't matter. Rosie was relieved he hadn't taken offence, and privately she didn't think he loved her to distraction anyway. She realised suddenly that he had never mentioned the word love.

Daisy's small voice, so newly heard, made Rosie jump. 'Daisy wants to go home. Show Ma Daisy's picture!'

Rosie turned to her with relief, giving the child a little hug. Her presence, that had sparked off Bennett's sudden amorous moment, also relieved the tension of the last awkward minutes.

'And so you shall, darling. We'll take the rose picture as well, and give your Ma a big surprise, won't we?'

She held on tightly to Daisy's hand as the two of them left the schoolhouse and walked towards Briar Cottage. Rosie wished desperately that Bennett hadn't started up all the churning emotions inside her. Guiltily, she knew they weren't even on his own account, but they had inadvertently revived all Rosie's turbulent feelings towards Will.

She was still bitterly hurt at what he had done and the way he had treated her like a whore. She flinched away from even thinking about it...but there were times in the darkness of the night when she awoke from a dream suffused in warmth and pleasure, still tingling from the fantasy of his sensual love-making. The dream-lover was so different from the man who had ravaged her, and yet he was the same—he was Will, holding her tenderly and caressing her, and bringing all her dormant senses to life in an exquisite surge of desire and love...the awakening was the more searing, remembering the cruel reality of that night. Whatever she had meant to him before, Rosie was sure she meant less than nothing now. He had never once tried to put things right between them, and she never stopped to think how her own defensive pride prevented him. He had used her, and he had had his fill of her. The softest, sweetest moments that came to her so poignantly in the night were always dashed by the bitter memory of the way it really was.

'Daisy's picture,' the child beside her repeated the words over and over as they walked, like a slow litany. Rosie concentrated on the thought of Jess's joy when she discovered her little daughter was no longer mute, and pushed everything else from her mind.

As soon as she reached the cottage she knew something was wrong. She could hear Mrs Guppey busily banging pots and pans in the kitchen, a sure sign of her agitation. In the small parlour her father stood tensely with his back to the fireplace, while in front of him Edwin had his arm firmly around Jess Lawrence's slender waist. Jess was pale, while Rosie could see the anger clearly stamped on her brother's handsome face. Her heart seemed to turn over. Surely Edwin hadn't chosen today to confess his love for Jess! It was bound to be a tricky moment, when Dunstan had wanted the best for his children and would be temporarily put out by this development.

Edwin and Jess had been so discreet until now. Rosie's guess was that her father had stumbled on the two of them in an embrace, and had probably blurted out words to enrage Edwin. She found out later it had happened just that way.

Her arrival with Daisy was both welcome and resented. Jess moved swiftly out of Edwin's protective arm and pulled her little daughter to her side, her eyes bright and hurt.

'Daisy means everything to me, Mr Nash,' she said in a tight little voice. 'And anyone who can look into a child's innocent eyes and see evil must be evil himself.'

'It's not the child that's at fault,' Dunstan said harshly.

'Nor the mother,' Edwin was suddenly shouting, in a way Rosie had never heard him round on his father before. She was shocked at coming on such a scene, and Daisy was obviously too frightened to speak now. Rosie saw the way she clutched at the two pieces of paper that had meant so much to her, and her heart grieved at the thought of losing the miracle...

'Stop it, please,' she heard herself gasping. 'Daisy and I have got something to tell you. Will you please listen?'

She had caught their attention, if unwillingly. Jess looked down at the flushed little face, uncertain now where it had been so excited before. Jess forced a smile, expecting the usual flurry of hand signs.

'What have you got to tell me, love?' she asked huskily.

Daisy swallowed, holding out the crumpled bit of paper. The fresh daisy had lost some of its petals from her hot little hand, and Rosie quickly helped her to spread the items out on the table. She willed the child to say the words, holding her breath as the small fingers began enacting their usual patterns and mimes. And then Daisy's mouth began to work.

'Daisy's picture,' she whispered slowly. 'Daisy flower. And Rose flower. Miss Rosie showed me.'

She said no more, because by then Jess was kneeling at her side and weeping all over her, hugging Daisy to her and kissing every bit of her face with love and gladness. No one in that tiny room could fail to be moved by the sight of her, and Edwin met his father's gaze over Jess's fair head with an unrelenting hardness in his eyes as he placed a sympathetic hand on Jess's shoulder. As if conscious of the other person who had been so gentle with her, Daisy suddenly twisted out of her mother's arms and tugged at Edwin's hand.

'Daisy's chair!' she said experimentally. 'Edwin made Daisy's chair!'

Edwin laughed, swinging her up in his arms. Openly defiant of his father's anger, he kissed the child as well. 'That I did, my little bird, and I'll make more things for you too! A whole house made of willow if it's what you want! Nothing's too good for our little Daisy, is it?'

The child laughed as he twirled her round in his arms. Inevitably, Dunstan's face softened a little, and Rosie wondered if he was remembering their own little Dorcas at that moment. Surely if Edwin did marry Jess Lawrence, Dunstan might find a certain pleasure in bringing this child into the family. It didn't seem the time for suggesting such a thing, however, and Dunstan's mind seemed to be caught on another matter, by the thoughtful expression in his eyes just then.

'Perhaps we had better leave this discussion until some other time,' Edwin began stiffly.

'No—Edwin, I would rather know right now why Mr Nash is so against me.' Jess was suddenly tremulous, and Dunstan Nash cleared his throat in embarrassment.

'I've nothing against you as a person,' he growled. 'I've always thought you likeable enough.'

'But not a fit person to be part of your family, is that it?' Her voice was a shade more shrill, and Rosie saw Edwin catch her hand and hold it tightly. 'Even though the vicar has forgiven me for something that was not my fault, and which happened years ago you set yourself up as my judge, do you? And it's clear from all that's gone on here that I'm condemned from the outset!'

'Jess, love, calm yourself,' Edwin muttered. She wrenched free of him, all the hurt of the past seven years smouldering in her eyes. She moved away from him slightly, and to Rosie she epitomised the frailty of all women at that moment, and Rosie felt a rush of sympathy towards her. If she herself hadn't been so fortunate, she might have been in the very same situation as Jess Lawrence. She intervened quickly.

'I never expected you to be so cruel, Pa, nor such a vicar's man! And if you can't see that Edwin and Jess are meant for each other, then you must be getting short-sighted too.'

'Be quiet, Rosie! Is this the way to speak to your father?' Dunstan snapped furiously.

'My father wouldn't have let anything stop him marrying the woman he loved!' she went on relentlessly, uncaring if he struck her or not for her insolence. Her eyes suddenly pricked with angry tears. 'And you've managed to spoil this lovely day for Jess and Daisy too. It's almost a miracle that Daisy has started to speak at last, and all you can do is rant and rage.'

'This has nothing to do with the child,' Dunstan said harshly.

'I thought it had everything to do with her,' Rosie said passionately.

'Leave it, Rosie,' Edwin stopped her flow with a grip on her shoulder. 'This is our business, and there's no need for you to be involved.'

'It's my business too, when my father dictates to us as if we were children! Are we not allowed to think for ourselves any more? I suppose it would raise our precious prestige in the village if I told you that Bennett Naylor has proposed to me. You wouldn't object if I were to be a school teacher's wife? That would be respectable, would it, Pa?' Her voice was scornful and bitter. It was so unlike Dunstan to be so dogmatic, and Rosie could only think he had been unprepared for all this that he had blurted out the first things that came to his head, and the argument had gathered momentum like wildfire.

A sudden movement from the kitchen broke the momentary silence, and Mrs Guppey poked her head through the doorway, her shawl slung around her shoulders, her basket over her arm.

'I'll be off now then, Mr Nash,' she

grunted. 'Food's keepin' hot, so don't 'ee let it spoil none.'

'Thank you,' Dunstan clipped the words, hardly noticing her. There was a sudden acute embarrassment between all of them. Then, before Jess could stop her, Daisy had sidled over to Dunstan and put her small hand in his large one, looking up into his angry face with trusting eyes.

'Edwin made Daisy's chair,' she repeated, obviously pleased with the phrase. 'And a baby chair for Daisy's doll.'

'Did he now?' Dunstan growled back.

The child suddenly reached for the wilting flower from the table and held it up to Dunstan. 'Daisy's flower. For you, because you're sad,' she said.

When he didn't take it immediately, Daisy's eyes searched the large body standing over her, and tucked the daisy stem in Dunstan's lowest waistcoat buttonhole. It lolled ludicrously over his stomach, and then Rosie breathed a great sigh of relief as her father's mouth began curving into a smile, and she knew that Daisy had done what none of the others had been able to do.

'Daisy had better stop and have some rabbit stew with us,' Dunstan gave the oblique invitation. 'Mrs Guppey always cooks enough to fill an army, so I'm sure we've enough for two more.' He looked directly at Jess. 'Will you stay, Jess?'

'Thank you, Mr Nash. Yes.' She spoke with dignity, and without the slightest hint of humility in her voice. Rosie had never admired her more.

'Will you help me set the table and ladle out the stew, Jess?' Rosie said quickly. 'Daisy can keep the men entertained.'

She had a shrewd idea that Daisy could charm the leaves from the trees if she had a mind to, and that Dunstan was going to be won over by the new Daisy pretty quickly. Leaving them alone, while Edwin went outside to fetch more logs for the fire, the two girls could hear Dunstan pointing out various items in the cottage, and Daisy's piping reply. It was a new game, and if he expected to catch her out, it was obvious that there was nothing lacking in Daisy's vocabulary now that she had found her tongue at last.

Jess caught hold of Rosie's hand, the quick tears springing to her eyes, her voice husky.

'How can I thank you, Rosie? To hear her talk like that is something I never dreamed of! And I'm sorry we should have spoiled your lovely surprise with all the upset.'

'You didn't spoil anything,' Rosie said gently. 'I'm so glad Pa seems to have accepted the situation now. You couldn't have expected it to be easy, but I'm sure that Daisy will tip the balance, Jess. You—you won't know that I had a little sister...'

'Edwin told me,' Jess nodded. 'He says your Pa doesn't like to speak of it because it upsets him too much. But I do understand, and if Daisy can help his grief, then surely her birth won't have been so terrible after all.'

Rosie's eyes were bright at the sudden hope in Jess's voice. She could only guess at the ordeals the other girl had gone through in this narrow-minded community.

'It will be good to have another sister,' Rosie said impulsively. 'Have you decided when the wedding will be?'

Jess shook her head. 'Not for a while. I've become too cautious over the years to want to rush things. Edwin and I want people to accept us gradually, so that in time they'll be the ones to ask when it's going to happen! We—we don't need the church's blessing to know that we belong, Rosie, though it's not the right thing for me to be saying to a young unmarried girl, is it? You must forgive me for being indiscreet. It must be something to do with this unusual day. Edwin and I have almost been accepted by your father—and my Daisy is talking at last! Can you wonder that I'm feeling slightly delirious?'

She began to laugh, and it was tinged with hysteria. Rosie handed her the dishes, thinking it best to give her something practical to do. When Jess had sobered a little, she questioned Rosie about her own news.

'What news?'

'You can't have forgotten that you told your father the school teacher had proposed to you, Rosie!'

Rosie's heart lurched. It had been said in a moment of anger, merely to taunt her father and make him realise how class-conscious he was appearing. She hadn't meant to tell anyone.

'There's nothing more to tell, Jess,' she said quickly. 'I don't really want to talk about it until I've made up my mind. It wouldn't be fair to Bennett for me to be discussing it.'

'That's fair enough,' Jess nodded. 'It would be a good match, of course,' she caught Rosie's eye and started to laugh ruefully.

'Now who's being materially minded!' Rosie said lightly. 'Let's take this stew into the parlour, or they'll be thinking they're not getting any food at all today. I don't know about you, but all this emotion is making me ravenous!'

For all her father's apparent change of heart towards Jess, and the unexpected delight he experienced in encouraging Daisy to string words together in her rather high little voice, Rosie knew he wouldn't be questioning her about Bennett Naylor until the family was alone. There wasn't very much she could say about it anyway, and although she had told Jess she didn't want to talk about it until she had made up her mind, her mind was in fact already made up. It had been from the minute Bennett proposed so unexpectedly.

She still felt a sense of duty towards him, and wouldn't like it to be known she had turned him down so readily. Bennett had a certain standing in the village, and it would hurt his pride to think Rosie Nash would rather fly to the stars than marry him! Or that she had been too certain of that fact to even give his proposal some thought and consideration. Better to let the question simmer for the time being...

Meanwhile this evening, that had started out so badly, was slowly developing into more of a family tableau, Rosie thought. The faces were different, the little group that gathered in the firelight as dusk settled could almost be compared with those halcyon days in Minehead, when Marjorie and Dorcas had been with them. Now it was Jess and Daisy, but the child's face glowed in the warmth of the fire, and Dunstan looked more relaxed than he had done in a long time as Daisy climbed on his knee after the meal, too innocent to sense any atmosphere among the adults, and too wise to let it deter her from seeking the lap of the leathery old gentleman with the chin that tickled her when she touched it.

Jess sat near Edwin, not touching, but hardly needing to. The love between them was so obvious now, and as the small secret glances passed between the two of them, Rosie felt a twist of envy, feeling that surely now everything would come right for Jess. While for her...in a strange way it made Rosie think more deeply of the way that she and Will Merrick had messed up their lives.

Will had made a terrible mistake, and she had truly hated him for it. But far deeper than the hate was the love she felt for him, which was as much a part of her as her own soul. She needed Will as a flower needed rain. The truth of it was at once so simple and so spectacular that she yearned to put things right between them. To know the joy of belonging once more, the way Jess and Edwin did.

She caught the smile on Jess's face just then, and smiled back. The euphoria seemed to surround the two of them at that moment, woman to woman, in a special feeling of empathy. Neither of them even gave a second thought to Mrs Guppey.

Chapter 14

Moule Inn was the scene of an explosive hubbub until late into that night. For once, old and young converged together, jostling to hear what was going on, as each tale became wilder and more impossible. Perce Guppey banged his jug of ale on the dripping table in front of him, and waited expectantly for it to be filled again by one of his listeners, since he was the one who had started this night's yarn-spinning.

' 'Tis no lie, I'm tellin' 'ee,' he declared, ruddy-faced with ale now, his thin nostrils positively quivering as they had done ever since his good woman came bursting into their cottage with her bit of news.

'Every man here knows the Lawrence wench had a dummy child!' someone scoffed. 'Do 'ee expect we to believe the babby's suddenly found a voice after seven year?'

'Seven year,' another spoke darkly. 'Don't that mean summat evil?'

The landlord dumped three more jugs of ale on the table between them, slopping yet more of the dark brew, but none of them heeded it.

'Let's have less of this evil talk,' the landlord said fiercely. 'I'll not have honest decent folk afeared to set foot in my Inn because o' this nonsense talk.'

'Nonsense talk, is it?' Perce Guppey's voice rose. 'When my old 'oman heard the dummy's voice for 'erself this very day! An' a thin pipin' little sound 'twere, by all accounts too. An' who conjured up the child's voice out o' nowhere? None but yon Rosie Nash.'

'What's this then, Perce Guppey?' Tom Kitch poked his head forward through the haze of smoke and fetid body odours. 'You were allus championin' the maid, as far as I can mind! Didn't you say a maid wi' a pretty name couldn't have nothin' sinister about her? They was your very words in this very place!'

'So they were, Perce,' Isaac Hale grunted.

Perce glared at them both, and at the small burst of laughter coming from the other quarters of the room. He'd come here agog with his tale, and he had no intention of letting them play it down.

'Mebbe I changed me mind then,' he snapped. 'All I'm tellin' 'ee is that the dummy child's been chatterin' away in the Nash cottage when she never uttered a word afore. An' there's summat else too. The young Nash feller's been sniffin' round Jess Lawrence an' means to wed 'er!'

'What's that? Make an honest woman of Jess Lawrence? Well, that's a turn-up.'

'An' the school teacher's made an offer for young Rosie Nash an' all.'

Perce was running out of steam now. Truth to tell, he'd hardly been able to comprehend all his missus was telling him earlier when she'd come home from her skivvying at the Nash cottage. Her side ached so much from the stitch, and the breath was short in her stocky little body, and it had taken her a while to recover herself. But he thought he had all the tale right...

Tom Kitch suddenly decided to take it seriously, and with the backing of the church caretaker, everybody else thought he should do the same.

'Vicar should be told about this,' Tom said sternly. ' 'Tis right what Perce Guppey says. 'Tain't normal for a child that's been dumb for seven years to find her voice all on a sudden. Vicar should have his say on it.'

'Didn't doctor say the child's voice

might come to 'er sometime?' Isaac said dubiously.

Tom snorted. 'Doctors! Quacks, all on 'em! How can a voice come to a body that's never had one unless 'tis by magical means? Tell me that, you dunce-noddle!'

There was a general drawing in of a score of breaths. The door of the Inn opened to let in a late-comer, bringing in a sudden gust of wind with him. The lantern lights swayed, flickered and dimmed for a moment until they righted themselves, and it was as potent as an omen to their fertile minds.

' 'Tis all back to they Nash's,' someone muttered.

'They say she teaches the children to draw black images of each other. Who's to say which of us ain't been drawn by *her*, me boys? Mebbe all our images be pinned up at Briar Cot ready for the maid to stick pins in as the fancy takes 'er.'

'Mebbe she and the school teacher be in league together. Teachin' our babbies the black arts. None of us be safe if 'tis the case.'

'Bloody hellfire! What's that smell?' someone shouted fearfully. 'The Lord help us. 'Tis a sign that there's a witch among us doin' her evil work.'

A series of small rapid explosions came from behind the group of crouched

322

tense figures, almost grotesque in their sudden terror as each peered round at his neighbour.

'God dammit, Isaac,' Tom Kitch roared out. ' 'Tis nobbut your stinkass of a grandson fartin' like gunfire enough to waken the dead. What be 'ee feedin' him on? It stinks worse than mouldy cabbage-water!' At times like these, Tom forgot his dignity as church caretaker and proved he could cuss with the best of them.

Cyrus Hale grinned around at the flushed old faces. Egged on by some of the younger men, it had been a laugh to let the old loons think the foul smell was sent by the witch. If he dared he'd tell as to how Rosie Nash had threatened him and Seth and Doughey when they'd tried to find her witch-mark, but truth to tell, he didn't dare. Not now that he was the only one left of the three to tell the tale. Instead, he resorted to his usual mockery.

'You're all daft to think Rosie Nash can work magic,' he slurred. 'Anyway, even if she can, I reckon I be safe against her. Witches can't abide iron, so mebbe you'd all best come into the smithying along o' me, eh?'

'Stop that talk, young Hale,' Tom Kitch snapped at him, furious at being made to feel foolish and to have let himself down.

He got to his feet, making a sudden decision. 'I'm for seein' Vicar about all this talk. Who's for making a deputation right this minute and gettin' it sorted? I fancy none on us will sleep easy tonight unless we do.'

'Vicar won't be none too pleased at bein' disturbed so late.'

'He'll feel less easy if we all come to mysterious ends by havin' pins stuck into black images, won't he?'

In seconds the Moule Inn was deserted, and a trail of men walked determinedly towards the vicarage, hammering on the door as if all the devils in hell were at their heels. In a few minutes an upstairs window opened, and the vicar's head appeared in a fury. In his floppy-tailed nightcap he looked less of a tyrant and more of a ludicrous fop, but none of the frightened group registered it too minutely. Fear had swept through them like a forest fire, and all they wanted was for someone to quench it as quickly as possible.

'What's to do?' Vicar Washbourne thundered, incensed at being disturbed from his habitual early night's slumber.

'We must talk with 'ee, Vicar,' Tom took on the role of spokesman. ' 'Tis urgent, and a matter that concerns the whole village.'

'Then it had best be a sound one,'

the vicar retorted grimly. 'Wait there a moment.'

He kept them waiting five minutes while he donned his day clothes. In the white moonlight they shuffled their feet nervously, and conversation dwindled now that it wasn't fired with the aura of the Inn and the slurpings of ale to give them courage. When the vicar threw open the door, they almost recoiled for a moment from the towering effect he made in the entrance, a lamp in his hand, and then as he told them sternly to enter, they filed in one by one like penitents.

Once inside, it was a different matter, as he sat at his desk and demanded to know what had brought them to his door at this hour. Then it seemed they all wanted to speak at once.

' 'Tis the Nash maid, Vicar.'

'Workin' magic on the dummy to make her speak.'

' 'Tis the devil's work, Vicar. An' so 'tis her teachin' of the children to draw the black images.'

'The young one's to make an honest woman of Jess Lawrence, so 'tis said, but there's no undoin' what was done to 'er, so what's to make on it all, Vicar?'

'Be quiet, the lot of you!' Vicar Wasbhourne roared out, his voice reverberating around the timbered walls.

He glared at each cowering man, his black eyes glittering and condemning. 'You come here to this sanctuary, sodden with drink and blubbering about tales of witchcraft and fornication, and ruining the sleep of a man of God! And you call yourselves Christians, do you? You call yourselves *believers!* Then why do you not believe the things I've told you from the pulpit? Does a witch come willingly to worship in church each Sunday, come rain or shine, which is more than some of you can manage! Does a witch place her hand on the Holy Book at my command and repeat the denial of all you would accuse her of? Have you no trust in your own eyes and ears? If not, then I wash my hands of you all. I would be better use in a parish that was not so steeped in ancient superstition that it saw evil in every whisper of the breeze!'

After a stunned moment, the commotion began again.

'You cannot mean to leave us, Vicar! 'Tis the last thing we want.'

'We only wanted your guidance, Vicar. Now that we have it, we feel easier in our minds.'

'Aye, your reassurance be what we needed to clear our minds, Vicar.'

'Then remember it the next time you're tempted to listen to the devil!' This time Vicar Washbourne's voice seemed to swell and magnify in the room as he pursued his point, which was fast taking on the semblance of a miniature sermon. Now he had them here, they would hear him out. If his night was ruined, then theirs would be one to remember too.

'Make no mistake, my friends, the devil is working in each and every one of you if you can see nothing but darkness around you. The devil has put black thoughts in all your hearts, and you must stamp them out before they eat away at your very souls. Look upon this night as a testing time, and resolve to come through it whole.'

As he paused for breath, the village folk looked shiftily at each other.

'What of the black images, Vicar?' Tom Kitch dared to query. 'Folk will be sore afeared of them now they know of them.'

Vicar gave him a sour look. 'It's clear you've not travelled far from your humble surroundings, Tom Kitch, or you would know of the fashionable practice for young ladies of idling their time away in the drawing of silhouette likenesses. In London and the big cities, and in every great house, such an accomplishment is as much admired as playing an instrument or stitching a fine seam. Were you more knowledgeable, all of you, you'd have realised it without resorting to this ludicrous panic!

'You may all be ashamed of yourselves for the work you have done this night. I advise you all to make light of it among your fellows before I see you in church again! Never fear that if the evil talk is still prevailing by the coming Sunday, God will know of it, and through me, will punish you for it. In listening to the devil, you are the evil ones! And now you will leave this place and I will pray for your souls, in the vain hope that it is not too late for their redemption.'

As the vicarage door slammed behind them, the group moved away silently, to pause outside the gate and gather up their senses.

'That fool, Perce Guppey, wi' his fairyin's,' one growled, glaring at Perce in the moonlight. 'What did 'ee mean by it, you loon, making all on us look such fools?'

'You all believed it,' Perce snapped.

'An' now we don't,' Tom said grimly. 'Not unless we want Vicar's wrath coming down on our heads. All he said made sense, at least to me. If the rest of you couldn't understand it, then mebbe you should all go back to school and do a bit o' learning as well. It seems Rosie Nash has got Vicar's backing, so there's an end to it.'

They walked on back to the Moule Inn

to report to the waiting drinkers all that had gone on. Cyrus Hale wiped the back of his sleeve across the film of froth on his lips, and belched noisily as he listened.

'It still don't change one thing, though, do it?'

Tom Kitch stared at him with open dislike. Poor Isaac, to be saddled with such a spawn, he was thinking.

'And what's that, me clever lad?' Tom snapped.

'Just that whether Rosie Nash is what she seems or not, fact is she allus manages to stir up a hornet's nest among us, don't she? You ain't goin' to deny that, I s'pose? One way or another, her name allus crops up when there's trouble about.'

The landlord decided he'd had enough talk about Rosie Nash in his establishment and told them to shut up about her, or he'd turn the lot of them out into the night. More than one felt a sneaking relief at his words, half thinking they'd get no sleep that night if these eerie tales didn't end.

'Anyway, I daresay Vicar will twist it all to God's work,' Cyrus couldn't resist adding, before the landlord pointed him the door. 'The dummy's voice will be one of God's own miracles, not the result of witchcraft. 'Tis up to we to choose which we want to believe, ain't it?'

The old goats were swayed as easy as the willows, Cy thought derisively. Vicar only had to say the word, and all their spunk disappeared in a puff of wind. Resentment still curdled his gut whenever he thought of Rosie Nash. He'd been made to look more of a fool on her account than any of these yokels, and got a few beatings because of her too. He wasn't done with her yet.

While the Moule Inn was agog with Perce Guppey's news, Dunstan Nash eyed his daughter speculatively. He was calmer now, and as he saw the quiet grace with which Jess refused Edwin's offer to see her and Daisy home, he felt a grudging admiration for the milk-girl, and knew that all Rosie's harsh words to him were justified.

'So Bennett Naylor has proposed to you, has he, girl? And without asking your father first!' He tried to sound jocular, and saw Rosie shrug her fine shoulders.

'It makes no difference, Pa. I didn't accept. I didn't really refuse either, I suppose. I merely said I'd prefer our relationship to go on the same as usual,' she told him. 'We work well together, and I admire him and respect him, but...'

Dunstan gave a sudden smile. It would have been an admirable match, but his heart warmed towards his daughter at the words she left unsaid.

'And if your mother were here, she would have said the worst betrayal of yourself would be to marry for less than love. Am I right?' he said gently.

Rosie went to him and put her arm around his shoulders, pressing her soft lips to his cheek. 'That's right, Pa. You do understand, don't you? And you must see how it is for Edwin too.'

She held her breath as he nodded slowly. Edwin was still tight with anger over his father's reception of Jess, despite the softening of his attitude, and Rosie badly wanted the three of them to be back on friendly terms.

'Aye, I understand, and I was probably a bit hasty earlier,' Dunstan said heavily. 'But there's something else I want to talk to you both about, if we can get all this talk of nuptials out of the way. Something that's becoming more urgent, and that's the question of taking our basketware to London in time for the exhibition. I was caught by an idea when Edwin was talking a while back.'

Edwin looked at him with less resentment now.

'You were dallying with the child— Daisy,' Dunstan went on. 'And saying you'd make her a whole house of willow if she wanted it. And it occurred to me that Nash Baskets is a poor title to advertise our goods. What do you say to changing it to House of Willow?'

'I like it!' Edwin's enthusiasm was obvious. 'It has a dignity about it, Pa, to make these London folk sit up and take notice. You're absolutely right.'

'Good. Then, Rosie, this is where you come in,' he looked across the table at her. 'You said that Bennett had a friend in London who was expert at the copper-plate, and would provide some cards explaining our work methods from beginning to end. Since you've become so adept at your drawing, perhaps you'd consider making some sketches of it all, including the way the withy beds look in the fields, through to the finished article in our workrooms. Each card to be headed House of Willow. What do you think?'

'Oh, Pa, it sounds marvellous!' Her eyes were shining, not least because the three of them were united again in a common venture. 'It will need to be done very soon. I can begin on the rough sketches this very night, and I'll ask Bennett to write to his friend with the details tomorrow. Perhaps Edwin will outline the words you want to use. Make it as concise as possible, Edwin. Folk won't want to be blinded by country terms they don't understand. But I'm sure it will be an added attraction, Pa. How clever you are to have thought of it!'

'I've thought of something too,' Edwin put in. 'You saw how charmed Daisy was that I'd made a tiny doll's chair to go alongside her own. I like working the tiny pieces, Pa. I'd be quite willing to make a whole range of miniature articles to match the regular pieces we sent to the exhibition, for a child's use. It would be a novelty to have toys made out of willow, and lighter for a child's small hands than wood.'

'It sounds an excellent idea, boy,' Dunstan said at once. 'I think the House of Willow stand will be one to reckon with after all.'

'I could ask Jess to make matching cushions for the chair seats and the baby's cradle if you like,' Edwin pursued. 'She's a first-class needlewoman, and would love to feel useful in our endeavour, I'm sure.'

Rosie held her breath, wondering how this suggestion would be received by her father. She said quickly that it would certainly enhance the look of the goods, and that she herself would have no time to make cushions. Dunstan gave a short nod.

'Then perhaps you would ask Jess when you see her next, Edwin,' he said, and in doing so they knew he had given his approval to the courtship as well as the industry.

'This calls for a celebration, Pa. A bottle

of home-made wine, I think, don't you? To the success of the House of Willow and all its contributors!' Edwin was jubilant now, and the three of them spent several happy hours making plans over the mellowing elderberry wine. By the end of the evening the proposed wording and sketches for the exhibition cards were roughly planned out, and exact details of the basketware to be exhibited were decided on. Much of it was already finished in the workshop, but Edwin would start immediately on working the smaller items. In his mind's eye the stand would be colourful and different, with the willow toys and with Jess's bright cushions to add to the stand's appeal.

'That's enough for one night,' Edwin said at last, flexing his shoulders when the cards were ready for showing to Bennett and passing on to his friend in London. 'I feel we've made some momentous plans here, Pa. A turning-point in our fortunes, perhaps.'

'Let's hope so. At least we've come to some amicable decisions. I wish your mother could have been part of it.'

'She is, Pa,' Rosie spoke softly. 'While you have Edwin and me, she'll always be a part of us.'

She didn't dare to say that although Daisy could never take the place of Dorcas, perhaps in time the child would allay much of the grief the family had endured at that terrible time.

She left the menfolk together and went upstairs to bed. Inside the cool sheets Rosie let her thoughts drift to Will. The feeling that all the ice around her heart was melting was still with her, and the memory of his attack could even fill her with a strange wild excitement. Will had wanted her so savagely on that night, driven on by his need to hurt her in body as he felt himself to be hurt in his pride.

Her body had been so unready for him...yet her own passionate nature had responded involuntarily, however mutely. During the intervening months Rosie had been able to forget some of the horror of Will's possession, even to think instead how such a union would be heightened by love and mutual desire.

As she dreamed, on the edge of sleep, she could almost taste the salt of his skin as his hand pressed against her mouth. She could relive again, without the fear she had felt then, the sensual invasion of her body, and Will's seeking lips on her breasts. Abandoning herself to the pleasure of it without the pain, and suddenly aware of the deep, rippling sensations that spread through her lower regions in a hot, languorous flame of sweetness, as if she was suddenly riding on the golden, shuddering crest of a wave, explosively exquisite...

'Will, oh Will,' Rosie moaned softly as the powerful sensations receded, leaving her lulled into a strange mixture of comfort and emptiness. Without him beside her, her arms reached out aimlessly, needing him with all the woman in her crying out for his love. How foolish they were to let anything or anyone come between them. Such foolishness was for children, and there was nothing childish about Rosie's feelings for Will, nor his for her, as she knew very well.

The rift between them must be mended, she thought, as sleep claimed her. And mended soon. No one else existed for her save Will Merrick, and she made a private vow to herself that she would marry no one but him.

She wondered if he thought of her as often as she did of him. If Will's dreams were as pleasurable as hers... She felt no false modesty, which mildly surprised her... but it was one more reason to believe that what she felt for Will was a deep and lasting love, or else it surely would not be so.

The next few days were so busy that Rosie knew she could make no suggestion about going to Merrick farm until the school week was over, so she planned to visit the farm on Saturday afternoon.

Bennett was delighted with the cards she and Edwin had roughed out, and sent them off immediately to his friend in London for completing. Rosie's small sketches were done separately to be stuck on the finished display cards in the manner shown on the roughs.

People seemed to be more smiling than of late as she passed, she reflected. Often they encouraged Daisy to speak if the child was with her, just to hear the phenomenon, and when folk congratulated her, she assumed it was on account of the way the connection of their two names had led Daisy into saying her first words, and not because they believed her to be affianced to the school teacher. The vicar had affirmed that the miracle was God's work and not the devil's, and the villagers of Moule were feverish to follow his lead as usual. Besides, it was easier on the senses to believe that no witch walked among them.

On Saturday afternoon Rosie announced that she was going to visit Mrs Merrick at the farm to discuss her stay there while the men took the basketware to London for the opening.

'You're not objecting then, Rosie?'

Edwin commented. 'I thought your first reaction was unfavourable.'

'It's a woman's right to change her mind, as you should very well know,' Rosie retorted lightly.

'And a man's lot to be constantly perplexed by them,' Edwin grinned back, secure in the knowledge that his Jess wasn't about to change her mind about anything. He still marvelled at the fact that he had been the one able to unlock Jess's frozen heart and reveal the warm sensitive woman within. He loved and cherished her, and all his own feelings were reciprocated. The future looked very bright to Edwin, and he wished his young sister could be as happy.

There were still times when Rosie looked too old for her years, as if something weighed heavily on her like a millstone. Then at others he told himself he was imagining things, when she became as animated as she had done recently over Daisy's transformation and the plans for the new House of Willow. Rosie needed a young man, Edwin thought, and hoped privately that it would not be the school teacher.

For all Bennett Naylor's eloquence and style, Edwin was certain he was not the man for his passionate sister. Bennett would be a thoughtful and caring husband...but with none of the earthy soul-mating that made a man and a woman's union almost spiritual in its perfection. Fire and tenderness—the combination was vital. He had found it in Jess. He hoped sincerely that Rosie would find it too...maybe in the days she would spend at the Merrick farm while he and Dunstan were away, she would have time to reflect and think again about Will...

Rosie had the same thoughts in mind as she and Boy walked towards Merrick farm on that sunny end-of-March afternoon. The blustery wind of the past few days had lessened, and the breeze was almost warm as Boy bounded ahead of her. Trees were networked with an early green tracery, and everywhere the coming of spring was more and more evident. Rosie felt almost light-hearted as she neared the farm, filled with anticipation at seeing Will. As yet she had no idea how she was going to tell him she had forgiven him for the night of the fair and Cory's lies that he had believed so readily. Somehow she had to let him know delicately that her feelings for him hadn't changed.

She felt oddly reticent, as if all the modesty she had brushed aside in her dreaming hours had suddenly reappeared. It was one thing to want Will...it was another to confront him and tell him so! It was something a young lady didn't do—or was this one of those times when a young lady forgot her inhibitions and behaved more like a woman! Rosie's mouth curved into a smile as the thought struck her, but she still felt nervous as Boy began to bark and Farmer Merrick straightened his back from the animal feed he was mixing in the barn, and looked at her with genuine pleasure.

' 'Tis good to see 'ee, my dear. I were only saying to Missus and our Will that 'twere some time since you came visiting. I daresay you've been too busy with your school teacherin' an' all. Missus has gone visiting a sick neighbour, but she'll be back afore long. Our Will's somewhere about, if 'ee wants to go looking for 'un.'

'Thank you, Farmer Merrick. I expect I'll find him,' Rosie said quickly, before the man offered to come into the farmhouse with her to make stilted small-talk. Besides, it was Will she had come to see, and the sooner she found him before her nerve failed, the better.

'We're that pleased you'll be stayin' wi' us while your men be gone to Lunnon, my dear,' Farmer Merrick called after her. She waved back, and began hunting round for Will. She hadn't seen him in any of the fields, where the new young withies were sprouting well in the marshy conditions.

There were more barns and outhouses...she found him inside the third one she tried, where the scent of hay was dry and dusty and fragrant.

'Hello Will,' Rosie said softly. She could feel the beat of her heart as she faced him, and it gave a leap of excitement, remembering the sensual dreams of him that had brought him so close to her, so real in her imaginings... He was so darkly masculine against the dim interior of the barn, his strong jaw-line jutting out aggressively as he turned to face her. And then she ran her tongue around her lips in a nervous movement as she saw that his face was unsmiling.

'So you've decided to wed the school teacher, have you?' he began abruptly. 'I daresay he's got far more to offer you than a farm-boy. You'll no doubt be anxious to get to London and get acquainted with his sister and all her fancy friends now. I daresay we'll hardly know Miss Rosie Nash when she comes back to Moule after the excursion—*if* she comes back!'

Rosie gasped at the stinging accusation in his voice. 'Who says I'm to marry the school teacher?'

'Jess does, and I've no reason to doubt her word in the state of seventh heaven she's in these days. All the Nashes will be heading for church together by the sound

341

of it. Who does your Pa have in mind? Can't you find a widow-woman for him to tie his coat-tails to?'

He oozed sarcasm, and if Rosie hadn't been so upset she might have realised that Will spoke so harshly out of his own pain at losing her to Bennett Naylor. But she saw nothing but his sneering, and the thought of her father replacing her gentle mother was enough to goad her into a reply she didn't want to make, and bitterly regretted as soon as she had made it.

'At least Bennett has some manners when it comes to women,' she whipped at him. 'He has no need to come skulking into cottages after dark like a sneak-thief! Bennett knows how to treat a lady like a lady—with respect!'

She saw Will's face redden furiously. 'Oh aye,' he muttered savagely. 'Then you've got what you wanted, haven't you? I wish you well of him, but don't bother inviting me to the wedding because I won't come. Not when 'tis me you should be wedding.'

'You're a fool, Will Merrick,' Rosie said in a wild rage. 'But if you think you're leaving it all to me to spell out, then you can wait till the cows curdle their own cheese! I've never met such a stupid, aggravating—'

'Don't come here treating me like dirt

on me own farm,' Will suddenly shouted at her. He moved towards her, his hands gripping her arms like iron bands. Why didn't he just bend his head and take possession of her mouth the way he had done of her body? He'd know soon enough then by her response whether or not Will Merrick was the man for her! He'd know by the way she melted into his warm embrace that the thought of Bennett Naylor holding her like that was as meaningless to her as a scattering of moonbeams... When he made no move towards her, and continued to glower at her, Rosie stamped her foot in frustration.

'Go on!' Will jeered in desolation, because it was the only way he could trust himself at that moment. 'You wrenched your ankle once before by the same artful wiles. Are you planning to try it again?'

That time it had ended in a kiss, and an unspoken feeling of commitment between them both that seemed destined to remain unfulfilled. Rosie stared at him numbly for a moment, and then twisted out of his arms as she heard his mother's footsteps approaching, and her homely cheerful voice calling her name.

'Why shouldn't I treat you like dirt, Will Merrick?' She ground out the words. 'If you behave like the scum of the earth, you must expect to be treated like it!'

She rushed, trembling, out of the barn and left him there, feeling as if her heart was breaking. She had come here on a cloud of euphoria, and now she felt as if she was in a whirlpool of plunging emotions once more. And Will couldn't love her after all, she thought bitterly. Oh, he'd said it should be him that she was wedding and not Bennett...but the aggressive way in which he'd said it made it seem as if he thought he owned her, because of that one act of love that suddenly didn't feel like love any more.

Chapter 15

Vicar Washbourne seemed to have worked his magic among the villagers once more. Even though Rosie and her menfolk were unaware of the rumpus at the Moule Inn and afterwards, she was beginning to think of the vicar as their anchor. Whatever the uneasy murmurings about her family during the week, by Sunday morning it resolved itself into pleasantries and smiles and nods...

Everyone seemed aware of the attachment between Edwin and Jess by now, and contrary to what a few old diehards muttered, most of them were approving of the match. Poor Jess had done her time of penance, and if she was safely wed then no other honest woman in the district could fear her own man's eyes would stray to the skirt of a loose woman. Such was the logic of Moule.

The time was quickly drawing near for Dunstan and Edwin to take their goods to London in the cart, and Rosie and the dog would stay at Merrick farm. She had made renewed protests about it lately, but Dunstan was adamant.

'What would Mrs Merrick think if you chopped and changed your mind all the time? I won't have it, Rosie,' he said firmly. 'If there's trouble between you and Will, you'd best get it over with and get back on a friendly basis. It seems I was right in not allowing the two of you to go courting. You behave more like cats at each other's throats, and that's no way to start a marriage!'

Rosie avoided his eyes and hoped he wouldn't see the bleakness in her own. She had recently seen Will chattering and laughing with several village girls on the old stone bridge at just about the time she left the schoolhouse. He often came to the village on some errand or other, but Rosie guessed bitterly that he made a point of flirting with the village girls for her benefit.

She didn't let him see by a flicker that she was affected by it in the least, though it cost her dearly to walk straight past the group without looking their way. Especially when she heard their giggles following her, and little Daisy Lawrence tugged at her hand and demanded to know why they didn't stop and talk to Will, and asked why Rosie didn't like him any more.

Mrs Merrick made her so welcome at the farm that it was even more embarrassing to try and avoid too much contact with Will, when all her instincts strained against it. She longed to throw herself into his arms and beg him to end this stupid feud between them, but her pride wouldn't let her.

'I'll go to the schoolhouse with Jess in the mornings, Mrs Merrick,' Rosie said at once, when the suggestion of Will taking her arose. 'It's more convenient, and I wouldn't want to put Will out.'

'It wouldn't put me out,' Will said distantly. 'But you must suit yourself. I wouldn't want to force my company on you.'

'Nor mine on you,' she countered, her voice freezing.

Mrs Merrick looked from one to the other in exasperation. 'You two be more like sparring partners than any other kind! I'm for knockin' your heads together our

Will, for being so uncivil to a guest in the house! Rosie will be glad to get up among they fancy ladies in Lunnon after your bits of showin' off!'

'Best place for her then,' Will lumbered out of the farm kitchen, unheeding his mother's outraged shouting for him to mind his manners, for he wasn't too big to get a clout from his father, either. Rosie sat at the table finishing her breakfast, smarting at Will's treatment. And hearing his mother apologise for him didn't help either.

'It's all right, Mrs Merrick.' Rosie forced back the thickness in her throat and the salty threat of tears. 'Will and I just don't get along too well any more, so it's probably best if I keep out of his way. It's nobody's fault, really!'

What would the buxom farmer's wife think if she knew of the times Rosie had lain sleepless in the strange bed at the farm? Listening to the different sounds and wondering if she dare to creep along to Will's room and try to put an end to all the barriers between them...though she never would, of course. It would be too shaming and too risky. The good farming folk would be scandalised at such behaviour, and so would her father...

Instead of enjoying these days at the farm, Rosie found them an ordeal. Where

Will went at night she didn't know, but each night she was there he found other amusements that kept him out until very late. The thought of those laughing village girls was enough to make her burn with jealousy, but she wouldn't give him the satisfaction of asking him.

A letter arrived for her from Alice Naylor during the time her father and brother were away. Bennett received it with his, and Rosie's face flushed with pleasure and a little alarm as she read it.

'Do you know about this, Bennett?' she asked quickly. 'About the—soirée—that one of your sister's friends is arranging while I'm in London? I'm to be invited, and—Alice—hopes I may stay on a little longer than the brief excursion trip. She says it would give her pleasure to show me a little more of London. It's very good of her, Bennett, but...'

'But what? Why should you hesitate? Alice will be charmed to escort you about town.'

'As the little country cousin?' Rosie's face was tinged with a different kind of colour at the thought. 'Or as something else? What exactly have you told her about me, Bennett? About—us, in particular. I hope you haven't given her any false impressions.'

He felt a brief regret as the confused

expression filled her lovely eyes. Bennett wasn't a passionate man, but there were times when he'd dearly like to fold her in his arms and comfort her, even though he suspected more and more that his feelings were more of a kindly uncle than those of a lover. Even so, Rosie was truly a flower among the young women of Moule, he thought poetically. He cleared his throat.

'Alice knows of my deep regard for you, Rosie, but I have said no more than that. She knows we work well together here, but I fear she thinks me altogether too much of an old stick-in-the-mud to change my ways now,' he said delicately. 'I hope I've described you as my dear friend.'

Rosie put her soft hand on his arm for a moment.

'That's just the way I think of you, Bennett,' she was quick to say. 'The way I always want to think of you. But if I'm to attend the home of Lady Lydia Fitzgerald, I shall have other things to think about. I can't let my family down by appearing in country clothes—and I fear I've rather neglected my appearance lately. I know my father would want me to look my best. Perhaps I should go to Bridgwater and find a dressmaker.'

'Allow me to take you, Rosie, please. It would give me great pleasure to do so.'

'Then I accept! Perhaps we can go on

Saturday, Bennett. The men will still be away, but it will give me something to do and keep me out of Mrs Merrick's way at the farm.'

And out of Will's sight too. And if he knew she was going into Bridgwater with Bennett Naylor and put the wrong interpretation on it, so much the better. When Bennett told her he would hire a trap and fetch her himself, she didn't object to that either, though she felt a little guiltily that it was putting him to a great deal of trouble and expense. But Bennett glossed over it so smoothly, and said nostalgically that it would remind him of the days when he escorted his mother and sister to similar establishments in London, that she could hardly object. By now Rosie realised that such expense would mean little to Bennett Naylor. His background was clearly very different to hers, and she thought of the coming excursion to London with a mixture of excitement and awe.

She informed Mrs Merrick of her plans for Saturday when she arrived back at the farm on Friday afternoon. The men were drinking tea from the huge endless pot that seemed to be always on the go. She saw Will's face darken as she mentioned Bennett's name, and couldn't resist elaborating.

'Bennett is so used to the elegant dresses of the London ladies, he will be such an asset when I visit the dressmaker's, Mrs Merrick,' Rosie said airily. 'He has such good taste.'

'Poncey's more the word for it,' Will growled beneath his breath. Rosie heard him very well, but looked at him with wide innocent eyes.

'Did you say something, Will?' Her voice was sweet as sugar. 'I daresay you'll want to dress up a little too, for the excursion to London.'

'What makes you think so?' he snapped. 'If folk can't take me as I am, they can do t'other thing. I'm not making myself up to be a dandy just for the other folks' benefit.'

'Stop that, Will,' his mother scolded him. 'You're such a grouch these days! And you take no notice of 'un, Rosie, my dear. Our Will won't be going on no train looking like the country clod, if I know 'un! He'll be wantin' to tidy up a bit for all they fine ladies and gennulmen.'

Will's eyes grew suddenly speculative as he glanced over Rosie's taut young figure.

'Aye, there's that, I s'pose,' he drawled. 'There'll be some pretty young maids about the town who'll be ready to try out a bit o' sport with a country boy.'

'That's enough o' that coarse talk, Will,' Mrs Merrick's cheeks went an angry red, while his father chuckled appreciatively. 'Just remember to act respectable and leave the lechering to they that knows no better. You may live among the animals, but that don't give 'ee cause to act like 'em!'

Farmer Merrick laughed out loud now. 'All right, mother, that's enough sermonising for now! You'll be in competition wi' Vicar next off! Leave our Will to sort out his own life, and stop embarrassing this young maid!'

Mrs Merrick looked across at Rosie in some consternation, not realising how determinedly she and Will were avoiding each other's eyes at his mother's censuring.

'Rosie, love, I'm sure I meant nothin' of the kind. You'll know how families be, and 'tis only because we think so warmly of 'ee that I forgot myself and chattered on so.'

'It's all right, Mrs Merrick, really!' She was well aware that Will's taunts had been for her ears only, telling her that she wasn't the only fish in the sea... She caught sight of Boy, wagging his tail furiously near her feet, and seized on him as an excuse to get out of the kitchen. 'I'll just let the dog out for a run. He looks as if he needs it.'

She almost fled out of the kitchen, her heart beating unevenly. She and Will seemed to have a penchant for scratching at each other lately, and her nerves felt ragged because of it. Her father and brother were due back from London on Tuesday, and Rosie knew it would be a relief to see them again. The time at the farm had been as awkward as she had expected. Perhaps it would be a good thing after all to stay in London for a week or two, if Alice Naylor would have her. She felt the need to get away from the close community atmosphere of Moule, with all its turbulent undercurrents of feelings that were as perverse as a moorland breeze. It wouldn't hurt Will either, Rosie thought keenly, if he thought part of the attraction was Bennett's family, and the desire to better herself.

She dismissed the thought that there was no one better for Rosie Nash on this earth than Will Merrick. And that to cut him down in her mind was as meaningless as thinking she could ever marry Bennett. But it wouldn't hurt him to sting a little...

She chased Boy in and out of the fields as the dog led her a dance, glad to be frisking in the April sunshine that still lingered into early evening. Rosie's cheeks glowed, and she felt instinctively that no city fug could ever compare with this clean air, scented with new grass and the vigour of things growing and replenishing themselves in the cycle of the seasons.

In the nine months that the Nash family had lived at Moule, the new withy crop was beginning to leaf, in time for the next round of auctions. Everything the same and unchanging in the way of the country.

Boy suddenly pricked up his ears at a sound too high-pitched for Rosie to hear, and then he went haring away from her, tail vibrating with ecstasy. She raced after him, calling his name, but when she saw he went towards the farm, she slowed down with a hand held to her side where a stitch caught at her.

'Where are you, Boy?' she called in annoyance as she reached the barns. She suddenly saw his tail sticking out of one of them, and ran to take hold of him. And then stopped short as she saw Will kneeling down and stroking the dog's head.

'He's decided to make friends with me,' Will said abruptly, and Rosie knew he was referring to that night when Boy had growled so worriedly, not understanding what was happening between two people he liked.

'So I see.' Rosie wasn't sure how to reply. Did Will mean he wanted her to do the same? If so, he must make the first move. She stood motionless, waiting. And willing him to act a little more humanly towards her.

'I've been told to say sorry for my uncouth manners,' he went on, but from his tone Rosie felt the apology sounded more like an insult. 'So I'm saying it.'

She stepped inside the barn, suddenly tired of all the badgering between them. She stood very close to him, the sharpness of her breath making her breasts rise and fall in a way he didn't miss from the tightening of his jaw.

'Are you, Will?' she asked breathlessly. 'Are you really sorry for all the differences between us? I know it must have been a shock when Jess told you about Bennett and me—just as I didn't like it when I saw you flirting with the village girls.'

She knew she had made a mistake as soon as she said it. If only she had bothered to make it plain that she didn't intend marrying Bennett...but Will didn't give her time for that now. She saw his mouth twist, and then he pulled her to him, not tenderly as she might have wished, but with an arrogant possessiveness.

'Why didn't you like it, Rosie? Were you worried they might be getting all my loving? Did that bother you then?' He spoke with crude seduction, and she struggled to get out of his embrace. He wouldn't let her go, and held her tight, his eyes hard and mocking.

'Do you think I care how you pass your time?' she flashed out at him. 'You can have a dozen girls for all I care!'

He paused for a split second, anger sparkling in his handsome face. 'Well, just so's you won't forget me, Rosie, when you're poncing about with your school teacher, here's something else to remember me by.'

His head bent towards hers, and he was pulling her closer to him, the hardness of his body nearly knocking the breath out of her. One hand slid upwards behind her thick hair, his fingers raking through it until her scalp tingled from his touch, and long shivers trailed all over her body. His mouth fastened over hers in a savage kiss, forcing her lips apart, and then she felt the tip of his tongue moving against her own, warm and sensual and earthy like Will himself.

His body moved against her too, in little seductive spirals, moulded against her like a second skin. The hot thrill of desire inflamed her senses as her knuckles clenched behind his back and pressed into him. She could think of nothing else at that moment but that the dream was coming true and she was here in Will's arms once more...nothing else but the pleasure and ecstasy that his touch gave her...for there was no one and nothing in the world for Rosie but him, and she knew it with a mind-shattering certainty. She belonged to him...

'Will! Get over here wi' me a minute!' Farmer Merrick's voice bawled out from the yard, and Rosie was suddenly pushed roughly aside.

Will breathed heavily, but there was no softening in his eyes as she had hoped, as he answered his father's call and then glared at her flushed face. 'See if your school teacher can measure up to that!'

She stood as if transfixed as he strode away from her. Those last moments had been so momentous for her, Rosie could hardly believe they hadn't meant as much to him. He had shamed her all over again if he had just meant that kiss to be a taunt, which seemed most likely now. Rosie smothered a sob and rushed into the farmhouse with Boy at her heels, and, glad that Mrs Merrick was out of the kitchen, she ran up the stairs to the sanctuary of her own room.

For a moment the shock of it still held her rigid, and then she seemed to crumple onto the bed, and lay on it in a fit of weeping. Will could have no real feelings for her at all if he could act that way. Or if he did, then the feelings were of lust and hate, with no love towards her at all. She could hardly believe he could be so cruel, but now she knew that Will was capable of hurting her more than just physically. The mental scars he inflicted on her were like little needle jabs, and just as damaging.

She called down to Mrs Merrick that she had a headache, and stayed in her room all evening, guiltily allowing the good lady to bring her a powder and some hot soup and bread. She needn't have bothered, however, for Mrs Merrick told her shortly that Will had gone off in a huff once more, and she didn't know what it was that had got into him lately, but she wished it would hurry up and go away!

To Rosie's heightened nerves, the country woman's words seemed to point her even more firmly in the direction of London. And long into the night Rosie lay with tear-dampened cheeks on account of Will Merrick.

By the time Dunstan and Edwin returned from London on Tuesday they were so keyed-up with enthusiasm that they hardly noticed that Rosie was paler than usual. They were so full of their descriptions of the great crystal palace that was to house the exhibition, and of the stand where their own House of Willow basketware was to have a prominent position due to the intervention of some unknown lady, that they talked long into the night, with only the briefest of comments from Rosie. Until at last she was drawn into their own excitement, and told them how Bennett had taken her into Bridgwater on Saturday for the ordering and fitting of some new clothes.

'I hope you don't mind, Pa,' she went on. 'But Bennett's sister has asked me to stay a week or two if I like, and her friend, Lady Fitzgerald, is giving a soirée for my benefit! I thought I had better have some smart dresses. I didn't want to let you down.'

'Of course it's all right, my love!' Dunstan said at once. 'But Lady Fitzgerald, you say. Edwin, isn't that the one?'

'It is!' He frowned slightly. 'Oh well, what does it matter? If we have Bennett and his sister to thank for mentioning our name in high society, then thank them we will. It's our work that must still stand the test of competition, and you never saw such varying items that are arriving daily, Rosie. The whole place is like an Aladdin's cave already.'

She was a little put out that their family should be even more beholden to Bennett's connections. But since he hadn't pursued his proposal to her and seemed quite content to be the friend he had always been, Rosie decided it would be foolish to resent the benefit to her family's business because of Bennett's name and his sister's influential friend.

'What were the display cards like?' she asked. 'Did the man do them well?' Another obligation, Rosie thought uneasily. If Bennett had been less than honourable, he might so well have made capital out of all this.

'They're admirable, Rosie,' Edwin said enthusiastically. 'Your drawings were so clear, he cut round them and stuck them onto the cards with his copper-plate. They look very effective, and trace the whole sequence of growing the withies to the actual production of the baskets. You'll be pleased when you see them, and with the display of the goods as well. Jess's cushions liven up the whole stand. I only wish she could come to see the exhibition, but she won't leave Daisy, and feels it would be too overwhelming for a child.'

'But you weren't overwhelmed by it all?' Rosie smiled at her brother. 'By the big city and the smart people?'

'Why should I be?' he retorted. 'My life revolves quite smoothly without any of them, but you only have to glance about to know the smartest folk need us and our craft! And from the interest taken in our stand, I guarantee that the House of Willow is one to be reckoned with.'

Dunstan laughed. 'It would take more than city folk to frighten Edwin off, Rosie, and rightly so. We're all the same beneath the fancy clothes, and it's as well to remember if if anyone of them tries to intimidate you, darling!'

'Rosie won't let that happen,' Edwin grinned. 'She's got too sharp a tongue for that.'

She wasn't sure if it was a compliment or not, but she could see that Edwin was dying to go and see Jess, and began making elaborate remarks about needing to stretch his legs. She couldn't resist teasing him.

'I've never known you to be so restless, have you, Pa? Why don't you just say you want to see your lady-love, and go and leave Pa and me in peace to talk over what I'm costing him in new dresses! I'm sure Jess will have some supper for you tonight.'

Maybe more than supper... Rosie didn't know how far their relationship had gone, and it wasn't her business to enquire. She only knew that when the two of them had been together for a time, there was a glow about them that she envied. And it was obvious from Edwin's eagerness now that it was Jess he was longing to see.

'Tell me more about London,' she said to her father quickly, not wanting to dwell on the cosiness of Jess and Edwin together.

'Was it very grand, Pa?'

'Oh yes, in parts,' he nodded. 'Though the Lamb Tavern where Edwin and I stayed was modest enough, and I daresay there are as many rowdies as anywhere else. It's the same place that the excursion folk will stay at, so we thought it was a good idea to take a look at the place. The folk from Moule won't be overawed by it, though they will be by the size of the exhibition. It really is a staggering sight, Rosie.'

'It must do you some good, Pa. Custom hasn't been too marvellous here, has it?' she ventured to say for the first time.

'Not altogether,' Dunstan admitted. 'They're a strange breed of folk here, Rosie, and a stranger is a stranger until the day he dies, in my opinion.'

'Even when his name is Nash?' she said wryly. 'I thought that was the cause of the trouble. They're too steeped in old superstitions to take people for what they are.'

'Well, don't let's get morbid tonight, darling.' Dunstan noticed the pallor in her face now, and sought to cheer her up. 'It's a shame we won't be in London to see the opening of the exhibition, for it's to be a real spectacle by all accounts. The Queen and the Prince and all the royal family are to be there, in a grand procession through the parks, and the whole thing is to be given the royal blessing. Properly so, since it's Prince Albert who has created the whole concept of the exhibition.'

'Is it as huge as the newspapers say?' Rosie asked, remembering the cuttings Bennett had shown her.

'It's a gigantic house of glass, and they say the area of it is four times that of St Peter's church in Rome. I don't know the truth of that, of course, but it's certainly a beautiful and impressive sight when the sun is shining on it.'

He looked at her thoughtfully. Sometimes Dunstan thought his daughter too looked as fragile as that house of glass...he could only hope she was possessed of the same innate strength as that other masterpiece. But something had certainly changed his daughter in recent months. It was as if he could no longer reach her in the way that a father was always closest to his daughter. Somehow she always managed to keep him at arms' reach, and he felt a sadness at knowing it. Rosie was no longer the carefree child she was, nor even the lovely young girl on the brink of womanhood that he had expected to be curbing a little. This new Rosie was a secretive, haunted person in a way he couldn't fathom. She was nonetheless alluring for all that, despite her sometimes severe mode of dress these days. In a way it only enhanced her womanliness. But there was something troubling her, and Dunstan mourned the fact that the closeness of father and daughter they had once shared, when his girl-child had run free over the moors and headlands of their old coastal home, seemed lost to him for ever.

'Did you enjoy your stay at Merrick farm, Rosie?' He saw her flinch, though she made a great pretence of playing with the exuberant dog on the floor, pleased to have all his humans surrounding him once more.

'It was fine,' she said in a muffled voice. 'Mrs Merrick made me feel very much at home, and I like Farmer Merrick a lot, Pa.'

And Will? Dunstan wanted to ask her, but didn't dare. Something about her tense attitude told him at once that Will was behind all Rosie's disturbance. And he knew this was something she must sort out for herself. He had believed until this minute that she was merely biding her time and exerting her femininity before giving Bennett Naylor the answer to his proposal. Now, Dunstan knew instantly that it would never be the answer he wanted. Every instinct in him told him so, whatever had happened between Rosie and Will. Bennett Naylor wasn't the man she wanted.

As always when he felt the need to think Dunstan felt the urge to be out in his workshop, among the withy rods and half-made baskets and tools that were his life, finding in the continuity of his work a solace whenever things were at their lowest. He got awkwardly to his feet now, muttering to Rosie that he just thought he'd take a look around outside and see that everything was in order in the workshop and outhouses.

She understood him so well. Knowing he longed to help her and didn't know how. Sensing that he hardly knew her any more, which to Rosie wasn't so surprising, because she felt she hardly knew herself any more. Nor anyone else for that matter. She certainly didn't know Will, not now. He had been a part of her and yet she didn't know him. She only knew he didn't want her any more. He had discarded her as carelessly as a worn-out glove, and it hurt so much...so much...

Rosie suddenly bent and buried her face in the warm thick hair of the blissfully stretched-out dog. At that moment she made up her mind to stay in London if she was asked, at least for a little while. Maybe it would help her to come to terms with Will's rejection of her... She choked on a sob, knowing it would take more than a few weeks away from him. If she lived a lifetime without him, it would still be Will Merrick who held her heart.

The dog's throaty little noises of sympathy went completely unheeded as her hands dug into his comforting rough coat. At that moment Rosie wished passionately that she had all the magical powers that the village accredited her with. If it were so, she would wish for nothing more than that Will Merrick wanted her for his own true love once more. Right then, the one thought seemed as impossible as the other.

Chapter 16

'Today is the first of May,' Bennett beamed around the schoolroom at the scrubbed faces in front of him and Rosie. 'Can anyone tell me anything about today?'

Half a dozen hands flew up in the air.

'We go a-May-gathering.'

'We choose the Queen of the May.'

'We sing an' dance around the maypole.'

Bennett had to stop them with a laugh. 'Well done. Yes, we do all of those things, and those are the traditional things. But something very special is also happening today, in a place far away from here. We've been talking about it, and Miss Rosie has been drawing pictures for you all to see. Can anyone tell me what it is?'

'Summat up Lunnon, sir,' one of the boys shouted out. 'This 'ere exhibition thing.'

'That's right, Luke.' Rosie had to admire Bennett at that moment for not letting his mouth quirk into a grin. The drawings she had done were pinned all round the walls, and the children glanced their way obediently, but in reality she guessed they would be more eager to pursue their usual country Mayday rituals.

'Here's the Queen in her carriage,' Bennett pointed out the scene. 'And here's the huge glass building where so many things will be exhibited that it would be impossible to count them. There will be silks from India, and the greatest diamond of all, the Koh-i-Noor diamond, will be on view. There will be machinery of all kinds, as well as paintings and basketware from Somerset, made by our own Miss Rosie's family.'

The children were becoming restless. Mayday was warm and sunny, and they wanted to be out of doors in the fields, not listening to Bennett's enthusiastic voice telling of something so remote to them they could hardly comprehend it. Rosie could see their attention wandering, but

Bennett would have his say. Finally he realised there was much fidgeting going on, and said mildly that when they had expended all their energy outside, they could come back and try copying Rosie's excellent silhouette drawing of the Queen. At least his school would be informed of what the head of the realm looked like, even if they lacked interest in this important day. He spoke with resigned sarcasm.

'My Ma says I'm not to go doin' no silhouettes, sir,' Vera Yandell's shrill voice rang out. 'My Ma says 'tis the devil's work to do such pichers, and 'tain't right to do the black images.'

Rosie felt a thrill of shock at the words. Every time she thought she was totally accepted in the village and the nonsense about the witchcraft had died down, something reminded her all too sharply that it still simmered beneath the surface. It was like a festering sore, ready to flare up into an angry eruption at any time. She glanced at Bennett, who was frowning with annoyance. Vera Yandell was a particularly irritating child, and Rosie saw Daisy and several others hiding their mouths behind their hands in a giggling fit at Vera's defiance.

'Then you'll just draw the outline without filling in the shape,' Bennett retorted, not to be thwarted by this chit. 'I presume your mother won't find that offensive? And anyone else who finds their regular schoolwork amusing or distasteful had better stay behind and think about it for an hour, while the rest of us go out and enjoy the Mayday revels.'

His words effectively shut them up. He gave a nod and they all went outside boisterously. As they followed, Bennett squeezed Rosie's hand for a moment.

'Don't let them upset you,' he murmured. 'It's no more than ignorance that puts such ideas into a child's head.'

She gave a half-smile, knowing that ignorance could be as powerful a weapon as truth. But the brief shadow passed as she and Bennett walked through the village street with the long straggling line of children, to let them go whooping about in the fields to gather whatever sprigs had even the smallest amount of leaf or blossom, with which to decorate themselves and their classroom.

In the schoolyard they danced around the maypole, chanting their songs to welcome the return of the sun. And then Bennett announced that Daisy Lawrence was this year's Queen of the May, and she wore a crown of flowers on her head for the rest of the day.

Rosie was pleased that Daisy had the

honour, and this year of course she would be able to run home to her mother and tell her the exciting news with a tongue that seemed to become looser with each passing day. And if Vera Yandell scowled with disappointment and gave Daisy a sly pinch that had her howling with rage, while Vera hissed at her that she was teacher's pet and mebbe a witch's pet too, neither Bennett nor Rosie heard it.

At the end of the day, when most of the children had gone home and Daisy waited while Rosie cleared up the various drawings and scattered garlands, her brow puckered a little as she saw Vera's deliberate outline of Queen Victoria without the shading of the silhouette. It was a grotesque likeness, for Vera had no artistic ability at all, but the child's defiant words were still clear in Rosie's mind. How could it be the devil's work to do something that was being done in many a fine drawing-room in fashionable circles! Ignorance would have it so, and the thought could make Rosie shiver as if something crawled over her flesh.

While the village children were making their Mayday garlands, a fête of a different kind was being enacted in a distant city. London was at its most effervescent on the first of May, when the royal procession set off in nine state carriages at eleven-thirty in the morning, on its way to Hyde Park and the opening of the exhibition. It rained a little, but by the time the procession arrived the proverbially lucky 'Queen's weather' changed the rain to sunshine, and the great gleaming crystal palace glittered in sunlight. The scene was a kaleidoscope of colour and light, the framework of the building in pale blue with touches of scarlet and orange, and flags of every nation adorning the immense three-tiered structure. The Marquess of Breadalbane declared the exhibition open on the Queen's behalf, while she sat grandly attired in her royal robes on the throne at the northern end of the huge transept. A fanfare of trumpets blared out, to be followed by resounding cheers. When the royal procession had withdrawn, the choirs sang the Hallelujah Chorus, their massed voices almost muted by the sheer size of the building and the milling spectators.

Among the first day visitors was a group of elegant ladies and gentlemen who studied the exhibition catalogue minutely, looking for one particular name.

'There it is, Lydia,' Miss Alice Naylor said to her friend, Lady Fitzgerald. 'House of Willow, exhibits of fine basket-ware by Dunstan and Edwin Nash, of Moule, Somerset.'

'Good,' Lydia said mischievously. 'Then let's have a little sport, shall we? One basket is very like another, but I've primed up my young men and gels, and Vivian too, when he can stop ogling them, to voice their approval loudly. We'll let these country simples have a moment's glory!'

The group surrounding her like attendant worker bees laughed loudly. Lesser beings looked their way and noted them down as leaders of fashion and elegance, and allowed them their frivolity. This was no day for resentment against those who seemed to skim along the cream of life anyway, they thought grudgingly. Today was a day for merriment.

Lady Lydia led the way forcefully through the crowds, the rustle of her silk gown and the occasional jab of her parasol clearing the way effectively. If Alice sometimes thought the lady was almost objectionable, she knew of her good points too, and refrained from comment. Lady Lydia upheld several worthy charities with her name and a little of her fortune, and was known to be a good friend when needed, for all her eccentricities.

There was already a passing interest in the stand of the House of Willow. The attractive copper-plate cards, with Rosie's clear drawings attached, were bringing murmurs of approval from people who had never given a moment's thought before now as to the origins of the baskets they carried daily. More fashionable folk too suddenly realised that the wicker chairs and plant stands and bird cages, so beloved of current fashion, had their beginnings in the humble Somerset earth and in the hands of craftsmen.

The young officers and pretty young women with Lord and Lady Fitzgerald were already proclaiming loudly the merits of the Nash baskets, giggling behind their hands as they followed their instructions. Give the country men a run for their money, Lady Lydia had ordered, and let them earn a copper or two of the wherewithal.

Now, Lady Lydia's eyes widened a little as she took in the carefully thought-out selection of basketware. The beautifully made cradle with its soft patchwork cushion base and pillow was not the kind that generally graced London mansions. Nor the sturdy basket chair alongside. Each piece was made to a regular pattern of light and dark willows, which Lady Lydia saw through her lorgnette were called withy rods, according to the adjacent cards.

There were log baskets and carrying baskets, trays of all sizes, even a windmill made out of withy rods. A lidded workbasket had the same patchwork cushion inside as the other items, giving the stand a look of unity. There were small tables and bread baskets, each finished with the distinctive Nash border, and beside each piece displayed was a miniature item of the same, either for a collector's showcase or for a child's amusement. Dunstan and Edwin had excelled themselves, and suddenly there was a new respect in Lady Lydia's eyes.

'It seems we underestimated the country-folk,' she said slowly. 'I would say this work is very fine indeed, would you not agree, Vivian?'

'Absolutely, my dear. A babe would sleep happily in such a homely cradle! Even the tiny one has rockers to match, do you see? Some skilful fingers have been at work here.'

Gradually it dawned on the rest of the group that their hosts were no longer funning, but were genuinely impressed by what they saw. And such was the Fitzgerald's magnetism that the ripple of excitement generated by the basketware stand irradiated to others nearby, then further among the crowds, until it seemed that the name of the House of Willow was on every tongue. If the spectators had not already seen the stand, then it was one to which they must all make their way, since word was out that it catered to the latest fad, and to it was added the originality of the miniature ware.

Such stunning exhibits as the Koh-i-Noor diamond might be perfection, but were as unattainable as the sun and stars, while basketware made by the House of Willow was within much humbler purses' reach, as well as pandering to the whims and fancies of an aristocracy ever looking for something new and different...

'Lydia, my dear, I do believe I have found the perfect answer to the decor at the new gentlemen's sporting club,' Lord Vivian remarked. 'I shall put it to the committee. What could be more appropriate to the town club of our members with country estates than tables and chairs made from country craft? What do you think, m'dear?'

'I think, since you are chairman of the committee, it's almost certain to be approved,' his wife said dryly. 'Unless the rest of them want your patronage removed!'

Lydia turned to her friend, Alice.

'Perhaps we may invite the Nash men to our little soirée after all, Alice,' she observed. 'If their work is to be so highly sought after because of Vivian's interest, then it would only be common courtesy to bring them along with your little gel.'

Alice hid a smile. What Lydia really meant was that if the House of Willow was to become a fashionable name in London society, then the Fitzgeralds would want it to be known that they were the ones to initiate it all. And how better than for the Nash family to be seen in the elegant Fitzgerald mansion!

'I'm sure Rosie would be more relaxed if her father and brother were there as well,' Alice nodded.

'Has Bennett popped the question yet?' Lydia demanded to know, as they made their way through the teeming Londoners and foreign visitors on this first frantic day of the exhibition.

'He hasn't confided in me if he has,' Alice replied a little tartly. It was clear that little Rosie Nash might suddenly appear more of a suitable wife for Alice's extraordinary brother, who was content to bury himself in that marshy county of Somerset, if her connections were to be renowned craftsmen of importance in the city! Lydia's transparency irritated Alice.

'If you will give me the address, I will write to this Dunstan Nash myself,' Lydia went on. 'Though I daresay the name and the village will do. It's probably no bigger than a pocket handkerchief.'

She dismissed it with a careless wave of her hand, and brushed away two urchins who came begging at her skirts for a penny. Lydia's charities were of her own making, and right now the most deserving of them was the Nash basketware that she was determined to see got its rightful recognition. How could it hope to succeed in the depths of the country so far away from everything! That Vivian had thought the same on his own account was an added incentive for the Fitzgeralds to be patrons of the newly discovered House of Willow.

On the middle day of June all forms of transport made their way to the railway station at Bridgwater, some few miles north of Moule. Bennett had organised his travellers' club well, and all were paid up for the train excursion and the nights' lodging at the Lamb Tavern in London. He and Rosie Nash would be staying at his sister's house, which fact was causing Will Merrick a deal of annoyance.

There was nothing he could do to change things, but for much of the tedious, rattling train ride to Paddington Station he sat morosely, staring out at the changing countryside, and wishing he and Rosie were to be lodging in the same place. Not that he'd think of asking her. Not now, with the prickliness between them sharper than a porcupine's back. Instead, when the chance arose, he smiled and jawed with the two young women whose father owned Moule haberdashery, and who had agreed to let them accompany him on this long journey.

They were stupid, giggling girls, and they quickly bored Will, but if paying them attention was annoying to Rosie, which he believed to be the case, then flirt with them he would! Rosie and the school teacher and her two menfolk seemed to be a very cosy foursome, he noted, with their heads together most of the time in a way that excluded everyone else. Bennett Naylor might have organised this excursion, Will thought, but it wouldn't endear him to the village if he thought himself too good to talk to the rest of them.

As it happened, Dunstan had only just shown Lady Fitzgerald's letter to Bennett and asked him to comment on it. That the letter, with its crested heading, had come as a complete surprise, was an understatement! Lydia had taken her time in writing, advised by her husband to wait until he had arranged things with his committee meeting. This entailed the members touring the exhibition stands and approving the House of Willow basketware to Vivian's satisfaction, and now Lydia was able to word her letter in a way to suit both herself and her husband.

'Dear Mr Nash,' she had written in a scrawling hand. 'My husband and I are very impressed with the craftsmanship displayed at the exhibition by yourself and your son. We understand that your daughter is to stay with our dear friend, Miss Alice Naylor. As we have arranged to give a soirée for the girl's benefit, we would deem it an honour if you and your son would join us also. I think you may be agreeably pleased at what we have to say to you.'

'Do you know the lady, Bennett?' Dunstan asked as the train thundered east. 'She gives no real details about anything.'

Bennett laughed in understanding. 'That's just like Lydia. She delights in thinking up schemes and surprises to liven up the day, as she puts it. Why Alice puts up with her, I don't really know, but they're old friends, and I'm sure all the information you'll need will be forthcoming. Just leave it all to Lydia.'

'I'm not sure I like the thought of waiting for some Lady's whim,' Edwin said shortly. 'I prefer to be in control of a situation. We may not be available for this soirée or whatever it is.'

'You'd be advised to be available, Edwin,' Bennett assured him. 'If Lady Fitzgerald has taken an interest in you, it can only be to your benefit, believe me.'

'Please listen to Bennett, Edwin,' Rosie put in swiftly. 'I must confess I was not looking forward to this particular evening. If you and Pa are there, I shall feel easier about it.'

It wasn't the speech of a young girl in love, Bennett thought ruefully. But by now he had almost discarded any hopes that Rosie might learn to love him after all, in a gentle, comfortable marriage of their minds as well as their bodies. He knew instinctively that such a marriage wouldn't be enough for her, and that reluctantly her stormy nature would prove too much for him to handle after all. He was perfectly happy to be her admiring friend, just as she wished, but a friend who could smile warmly at her and put an arm casually around her shoulder on rare occasions, and never realise what a different connotation might be put on the gesture by an observant farmer's son.

Once the train arrived at Paddington, Bennett repeated the instructions he had already given out several times, using the school teacher's method of frequent repetition to drum it into their heads. A conveyance would meet them at the entrance to the station, with a man holding a placard with the words Moule Club written on it. He would show them where it stood, and from then on it would be at their convenience for their stay in London, taking them to and from the exhibition each of the two days from tomorrow. If they wanted to go elsewhere they must find their own means, but the conveyance would deliver them between the Lamb Tavern and Hyde Park at given times only. It was all perfectly clear. Bennett just hoped they weren't so bewildered by the occasion, and the mass of people at the huge glass-domed station, that they forgot everything immediately.

'Goodbye Pa—and Edwin,' Rosie said with a catch in her throat, as she and Bennett walked with the rest of the Moule crowd to the outside of the station. She felt a little as if she was being cast adrift from all she knew and loved at that moment, and her eyes sought and found Will's, standing stiffly alongside one of the haberdasher's daughters, and Rosie watched him deliberately turn away, with a little sinking feeling in her heart.

'You enjoy yourself, Rosie,' Dunstan said a little roughly, and Rosie guessed that he saw her unease. She forced a smile. This was no way to behave on this marvellous adventure!

'And we'll be seeing each other again very soon,' she told him. 'Tomorrow morning at the exhibition.'

'Don't worry, we'll be there to meet the rest of the party,' Bennett assured them all. 'And now I really think Rosie and I had better leave. My sister's carriage has arrived for us.'

Rosie hardly needed to see Will's mouth twist. Bennett's comment seemed to say it all. She was being whisked away to the gloss of his world, while Will and the others, including her own father and brother, went off to the rowdiness of the Lamb Tavern. Edwin had said it was all right for a short stay, and that they were lucky to get in anywhere, with London bursting at the seams with visitors for the exhibition.

But a while later, in the spacious elegance of Alice Naylor's home, the contrast between her surroundings and the Lamb Tavern couldn't be more marked. What was the matter with her, Rosie asked herself? She shook herself out of her introspective mood, and knew that if it hadn't been for Bennett's connections, she too would be staying in far less comfortable rooms than these! She loved everything on sight, and Alice Naylor was agreeably surprised at Rosie's quick wit and fresh charm. Her voice was softly modulated, the accent warm and not over-countrified. It was also quite clear, to Alice's faint relief, that the girl was not in the least in love with Bennett. She was charming, but far too young for him, of course. The certainty that Rosie's heart was still intact as far as her brother was concerned made Alice especially warm towards her.

'We are to have visitors for afternoon tea, my dears,' Alice included them both. 'Lady Fitzgerald is dying to see you, Bennett, and to meet you, Rosie. She and Lord Fitzgerald will be arriving about four o'clock.'

Rosie smiled nervously. Never having met any of the aristocracy before, she felt very apprehensive. Her feelings obviously showed.

'Don't worry, Rosie, Lydia will love you,' Bennett smiled reassuringly.

'How—please forgive my ignorance—but how do I address her?' she asked, her cheeks flaming. She hadn't expected this meeting to happen so soon. There was so much to get used to so quickly. The crowds, and the strange, quick voices with their incomprehensible language...it was English, but the phrases didn't make sense to her, and it was only later that Bennett told her it was the peculiar rhyming slang that Londoners used. Added to that, the noise... Rosie had given no thought to how noisy the city would be. Every sound seemed magnified because people shouted so much, and because of the volume of traffic on the cobbled streets. The sounds of wheels were magnified even more because of them. In the ride from Paddington it seemed too that every street was burdened with costermongers selling their wares; from baked potato men and coffee stalls, to organ grinders with gaily dressed monkeys perched on their shoulders, and street acrobats in danger of being crushed by the traffic. London was a bewildering cacophony of noise and smells and people, and Alice Naylor's house was a haven of peace right now. Rosie had never expected it to be quite so strange.

She heard Bennett's understanding voice. 'Just call her Lady Lydia, Rosie, and stop looking so worried! She won't eat you, I promise!'

'You'd like to see your room, my dear,' Alice was saying briskly, and the next minute a maid appeared in answer to her bell summons, bobbing neatly to Alice and waiting for instructions. Rosie was almost agog at the sight of the girl in her prim black dress with the starched and frilled white apron of dazzling whiteness, as she was at this beautiful house. She was told to follow Maisie, and come down as soon as she had refreshed herself, as Alice delicately put it.

By the second flight of stairs Maisie had dropped her formal manner and grinned cheekily at Rosie. They were about the same age, Rosie realised, but this Maisie seemed years more worldly-wise than she was. For the first time Rosie knew what city folk meant when they referred to others as country cousins. Folk here had a slickness that was missing in the country—for good or bad wasn't the point. They were just different, and at that moment Rosie was feeling very much out of her element.

'Up from the country, are you, ducks?' Maisie said. 'Nasty smelly place, ain't it? I went there once. Got me boots all covered in shite-diddley-dite. Up 'ere for the exhibition, are yer?'

'That's right,' Rosie said. 'My father and brother have got their work exhibited. The House of Willow.'

'My Gawd, Cookie was sayin' summat about that. Doin' well, ain't it? I ain't bin there meself. Might go before it's finished, I daresay,' she said unconcernedly.

Rosie looked at her in astonishment. Didn't Maisie realise this exhibition was just about the most exciting thing to occur in England for years! 'Don't you want to see it, Maisie?'

The maid shrugged. 'I'd rather spend me free time with me boy,' she winked at Rosie. 'He works down the fish market at Billingsgate. You got a boy, miss?'

It was obvious Maisie didn't give a

thought to Bennett Naylor being Rosie's 'boy'. He'd be too old and stuffy, and one of the 'nobs'. It was clear she'd quickly categorised Rosie as nearer her own class, and Rosie wasn't sure whether to be pleased or annoyed because of it. But Maisie wasn't waiting for an answer. She threw open the door of the biggest bedroom Rosie had ever seen, with a real bathroom alongside, with taps and running water in a basin, and a smart, elaborately decorated water closet besides. And this was to be exclusively Rosie's, for the duration of her stay. She was dazzled by it.

She told Maisie she would unpack her own luggage, wanting to be alone and to explore this vast room by herself. From the window she saw a park with shady trees and ladies and gentlemen taking the afternoon air. The whole area had an aura of quiet gentility about it, and it seemed no time at all before the sound of carriage wheels drawing up outside drew Rosie's eyes to the street once more. Her heart hammered fast as she heard a distant church clock strike the hour of four, and realised this must be Lord and Lady Fitzgerald. And she was up here skulking in her bedroom, instead of being downstairs to meet them.

Face flaming, Rosie made her way

quickly down the winding staircase, to find Bennett waiting for her below. Too late Rosie realised she should have changed out of her travelling dress into another, as she went into the drawing-room with Bennett and saw his sister's attire. But she had not changed, and there was an end to it. She felt distinctly uncomfortable as the two other people in the room turned to look at her, and felt a little like a pinned butterfly as Lady Fitzgerald examined her through a lorgnette, and Lord Fitzgerald's eyes widened with unexpected pleasure.

'So this is Miss Rosie Nash,' Lady Lydia said at last. 'Come here and let me see you properly. Turn around, gel!'

Rosie stood still in astonishment, and then pivoted once. Her blue eyes met those of Lady Lydia, and clashed momentarily. 'I'm pleased to meet you, Lady Lydia,' she murmured.

'Are you? Well, that's as it should be. What do you think, Vivian?'

Lord Fitzgerald gave a low chuckle. 'I think she's a very pleasing sight. She'll grace any man's dinner table.'

'So she will. You may put your ogling eyes back in place now,' Lady Lydia said severely. 'If her relatives are as handsome as Miss Rosie Nash, they'll do well enough.'

Rosie was suddenly furious at being spoken of as if she was a servant. As if she was practically invisible, instead of being a guest in this house. And the inference that her father's and brother's work might depend on the kind of impression they made to toffee-nosed people such as these, angered her anew. She forgot all about being nervous, her eyes flashing at the newcomers.

'They already do well enough at home, Lady Lydia. Their work has the mark of quality, and there are none finer than the House of Willow baskets.'

'They certainly have a champion in you!' Lady Fitzgerald gave a sudden laugh. 'I like a young gel of spirit. I like you, Rosie Nash. You could teach some of these debutante gels a thing or two with their simpering ways. I'm eager to meet this father and brother of yours. If they're anything like you, I think we shall have a very lively soirée tomorrow night.'

'Tomorrow night—then I had better let them know in the morning,' Rosie began, her former anxiety about this meeting completely dissolved. Lady Lydia had a frank bossiness, but somehow it didn't annoy Rosie any more. There was an honest directness about her that she could relate to. She was about to learn of Lady Lydia's quicksilver whims as well.

As Maisie appeared with the silver teapot and began to pour out the five dainty cups of tea, Lydia suddenly clapped her hands, her eyes dancing with amusement.

'We shall let them know this evening, Rosie Nash! We shall all go in a party to this tavern where Bennett has arranged for their stay, and go slumming for an hour or so. What fun! Well, is it agreed? Don't you think it a splendid idea?'

'I'm not so sure, m'dear,' Lord Vivian began, but his wife waved him aside impatiently.

'Of course you agree, Vivian. Don't be tiresome. Rosie here will be happy to see her family again, I'm sure, and it will give the Nash men time to get to know us a little before coming to the house tomorrow evening. That's reasonable, don't you think? Bennett dear, give me your approval, do!'

'I can hardly do otherwise, Lydia,' he said with a dry smile. 'You'll get your own way in the end, as you always do, so we may as well all give in right away!'

Lydia beamed at him. 'You're a dear boy, as always, Bennett, and why some young gel hasn't wormed her way into your affections yet, I'll never know. Still, you could so easily have picked the wrong one, so perhaps it's better as it is. So tell me all about the country, Bennett, and you too, Rosie dear,' she said sweepingly, 'and when we've had dinner, we shall go off to this tavern. You did invite us for dinner, didn't you, Alice?'

'Naturally,' Alice replied, poker-faced. 'If you will excuse me for just a moment, I want to have a few words with cook.'

She moved quickly, to instruct cook that they would be five for dinner instead of three, and wishing she could stand up to Lydia the way Rosie had done so effectively. But she couldn't, and never would, and she knew she would continue to be Lydia's shadow for as long as their friendship lasted. It had its compensations, Alice comforted herself. It opened doors to a spinster lady that would remain firmly closed without the Fitzgeralds' patronage.

In the drawing room the quartet of people began to learn more about each other. Lydia, too, saw at once that Rosie would never marry Bennett, and put on her thinking-cap as to which of the young officers might be man enough for this vivacious, wilful young woman with the stunning blue eyes and peach-blossom skin. Clearly she was wasted on clod-hoppers, and presented in the right circles she could be positively breathtaking. Given more suitable clothes than the miserable rag she was wearing now, and with her hair coiffed more fashionably...the gel needed someone to take her in hand, and produce a swan from the little country duckling.

And Rosie was suddenly quailing at the thought of Will Merrick's reaction when she appeared at the Lamb Tavern that night, accompanied by this impossibly arrogant and condescending woman and her retinue. She knew only too well what Will would think. He'd think this had all been Rosie's doing, and that she was flaunting herself with her fine friends, just to show him how far beneath her she thought Will Merrick was.

If it was written in letters of fire across the sky, Rosie knew this night's visit could only widen the gulf that already existed between Will and herself. The gulf that seemed destined to be a bottomless pit.

Chapter 17

There was a rustle of excitement at the Lamb Tavern that evening. A fine carriage had drawn up in the courtyard outside, and necks craned to see the occupants.

' 'Tis a splendid sight, whoever the lady be,' one of the Moule villagers said excitedly. 'Can it be the Queen, do 'ee think?'

Guffaws of laughter followed his words. The grinning Cockneys at the next bench were enjoying these slow-talking clods and their wild suggestions.

'What would Queen Vicky be doin' round this dump of a night?' one sniggered. 'Ain't you turds seen no reg'lar ladies and gents 'fore now? Plenty o' toffs to be seen in the smoke, an' if you're wantin' to spare a copper or two, me an' Joe'll tak' yer round the sights.'

He realised no one was taking any notice of him any more, as the fashionable party made their way towards the tavern, amid a flurry of expectation for a good night's trade from the tavern-keeper.

' 'Tis your young maid, Mr Nash, sir,' the haberdasher said in astonishment, turning round eyes towards Dunstan and Edwin. 'Accompanyin' these fine folks. Well, I never did! Jus' fancy that now.'

Dunstan had half-risen from his bench as he too recognised Rosie through the thick green glass tavern windows. Edwin was already on his way to welcome the group into the tavern and tossing a request over his shoulder to make room for them. While the giggling daughters of the haberdasher suddenly realised that Will Merrick was no longer bothering to flirt with them, even in the half-hearted way he had, and was sitting bolt upright, his handsome face tight with anger.

A waft of perfume entered the smoky

tavern with the elegant group, and the gent waved a lace-edged handkerchief under his nose as if everything about the place was distasteful to him. Will saw Rosie's eyes seek him out, and he glared back, noting the school teacher standing protectively close to her.

Dunstan moved forward immediately, and waited for Bennett to make the introductions.

'Lady Fitzgerald, may I introduce Mr Dunstan Nash and Mr Edwin Nash of the House of Willow,' he said, then to the country men he introduced the lady and gentlemen and his sister, Alice.

'We are very pleased to make your acquaintance, my Lady,' Dunstan said gravely. 'And honoured that you come here this evening. May we offer you some refreshment?'

'I think not,' Lord Vivian began, but his wife waved him aside. She seated herself on the bench next to Edwin, leaving scarce room for the others to squeeze in.

'Oh, don't be so stuffy Vivian. Once in a while let's go native,' Lydia said imperiously, not even realising that she might offend by her words. The majority of the Moule folk were too goggle-eyed to notice anyway, and the others, who were used to the occasional spectacle of the gentry slumming it, soon turned back to their own pursuits.

'Lady Lydia,' Rosie said suddenly, 'may I introduce Mr Will Merrick, who grows the willows on his father's farm for our baskets?'

She indicated Will, wanting to bring him into the little circle, and not understanding just why he should look at her so hatefully. She was thrilled to be in such company, and failed to see that Will was humiliated by what he saw as her clumsy attempt to show him up. Lady Lydia was nothing if not an astute woman, and saw at once that there was something between these two, if only animosity at the moment.

She graciously acknowledged Will's abrupt rise to his feet at the introduction and his mumbled comment.

'Then I think it only right that Mr Will Merrick should be invited to our little soirée tomorrow evening too,' Lady Lydia said gaily. She turned to Dunstan. 'That is why we are all here, Mr Nash, to say that the frivolities will be tomorrow evening, and we look forward to seeing you and your son there—and Mr Merrick too. About seven-thirty, I think. You will all have spent a tiring day at the exhibition, but I hope you will not be too tired to enjoy a little diversion and see how we quaint city folk live!'

Her laugh trilled out, and Rosie felt

hot with embarrassment at that moment, sensing the faint mockery in the words. She hoped and yet dreaded that Will would come. She wanted him there...but if he was merely going to scowl the whole evening, it might be better if he did not come. When the party rose to go, after sipping barely a mouthful of the refreshment offered to them, she managed to linger on the pretext of saying a few words to her brother, and caught hold of Will's arm.

'Please come, Will. I'm told the house is magnificent, and if it's any more so than Miss Naylor's, I'm sure it will be something to remember. Don't be stuffy, Will, please.'

'Why should I want to come and look at other folks' houses?' he growled. 'From the looks of you, it's already made an impression on you. Some of us aren't so easily impressed, just because of a person's riches.'

'Is that what you think, Will Merrick?' she said in an angry whisper. 'Are you sure it's not that you think you'll be at a disadvantage because of the young officers and the fine manners at the Fitzgerald house? If that's the case, then you're quite right to stop away.'

'I haven't said I'll stop away,' he said disagreeably, and Rosie hid a smile, knowing that he would be there. In some ways she felt infinitely wiser than he, and not only because of her interest in book-learning and school teaching. But she was glad to be out of the tavern, and after bidding her father and brother goodbye, back in the lurching carriage on the way to Alice's house once more. On the way Lydia tapped at the driver to take them by way of Hyde Park, for Rosie to see the great glass building for the first time.

Although it was dusk now the immense structure still had a fairy-tale appearance as it loomed skywards, framed by an indigo sky and the darkening verdant grasses and trees of the park. The flags waved in the breeze, and Rosie felt a quickening of excitement, realising how vast was the undertaking, and just how many influential people would have examined her menfolk's work.

She fell asleep that night the minute her head touched the pillow, and was awake early the next day to the new and noisy sounds of a London morning, so different from the quiet of the country. It was impossible to linger in bed, and neither did she want to, with the prospect of the exciting day ahead. The maid assisted her with her toilet, and informed her that her mistress and Mister Bennett were already downstairs, both being early risers. They were to go to the exhibition soon after breakfast, since Mister Bennett had told Miss Alice that the travelling club would want to be there the whole day, though it was obvious from the maid's inflexion that most ladies and gentlemen wouldn't appear there until after midday.

Her tone did nothing to deflate Rosie's enthusiasm. She was faintly relieved too that Alice herself declined to join the Moule Club on the excursion to the exhibition. There was no need to put on airs, Rosie thought guiltily. They could just be themselves, and perhaps she could cajole Will into a better mood about the evening soirée. The thought made her spirits rise. At least she would be able to spend some time with him today!

She and Bennett met the rest of them at the appointed place. Already it seemed as if all roads led to Hyde Park and the great crystal palace that looked even more spectacular in daylight. The colours and fabrics of the different attire of the visitors added to the vivacity of the scene, and the Moule Club made its determined way to the entrance, as excited as any of them.

'It's a good thing you had all the ale you wanted last night,' Dunstan smiled at the haberdasher, known for his drinking capabilities. 'There's none allowed here, I understand.'

'You'll find plenty to quench your thirst,'

Bennett put in. 'There's tea and coffee, raspberry vinegar, soda water, ginger beer and orangeade and plenty more, all at sixpence a time. You'll find ices too, and sandwiches, pies and bread, butter and cheese if you're peckish later on.'

'Does he have the catering rights?' Will said shortly to Rosie, as they made their way across the summer grass. She looked at him in exasperation.

'Will, why are you so objectionable all the time?' she asked him. 'Can't you enjoy the day like the rest of us?'

'And the night too? Am I supposed to enjoy the prospect of being made to feel foolish in front of a collection of dandies?' The words were out before he could stop them, and he chewed his lip savagely. He didn't really care for Rosie Nash to know that he was agitated at the thought of attending the Fitzgeralds' soirée. Not least because he had never envisaged such a thing, and knew he would feel poorly turned out beside the young officers Rosie had mentioned. He despised himself for admitting he might feel inferior, and Will Merrick had never felt inferior to any man yet.

Rosie, who had worn one of her new outfits that day, and was feeling a little piqued because Will didn't appear to have noticed how fine she looked, began to think him as petulant as any of the children at the village school.

'Don't come then,' she moved away from him impatiently, and went to join her father and brother. 'I shan't miss you if you're in that mood!'

Once inside the building Rosie forgot all about her argument with Will, and stood in awe-struck wonder for a few minutes while her eyes took in the scene. The building was so huge it included three tall elm trees that were merely enclosed in the transept, giving an added dimension of space to the interior. The exhibits were so varied as to take the breath away, and it would take days to look at each one in anything like enough detail.

For her and her menfolk the House of Willow stand was of the most immediate interest, and passing through the great show-pieces Rosie felt a momentary unease that their own stand might seem homely and unimportant compared with the more valuable exhibits. She couldn't bear it if her father and brother's high hopes and pride were dashed...

She need not have worried. To Rosie's pleasure and astonishment the House of Willow stand was attracting considerable crowds, and she saw at once how artistically it had all been arranged, with the explanatory cards and her own drawings adding to the basketware and the gaiety of Jess's needlework.

Bennett recognised a gentleman of his acquaintance nearby, and introduced him and his lady companion to the Nash family.

'So you are the basket-makers,' the gentleman said. 'I congratulate you both on a fine display, and from what I've been hearing, substantial orders will be coming your way, dear sirs!'

He nodded and moved on, and Rosie felt her heart swell with pride as her brother smiled delightedly at her. It would all be worth while if the Nash name could be revered, instead of being slightly suspect as it was in Moule.

They spent the whole day at the exhibition, and were exhausted at the end of it. She and Bennett parted from the others, with Rosie urging Edwin to try and make Will relax a little and come to the soirée. Lady Lydia would be offended if he did not. And so would she... She caught the hint of laughter in her brother's eyes and grinned, knowing she was young and selfish enough to want the best of both worlds!

She wore a lovely gown that evening, especially made for the visit to Lady Lydia's house. It was of pale green watered silk, with fetching little bows of purple velvet around the hem and décolleté neckline. Above the neckline Rosie's creamy skin rose out delectably enough to attract every male eye, without being either blatant or unfashionable. Even so, she felt unnerved at the thought of being among so many elegant people, especially when Lydia's town house seemed like a palace to her, with its costly paintings of past Fitzgeralds adorning the walls along with genuine masterpieces.

She was glad to have the support of Bennett and his sister, and sought out her own kin among the groups of well-dressed women and fine gentlemen. The officers in their uniforms almost outshone their ladies, and Rosie found herself the centre of a small group of them. If she was flattered, she felt less so when she realised Will had arrived with her father and brother, looking very uneasy; but within minutes it seemed it was Will who was attracting the attention of the ladies. She was near enough to hear some of the conversation.

'Do tell us, Mr Merrick, how the willows are grown for the baskets! So intriguing to read about it at the exhibition! And you actually grow them, do you?'

'I do, ma'am.' Will kept a straight face as they gushed around him. 'Me and a hundred other farmers in the Levels.'

'Do they all talk like you, Mr Merrick?

Forgive me, but it's such an attractive accent! And what are these Levels? Is it not all horribly marshy in Somerset? I confess, it's a part of the country I'm not at all familiar with.'

Will smiled faintly. Oh, Rosie could just see how these city folk could be charmed by the sight of him tonight. Rudely healthy, his dark hair neater than usual, his blue eyes aglitter in this company where he had no wish to look or sound foolish, his strong, square jaw at a determined tilt. Dressed in suitable fashion, while not kowtowing in the least, he looked what he was—a dashing, virile young farmer, and to these ladies, young and frivolous and matrons alike, he was a novelty in a city hungry for novelties. Dunstan and Edwin Nash had their own circle of admirers wanting to know about the basket-making, but it was Will who held the bulk of the female attention that evening, and Rosie felt a burning jealousy at the way he was lapping it all up like a cat with the cream.

She heard him give his husky, throaty laugh, and she suddenly realised he was well aware of the fact that she was close by. He was enjoying all this, Rosie thought furiously! Enjoying the fact that, after hating the thought of coming here, Will Merrick was an unexpected success, and Rosie Nash was discomfited by it all!

'We call them withies, ma'am,' he went on in his slow, lazy drawl. 'And yes, the ground is marshy, and subject to flooding every winter, but the withies like their feet in water. It's the perfect crop for the wetlands.'

'You called it the Levels. What is that, pray?'

'Why, 'tis the term we use because of the nature of the land,' he turned to the pretty young miss who had asked the question, and Rosie didn't miss the way she coloured slightly, as Will's gaze took in the girl's slender shape and rested finally on her full red lips. 'You'll have heard of Sedgemoor if you've done your history, no doubt? Where the old battle was fought in the Duking Days? 'Twas a bad setting for a battle, with no cover for either side, since the land is flat and open, and in fact its best industries are just what Mr Nash's family and mine are engaged upon. The river Parrett flows in from the sea at Bridgwater, and the land is criss-crossed with ditches that we call rhines, giving plenty of rich, moist conditions for growing the crop. And you'll know that the basket-makers of Somerset are famous.'

The girl was listening with rapt attention. 'How fascinating you make it all sound, Mr Merrick,' she breathed. 'Mama, don't you think we should visit this part of the country that Mr Merrick has been telling us about? It's so tiresome in town this year, with all the visitors crowding into it. The country sounds heavenly!'

Rosie saw Will dart a mocking little smile her way. It implied that if Rosie Nash had her admirers flocking round her, then Will's attractions for the opposite sex were just as potent. Didn't she know that, Rosie fumed? He didn't need to try and prove anything to her... She was ridiculously relieved when the girl's Mama said coolly that the family would be travelling abroad as they always did, and that marshy farmlands would be no good for the family health, begging Mr Merrick's pardon.

Lady Lydia had also been listening to the various exchanges of conversation, and congratulating herself that bringing these countryfolk here tonight had been a burst of inspiration. When the House of Willow became famous, as she had no doubt it would, it would be firmly established that they were first introduced to London society at the home of Lord and Lady Fitzgerald. As yet Vivian had been tardy in obtaining orders for the House of Willow, being of a more thoughtful nature than his volatile wife, but she had no doubt that orders would come flooding in.

Lydia was also nothing if not an observer of human nature, and she was certain now

404

that there was or had been something of a close association between Bennett's young assistant and the farmer's boy. And while she acknowledged that they made a handsome couple, she was quite sure the girl could do far better for herself. The idea of making Rosie Nash her protegée was simmering in her mind as she watched the young officers buzzing around her like bees around a honey-pot.

As the Nash men drew near, in their gradual circulating of the drawing-room, Lydia spoke imperiously.

'Mr Nash, this lovely gel of yours deserves a season in town. It's appalling for her to be wasted in the country when you can see what a success she is! The gel positively glows in the right setting. What say you allow her to stay for a month or two? She would be adequately chaperoned, and it would amuse me to provide for her. Well, Mr Nash?'

Dunstan bit his tongue at the slight to his own background. By now he had assessed the kind of woman Lady Lydia was, and that her offer was genuine and kindly enough, if badly phrased. He looked at his daughter, who was truly shimmering tonight, he thought. Perhaps the lady was right...

'If it's what Rosie wants, then I have no objection,' he commented. 'But my daughter has a mind of her own, Lady Lydia, and you must ask her!'

'If she didn't have a mind of her own, I wouldn't want her,' Lydia retorted. 'I've no time for wishy-washy young women and the gel appeals to me. Well then, Rosie. What say you? Do you stay?'

It was one thing to toy with the idea in theory, and quite another to have it thrown at her so suddenly in the midst of this company! Rosie was non-plussed for a moment, aware of the intense look on Will's face as he too wondered about her answer. But why shouldn't she stay? Hadn't she wanted a breathing space while she sorted out her own turbulent emotions? She glanced at Bennett, patiently prepared to agree to whatever she wished.

'I'm not sure I can, Lady Lydia,' Rosie said swiftly. 'I'm needed at the school.'

'I'm willing to manage without you for a time, Rosie,' she heard Bennett say at once. 'One of the older girls can assist me as she did before you came. Please don't allow that to stand in the way of Lady Lydia's offer!'

Rosie wasn't sure if he meant that she wasn't really needed at Moule village school or not. She was about to say she needed to sleep on it before she decided on such a different way of life, when she saw Will lean towards the pretty young girl who seemed so besotted with him, and whisper something in her ear. The girl gave a small tinkling laugh, and the sudden warmth between them both put the words into Rosie's mouth before she could stop them.

'Then if I'm not needed at home, I'd be delighted to stay for a while, Lady Lydia, though I do hope Miss Naylor won't think me ungrateful after her generous hospitality.'

'My dear Rosie, of course I shan't,' Alice said at once. 'It will be a grand opportunity for you to share the Fitzgeralds' home for a few months, and Lady Lydia and I see so much of each other, I'm sure we shall still be very much acquainted.'

Besides, Rosie thought privately, since she had no intention of marrying Bennett Naylor, her moving out of his sister's house would relieve them both of the slight feeling of embarrassment that the situation produced.

'That's settled then, and I shall draw up a programme of events immediately,' Lydia said with her usual verve.

Afterwards, Rosie couldn't really have said why she had accepted so readily. Her mind had been half made up before, of course, but it had needed that small trigger of Will's attention to the other girl to make her piqued enough to agree. It would be exciting and invigorating, if Lydia's own enthusiasm for it was any pointer, and Lady Lydia clearly saw Rosie's emergence into London society as her new cause... But when the time came for everyone else to board the train at Paddington Station for the West, and Rosie and Alice Naylor were saying goodbye to their respective menfolk, Rosie felt a sharp pang at being parted from all she knew and loved. Especially Will... When Dunstan and Edwin had each hugged her and she had made them promise to write to her, there was a chance among the milling crowds on the station for a few minutes with Will. They were pressed close by the groups of people, and she risked putting her hand on his arm, forgetting their animosity in the realisation that it might be months before they would see each other again.

'I shall miss you, Will,' she said with a catch in her voice. She looked up into his eyes as if she wanted to imprint his image on her memory for ever, just as if it wasn't already imprinted on her heart. Right now, at the moment of parting, Rosie regretted every foolish misunderstanding that had ever occurred between them.

'You won't have time to miss me,' he

said roughly. 'You'll be too busy with your new friends.'

'But never too busy to forget the old, Will.' She pleaded with him to say something, anything, to let her know he would miss her too. In the end, she gave up all thoughts of pride, and asked him, 'Won't you miss me too, Will, just a little?'

The fierce look he gave her made her flinch. Had everything between them meant nothing to him after all, she thought raggedly? Even the momentous night he had seduced her...had that meant so little to him too? Were men such different animals to women then, feeling nothing but the physical needs of the moment, and knowing none of the glory of love, only the savagery of lust? At that moment, Rosie believed it to be so.

'I'll miss 'ee,' Will resorted to the local dialect he rarely used. 'Like a thorn under my flesh, Rosie! We've done nothing but irritate each other for so long now, a time apart is all to the good. I wish 'ee well of your time in London, and I daresay you'll be far above the likes of we poor countryfolk when you return to us. Or perhaps you won't be returning at all, if one of they fine officers catches your eye again.'

'You're a fool if that's what you think,

Will,' she said, choking a little.

'Aye, I'm a fool. A country, clod-hopping fool,' he said calmly. 'And you're Miss Rosie Nash, who's going to stay with the real lord and lady for as long as it suits 'em both. Wouldn't you say that puts us as far apart as 'tis possible to be?'

Rosie swallowed the choking lump in her throat. They were saying all the wrong words to each other. She wanted to clasp him in her arms and tell him she would never want anyone but him. She wanted to feel his mouth on hers, and the young strength of his body pressed close to hers. She wanted...oh, she wanted...

'Will you write to me?' All her pride seemed to be scattered to the four winds now as she asked the question.

'I was never any good at letter writing. Never had the cause for it. You'll find out all you need to know about Moule doings from your father and brother—and I daresay the school teacher can pen a fine letter.'

Just as she had done in the withy field so long ago, Rosie felt a wild urge to stamp her foot at the frustration she felt. Will Merrick was without doubt the most irritating, impossible man on God's earth, and she hated him as much as she loved him. The knowledge of it swept over her as

410

insistently as it had done before. However much she hated him, it was as nothing compared with the burning love she felt for him, and always would. It was a deep-rooted basic love that eclipsed all others, and he was too blind, too stubborn to see it. What did a little time in London matter, compared with the certainty in her heart that they were destined to spend eternity together?

If she could have read Will's mind then, she would have seen all the black despair he felt at seeing her slipping away from him, and unable to do a thing about it. Will Merrick wouldn't beg a woman to marry him and live in a farmhouse, when so many dazzling opportunities were open to her. To his mind, Rosie had already made her choice, and the constant company of the foppish aristocrats would turn her head as surely as night followed day. Rosie would have no time for him now. Rosie was already part of another world that didn't include him...

A sudden flurry of activity told them the train was about to leave, and the Moule travellers who weren't already on board had better do so at once. The onlookers seemed to press forward in a bid to wave their last goodbyes, regardless of being enveloped in a great cloud-burst of steam and smoke from the engine.

Rosie found herself pushed closer to Will, and for a moment his arms went out to steady her.

It was more than either of them could do to resist the contact. Cocooned in a gauzy haze of steam, she felt the swift pressure of his lips on hers, and the sweet familiarity of his touch. Her response was immediate, her young body yearning towards him, her soft lips delighting in this unexpected, poignant farewell. It lasted barely seconds before other hands were hauling Will onto the train, and Alice Naylor was urging her to stand well back from the billowing, lung-filling smoke.

There was no time to speak of love, but love was in Rosie's heart and in her eyes as she tried to make out Will's shape in the window of the train as it chugged slowly out of the station. She wondered desperately if he felt it too, or if, from the dark, anguished exclamation he made as he left her, he was regretting he had made even that one small concession towards her. One kiss...as the train took him away from her, Rosie felt as instantly deflated as she had felt ecstatic seconds before. As if with Will's leaving, all the life-blood was draining out of her. It frightened her a little to know that one person could have such power over another, without even caring.

Chapter 18

The few weeks Rosie had originally intended to stay in London stretched to three months. Lady Lydia had arranged such a round of entertainment, theatre going and parties, strolls in the parks where they would meet the young officers, and more visits to the exhibition, where they even glimpsed the Queen and Prince Albert on one occasion, that the time flew by in a whirl of frivolity.

Yet Rosie couldn't say she was altogether comfortable in her new surroundings. Lydia was generous in the extreme, insisting that Rosie had gowns and bonnets and muffs made up for her by Lydia's own dressmaker, and on the surface she looked the typical young lady of fashion, admired wherever she went.

Early on she had a moments' awkwardness at one of the Fitzgeralds' party evenings, when one young lady after another performed on the pianoforte, or sang a ditty, or recited... Rosie began to feel inadequate, having few musical talents, when she remarked that she was quite adept at drawing a silhouette likeness.

The materials were brought to her at once, and she charmed everyone by her lightning pictures of host and hostess, and anyone else who was interested.

'You constantly surprise me, Rosie,' Lydia said with pleasure, ever interested in something new. 'Can you also draw from memory? I fancy Miss Naylor would appreciate a likeness of her brother!'

'I have already done one for her,' Rosie said at once. She thought quickly of the Moule folk. 'There are some real country characters in my village. Would you care to see my impression of one or two?'

They crowded round, eager to see her slender fingers at work. Vicar Washbourne came first, of course, that saturnine face with the hawk nose and dominant personality...then Will's buxom mother, plump and homely as a pigeon pie... Sketched with affection and never with malice, the likenesses sprang to life for the townfolk to admire. Rosie drew Daisy's small, pretty profile, with the wayward tresses of fair hair curling round her neck, then the ancient, craggy outline of old Isaac Hale...

Suddenly she didn't want to do any more. Isaac Hale reminded her too much of Cyrus, whom she hadn't thought about for weeks, and never wanted to think about again. She asked to be excused from any

414

more, and those dandies who had been lucky enough to have their likenesses of themselves drawn were well pleased by their apparent exclusivity.

Rosie took the Moule silhouettes to her room that evening, smiling gently at Daisy's profile, and filled with a sudden longing to see her again and hear her piping voice. The vicar's face made her smile. Mrs Merrick's made her wistful, linking her inevitably with Will. While Isaac Hale... Rosie gave an unaccountable shudder. For an uncanny moment she could smell the odorous grandson, Cyrus Hale, as his arms closed round her on the first occasion he'd pretended to save her from the rhine. The whiff of the smithy and his own animal sweat could still permeate her nostrils as if he stood close to her... Rosie found herself tearing old Isaac's likeness into a score of pieces, as if it was Cyrus himself she destroyed.

The feeling of unease as she lay in bed that night wouldn't go away. Why should thoughts of Cyrus disturb her? He was many miles away, and couldn't hurt her here. Yet it only added to the growing feeling that it was time she went home. Lady Lydia was kindness itself to her, but London wasn't home. All the splendid sights she had seen, and the way Lydia dressed her up like a little pet, couldn't compensate for her own family, and for people who were more real to her than these smart ladies and gentlemen with their fads and fancies that changed direction like the wind. Rosie secretly found them all shallow, and she missed home. Most of all, she missed Will.

True to his word he hadn't written one letter to her, and she couldn't bring herself to break the silence between them. She had gleaned news of him through her father and brother, and occasionally Bennett had referred to him, as if knowing how badly she would want news of him. But none of them said what she most needed to know...whether Will missed her in the way she missed him. If he still thought of her at all, still loved her, and needed her...and she would never know, stuck here! She might as well be a million miles away from home, and despite her frustrations she didn't quite know how to tell Lady Lydia that she wanted to go home, without sounding terribly ungrateful.

In early September a letter came from Edwin that enabled her to do so without further thought.

'Jess and I have decided to be married in October, Rosie, so I hope you'll be coming home in good time for that. We want to ask a favour of you and Pa. Will you have Daisy to stay at Briar Cottage for a week or two after the wedding, so that Jess and I can have a little time on our own?'

Rosie went immediately to see Lydia in the morning-room where she was reading her own correspondence, and told her Edwin's news, adding that she felt she must return home very soon now in order to help with the preparations.

'Of course, my dear, though I shall be sorry to see you go. I had hoped you might feel inclined to stay for ever, but I see by the eagerness on your face that home still tugs at you, Rosie!'

She blushed. 'Please don't think I'm being ungrateful, Lady Lydia.'

Lydia waved aside her embarrassment with an airy gesture. 'Of all things, child! Naturally you must go home whenever it suits you, and if no young man has caught your eye by now, then could it be that there's someone in the country who will be waiting impatiently for your arrival?'

Rosie smiled wanly. 'I'm not sure.'

'Then make sure, gel! I thought you were a gel of spirit like myself! There are more ways than one of getting what you want. And here's something else to cheer you up—another letter for you tucked amongst mine. Sit in the window and read it, my dear.'

For a moment Rosie's heart leapt, and then she saw Bennett's precise handwriting on the envelope. She seated herself on the window-seat where it was warm and sunny, and perused Bennett's lengthy paragraphs, skimming much of the letter with a guilty feeling, until she suddenly sat upright, all the warmth of the day disappearing and leaving her with a chill, eerie feeling.

'The village goes on much the same, Rosie,' Bennett told her. 'Except that a week ago old Isaac Hale dropped down dead over his jug of ale in the Moule Inn. He wasn't even ill, at least no more than usual for a man of his years, when suddenly he looked as if he was seeing a phantom, according to the tales of his fellow drinkers, and fell across the table, cold as mutton.'

A week before Bennett had written to her... Rosie calculated how long the letter had taken to reach her, and knew that old Isaac would have died around the time she had been drawing the silhouette likenesses of the village folk. The night she had ripped his likeness into a score of pieces as if she was physically destroying Cyrus Hale himself...

She felt herself begin to shake. It couldn't be true, could it? There was no dark spirit inside her making her capable of doing this dreadful thing, was there? It was all coincidence, nothing more...just a horrible coincidence...coincidence...

'Rosie, my dear, are you ill? Bless me, but you're trembling from head to foot. You certainly won't be able to travel if you have the ague. Or was it bad news in the letter? Tell me at once if it was that?'

Rosie focused her eyes on Lydia as if coming out of a fog. The shivering began to subside. The shifting ground beneath her feet settled into position once more and became the carpet in the Fitzgeralds' morning-room. The sun shone in a blue sky outside, and the spectres of superstition receded a little. If she allowed herself to believe in them, she was being as gullible as the villagers themselves...

'It's a letter from Bennett, Lady Lydia, containing nothing more alarming than news of the village and the children, and the death of one very old man. It was just the combination of news that gave me a sudden shiver, that's all. I didn't mean to alarm *you!*'

The excuse sounded feeble enough, but Lydia was too taken up with her own letters to query Rosie too deeply, to Rosie's relief. She glanced through Bennett's letter again. There was another part that should have commanded more of her attention. She frowned as she re-read it.

'Far be it from me to ask you to hurry home, Rosie, when I'm sure you will be having a wonderful time with Lydia. But

419

there are times when I certainly need you here! Now that the novelty of Daisy's speech has worn off, the child has become very naughty indeed. Several times she has played truant from school in the company of Vera Yandell, who is not a good influence on her now. It's rather odd how the two of them have formed a friendship, but each seems to lead the other on, unfortunately. I fear it is an attempt on Daisy's part to regain some attention, and the situation is sometimes very vexing.'

Poor Daisy, Rosie thought at once. Despite the other children calling her dummy when she refused to speak, at least she had a kind of uniqueness then. Now she was just one of a crowd, and was clearly rebelling to make herself noticed again. The thought strengthened her resolve to go home, and she put all thoughts of Isaac Hale's untimely death from her with a determined effort.

When Alice heard the news, she wanted to make sure Rosie waited for Bennett to make the journey to London to fetch her, and to make a brief visit to his sister. But Rosie would have none of it. She had called on Alice on a private visit to inform her of her decision, and looked at her frankly now.

'Please don't ask him on my account, Alice,' she said gently. 'You must know

420

by now that I am not destined to marry Bennett, fond though I am of him. If he were to fetch me it would give people the wrong idea, I feel, and besides, I know he won't want to leave the school in the hands of one young pupil assistant for any length of time. I am quite capable of travelling alone, and my father will meet me in Bridgwater.'

Though her voice was quiet, it was quite determined. Alice realised it, and was struck anew by the girl's poise and dignity. Compared with some of the brainless young things who graced the drawing-rooms of houses like the Fitzgeralds', Rosie was a credit to her family, and Alice felt a brief regret after all that her brother hadn't captured this young girl's heart.

Lydia insisted that Rosie took all the new gowns and gifts home to Somerset, and was escorted to the train with much ceremony on the morning of her departure. Rosie was touched by Lydia's obvious sorrow at her leaving, and knew that she would never forget her kindness. An elderly acquaintance of the Fitzgeralds was also travelling West, and Rosie was put in his care for the long journey, along with her trunks and baggage. But no amount of sadness at leaving her new friends could deny the soaring joy inside her that she was going home. To her father and Edwin, and to the little cottage that could fit in one room of the elegant Fitzgeralds' home, but was still dearer to Rosie for all that. And there was more...she was going home to Will.

The one person Daisy Lawrence could relax with was Will. Will didn't sit all dreamy and still like her Ma did sometimes now. Will didn't ignore her the way Edwin did occasionally, when he said he wanted to talk to her Ma and not to Daisy. Will didn't have twenty other children on his mind as well as her the way that Sir did... Will hadn't deserted her as Rosie had, and Will didn't think her friend Vera Yandell was so awful and rude as Mr Nash had once told her she was...

On the days when she went missing Daisy could sometimes be found in the withy fields, her small body completely hidden among the rustling swaying rods, in full leaf now and nearing maturity. It was a game Daisy liked to play, to pop up suddenly like a jack-in-the-box in front of Will Merrick, and she had dragged Vera Yandell there once or twice to show her the wonderful new hiding-place she had found.

'You'll sink down in the marsh when the ground gets soggy,' Will warned her. 'Then you'll be gone for ever, and we won't have no Daisy at all!'

'Shan't come here when it's soggy then,' Daisy chanted back precociously. 'You can't find me, Will!'

She bobbed down among the rods and out of sight. He made a great to-do about searching for her, knowing full well the general route she had taken, and then swung her up in his arms like a little rag doll. She squealed with delight, her fair hair flying round her shoulders, her skirts swinging out beneath her overall. He was as tall and strong as Edwin now.

'I know something you don't,' Daisy chanted on when she could get her breath.

'Bet you don't,' Will said arrogantly. 'What does a whippersnapper like you know that a grown man don't!'

'Rosie's coming home, that's what!' Daisy said triumphantly.

He put her down among the withies, his face suddenly still with thinking, like her Ma's sometimes went. She could hear the sound of his breathing, as if he'd just been running a long way.

'How d'you know that?' Will growled at her.

'Ma told me! I know something else too. Ma's goin' to church with Edwin to get married, and I'm to stay with Rosie and Mr Nash for a coupla weeks. Why do I have to, Will?' Her voice grew resentful.

'Because married people want to be

alone for a time, that's why.' Will had that grouchy voice of his again, Daisy noted, as if he was angry with her for some reason. She pouted defiantly.

'I shan't stay. I'll run away.'

Will grabbed her wrists hard, making her squeal with fright this time. 'No, you won't. You'll stay at Briar Cottage and do as you're told and not make a fuss, do you hear? And if you don't behave yourself I shall come and thrash you with a withy rod!'

She didn't believe him. He was her hero, her sun-god, and the mischievous grin spread across her face. But he didn't smile back, and he made her promise to be good for Rosie.

'And for your Ma and Edwin too,' he said as an afterthought. 'They'll want to know you're behaving yourself, so you just remember all I said.'

He was remembering all she had said too, as he went home that day. Rosie was coming home. It shouldn't matter a damn to him. By now she had probably put on airs and an affected accent like that Lydia woman, and was used to the company of officers and gentlemen. Why should she ever look at the likes of Will Merrick again? It shouldn't matter a damn to him that she was coming home...but it did.

He was still too vividly aware of the

way she had felt in his arms, and of the way she had become so entwined in his heart, that he could hardly think sensibly about her any more. Either he became angry with himself, because of what he had done to her at the cottage that night, allowing himself to be deceived by a gypsy's lies; or else he was angry with *her*, just for being what she was, the sweetest, most adorable, most alluring woman in the world... Somehow Will found himself blaming her for just being herself, when at the same time she was everything he wanted. If this was what love did to you, he thought savagely, this deranging of the senses, then a man was better off without it! By now she would have grown too far above him anyway. If she didn't come home full of airs and graces, she'd probably be coming home to marry the school teacher after all. He was filled with a sense of doom and frustration on all sides.

As for Rosie, the day couldn't pass quickly enough. Had the journey to London seemed so tedious? All the way home her nerves seemed to be at fever-pitch, and she made only nominal conversation with her travelling companion. All she wanted was to be at home, and stepping out of the train at Bridgwater station to be enveloped in her father's warm embrace was enough to bring the stinging tears to her eyes.

'Here now, what's all this?' Dunstan said, his own throat thick, for they had never been parted for so long before. 'What will folk think—an elegant young lady of fashion brimming over with tears?'

She hugged his arm. 'Is that how I appear, Pa?' Rosie inquired shakily. 'I feel more like a lost soul come home and nothing more!'

Dunstan laughed understandingly. 'It will take a little while to re-accustom yourself, my love, but we're all eager to see you again, and yes, you look very fine! You'll outshine the bride if you're not careful!'

'Oh, I mustn't do that, Pa,' she said quickly. 'Are they very happy?'

'Of course,' he said dryly. 'So much so as to be unaware of anything else around them, which is a state only to be expected.'

'Is it?'

How unreal it sounded, how enviable, Rosie thought in a moment of bleakness. Would such a state ever happen to her? She had thought it had, once. Now it seemed as remote as the moon and stars.

The ride home took some time, and through it Rose gradually recovered herself. The first euphoria had vanished, leaving in its wake a strange lethargy. Jess and Edwin were in some seventh heaven of their own. Dunstan was telling her now of a letter that had come from London recently with some orders for the House of Willow that had made him and Edwin jubilant. Her family was more than content. Only Rosie felt uneasy, as if fate hadn't finished with her yet. It was a feeling that wouldn't leave her during the next few days, when she was re-acquainted with home and school, and folk who remarked about the new and handsome Rosie Nash, and pupils who were almost too awed to ask her questions about London and the exhibition until she made a point of discussing it with them.

Everything was as it was before, and yet everything had changed. She was not the same, except in one respect. She still loved Will Merrick, but he hadn't even bothered to come to the cottage to welcome her home. It would have been a neighbourly gesture, considering the connection between his family and hers. She didn't see him until she went to church with her family on Sunday, and then it was more than she could do to resist turning her head a little to see if he was there.

He stared straight at her, unsmilingly, and she felt the hot colour rush into her cheeks. She tried to smile at him, but he unnerved her so, she just couldn't. Instead, she let her gaze wander around the cold stone interior, seeing folk who nodded or smiled or looked plain curious at a body who bore the unmistakable mark of the city dweller in her clothes and hair, and for a moment Rosie wished she had worn something plainer than the fine silk plaid gown Lady Lydia had insisted on buying her, with its matching bonnet and lace gloves. She was altogether too fine, Rosie realised desperately, and it might very well antagonise these good people all over again...

Her eyes were drawn as if irresistibly to where Cyrus Hale sat glowering at her, his arms folded flat across his chest. The empty seat beside him reminded Rosie of his grandfather's death, and she gave a shiver, turning swiftly to the front of the church as Vicar Washbourne entered, his powerful gaze covering the whole of his congregation in one sweep.

'Let us welcome back our lost sheep into the fold,' he began at once, his voice resounding around the walls. 'And give thanks to those who see the error of their ways before it is too late.'

The text mystified Rosie until she realised that Jess and Edwin's approaching wedding was the subject of the day's sermon, and that Jess wasn't to get away

428

scot free without some reference to her past, even though the vicar had agreed to marry them in church, providing it was to be a small ceremony and in the best of taste. He dictated to them all, Rosie thought indignantly, but, stealing a glance at Jess's flushed face, she knew her future sister-in-law had been indoctrinated in the vicar's ways for too long to do anything but submit. And from the way Jess held on tightly to Edwin's hand, Rosie suspected she had begged him not to make a fuss, but to let things simmer. Once they were safely wed they would be a complete unit, Jess would be respectable, and Edwin part of the community proper.

It wasn't until the service was over and the congregation spilled out into the September sunlight that Rosie had any chance to speak to Will. And then his gaze seemed both aggressive and defensive as she broke away from her family to approach him.

'Why haven't you come to see me?' she asked at once, brushing aside the conventions.

'Why should I? So you could tease me with your fine clothes and tales of the grand times you had in London?' he said mockingly. 'Or to hear that you've decided to wed the school teacher after all? It's all we hear at the farm these days, what with Jess's wedding and Rosie Nash coming home. Ma's wanting you to come to Sunday tea.'

'How gracious you are, Will Merrick! Is that meant to be an invitation?' She could be as sarcastic as he, though her blood was racing at the thought of going to Merrick Farm that afternoon.

Out of the corner of her eye she could see his mother bustling towards them, a beaming smile on her face. Mrs Merrick stooped to kiss Rosie's cheek, then stood back to admire her.

'My, what a fine young lady you look, Rosie my love! Has our Will asked 'ee over for Sunday tea? You'll come, won't 'e? Farmer an' me want to hear all about Lunnon, and we can get precious little out o' this spark!'

'I'd love to come, Mrs Merrick,' Rosie warmed to her as always.

'That's right then.' She glanced from one to the other, her mouth pursing at the stupidity of young folk who couldn't see the wood for the trees. She spoke decisively. 'The nights be drawing in already, so our Will can take 'ee back later, my love. We'll have enough jawin' to take us into evening, I'm sure!'

For a minute Rosie thought he was going to argue, then he shrugged and said he'd see her later. Well, that was something, thought Rosie, smiling at Mrs Merrick as if they were two conspirators. As the Merricks moved off, a voice she detested sounded behind her.

'Nice to see 'ee, Miss Nash,' Cyrus Hale said gloatingly. Rosie whipped round to see his lecherous eyes taking in every bit of her. His hot eyes made her want to fold her arms about herself, but she met his gaze steadily, not wanting this oaf to know how sorely afraid she was of him still.

'I was sorry to hear about your grandfather,' she said with a tremor in her voice, remembering the strange feelings she had had on receiving the news. Cy gave an uncaring shrug.

' 'Twas 'is time to go, weren't it? I ain't a'grievin'—not unless you were thinkin' o' consolin' me, Rosie? That 'ould be a different notion!'

His guttural voice deepened to a throaty leer. She moved away from him quickly as she saw her father and brother looking around for her before going home. She wouldn't deign to answer this pig... His words floated after her.

'What a shame you missed the fair, Rosie! Somebody was asking after 'ee.'

She didn't want to think of Cory Pendle. The brief liaison with the gypsy seemed part of a different life now...and it was through Cory and Cyrus Hale that Will had come to the cottage that night, filled with drunken rage and lust-bent...it was because of those two that the sweet, fragile love between herself and Will had been besmirched...

'Rosie? Are you all right?' Jess's face suddenly seemed to loom in front of her as she stumbled a little.

'I'm fine, Jess.' For a moment she had wished she really could put a spell on the two she hated most, and was immediately appalled at herself for even thinking that way.

Jess smiled in relief. Nothing could dismay her for long these days, not even the vicar's snide remarks. In a few weeks now she would be Mrs Edwin Nash, and the very name had the sweetest sound for Jess. Rosie was merely tired after the hectic time in London, and needed time to resume her more placid life in the country, that was all...

At Merrick Farm that afternoon and evening Rosie was in sparkling form, delighting Mrs Merrick with tales of the exhibition and the fine ladies and gentlemen who paraded like peacocks in the park, and describing the Queen and her handsome Prince...finally being persuaded to draw a silhouette profile of each royal person for the Merricks to hang

432

on their wall. Mrs Merrick was charmed by everything she heard, as excited as if she had actually been to London herself. Farmer Merrick indulged the two of them, while Will added in a word now and then, so as to let his mother know he too had seen some of the wondrous sights Rosie described so vividly. But at last the shadows lengthened and Rosie said she had better go home, looking expectantly at Will.

For a moment she thought he was just going to sit there, then he rose and said abruptly he'd see her home in the farm cart. Rosie wished their relationship was as easy as Jess and Edwin's, but somehow she and Will seemed ever more strained with each other. Even when she sat beside him in the cart, his thigh bumping against hers as the horse jogged along on the rough track, it was almost impossible to believe his arms had ever crushed her to him in the wildness of passion. They were so close, and yet she felt she would never reach his heart again...

For Will the nearness of her was a sweet torment to his senses. Rosie was such a fine young woman now, seemingly far above him with her silk gown and the subtle scent of her teasing his nostrils. He was more tongue-tied than he had ever been with a woman before, and knowing it angered him. He felt unmanly, unable to make the feeblest conversation with her in the fear that she would be comparing him unfavourably with the new gentlemen friends she had found in London.

As if she could read his mind, Rosie suddenly rounded on him. 'Are we going to continue this journey in total silence, Will?' she demanded. 'You weren't so quiet when you were chattering to the haberdasher's daughters, I remember! Nor the pretty young girl at Lady Lydia's soirée! I don't fancy the cat got your tongue that night, did it?'

'I'm surprised you even noticed,' Will retorted. 'You were too busy flirting with the officers.'

'Flirting! I was merely being pleasant and trying not to appear the country cousin, that's all.'

'Is that how you thought I looked then?' He took her words as a slight against himself, and Rosie fumed at his stupidity.

'Oh no, Will dear,' she oozed sarcasm. 'You must have known what a success you were with the young ladies of fashion! I'm sure there are one or two even now who are sighing over Will Merrick!'

'Good,' he said grimly. 'It's nice to know.'

'How ungallant you are, Will,' she cried.

'You don't care how many hearts you break, do you?'

'Why should I?' He was too pent-up with the disturbance of his emotions to care what he said to her. 'Neither do you, Rosie. We're two of a kind, aren't we? Only it doesn't matter to you if you left the London dandies pining for you, does it? You had the school teacher to come back to, didn't you? I hope he doesn't mind taking second-hand goods.'

Her hand lashed out and struck him on the cheek before he said another word, and then she was pummelling at his chest furious and humiliated beyond words. He was the one who had seduced her, and now he had the gall to taunt her with it...

'You bastard, Will Merrick,' she screamed out when she could get her breath. 'That was a filthy, despicable thing to say, and just what I might have expected from a farm-clod like you! Get back to your pigs where you belong, and don't ever speak to me again, do you hear? I wish I'd never set eyes on you!'

She slid out of the cart and began running the last half mile home, tears streaming down her cheeks. Her harsh sobs made her chest ache, and the dampness of the September evening was seeping through her shoes. All around her the notorious wraith-like mist of the Levels heralded the start of less clement weather, and somewhere a dog howled in the night. Any other time Rosie might have been frightened...but right now all she wanted was to get away from Will and the shock of his words. All she wanted was to crawl home like a wounded animal, thankful to her soul that Edwin would be with Jess and her father browsing in his workshop among his baskets, so that they wouldn't see the distressed state she was in. She couldn't have faced either of them. They were men too, and a feeling of bitterness against the entire male sex was chilling her right through. After Will's degrading taunt she hated every one of them...and the bitterness went too deeply for her to recognise Will's frustration for what it was.

He didn't love her, she thought, every nerve-end trembling as her mind screamed out the truth of it. He never could have loved her, and it was all a sham. Her beautiful girlish dream that she and Will had found a true meeting of minds and souls was just so much nonsense...dreams were for children, and all a man wanted a woman for was her body. There was nothing more. Love didn't exist. Love was just another word.

Chapter 19

Jess and Edwin were married very quietly. Apart from Jess's small daughter, the Nash family and the Merricks, whom Jess counted as her closest to a real family, only a dozen curious villagers sat in the back of Moule church as Vicar Washbourne pronounced them man and wife. Rosie felt the stab of tears very close to the surface as she heard the couple make their vows, unable to resist stealing a glance at Will, who sat stiffly some yards away from her. As if this ceremony had no particular meaning for him, and he wasn't imagining, as Rosie was, that it might have been their two names the vicar was pronouncing in a loud voice now, letting all know that those whom God had joined together were united forever in His sight and therefore blessed.

Outside in the crisp October morning a small crowd of villagers had gathered to watch the occasion, and to wish them well. Jess Lawrence Nash was now respectable, despite all. The inference was clear to see on some of the gnarled faces, and the children jumped up and down in the excitement that a wedding brought into their drab lives. Vera Yandell winked at Daisy Lawrence and gave her a sly pinch as she passed to let her know in spite of her finery that day Vera was still boss.

The entire wedding party went back to Merrick Farm for cake and wine, since Mrs Merrick had insisted on Jess having things done rightly. By now Daisy was becoming fretful and naughty, and Rosie was glad to take charge of her, partly to rid her mind of the disturbing images of the glances between Jess and Edwin, that said all too clearly how much they wished this party to end so that they could be alone...partly because it was obvious that Will didn't want her around, and if he didn't want her, then she wouldn't want him, Rosie thought rebelliously...only she did, she *did*.

'You'll have heard I'm travelling to London the day after tomorrow, Farmer,' Dunstan said congenially over the wedding feast.

'Jess were telling us,' Farmer Merrick nodded. 'To do wi' this 'ere exhibition, I'm told.'

Dunstan nodded. 'The exhibition has finished this month, and the people that Rosie stayed with have contacted me. It seems the House of Willow was a great success, thanks in no small measure to Edwin's tiny pieces of workmanship, and

438

Jess's help with the fabric work!' He acknowledged both of them by raising his wine glass, and Rosie saw how they glowed at being classed together even in such a peripheral fashion.

'An' you'll be gettin' lots of orders then, will 'ee, Mr Nash?' Mrs Merrick asked.

'I believe so. Lord Fitzgerald is chairman of a committee for a gentleman's club in London that is now expanding to have branches all over the country. It seems they have decided that the House of Willow furniture is exactly right for use in their sporting rooms, where they wish to keep to a country theme. I am invited to stay at the Fitzgeralds' house in London to discuss designs and to sign contracts for firm orders. There's no doubt that Edwin and I will be kept very busy, and we shall naturally place as much of the withy ordering your way as we can, Farmer.'

'Aye well, you did right by we at the auctions,' Farmer said comfortably. 'An' nothin' gives Will an' me more pleasure than to see our various businesses flourish so well together.'

Rosie glanced at Will. From his expression it looked as if he didn't know the meaning of the word pleasure, and she sensed that he wished himself as far removed from any association with her family as possible at that moment. The old Rosie might have felt an urge to stamp her feet and rage at him, but in the past few weeks she had been aware of a growing sadness for the love that had blossomed and died. She thought of it almost tangibly, as if she had held its fragile beauty in her hand and seen it crumble to dust. She ached inside because of its loss, feeling it with the same sense of grief and despair as she had the death of her mother and little sister. Those times Dunstan and Edwin had shared her grief. This time she was entirely alone, unable to confide in anyone. Edwin was too full of his own joy, and rightly so...and Dunstan so invigorated with the prospect of the visit to London and all it entailed that Rosie knew it would be unfair to burden him with her cares at such a time.

She was thankful when the party came to an end, mainly because of Daisy's tiredness.

'You'll be glad of her company while your Pa's away up in Lunnon,' Mrs Merrick fussed around finding coats and bonnets. 'You'll be all right now, will you, Rosie? You know you're always welcome to stay here, and the child too, while Jess and Edwin have a little time to themselves.'

'I'll be fine, thank you, Mrs Merrick,' she said quickly. 'Daisy and I will enjoy ourselves. We'll come to no harm, and

Edwin will be coming to the workshop every day.'

It was only the nights that she would find difficult...nights when Rosie knew full well she would be envying her new sister-in-law in the arms of her husband... She realised she was clenching her hands, knowing that however uneasy she might feel at Briar Cottage with only Daisy for company, she could never stay at Merrick Farm again. The thought that Will was so near in truth and yet so far in spirit would be unbearable.

' 'Tis a pity you don't have a dog for company no more,' Mrs Merrick went on. 'Gettin' caught in a trap like he did while you was away too. Farmer an' me was saying you should have another to take his place.'

'One day perhaps.' Why didn't they let her go, Rosie thought wildly? She wanted to get away...to be home...to stop thinking... At last Daisy was sitting between her and Dunstan in their cart, and Jess and Edwin rode on ahead, their own cart decked with ribbons and streamers, to wave goodbye to them at the gate of Jess's cottage. Edwin and Jess's cottage now, Rosie amended, since it had been decided he would move in with her and Daisy and enlarge the place gradually.

She wanted to be home, to put Daisy

to bed in Edwin's room, and then to start on her father's packing. She didn't want time to think, to brood, to dream...but it was impossible to still her dreaming in the soft, dark, wakeful hours of the night, and to prevent the images of Jess and Edwin from becoming Will and herself... If Vicar Washbourne would condemn her for a wicked harlot for harbouring such thoughts, then let him, but the one place the vicar couldn't intrude was the privacy of her own thoughts.

Dunstan insisted that he would be back as soon as possible, though Lord Fitzgerald had intimated in his letter that it would be useful for the basket-maker to visit the various gentlemen's clubs within reasonable travelling distance from London with him, to get a better idea of what was required. Then there were the designs to be roughed out and approved—all in all, it must needs take several weeks...

'Don't worry, Pa,' Rosie told him on the morning of his departure. 'Briar Cottage would be full to bursting with all Daisy's paraphernalia about and your designing materials too. It's far better that you do it in London at the Fitzgeralds'. You'll have calm surroundings and I won't be on edge thinking Daisy's disturbing you all the time.'

'The little minx is enough to disturb

anyone. Don't let her run riot over you, Rosie. I've asked Will to stop by each morning and check on you, since he's taking over Jess's milk delivery for a few weeks to let her and Edwin settle in to their new life.'

'You shouldn't have done that! I don't need anyone checking on me.'

'It's done, Rosie,' Dunstan said calmly, wanting no arguments. 'The Merricks agreed to it readily, and it will put my mind at rest.'

'I'm not so sure it will mine, to have him knocking at the door at the crack of dawn!' she said tensely.

'You'd be awake anyway. You always are when Jess comes by rattling the churns.'

'But not at dawn! Farmer said Will's intending to start before daylight so as to get back to his own work. They're starting on the withy cutting very soon. Oh Pa, I wish you hadn't done this!'

But he'd done it and there was no changing his mind. And if Rosie had intended staying in bed and merely calling out to Will that all was well each morning, she had reckoned without Daisy's excited clamouring to see Will, her idol. It ended with Rosie stiffly offering him tea and bread, and him accepting just as stiffly. Of the three of them only Daisy appeared normal, and that was only when Will was around. For the most part she was wilful and irritating, and by the end of a week at Briar Cottage, wanting to know when she could go home with her Ma.

'You know what Edwin said,' Rosie said crossly. 'In two or three weeks' time, when Grandpa gets back.'

Daisy had started calling Dunstan Grandpa to his amusement. She glared at Rosie now. 'I want to be with my Ma. Vera says I'm a teacher's pet 'cos I stay with you. Why can't I go home?'

Rosie sighed. All her natural flair with children seemed to be deserting her lately, and she could only feel impatience with Daisy.

'Because you've been told to stay here, that's why,' she snapped.

'Why can't I stay with Vera?' Daisy's voice rose. 'Vera's Ma 'ould have me.'

'Because I'm your auntie now as well as your teacher, Daisy, and you're to do as you're told.' The child was driving her to distraction with her whining ways. 'If Vera says you're a teacher's pet, it's only because she's jealous, and jealousy's a bad thing. You see too much of Vera Yandell.'

'You won't stop me seeing her. She's my friend!' Daisy was shriller than ever, her small body as tense as a tiger ready to spring as she faced Rosie with defiant

444

eyes. Rosie gave a long sigh.

'Nobody's trying to stop you seeing her. But you should have other friends as well.'

'Don't want no other friends,' Daisy's lower lip jutted out mutinously. 'I don't like you no more.'

'I don't like you much either,' Rosie said calmly.

Daisy gasped. 'Yes you do! Grown-ups have to like children.'

'Why do they? Is there a rule about it?'

She was answered by Daisy rushing out of the cottage like a little whirlwind, as she heard Edwin approaching for his day's work at the workshop. Rosie wilted. All this drama before they had even got to the schoolhouse that day. Five minutes later Edwin came in, holding a tearful Daisy in his arms, won over by her apparent fretting for Jess.

'Will you be all right if she comes to us, Rosie?' he said at once. 'I don't like to see her like this, and Jess wouldn't want it.' He missed the little triumphant dart Daisy threw at Rosie.

'She's all right here,' Rosie said sharply. 'She's playing on your feelings, Edwin, and you're a fool to give in to her.'

Daisy started wailing at once, and Edwin tightened his arms around her, looking at

445

his sister in some surprise.

'You've got very hard, Rosie! Then I'm a fool, but Daisy comes home with me after school today, and I'll bring her along here in the morning for you to take her to school. I'm not having her upset like this.'

There wasn't a thing Rosie could do about it, and once again Daisy had got her own way, and antagonised Edwin against her into the bargain. Suddenly Rosie just didn't care. Let her go home. She'd prefer to be on her own anyway. In the past few days the irritation of having Daisy around had been intensified by the onset of bad weather. Incessant rain and heavy grey skies had combined with whipping cold winds to make even the best of tempers fray. Daisy had whimpered in the night, wanting Jess, and unused to being disturbed so often Rosie had felt bad-humoured and over-tired. She knew she wasn't giving her best at the schoolhouse, and was vaguely surprised that Bennett hadn't mentioned it. No, she couldn't say in all honesty that she would be sorry to hand Daisy over to Edwin and Jess!

They plodded along the lanes towards Moule that morning without speaking, their boots barely keeping out the dampness, their shawls pulled tightly around their shoulders over their top-coats. The whole

446

of the earth seemed a spongy mass by now, and what were once green fields were already sheets of grey water where the Levels held them captive. The only crop that would be flourishing well was the withy crop...and Rosie surmised that the withy beds would be even more sodden very soon, as the river Parrett looked ominously near to bursting its banks.

Last week Bennett had given the pupils a history lesson, in which he had told them of the time of the great rushing tide known as the Bore, when the sea had rushed in along the river at Bridgwater in 1799 in a furious avalanche of water, overturning ships large and small and destroying all in its path. The children had been enthralled at hearing the tale, but Rosie felt a sudden uneasy premonition as she eyed the rising water and the steady, monotonous drizzle of rain that almost blinded them as they neared the village. If it should happen again, and she was at the cottage alone... Rosie felt a flicker of fear. Perhaps she should go to Merrick Farm after all. Or at least think about it.

The farm would be safe, sitting on the upward curve of the saucer in which Moule stood. The farmlands were on the flat, but the buildings themselves would be out of harms' way. Jess and Edwin and Daisy would obviously go there if danger threatened. She would be alone in the cottage...angrily, Rosie knew she was beginning to panic before anything happened! Village folk went about their everyday business, splashing about in stout boots and grumbling...how would it look if Rosie Nash the school teacher admitted she was scared to death by a bit of water!

The bad weather continued. Occasionally the wind lessened, so that the grey sheets of water covering the fields seemed more like motionless glass. The ripple of the smallest breeze across their gleaming surfaces then was almost startling. But the respite never lasted long, and soon the moaning gust would begin again.

Daisy had gone home with Edwin and Jess, and at least Rosie's sleep was only disturbed by the force of the wind now, and not Daisy's plaintive whining in the night. Soon Dunstan would be returning from London, and Rosie was counting the days. From his letters the visit was a success, and she couldn't begrudge him his sense of achievement and pleasure.

She couldn't have said just what awoke her before daybreak one morning. A small sound...a cracking of twigs...a sense of someone else's presence...an instinct of self-preservation...

Whatever it was, she lifted her head

sharply from her pillow, getting a crick in her neck in the process, and balanced on one elbow for a few seconds, listening, listening...trying to hear above the drumming of her heart. A pulse beat wildly in her throat and in her head. It seemed to spin sickly so that she felt dizzy for a moment, and she swallowed back the dry taste of fear. For one heart-stopping moment the far-off echo of a gypsy woman's hacking voice seemed to fill her head to bursting, blotting out all else, clamouring to be remembered.

'...a dark-haired man who means you harm...beware the dawn, my pretty maid... beware the dawn.'

Rosie's heart lurched as she realised the hour of dawn was fast approaching. If the rain clouds had been less oppressive, the morning might have been lighter by now, the sky tinged with the unearthly colours of pink and gold, and blue emerging daylight. As it was, there was only a subtle lightening of shadows, and the sudden sound of a hated voice, calling and whispering her name in a way that filled her with instant terror.

'Where be 'ee, Rosie Nash, my pretty wench? 'Tis time you and me had a reckonin'! 'Tis time I were paid for the loss o' poor Doughey Pond and Seth Weaver, and my dozy ol' Granpappy. None on 'em would have gone if tweren't for thee, Rosie Nash. I reckon as 'ow you owed I summat, an' I'll take your maid's ring for payment. The thought on it makes I fair bust my breeches, so you just come an' see what's awaitin' for 'ee, my pretty!'

The voice was hoarse and guttural, and Rosie suddenly sensed that it was thickened with drink. She had heard tales that Cyrus Hale had taken to drinking bouts lasting all night long since his grandfather had died, and went wildly about the village hollering and bellowing in the small hours, to the outrage of decent folk and the verbal lashings of Vicar Washbourne. It was the first time he had come to Briar Cottage...

Rosie slid out of bed, tight with fear, pulling a dressing-robe around her nightgown. She was thankful Daisy wasn't here, for this drunken lout's blundering intention would be enough to deaden the child's voice again, and this time for ever. At the same instant Rosie wished desperately for someone's aid. Never had she felt so isolated or so afraid. Her teeth were chattering in her head as she edged to the bedroom door and peered out through a chink of it.

Cyrus was downstairs, lurching about, unsure of the plan of the cottage. He stumbled against furniture, cursing loudly each time he struck his shins. She could hear his laboured, unsteady breathing, and then her heart missed a beat as he reached the stairs and began to climb.

'Be 'ee all ready, my pretty wench? Nice an' spread an' juicy? It makes my mouth water to think on it! Come on now, pretty pretty, where be hidin' yourself?'

Even if it had done her any good to scream, Rosie couldn't have done so. Her tongue seemed stuck to the roof of her mouth with fear. Her blood pounded in her ears and her fingernails dug sharp crescents in her palms. There was no escape, she thought hysterically. She was trapped like a fly in a spider's web, only Cyrus Hale was far more deadly, more odious... She could smell the stench of him already, the strong, stale smell of drink, and the unwashed body stink of him. The thought of him touching her, of his hard, writhing, sweaty body clamped tightly against hers, sent a wave of nausea running through her. She would kill him first...

There was one small sliver of hope as she heard him reach the small landing at the top of the stairs. The cottage was modest enough, but it had three tiny bedrooms, and Cyrus would be unsure which way to go now. If she remained very still, and luck was with her, he would go into one of the other rooms, and she could race down the stairs and away from him. She would go to the village...the vicarage...anywhere to get away from this lascivious monster. She held her breath as he paused at the head of the stairs, muttering in gleeful prospect of what was to come.

She could almost hear him sway. Oh, please God, let him fall downstairs and break his neck—the wicked thought was in her scattered senses before she could stop it. She heard his heavy breathing steady a little, and Rosie's own breath became a tight ball of pain in her chest as she tried not to make the slightest sound. For the moment she could bless the darkness of the pre-dawn and the gusting wind that stifled her threatened sobs. There was only the width of a door between them, and the mounting tension was becoming almost unbearable. If some sixth sense told him which room was hers she would be doomed...

'Sweet pretty, pretty,' she heard him coo in the coarse guttural voice that made a mockery of the words. 'You an' me be due for a cockin' you won't forget. 'Tis my mark that'll be on 'ee soon, witch-wench, straight up that soft velvet passage. Do 'ee start to feel the itch for it yet, my pretty?'

The sudden sound of a boot kicking open a door made her jump with fright.

But it wasn't Rosie's door, and seconds later she heard him pawing about in Edwin's room, searching for her...

She sprang into action as if catapulted from a cannon. She wrenched open her door and fled downstairs as if all hell's demons were after her. In Rosie's mind, Cyrus Hale was no less. In her fright she fell over tables and chairs that he had knocked about, sobbing now as she heard him lumbering after her. Her attempt to escape suddenly seemed pitiful, for he was too strong and determined for her, and even his drunken state only seemed to give him added brute strength to do what he had come for. He bounded down the stairs two at a time just as Rosie found the parlour door and fled through it into the stinging rainswept dawn. The darkness was lifting, but she was blinded by wind and rain, the sobs torn from her throat as she stumbled outside the cottage over sinking muddy ground. She didn't know where she was going. Somewhere in the recesses of her mind she screamed for Will. Why wasn't he here? It was dawn, and he should be trundling along the muddy lanes with the milk cart—Will, Will...

'So 'tis sport you'm wanting, be it, pretty maid?' Cyrus Hale's voice jeered closed behind her. ' 'Tis all the same to I where you be. I can screw 'ee just as well in the mud as in a soft feather bed. 'Tis your back that suffers when I be drivin' home!'

She heard the lecherous laughter as the thought inspired him. In the fierce gale the workshop door was swinging open on its hinges, and as she heard him lose his footing and sprawl headlong on the slippery ground, Rosie fled inside the workshop, stumbling among the offcuts of withies strewn over the floor. If she hadn't had the mute sense to slide her feet into soft slippers, they'd have been cut to ribbons. As it was she felt the sharpness of the cut rods against her feet and bit her lips to stop from crying out. Maybe he wouldn't find her here. Maybe he hadn't seen where she went, and would go flailing off towards the village looking for her...

His dark, menacing shadow suddenly filled the dim, dawn-lit doorway, and Rosie fought hard to stifle a scream. He wouldn't be able to see her yet in the darkness of the workshop, but she suddenly heard him kick the door shut. His harsh breathing was echoed by her own, that was emitted in a sudden sob she couldn't resist. She heard his soft, triumphant chuckle.

'So now we'm together, pretty maid, and 'twill be all the sweeter for the waitin', like an apple ripe from the tree. You been ripe for I for a long whiles, Rosie Nash, an' I aim to do all the tastin' I want.'

She edged away from the sound of his voice, backing into a collection of baskets tied on the wall for tidiness, and he followed the sound. Her eyes were dilated with fear that those groping hands would reach their target, and that fleshy mouth would fasten over hers, forcing her lips apart and filling her mouth with his spittle. Her mind refused to think further, of the greater violation of her body by his...her hands were outstretched as if seeking help...they found the nail on which hung her Pa's cow-horn filled with grease, and his sharp bodkin.

Her fingers closed round it, but even as she wondered if she would dare plunge the point of it in another's flesh, her shaking wet hands let it slide out of her grasp, to fall harmlessly among the offcuts at Cy's feet.

He paused, sensing her whereabouts now. Outside the sky was imperceptibly lightening, and the outline of her shrinking body in its pale dressing-robe, pressed damply to her skin, was just visible to him. She saw him straighten and swagger towards her, taking his time, knowing her Pa was away and her brother wouldn't be here for several hours. Knowing all about young Daisy going home to her own Ma and sweet Rosie being alone, because he had made it his business to find out. Biding his time—and his time was now...

'Don't...don't...' her voice was a ragged thread of sound. She was begging and she knew it. Her answer was a whipping of his hard blacksmith's hand from one side of her face to the other, almost knocking her senseless. She almost prayed that it would be so. Better to be beaten to a senseless pulp if this animal was intent on ravishing her, than to be forced to feel every moment of his enjoyment of her...

She was almost unable to move. Her legs were leaden, every breath a painful effort. It was as if she saw the devil himself leering towards her, and she was the helpless victim, doomed and in his power at last. She swayed dizzily on her feet as his hands groped at the neckline of her dressing-robe tearing it open. To her dazed mind he was slavering over her and all her bones were crumbling...her shivering hands sought to hold on to something, anything, for support... They reached a hard, cold object on the bench and her fingers closed around it.

She felt the hot, clammy touch of his hands on her skin, and lunged forward with all her strength, crashing her father's iron across the side of Cyrus Hale's head. He didn't even cry out. One second he was pressing against her, and she could feel the rise of his manhood pulsating against her, pushing her backwards...the next all the pressure had gone and he was falling like a stone among the withy offcuts, and Rosie lost her balance, falling across him, the wild sobs in her throat the only sound apart from the moan of the wind outside and the sheeting rain.

For a few seconds she lay prone, gathering up her senses and trying to regain her breath. Then the knowledge that she lay across Cyrus Hale's inert body filled her with a new horror, and she struggled to move away from him. She shivered from head to foot as she realised her hand had been touching Cy's head, and there was a new warm stickiness on her fingers.

Without thinking she thrust her hand to her mouth in terror and tasted the blood. She spat out violently and rubbed at her mouth to rid herself of it. But it still remained...the taste and the smell of blood. In total hysteria Rosie turned and rushed out of the workshop, knowing she had killed Cyrus Hale, and in a superstitious village like Moule such an action would be a death sentence, whatever the circumstances. A death must be avenged...

Her mind was exhausted and confused.

All she could think of was being as far as possible from the thing inside the workshop. To run and run... Her face was stung by the blinding rain and she never noticed it. Ground mist loomed and receded and carried the voice of the wind through her senses, until it seemed as if all those old ghosts who had once lived and fought and died on the Somerset Levels jeered and taunted and condemned her with one voice. She would lurch about, her slippered feet squelching deeper and deeper in the spongy ground until she sank below the dank waters of a rhine, enmeshed in weeds and forgotten... It was the only clear thought in the tangle of her mind. It seemed so inevitable now that she paused for an instant in her wanderings, as if seeking the direction of the rhine, moving towards her destiny...

As her footsteps faltered, Rosie heard the thunderous sound of hoof-beats, muffled by the soft ground, but seeming to fill her head. There was the sound of clanking metal, the clash of steel, the harsh male voices...the squeal of horses, frightened at being part of a battle scene...

'Rosie, for God's sake, what are you doing here? I bloody near ran you down!'

Strong arms suddenly held her tight, and her dazed eyes were looking into Will Merrick's face. In the pale morning he looked ashen, but no more than she did. She could hear the snort of the farm horse nearby, alarmed at being pulled up so short when Will had suddenly caught sight of her like a wraith in the dawn mist. One of the milk churns had fallen from the cart and spread its contents in a creamy pool over the mud.

There was no devilish trickery of the Duking Days here. No re-enaction of the bloody battle with past Nashes to live out their fantasies in her. No horses, only a frightened farm horse. No clash of steel, only the clattering of the milk churns. No blood-chilling soldiers bellowing to victory—only one voice...only Will's voice...

Rosie clung to him, her sodden garments chilling her through, her fingers like claws in her relief at finding the one warm human being she needed. She still couldn't think coherently, and when she spoke, the words were like babbling gibberish.

'In there—in the workshop, Will. He came—like the gypsy said. Beware the dawn, she said—a dark man to do me harm. And—and another to save me. But you can't save me, Will! Nobody can save me when I'm so wicked! He's dead, you see. I killed him. I killed him, Will.'

He clamped his hand across her mouth as her voice began to rise. She frightened him.

They were quite close to Briar Cottage, though God knew how long Rosie had been wandering out here. She looked as if she had been going round in circles for hours and she was badly shocked. She was imagining things too.

'Who have you killed, Rosie?' he asked gently. 'There's nobody who'd want to do you harm—and you could never be wicked.'

'I am!' she said shrilly. 'In the workshop, Will.'

'I'd better take a look then.'

'No! Don't go in there. I can't go in there. His eyes were still open. They'll look at me and gloat. Don't make me, Will!'

His arms tightened around her still more, his face more troubled than it had ever been. Something was badly wrong, but he still couldn't believe what she said. Something had frightened her and her vivid imagination had done the rest. It was easy on such a night, and she shouldn't be in the cottage all alone...

'I can't leave you out here,' he said practically. 'And there's nothing in the workshop to harm you while you're with me. You trust me, don't you, Rosie?'

She nodded mutely, her large frightened eyes brimming with tears. Spiked with rain, her lashes lay black against her cheeks. Will ached to comfort her, but

460

not yet. She was still too caught up in that strange other world she had invented to be comforted, and he had to know the truth of it. If there was anything dead in the workshop, he had to know it. He kept his arm around her and helped her on to the farm cart, and took her the last short distance to the cottage. Once there he lifted her down, and held her tightly as they opened the workshop door cautiously.

It was nearly daylight now, and Rosie kept her eyes tightly shut, unable to look down at Cyrus Hale. By now the blood would be filling the workshop—a river of blood...and she was the murderess, the wicked one... Her heart pounded sickeningly in her chest, for now Will too would see her for what she was.

'There's nothing here, Rosie,' she heard him say. 'Open your eyes and look. There's nobody in here. *Look*, Rosie. Trust me.'

She heard the words, but she couldn't believe them. How could she when she had seen Cyrus Hale sink to the ground without a sound and seen the blood gushing from his head? He was here...he was here, and Will was forcing her to look. She began shaking again, and she felt the sting of Will's hand this time to quieten her screaming. She wasn't even aware she had uttered a sound until the

461

screaming changed to a quiet whimpering, and her eyes opened just a fraction, still afraid...

'But he was here, and I killed him,' Rosie stammered. 'Cyrus Hale came here, Will, he came to—to—oh, it was horrible, and I struck him with Pa's iron—see, here's the blood on it.'

She touched it and dropped it with a thud among the withies. That much was true...Will's arms closed around her again, and the slow relief began to fill her as he spoke deliberately as if to a child.

'Well, you may have struck him, but you certainly didn't kill him, Rosie. You probably stunned him, but he's too tough to die from a single blow. He'll have slunk off home by now, feeling pretty sick, and I'd say he only got what he deserved. You should have done the same to me.'

He stopped speaking as she turned her eyes towards him. Thankful to his soul, he saw that they had lost that awful blankness now, and were registering what he was saying to her. All the guilt he ever felt was welling up in him now, and she gave a small sob as she leaned against him. Without words, he knew she forgave him everything. Miraculously, they were together again.

Chapter 20

The embers of the previous night's fire still glowed redly in the hearth. Will prodded some dry sticks beneath the logs until it flared into life, and quickly righted the upturned furniture. The oil-lamp he had lit threw a soft warmth around the room. Rosie stood exactly where he had put her, hugging the tattered dressing-robe to her body, still shivering uncontrollably. Shock was evident in her face, and Will knew she had to get into some dry clothes before she became ill.

When he spoke to her it seemed as if Rosie was incapable of thinking for herself. She pointed mutely to a chest in the corner when he asked about dry towels, and upstairs to her room when he mentioned her clothes. There was no help for it, he thought grimly, and if Edwin came to the cottage early that day, he must explain as best he could what was happening here...

First he gently removed the torn dressing-robe, and then bade Rosie lift her arms for him to take off the soaking nightgown. She looked at him dazedly for a moment.

'Trust me, Rosie,' he said yet again in a husky voice. 'You need warmth and dry clothes and a hot drink. Wrap yourself in towels and sit by the fire while I see to it all, please, love. No one will harm you, I promise you.'

As far as was possible he wouldn't even let himself think of her as a woman, as she lifted her arms with slow obedience to do his bidding, and stood before him with trusting eyes while he wrapped the warm towels round her. Now was not the time for the sight of her to stir his senses, though he felt he would never forget the almost waxen perfection of her body, the milk-white breasts with their frozen rosebud tips, the curving seductiveness of her, the sweet haven where he had once soared to heights of pleasure... Will knew that one false move on his part now and Rosie's brittle hold on sensibility would be shattered for ever. And he loved her so much...

As she stood limply within the circle of his arms, in the warm cloak of the towels, she raised her soft, drowned eyes to his for a moment. As if she knew instinctively that nothing she said or did would be misconstrued or taken advantage of, she whispered against his cheek, 'I love thee, Will,' unconsciously using the local patois, and her lips brushed his. They were cool, denying for the moment the hidden fire of her. He refrained from crushing his mouth to hers with a great effort, content merely to hold her, glad to his soul of her need of him.

'No more than I love thee,' he answered hoarsely, 'and will do to the end of my days, Rosie. There's nothing I want more than to have you as my wife, and if you tell me now that you prefer the fine London gentlemen or the school teacher, then I'm as lost as that evil Cyrus Hale.' He felt her shudder in his arms.

'Don't speak of him, Will,' she whispered. 'Nor of the others. They don't exist. There's only you, Will, from the first moment.'

This time he kissed her with more passion, but still holding himself in check. Her sweet body was crushed to his, and he could feel the softness of her breasts and all the warmth returning to her limbs. And God, how he wanted her... He spoke thickly against her mouth.

'Rosie, get yourself into your clothes, for God's sake, before I do something rash. Your brother will be here soon, and we had best set the workshop to rights, unless you want to tell him all that happened.'

As he expected she shook her head vigorously. The shame of Cyrus Hale's assault wasn't hers, and yet she felt it as keenly as if it was...and besides that, she thought she had killed him. He might still be badly hurt...she couldn't forget that so easily, but neither could she confide in Edwin or anyone but Will. She never wanted to see or hear about Cyrus Hale again.

She moved reluctantly out of Will's arms, and he sighed with relief, not knowing how long he could have gone on merely comforting her. She dressed quickly while he made them both some tea, and then he went to the workshop to clean Dunstan's iron and get rid of the small patch of stained withy offcuts.

'Edwin will see that you're shocked, my love,' he told her, when she sat on the settle with his arm about her. 'It's best that we concoct a tale of your having heard the milk-cart overturn and came rushing out in your nightclothes to see what had happened. At least the spilt milk is evidence of such an accident, and better a white lie than the truth.'

She nodded, safe in the crook of his arm. With the fire's blazing warmth and the miracle of Will's love restored to her, Rosie could agree to anything, lulled into a blissful sense of well-being and thankfulness. The next wedding at Moule church would be hers and Will's...the unbelievable had happened, and she thanked God for the mysterious ways in which He worked.

By the time Edwin arrived with Daisy, Rosie had recovered quite well from her experiences. There was still a pallor in her cheeks, despite the fire's heat, but that was easily explained away by the accident to the milk-cart. Will did most of the talking, and spoke quickly to allay any suspicion on Edwin's part.

'It all made me late with the milk-round, and seeing Rosie was so stunned, I thought I might as well be really late and wait for you, Edwin. There's nothing I can do at the farm in this weather, and I'll take Rosie and Daisy into the village on the cart in time for school if you like. There's another thing too. The weather looks real bad, and if Rosie's agreeable I'll meet her this afternoon and take her back to the farm to stay till your Pa gets back. It's worrying for her to be here alone.'

If Edwin thought it a mite odd for Will Merrick to be suddenly so concerned for his sister's welfare, he caught the sudden softening of his glance towards her, and the flush on Rosie's pale face. Well, *at last*, Edwin couldn't help thinking... He agreed that it was the best idea.

'I want to stay at the farm as well,' Daisy piped up. 'Mrs Merrick always lets us stay when the wets come badly. Can I come with you, Will?'

'What, tired of your new Pa already?' Edwin grinned at her. 'All right, if Will says it's all right. From the look of it, we'll all be at the farm before long anyway.'

He and Will flashed an anxious look at each other. Flooding was an annual occurrence on the Levels, but some years were worse than others, and some folk in the village had already moved out, by all accounts, to await the coming of better weather. Others had seen to the plimming-up of small wooden boats, kept ready in back yards for just such an emergency.

So when Will had deposited Rosie and the child at the schoolhouse and promised to be outside for them when school was over, Rosie discovered that the pupil attendance was sadly depleted. There was only a handful of children there, and Bennett Naylor came to a quick decision.

'We'll carry on for today, Rosie, but if this rain goes on all day again, we'll close the schoolhouse for the time being. I think it's best for the children to be at home with their parents in case any of them decide to move out of the village in a hurry. We'll write a note for each child and inform them verbally for those parents who are unable to read.'

'Is there real danger, Bennett?' Rosie asked anxiously.

'If the Parrett bursts its banks, there's nothing to stop it surging through Moule,' he said grimly. 'It's happened before, though not while I've lived here, but I've heard tales of it, and I think it's best we keep the children's spirits up with singing and play-acting today, for little ears are listening.'

It was hard to keep cheerful, knowing that danger could be imminent. Wasn't it better to evacuate the village right now, Rosie demanded of him? But Bennett told her that wasn't Moule's way, nor Vicar Washbourne's either. Vicar and the Good Lord would alert them all in time, Bennett said somewhat dryly...and Rosie hoped cynically that he was right. The river habitually rose higher than at present before anyone left their homes, she was told, but as the day wore on the blackening sky left her in no doubt that there would be no more school until all danger was past. She was glad to see Will collect her and Daisy that afternoon. They would be safe at the farm...

High tide was expected soon after school closed for the day. Rosie remembered what it was like, seen far below from her vantage point on the Minehead cliffs, the sea a churning, foaming mass of mountainous waves crashing against the rocks. She had seen small boats disappear without a trace, and large ships flounder. She tried not to imagine that same sea surging up the Channel and finding an inlet in the river Parrett, wide-necked at first and then funnelling its way through Bridgwater and twisting its way through the Levels with the village of Moule directly in its path... By the time the sea reached Moule, it would be a gigantic wall of water...

Rosie turned gladly as Will arrived at the schoolhouse. Most of the children had gone home by then, with Daisy and her friend Vera Yandell, busily whispering in a corner. Rosie called them thankfully, and buttoned Daisy into her coat, telling Vera to get along home as quickly as she could now. She saw Vera give Daisy a sly pinch.

'All right, teacher's pet,' the girl hissed gleefully. 'Teacher's pet, witch's pet.'

'All right, Vera, run along now,' Bennett snapped. He eyed Will Merrick, knowing immediately by Rosie's reaction to him that his own cause was lost for ever now; and because it was a fact, ruefully cursing himself for missing his chance. But he nodded amiably to Will, wishing him a safe journey home with his two charges.

'We'll get on quickly,' Will began, and

then his head jerked back as the sound of church bells sounded, distantly at first and then closer, each bell ringing out its own voice, jangling against the next as one church and then another took up the warning until it became a great cacophony of sound.

'What is it?' Rosie gasped, as Moule's own church bell pealed out, almost deafening them in its urgency.

'There's no time to get to the farm,' Will rapped out. 'It's the warning that the surge tide is approaching.'

'What shall we do?' Rosie said in panic. 'The cottage is right in its path, the same as the village.'

'The church!' Will was shouting instructions as the few remaining people in the schoolhouse looked to him for instruction. ' 'Tis the highest building around, where all go for sanctuary at such times. Come on—quickly—there's no time to lose.'

Vera Yandell had paused uncertainly at the door as the church bells rang out across the flat wetlands, but now Bennett grabbed her hand as Rosie made for the door. Will had scooped Daisy up in his arms, and the five of them raced for the higher mound of land upon which Moule church stood. Soon it would be an island for the few hours until the water receded with the ebb tide, and all roads led to the church now as Rosie was jostled on all sides by villagers all seeking refuge within its walls.

It only took a few minutes to reach the church, and already folk were huddled inside, some with a few possessions they had grabbed, others uncaring as long as they saved themselves and their children. No one could surmise how bad the flood would be until it came, and Vicar Washbourne was doing his utmost to calm the hysterical as best he could.

'We'll do no good by wailing,' he roared out. 'Have ye no faith in God's love? Ye all knew where to come when help was needed, so trust in the Almighty to save those within His house!'

'He'd turn any situation into an excuse for a sermon,' Will murmured in Rosie's ear. He said it to keep up her spirits as much as anything, because after her ordeal that morning she had lost what little colour she had, and her eyes were restlessly searching the packed interior of the church. Will gave her hand a comforting squeeze.

'Don't worry about Edwin and Jess, darling. They will have heard the church bells, and Jess would know immediately what to do. She and Edwin will be at the farm by now, perfectly safe, and they both know that you and Daisy are with me. We've been through this situation before, Rosie. They'll know we're at the church.'

'Will,' she turned troubled eyes on him. 'I wasn't thinking about Edwin and Jess.'

His arm slid around her waist, his lips brushing the velvet softness of her cheek, no matter how many village dames were looking on. Soon everyone would know that he intended marrying Rosie Nash, and as soon as possible. He felt her tremble against him.

'No one's going to harm you while I'm here to protect you, Rosie, and you're not staying at Briar Cottage alone again. You'll stay at the farm until your Pa returns.' He was aggressive in his defence of her. 'Cyrus Hale is probably miles away from here by now if he's got any sense! He'll know better than to try anything on again.'

But he'd need a refuge from the rising water as much as anyone else. Rosie knew it, just as Will did. Her eyes roamed around the groups of people. Nearly all the village must be crammed in the church by now, but not him. The sharp fear that she had killed him rose up in her again. Even if it hadn't happened straight away when she'd struck him with her Pa's iron, he may have been so dazed he'd wandered senselessly for a while and then slid into the mud and filth to drown. And if that was the case, then she had still killed him as surely as if she had stuck her Pa's bodkin into his heart...

'Are you unwell, Miss Nash?' Vicar Washbourne's face peered down into hers as if from a gauze-covered distance. 'Have faith, child. The waters have never reached the church yet, and at least your father's business is one to be spared, even if your pots and pans float about awhile. Baskets can be cleaned and dried and sold as good as new. Others may not be so fortunate.'

'He's right, Rosie. Our withies will come to no harm, and neither will your Pa's goods, so long as they're treated like Vicar says.' Will encouraged her to think positively. 'You and me—we'll survive no matter what happens.'

She looked at him dully. They would survive, so long as Cyrus Hale didn't ruin everything. The thought wouldn't leave her. It throbbed and festered inside her, and her fingers curled more tightly round Will's. He looked up at the vicar and spoke up so all around could hear.

'Once the village gets back to normal, Vicar, we want you to perform another wedding service if you will. Rosie and me want to be wed on the first dry Sunday.'

A murmur of approval ran through the groups nearest them. They made a handsome pair, Will Merrick and Rosie Nash, and a pair blessed in marriage by the church had an immediate place in the hearts of village folk. Vicar Washbourne nodded in satisfaction, and announced the news in a great bellow to cheer up the anxious villagers.

'You hear that, my friends? There's to be another wedding in Moule. church, so there's something to lift your spirits and think on. There's two young people not afraid to face the future, despite the dangers outside. And think further, all ye who know your bible as well as ye should—God sent another great flood in His wisdom, didn't He? And out of it the good survived and the evil perished. We here shall survive, my friends! So let us all raise our voices and sing to the praise of the Lord, instead of bemoaning our fate. If Tom Kitch is here, let him give out the hymn books to those that need them!'

Rosie heard the murmurs of good wishes from those nearest her and Will, and a little glow crept into her frozen heart. Her hand was still tightly held in Will's, and she felt his lips on her cheek once more.

'Now everyone knows,' he whispered against her skin. 'There's no one to divide us now, my sweet Rosie. We have Vicar's blessing.'

A loud gust of wind took his voice away as the great oak door suddenly opened and was thrust shut again, and Rosie's heart gave a sickening leap in her chest as she saw Cyrus Hale leaning against it. He was as dishevelled as ever, his hair wild and his evil little eyes gleaming with hate in his fleshy face. Normally florid, it was pale as death now, except for the ugly blackening bruise on his cheek. His shapeless clothes and leather jerkin were muddied beyond recognition, and after Vicar Washbourne's first involuntary look of distaste at the fellow, he strode towards him.

'Come you in, my son, and find a corner to rest until the danger is past. You must be the last to find sanctuary, and will have missed the announcement of future nuptials between our two young friends here.' He spoke pompously, covering his dislike.

Oh no...oh no...Rosie closed her eyes for a moment, wishing she could blot out the sight of Cy's head suddenly swivelling towards her and Will. Wishing desperately that she had killed him after all, and hating herself for the wickedness of it. She saw Cyrus Hale walk slowly towards her, and to her horror he began to laugh with a harsh guttural sound. The vicar put a restraining hand on his arm, thinking he was ill, but Cyrus angrily shook it off. He swayed on his feet as if he was drunk, but Rosie knew instinctively that it wasn't drink filling his mind with evil revenge at that moment...

'Gettin' wed, is it? That whore?' At his ringing words, there was a loud gasp all round, and Rosie felt the tears spurt from her eyes. Cyrus jabbed a finger at his temple. 'You see what she did to I, this fine school teacher o' yourn? Pretty nigh killed I, she did, an' here's the wound to prove it.'

'And why did she nearly kill you, Cyrus Hale?' Will was suddenly on his feet, standing in front of Rosie, his dark eyes blazing. 'Why don't you tell these good people the rest of it? How you went to Briar Cottage, knowing Rosie was there alone, and tried to seduce her? If she's marked you, it's no more than you deserved. If I had been there, I'd have killed you with my bare hands.'

'An' I'd break your head as soon as look at 'ee, you poncey farmer's boy,' Cyrus shouted. 'Ask your fancy piece about the gypsy if you think she be so pure. You're welcome to 'er if 'tis tainted goods you want!'

His answer was a crashing fist in his gut as Will threw himself on him. It winded Cy for a moment, and he went staggering backwards into a group of people. Children were screaming, and there was a sudden uproar in the church as the men surged forward to pull the assailants apart. Above it all, Vicar Washbourne's voice roared out.

'Have you all forgotten that this is the house of God?' he thundered. There was murder in the eyes of both Cyrus and Will at that moment, and the vicar strode between them, glowering at each of them, and at the rest of the people there. Rosie shook all over, sensing that the tenuous hold she had had on these villagers' goodwill was fast slipping away with Cyrus Hales' vindictive words.

'How dare you come here and defile those hallowed walls!' Vicar Washbourne roared on to Cyrus Hale. 'We want no talk of whoring here, nor condemnation of another. This is not the night, when all our souls are in danger, and I'll have none of it, do you hear me, blacksmith? And you, Will Merrick, I hold your family in fine esteem, so I'm inclined towards believing the tale you told of this cur's intention, but that's no reason for turning God's house into a brawling place! Now, if the two of you have calmed your tempers, then I'll ask these good folk to leave go of you, and I'll see you settled in opposite ends of the church for the rest of the time we're here!'

For a moment Rosie thought it was going to happen as he requested. The men let go of Cyrus and Will gingerly, and Will immediately returned to her side, to put his arm protectively around her. Thankfully, Rosie saw that Bennett had Daisy on his lap, with her friend, Vera Yandell, looking agog at such excitement. Cyrus shook off the restraining hands on him and glared all round.

'You're all witch-charmed, you fools,' he shouted, 'and none of 'ee can see it! Well, I ain't waitin' round no longer while the likes of Rosie Nash be among 'ee! There's plenty o' folks'll be glad o' my services, and I be gettin' out while I can. You'm welcome to 'er and 'er kind!'

Before anyone could guess his intention, Cyrus had twisted round and lumbered towards the church door, wrenching it open, and lurching out into the night. A dozen men made to follow him and bring him back, and as many more stopped them, forcing the door shut. Outside the rain fell in a torrential downpour.

' 'Tis no use. If he wants to go, 'tis his choice.'

'He were allus a bad un. Good riddance, I say.'

'Best off wi' the gypsies, like he were allus threatening, now his Granpappy's gone.'

Will spoke softly in Rosie's ear in the

midst of the uproar. 'Don't let it upset you, sweetheart. If he's gone from the village, then it's as they say, and good riddance to him.'

'But he's done the damage, Will,' her lips trembled so much she could hardly say the words. 'Folk were pleased at hearing we were going to be wed, and now I can see by their faces that they're divided once more. I'll never be accepted here, never.' Her voice broke on a sob, because suddenly it seemed that acceptance at Moule was an insurmountable obstacle that Rosie could never hope to cross. Cyrus Hale might as well have done his worst to her back there at the cottage, because she was as surely damned.

She felt Will's strength as his arms tightened round her, but there was no comfort he could give her at that moment. The gypsy had been right after all, Rosie thought bitterly. Beware the dawn...but the aftermath was worse, because she had glimpsed Valhalla, and now she wondered if she would ever dare to marry Will in the face of so many mistrusting villagers. She only had to look at them to see those who avoided her gaze since Cyrus Hale's appearance. And if her marriage to Will had bad repercussions on his family and livelihood, then perhaps it would be better if she too went away, like Cyrus

Hale... The twist of it was that he *had* marked her...

'Listen! Listen, all on 'ee!' A sudden shout went up among the babbling voices in the church. 'Don't 'ee hear it?'

They were quiet for a moment, and out of the darkness they heard a mighty roar, gathering in strength and obliterating all other sounds, of rain and wind and heartbeats. The surging tide was sweeping inland along the course of the river Parrett, and within minutes now the village of Moule would be flooded, and all at ground level submerged. A woman screamed. Folk shouted to God to have mercy, and Vicar Washbourne took command by loudly intoning a prayer of his own making.

'Lord save us in our hour of need!' His voice was as strong as ever not betraying one flicker of fear. 'Save Thy servants, dear Lord, who adore Thee, and who worship here at Thy throne. We await Thy bidding in Thy house, Lord God Almighty, until Thou seest fit to let the waters recede. Until then, we commend ourselves to Thy hands. Amen. Let us sing His praises, my friends. Let us sing to the rafters!'

Fitting the action to the words, his voice rang out with the first phrases of the hymn, 'O God, our help in ages past'. There were few who joined in at first, but gradually some stalwarts began singing, their voices puny against the great roar of water outside the church, but others followed suit, giving their minds a task to do in the grip of fear.

Bennett Naylor had gathered his small flock of schoolchildren around him, and Rosie could see them all singing bravely. Except one. Rosie's heart gave a sudden jolt as she saw Daisy sitting mute and white-faced on Bennett's lap. Please God, don't let all this take her voice again, Rosie begged silently... The tragic thought made her give a small whimper as she tried to sing at the vicar's command. She felt Will's hand squeeze hers.

'I love thee, Rosie,' his voice whispered in her ear. 'Whatever happens, nothing can change that.'

'And I love thee, Will, so much.' A sudden scream of terror from those around the walls of the church stopped the singing instantly, as the splashing of water broke through the cracks of the doors and windows. The sound of the surge outside was as if it held all the wrath of God in its wake, and Rosie felt total panic as she flung her arms tightly around Will's neck and sobbed.

'Oh, hold me, Will, hold me.'

Chapter 21

In the moments of utter confusion, Vicar Washbourne's voice thundered out again. 'The Lord will protect all those that believe in Him.'

Rosie's eyes were still tightly closed as she clung to Will. His voice was right beside her ear, urgent and strong.

'It's all right, darling. 'Tis only the roar of the surge tide sweeping through, and the gusting of the wind sending rain flurries inside. We'll not be drowned in here. Once the surge has passed, the water will settle itself. We only have to sit and wait until it subsides. Believe me, Rosie.'

Believe in Will or God...to Rosie's muddled mind it was all the same at that moment. She shook so much it was as if she had the ague, but gradually she realised the babble of fear was dying down in the church, and relief was spreading as quickly as had the panic as Will's words proved themselves to be the case. The great surge of the flood tide had come, and though livestock and cottages would suffer, everyone who lived in Moule was in the sanctuary of the church. All save

Cyrus Hale...Rosie clenched her hands for a moment, blotting all vicious thoughts of him from her mind. If he had perished in the flood, then it was largely his own doing for lurching out there in the darkness. She smothered a sob, unable to rid herself totally of the hope that he would never worry her again... She felt Will's arms tighten around her.

'I told you we'd be safe here, Rosie,' he said gently. 'You'll have quite a tale to tell your Pa when he returns from London anyway. Those fine folk up there would never credit all this!'

He was cheering her as best he could, considering that Moule church was a cold and sombre place at night, with the candles flickering and villagers huddled together in family groups. For the moment the singing was stilled, and Vicar Washbourne announced that after a short prayer of thankfulness it would benefit them all to get a good night's sleep, before the unenviable task of sifting through flood-damaged houses and village shops began.

'Shouldn't we go looking for the young blacksmith, Vicar?' one man grunted, darting a look in Rosie's direction as if already blaming her for what they might find.

'In a few hours' time,' the vicar said shortly. 'Whatever God's will, it can make no difference to young Hale now. And in the midst of our thankfulness for deliverance, let us not forget that whomever He chose to live or die, it was His will and none other's.'

The prayer was of such length that Rosie's knees were sore by the time she rose up from them and settled back into the comfort of Will's arm for the night. The wind and rain had subsided at last, and there was a strange calmness outside. The vicar had inspected it, and informed them all to stay where they were until he gave the word that it was safe to venture out in the morning.

'We must do as he says, Rosie,' Will said. 'And if it's God's will that we spend the night together, then who are we to argue?'

She gave a weak smile. Spending the night together could be so different in other circumstances than these! And she would never sleep—sleep would be impossible—but she had forgotten the terror of the previous dawn when Cyrus Hale had come to Briar Cottage. Forgotten the fear of him ravishing her, and the driving sense of self-preservation that had made her nearly kill him. All that nerve-racked day, with only the knowledge that somehow she and Will had rekindled their love for each other to keep her sane, Rosie had been living on a knife-edge, and now that the threatened danger of the flood had come and gone, she slid into an exhausted sleep as gently as slipping into a warm blue ocean.

And when she slept, she dreamed...she was far away from the turbulent world in which folk looked at her in suspicion and fear. She was somewhere on that buoyant ocean with Will's arms around her and his love enveloping her. She was drowning in his kisses and the long pent-up passions that bound them together as surely as any marriage vow. She was soaring to heights of ecstasy she had never known...complete in the union for which God had fashioned man and woman...

She awoke with a little jump of her nerves, because the dream had been so real that she thought for a moment that she and Will had actually...here, in this sacred place, surrounded by all the outraged villagers of Moule... But Will's face was very close to hers and his eyes were closed in sleep, his breath softly warm on her cheek. For a few moments she watched him breathing, and for the first time in many months a feeling of belonging crept through her veins. If Moule would never accept her, there was one place that would always be her haven, where she would always belong, and it was here in Will Merrick's arms.

Rosie closed her eyes again, and this time she slept more peacefully, without the restless dreams to disturb her, and the next time she awoke it was nearly dawn. Folk around her were stirring from their slumbers, stiff and cold, and those who had the foresight to bring blankets snuggled into them more closely.

Near the door of the church a small knot of men were gathering under Vicar Washbourne's guidance. A rumble of voices reached out towards them, but Rosie was unable to hear what was being said.

'They'll be going out to see if anyone was caught in the flood,' Will murmured against her cheek. 'Everyone in the village was accounted for, but there may have been strangers passing through. There's always a counting before the womenfolk go back to their homes.'

'Do you—do you think they'll find him?' Rosie whispered.

They both knew who she meant. Will shrugged. He didn't care if the blacksmith lived or died, as long as neither event had any repercussions on Rosie. The men left the church, letting a cold rush of air into the place, and Rosie shivered.

'They'll find him,' Will said grimly. 'One way or another.'

They didn't have long to wait to know the answer. Running feet approached the church a short while later, and the news that Cyrus Hale's body had been found floating face down in the swollen river Parrett brought a momentary hush inside the church.

'Looks as if it'd been taken upstream with the surge an' knocked about a bit, then brought downstream agin,' one of the men said. 'Fair blackened an' bloated he be too. Vicar says to put him in the smithy for now, since the water's gone down through the village, so that's what us did.'

Rosie's breath caught in her throat. She couldn't even feel pity for Cyrus Hale, and she prayed that God wouldn't condemn her for it. Others were already doing that, from the sour looks on some of the faces in the church. Though there were still some who voted good riddance to Moule's most disliked character.

' 'Tis time we was getting out of here and back 'ome,' some of the villagers were saying now. 'Best see for ourselves what damage has been done.'

'Wait awhile yet, friends,' Vicar Washbourne's voice rang out. 'Wait until daylight, I beg you.'

'Wait wi' the likes of that one, Vicar?' one old crone spoke up loudly now, glaring

488

at Rosie and Will. 'She may 'ave turned young Merrick's head there, but I for one don't want to spend no more time in 'er company, no more than poor blacksmith did!'

A few mutterings of agreement followed, and Rosie's heart began to thud anxiously.

'Take no notice, sweetheart,' Will held her hand tightly. 'Vicar won't stand for such nonsense.'

'But we'll never change them, Will,' she mumbled. 'They'll always think I put a spell on Cyrus Hale. They're so *stupid!*'

'Hush, love. Calling them stupid won't help you.'

'Some of them aren't bothering to listen to the vicar anyway,' she gestured towards the door. 'So much for his influence when it's a case of fearing God or the devil!'

'Rosie, stop it! You'll be believing it yourself in a minute,' Will snapped at her.

Suddenly Bennett Naylor's voice rose above the general din inside the church.

'Has anyone seen Vera Yandell and Daisy Lawrence Nash? They were here a few minutes ago, and now they seem to have disappeared. If anyone sees them, will they bring them back to the school corner here please?'

Rosie jumped to her feet, a new fear clutching at her as she heard Bennett's words. Vera and Daisy had been so naughty and secretive lately, always running off and hiding in the most unlikely places, sometimes skipping away from school for an hour or more, or even a whole morning. But not now...surely not now... There were a few places within the church that they could hide, the vestry and the bell tower, or behind any of the pews or the pulpit...folk quickly searched in every likely spot and found nothing. Vera Yandell's mother began a low wailing, moaning that she should have had Vera safely with her, and not let her stay with the school teacher at all.

'Be quiet, Mother Yandell,' Vicar Washbourne snapped. 'The children were happiest kept together, and Mr Naylor kept them more amused than drivelling parents would have done through the night. There's only one thing for it. The two of them must have slipped out of the church a while ago, and the men had best go out again to look for them.'

Vera's mother suddenly turned a red-blotched face towards Rosie. ' 'Tis the witch's doing,' she screeched out. 'Our Vera was allus tellin' us how she draws they black likenesses at school, that be naught but witchraft to take away the soul of a person. 'Tis most likely the witch charmed our Vera to go out into the darkness an' be drowned, like she did to that poor young Cyrus.'

Rosie's heart was pounding so fast she could hardly breathe. She leapt to her feet, away from Will's restraining arm, as a small crowd of village folk seemed to move in a menacing circle towards her at Mrs Yandell's outburst. And then, as if all reason left her, she was screaming back at the woman, her voice choked with memory and grief.

'You fools, all of you! If I hated children that much, do you think I'd spend my days trying to teach them to read and write and be less ignorant than their parents! Do you really think that if I wanted to do evil to Vera that I'd let my own step-niece go off with her into the darkness and the danger? And if I was a witch, do you think I would have let my own dear little sister be dashed to death on the rocks below my home at Minehead six months before I came to live in this terrible, superstition-ridden hell-hole? If you think I'm wicked, then look at yourselves for a moment, and try using your brains to think sensibly for a change. My family has nothing at all to do with any past Nashes that ever lived here, good or evil! I wish we'd never come here. You're the wicked ones, not me! And what are you all doing now, instead of going to look for the two children who are missing?

Are you afraid of a little water as well as an innocent girl? Well, I'm not afraid. I'm going to look for Vera and Daisy.'

She stormed through the dumbstruck folk with Will right behind her. None of them knew about Dorcas until now. It was a pain too deeply embedded in her heart to relate to strangers, and the tears nearly choked her as she wrenched open the church door and rushed through it. She hated them all for forcing her grief to the surface again. She felt Will catch at her arm and grip it tightly.

'Go steady, sweetheart. That was quite a speech you made, and you'll need time to catch your breath.'

'I don't have time, Will,' Rosie said bitterly. 'I must find them. If anything's happened to Daisy—to either of them—I shall feel the blame, even though I know I don't deserve it. But oh, the weight of their hatred is beginning to wear me down, Will. I'm so afraid—despite what I said.'

Tears streamed down her face as the chill dawn air snatched at her cheeks and hair. Another dawn...this one oddly still. The mound of land on which the church stood had been isolated like an island during the night, but now the water had gone down considerably and the Moule cottages stood like thatched sentinels floating on the waterlogged ground. All around them, as far as they could see in the pale light, the fields were grey sheets of water that would take days to recover. Roads were beginning to be visible, and Rosie suppressed a shudder, remembering that Cyrus Hale's body would be lying in the smithy where the men had placed it earlier.

Will took command as he saw her sudden glassy-eyed stare and the disorientation that surrounded her. Behind them small groups of men were appearing at the church door, talking loudly of their intention of seeking out the two small girls and deciding on plans of action.

'At least you've stirred up something here, Rosie,' Will said. 'Between us all, we'll find them, and they'll be safe. Young Vera's got a crafty head on her shoulders, hasn't she? She and Daisy will be somewhere safe, and watching everyone paddling about looking for them and thinking it's all a huge joke. Come on, let's get started for the village.'

Their feet sank into the spongy ground, the wetness oozing immediately over their boots, freezing in the early morning. Stiff from the night's uncomfortable sleep, at least it was a relief to stretch their limbs and be away from the rank, cloying atmosphere of the church, where so many tightly-packed bodies had made it resemble a sheep pen. They began calling Vera and

493

Daisy's names, but as if to mock them the wind suddenly sprang up again, and little flurries of rain stung their faces and carried their voices with them.

Ahead of them they could see the village men calling outside every cottage and getting no response. Rosie's teeth were chattering and she clung to Will's hand as they moved quickly along the sodden lanes.

'They won't come out for the men,' she stuttered. 'They'll be too afraid of a scolding.'

'So they should be,' Will said shortly. 'Little idiots, to slip out like that.'

'Oh, don't be angry with them, Will. I'm so afraid they may have tried to go back to Briar Cottage and fallen in the rhine. It's my worst fear.'

'It's unlikely. Even Vera wouldn't be so stupid!' But he looked uneasily towards the grey mass of water leading away from the village towards Briar Cottage and the distant hazy outline of the hills rising behind Merrick Farm. The road was passable by cart now, but if two small girls had tried to find their way to Briar Cottage before daylight, anything could have happened to them. He didn't want to think of it, but it was a thought that couldn't be overlooked.

The men were still shouting for the girls, and then to each other that they had found nothing. Will hesitated. His horse and cart were safely tethered in the lee of the church, and they could risk going to the cottage... He opened his mouth to suggest it when Rosie suddenly gripped his arm more tightly.

'I've just thought where they might be, Will,' she spoke breathlessly with sudden hope. 'There's a cubby-hole in the schoolhouse where we keep chalks and boards. It's big enough to hide two children, and I've known it done before. Vera would know it.'

'Come on.' Will started to run through the sloshing water and mud, along the street to the schoolhouse. He pushed open the door and they rushed inside, calling out the children's names. There was no reply, and then Rosie pointed to the small cubby-hole door in the corner. Her heart pounded as she ran to it, bumping against school desks and chairs and not noticing the bruises.

'Daisy, come out, please,' her voice was frenzied with fear. If they weren't here... She tugged at the small door. It normally opened outwards but was caught by the force of the water swirling around the schoolroom floor. It was fastened tightly...

'Will, they can't get out!' Rosie suddenly screamed. 'They're trapped in there by the water.'

'We don't know they're in there yet!' he shouted at her. If they were, they didn't answer, and he didn't want to think what that might mean, confined in a tiny space with no air. They couldn't have been there very long, but how long did it take to suffocate...? He looked round wildly for something with which to prise the door open and there was nothing.

'Stay there and I'll find an implement to get it open,' he ordered.

'Be quick. Oh, be quick.'

Will didn't stop to answer. He knew the need for speed as well as Rosie did. But where...the smithy! Will raced towards it, the incongruous thought flitting through his head that perhaps something of Cyrus Hale's could even yet be the saving of the missing girls. He snatched up an axe and then flung it down again. Smashing through the cubby-hole door might be disastrous if it was as small as Rosie said... He looked round frantically for something else. A crowbar! Will seized it and ran back to the schoolhouse, his heart feeling as if it would burst in his chest. He splashed across the room and forced the end of the crowbar between the small door and the jamb, needing to lever it in several places before it inched outwards and they could see the two small, huddled bodies inside.

Rosie gave a stifled scream, her hand over

her mouth, her eyes streaming with tears, but Will was still rapping out commands to her.

'Help me get them out, Rosie. They can't have been here long.'

As he spoke they heard Vera give a low moan, and Will lifted her out while Rosie scrambled to reach for Daisy. She lay so still and limp in her arms, so frozen and pale... Even as Rosie felt total despair wash over her and an agonising feeling of déjà vu, remembering her own sister's appearance in death, Daisy's eyelids fluttered open and she breathed faintly like a little bird...

'Rosie,' her mouth moved to whisper the name. Then, seeing whose arms held her, Daisy's own arms wound around Rosie's neck more tightly and the child began sobbing. 'Oh Rosie, we got shut in. It was all a game. Vera said it was just a game.'

'Hush darling, it doesn't matter now,' Rosie said, her eyes blinded by tears of relief. 'We'll get you back to the church now and talk about it later.' She looked at Will, who nodded, as the contrite Vera was also recovering. A few minutes later and it might have been a different ending. Each of them carried a child to the schoolhouse door, to be met by Tom Kitch and Perce Guppey, their faces gaunt as they took in the sight of them.

'They're safe,' Will said quickly. 'Rosie knew where they might have been hiding, and if she hadn't they'd have been dead by now. Pass the word that they're safe.'

The men shouted the words, and others took up the call, so that it was a chain of sound as joyful as the warning of the church bells had been ominous earlier. By the time Will and Rosie had reached the church with their precious burdens, the other searchers had caught up with them, and Vera's father had taken his daughter out of Will's arms to deliver her to her distraught mother at the church door.

'You've Rosie Nash to thank for finding her in time, Mother,' the man said sternly. 'I reckon as how we owe her a debt.'

Murmurs of assent filled the stone walls, but Rosie was past caring about the villagers of Moule. She was cold and aching, and more concerned with how Daisy fared. The child's colour was returning, and someone had the foresight to bring some bread and cheese from one of the cottages. It wasn't hot food but it was some nourishment at least, and the two girls ate hungrily. Rosie realised her own stomach was gnawing, as everyone else's must be, but with the coming of daylight they could all return home soon, and try to restore the ravages of the surge tide. She suddenly realised someone was speaking to her, and her head jerked up as she saw Mrs Yandell handing something to her.

'I'm thankin' 'ee, Rosie Nash, and though it's a mite late to be biddin' 'ee welcome to Moule, I'm doing it now. And I want 'ee to have this to keep out the cold and wet. You look near to frozen.'

The woman handed Rosie a blanket to wrap round herself. Rosie looked at her numbly, unsure about this change of heart after the woman's screeching accusations earlier. The horror of finding the two girls and thinking they were dead, and then the relief of finding they were not, was holding her in a kind of trance-like state now. It was as if she was watching and listening to everything in slow motion, as if her senses were still too jumbled to comprehend that others were approaching her now.

A dry pair of boots appeared to replace Rosie's saturated ones, and someone handed over a shawl. Then Mrs Guppey was rubbing Rosie's frozen feet with the shawl and lacing them into the dry boots, still warm from someone else's feet. It didn't matter.

Nothing mattered but the fact, slowly dawning on Rosie, that she was being ostracised no longer. That in their separate and homely ways the Moule villagers were offering what they had in retribution. To herself and to Will they were as warm and giving as they knew how, while the children were coddled by loving hands. Rosie's heart was suddenly too full, her throat too choked to whisper her thanks. She could only nod, and bite her trembling lips at all this sudden kindness.

A while later Edwin arrived on horseback, hurrying anxiously into the church, thankful to see that Rosie and Will were safe, his eyes seeking out Daisy and sweeping her into his arms.

'We've been at the farm,' he said briefly. 'But Jess won't be easy until Daisy is back with her. Is she well? She looks very pale. I mean to take her back on the horse. The roads are passable with care.'

He stopped, aware that something had happened here. Will explained briefly, and Rosie saw her brother's face whiten. She knew that he too must be remembering Dorcas and the heartbreak of that dreadful day. But this day was different. This was a new dawn, and slowly Rosie felt as if she was coming back to life. As if she had travelled a very long way, and now everything before her was outlined with startling clarity. Her inborn optimism seemed to tell her that all her tomorrows would be happier ones, especially with Will beside her.

'I want to go with Edwin,' Daisy was

snuffling. 'I want to see Ma and go to the farm.'

'So you shall, darling,' Rosie told her quickly. 'Hold her tightly in front of you, Edwin. We'll follow soon. I must collect some dry clothes to bring to the farm. Will has the cart.'

'Leave Rosie safely with me, Edwin,' Will took charge of her now. 'She'll be staying at the farm from now on until your father returns from London.'

She nodded swiftly. There was no argument. All she wanted in the world was for Will to take care of her. He must know it, but suddenly she needed a little time to be alone with him to tell him all that was in her heart. Thankfully, Edwin didn't object to Will's suggestion, and minutes later he set off with Daisy tied securely in front of him on the horse's back.

It was some while before the villagers were content to let Will and Rosie leave. She was their new shining star, and the change of mood was still enough to stun her as they asked when the wedding would be.

'Very soon,' Will smiled. 'As soon as Vicar can arrange it, and we hope you'll all dance at our wedding.'

As her hand stole into Will's, Rosie caught sight of Bennett sitting quietly with the group of children. His face was drawn, but Rosie didn't really think he'd mourn for too long at losing her for good. Bennett wasn't really the marrying kind. But on this day she didn't want anyone to be sad.

'I'd like the children to be there, Bennett, and to form a circle of honour. Will you arrange that for me? I'm sure they would like to do that.'

He agreed at once, glad to be of service. Then Vicar Washbourne spoke up, his voice ringing loudly around the stone walls, his gaunt features creasing into a broad grimace of a smile.

'Let us not forget to give thanks for this day of deliverance, friends. And for the safety of our children. And in doing so, let us not forget that Rosie Nash was instrumental in their saving. As well as capturing the heart of a fine young man, she has charmed us all with her sweetness and goodness, and in God's name I will be honoured to seal their union in His house. Let all come on the appointed day!'

'Amen.' The murmured word circulated through the church.

And at last they could leave, seated in the cold, damp cart and heading back carefully to Briar Cottage. Will had to concentrate on the journey through the splashing water underfoot, but Rosie was content to lean her head against his shoulder as strength and vitality returned to her.

Now that all the danger was over and they were alone at last, Will too felt the renewal of all that had lain dormant in these few perilous days, and the hunger he felt to make Rosie truly his overshadowed the more mundane need for food. His was a hunger of a greater kind.

Once they reached Briar Cottage they fastened the horse to the fence, and Rosie went immediately to the workshop, treading carefully on the marshy ground. Her action was partly compulsive, to see for herself that this was a place of pride and craftsmanship and no longer the scene of near-rape and murder; partly to assure herself that nothing had really suffered here from the onslaught of water.

The withy rods floated about, the offcuts in crazy spirals in the slurry, and the tied baskets nearest the floor were covered in filth and sludge. But they would all be workable and saleable once more when they had been washed and dried.

'Didn't I tell you, Rosie?' Will's arms closed around her, his voice strong. 'Your land and mine had the best of it. We're survivors, like the withies. Strong and supple and practically indestructable they are, like you and me. And nothing in this world is going to part us now, sweetheart. We were always meant to be together.'

'I know it,' she breathed. 'Oh Will, I know it!'

The glory of it was that he knew it too, echoing the romantic dream of hers that their lives were too closely intertwined for anything to separate them.

Slowly he bent his head and tasted the softness of her lips beneath his. She could feel the beat of his heart. Against her own, the sensation was of one heartbeat, one life-blood. Singly they were vulnerable. Together there was nothing they couldn't do. Joined in love, as perfectly as if they were two halves of the same being. Against her mouth, Rosie heard his small indrawing of breath.

'Oh Rosie, I want—I want—'

Her eyes were blue and luminous as a summer sky as she looked up at him, his face darkened by shadow, but so infinitely dear and familiar to her that she would know every contour of it blindfold.

'What do you want, Will?' she whispered, her heart still pounding in a reckless drumbeat.

'I want *you*, Rosie. To know that you belong to me for ever, and to blot out the memory of that other time. Can you ever forgive me for that?' His voice was suddenly rough with remembering, and she hushed him with a small kiss.

'There's nothing to forgive.' Her breath

caught in her throat. 'And what makes you think a man has the exclusive rights to wanting or needing?' The small note of arrogance died in her voice as she saw the rush of desire in Will's eyes.

Together they turned to leave the workshop, arms still entwined. Inside the cottage a thick layer of mud lay over matting and flagstones, and the place was cold and dank without the leaping fire to cheer it. They didn't linger there long. There was time enough to come back with brushes and soap for cleaning. Now was not the time...

They moved towards the stairs, and Rosie was aware of a deep trembling inside her. She was afraid...despite her need of Will, she was afraid. The only time she had known a man's body intimately, he had torn at her like an animal. Since then Cyrus Hale had nearly done the same... She gave an uncontrollable shudder, and inside her bedroom Will turned her into his arms.

'Trust me, Rosie,' he said gently, as he'd done once before. 'I love thee more than life itself. I'd never hurt thee.'

The fear subsided. She removed her damp clothes as quickly as her shaking hands would allow, and now a sweet wild tingling began to suffuse her whole body as she realised Will too was stripping off his clothes, and then they were rubbing at their chilled bodies with rough, stimulating towels to bring back the warmth and life to their limbs. Yet they hardly needed them. The flame that burned within them both warmed them more surely than any artificial means ever could.

The breath was coming shallowly in her chest as Will gently pushed her back onto her narrow bed. The first and last time he had lain with her she had known only fear and utter humiliation. Now, as his hands began their gentle caresses and his voice murmured soft words of love, her desire rose to meet his, their union as spiritual as it was of the flesh in those moments before she felt the hard weight of him covering her softness.

He entered her with an exquisite slowness, and she gave out a long, deep sigh of fulfilment. Her arms drew him down to her, her sensitive fingers stroking his strong muscled back, and his mouth covered her face with kisses as the rhythmic movements sent waves of sensual pleasure coursing through her.

This was her destiny. Rosie's dizzying thoughts were held and then shudderingly released as Will's passion took them to the edge of ecstasy, stunning all sense of reason in the sheer rapture of perfect consummation. There was only one thought flowing gloriously through her mind now. Will was hers and she was his. Now, forever, until eternity and beyond.

The publishers hope that this book has given you enjoyable reading. Large Print Books are especially designed to be as easy to see and hold as possible. If you wish a complete list of our books, please ask at your local library or write directly to: Magna Large Print Books, Long Preston, North Yorkshire, BD23 4ND, England.

This Large Print Book for the Partially sighted, who cannot read normal print, is published under the auspices of

THE ULVERSCROFT FOUNDATION

THE ULVERSCROFT FOUNDATION

. . . we hope that you have enjoyed this Large Print Book. Please think for a moment about those people who have worse eyesight problems than you . . . and are unable to even read or enjoy Large Print, without great difficulty.

You can help them by sending a donation, large or small to:

**The Ulverscroft Foundation,
1, The Green, Bradgate Road,
Anstey, Leicestershire, LE7 7FU,
England.**
or request a copy of our brochure for more details.

The Foundation will use all your help to assist those people who are handicapped by various sight problems and need special attention.

Thank you very much for your help.